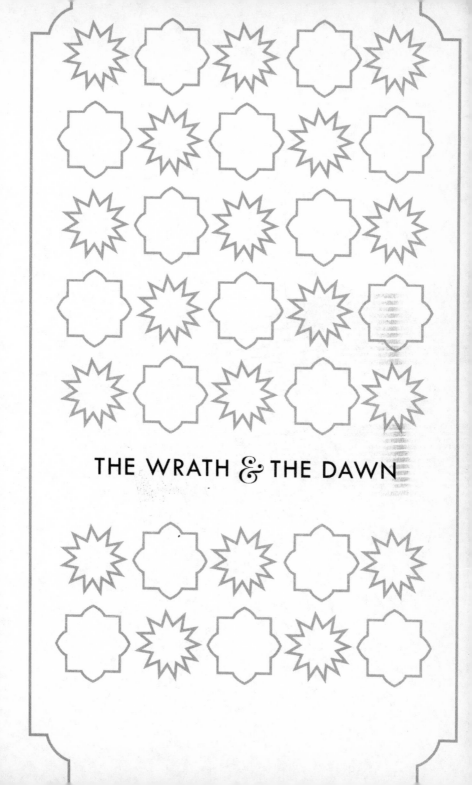

THE WRATH & THE DAWN

THE WRATH & THE DAWN

· R E N É E   A H D I E H ·

G. P. PUTNAM'S SONS • AN IMPRINT OF PENGUIN GROUP (USA)

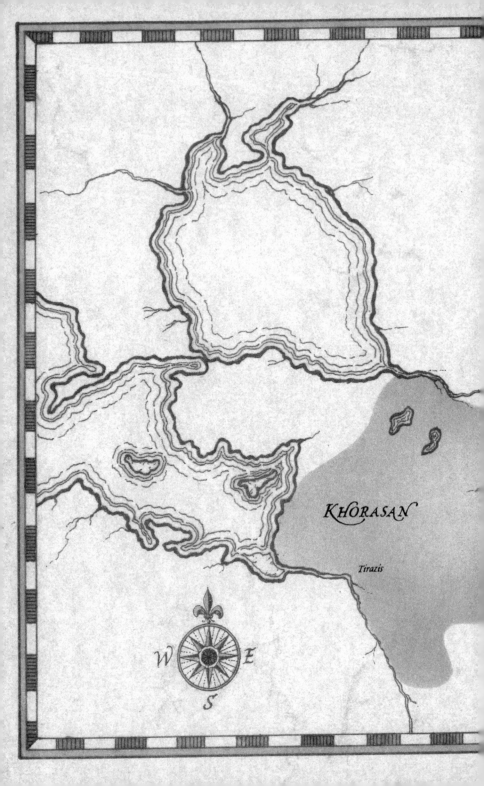

KHORASAN

Tirazis

W E
S

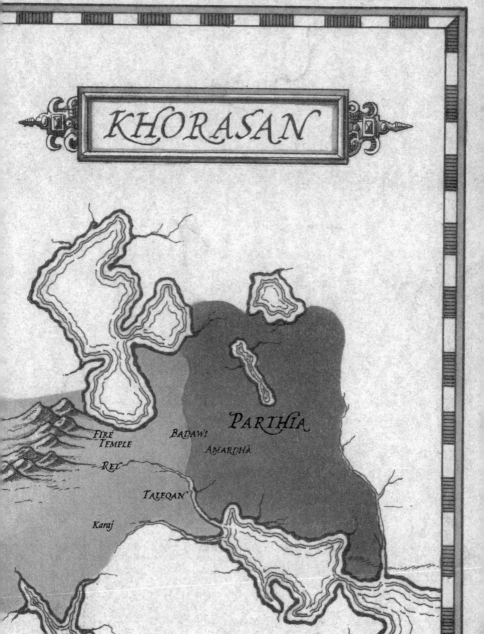

KHORASAN

PARTHIA

FIRE
TEMPLE

BADAWI

AMARDHA

REY

TALEQAN

Karaj

G. P. PUTNAM'S SONS
Published by the Penguin Group
Penguin Group (USA) LLC
375 Hudson Street
New York, NY 10014

USA | Canada | UK | Ireland | Australia
New Zealand | India | South Africa | China
penguin.com
A Penguin Random House Company

Library of Congress Cataloging-in-Publication Data
Ahdieh, Renée.
The wrath and the dawn / Renée Ahdieh.
pages cm
Summary: In this reimagining of The Arabian Nights, Shahrzad plans to avenge the death of
her dearest friend by volunteering to marry the murderous boy-king of Khorasan but
discovers not all is as it seems within the palace.
[1. Fairy tales. 2. Love—Fiction. 3. Murder—Fiction.] I. Title.
PZ8.A263Wr 2015 [Fic]—dc23 2014046249

Printed in the United States of America.
ISBN 978-0-399-17665-4
5 7 9 10 8 6 4

Design by Marikka Tamura.
Text set in Italian Old Style MT Std.

For Victor,
the story at the heart of mine.
And for Jessica,
the first star in my night sky.

I once had a thousand desires,
But in my one desire to know you,
all else melted away.

Jalal al-Din Rumi

PROLOGUE

IT WOULD NOT BE A WELCOME DAWN.

Already the sky told this story, with its sad halo of silver beckoning from beyond the horizon.

A young man stood alongside his father on the rooftop terrace of the marble palace. They watched the pale light of the early morning sun push back the darkness with slow, careful deliberation.

"Where is he?" the young man asked.

His father did not look his way. "He has not left his chamber since he gave the order."

The young man ran a hand through his wavy hair, exhaling all the while. "There will be riots in the city streets for this."

"And you will put them to rout, in short order." It was a terse response, still made to a somber stretch of light.

"In short order? Do you not think a mother and father, regardless of birth or rank, will fight to avenge their child?"

Finally, the father faced his son. His eyes were drawn and sunken, as though a weight tugged at them from within. "They will fight. They should fight. And you will ensure it amounts

to nothing. You will do your duty to your king. Do you understand?"

The young man paused. "I understand."

"General al-Khoury?"

His father turned toward the soldier standing behind them.
"Yes?"

"It is done."

His father nodded, and the soldier left.

Again, the two men stared up at the sky.

Waiting.

A drop of rain struck the arid surface beneath their feet, disappearing into the tan stone. Another plinked against the iron
railing before it slid its way into nothingness.

Soon, rain was falling around them at a steady pace.

"There is your proof," the general said, his voice laden with
quiet anguish.

The young man did not respond right away.

"He cannot withstand this, Father."

"He can. He is strong."

"You have never understood Khalid. It is not about strength.
It is about substance. What follows will destroy all that remains
of his, leaving behind a husk—a shadow of what he once was."

The general winced. "Do you think I wanted this for him? I
would drown in my own blood to prevent this. But we have no
choice."

The young man shook his head and wiped the rain from beneath his chin.

"I refuse to believe that."

"Jalal—"

"There must be another way." With that, the young man turned from the railing and vanished down the staircase.

Throughout the city, long-dry wells began to fill. Cracked, sunbaked cisterns shimmered with pools of hope, and the people of Rey awoke to a new joy. They raced into the streets, angling their smiling faces to the sky.

Not knowing the price.

And, deep within the palace of marble and stone, a boy of eighteen sat alone before a table of polished ebony . . .

Listening to the rain.

The only light in the room reflected back in his amber eyes.

A light beset by the dark.

He braced his elbows on his knees and made a crown of his hands about his brow. Then he shuttered his gaze, and the words echoed around him, filling his ears with the promise of a life rooted in the past.

Of a life atoning for his sins.

One hundred lives for the one you took. One life to one dawn. Should you fail but a single morn, I shall take from you your dreams. I shall take from you your city.

And I shall take from you these lives, a thousandfold.

MEDITATIONS
ON GOSSAMER AND GOLD

T HEY WERE NOT GENTLE. AND WHY SHOULD THEY BE?
After all, they did not expect her to live past the next morning.

The hands that tugged ivory combs through Shahrzad's waist-length hair and scrubbed sandalwood paste on her bronze arms did so with a brutal kind of detachment.

Shahrzad watched one young servant girl dust her bare shoulders with flakes of gold that caught the light from the setting sun.

A breeze gusted along the gossamer curtains lining the walls of the chamber. The sweet scent of citrus blossoms wafted through the carved wooden screens leading to the terrace, whispering of a freedom now beyond reach.

This was my choice. Remember Shiva.

"I don't wear necklaces," Shahrzad said when another girl began to fasten a jewel-encrusted behemoth around her throat.

"It is a gift from the caliph. You must wear it, my lady."

Shahrzad stared down at the slight girl in amused disbelief. "And if I don't? Will he kill me?"

"Please, my lady, I—"

Shahrzad sighed. "I suppose now is not the time to make this point."

"Yes, my lady."

"My name is Shahrzad."

"I know, my lady." The girl glanced away in discomfort before turning to assist with Shahrzad's gilded mantle. As the two young women eased the weighty garment onto her glittering shoulders, Shahrzad studied the finished product in the mirror before her.

Her midnight tresses gleamed like polished obsidian, and her hazel eyes were edged in alternating strokes of black kohl and liquid gold. At the center of her brow hung a teardrop ruby the size of her thumb; its mate dangled from a thin chain around her bare waist, grazing the silk sash of her trowsers. The mantle itself was pale damask and threaded with silver and gold in an intricate pattern that grew ever chaotic as it flared by her feet.

I look like a gilded peacock.

"Do they all look this ridiculous?" Shahrzad asked.

Again, the two young women averted their gazes with unease.

I'm sure Shiva didn't look this ridiculous . . .

Shahrzad's expression hardened.

Shiva would have looked beautiful. Beautiful and strong.

Her fingernails dug into her palms; tiny crescents of steely resolve.

At the sound of a quiet knock at the door, three heads turned—their collective breaths bated.

In spite of her newfound mettle, Shahrzad's heart began to pound.

"May I come in?" The soft voice of her father broke through the silence, pleading and laced in tacit apology.

Shahrzad exhaled slowly . . . carefully.

"Baba, what are you doing here?" Her words were patient, yet wary.

Jahandar al-Khayzuran shuffled into the chamber. His beard and temples were streaked with grey, and the myriad colors in his hazel eyes shimmered and shifted like the sea in the midst of a storm.

In his hand was a single budding rose, its center leached of color, and the tips of its petals tinged a beautiful, blushing mauve.

"Where is Irsa?" Shahrzad asked, alarm seeping into her tone.

Her father smiled sadly. "She is at home. I did not allow her to come with me, though she fought and raged until the last possible moment."

At least in this he has not ignored my wishes.

"You should be with her. She needs you tonight. Please do this for me, Baba? Do as we discussed?" She reached out and took his free hand, squeezing tightly, beseeching him in her grip to follow the plans she had laid out in the days before.

"I—I can't, my child." Jahandar lowered his head, a sob rising in his chest, his thin shoulders trembling with grief. "Shahrzad—"

"Be strong. For Irsa. I promise you, everything will be fine." Shahrzad raised her palm to his weathered face and brushed away the smattering of tears from his cheek.

"I cannot. The thought that this may be your last sunset—"

"It will not be the last. I will see tomorrow's sunset. This I swear to you."

Jahandar nodded, his misery nowhere close to mollified. He held out the rose in his hand. "The last from my garden; it has not yet bloomed fully, but I wanted to give you one remembrance of home."

She smiled as she reached for it, the love between them far past mere gratitude, but he stopped her. When she realized the reason, she began to protest.

"No. At least in this, I might do something for you," he muttered, almost to himself. He stared at the rose, his brow furrowed and his mouth drawn. One servant girl coughed in her fist while the other looked to the floor.

Shahrzad waited patiently. Knowingly.

The rose started to unfurl. Its petals twisted open, prodded to life by an invisible hand. As it expanded, a delicious perfume filled the space between them, sweet and perfect for an instant . . . but soon, it became overpowering. Cloying. The edges of the flower changed from a brilliant, deep pink to a shadowy rust in the blink of an eye.

And then the flower began to wither and die.

Dismayed, Jahandar watched its dried petals wilt to the white marble at their feet.

"I—I'm sorry, Shahrzad," he cried.

"It doesn't matter. I will never forget how beautiful it was for that moment, Baba." She wrapped her arms around his neck and pulled him close. By his ear, in a voice so low only he could hear, she said, "Go to Tariq, as you promised. Take Irsa and go."

He nodded, his eyes shimmering once more. "I love you, my child."

"And I love you. I will keep my promises. All of them."

Overcome, Jahandar blinked down at his elder daughter in silence.

This time, the knock at the door demanded attention rather than requested it.

Shahrzad's forehead whipped back in its direction, the bloodred ruby swinging in tandem. She squared her shoulders and lifted her pointed chin.

Jahandar stood to the side, covering his face with his hands, as his daughter marched forward.

"I'm sorry—so very sorry," she whispered to him before striding across the threshold to follow the contingent of guards leading the processional. Jahandar slid to his knees and sobbed as Shahrzad turned the corner and disappeared.

With her father's grief resounding through the halls, Shahrzad's feet refused to carry her but a few steps down the cavernous corridors of the palace. She halted, her knees shaking beneath the thin silk of her voluminous *sirwal* trowsers.

"My lady?" one of the guards prompted in a bored tone.

"He can wait," Shahrzad gasped.

The guards exchanged glances.

Her own tears threatening to blaze a telltale trail down her cheeks, Shahrzad pressed a hand to her chest. Unwittingly, her fingertips brushed the edge of the thick gold necklace clasped around her throat, festooned with gems of outlandish size and untold variety. It felt heavy . . . stifling. Like a bejeweled fetter. She allowed her fingers to wrap around the offending instrument, thinking for a moment to rip it from her body.

The rage was comforting. A friendly reminder.

Shiva.

Her dearest friend. Her closest confidante.

She curled her toes within their sandals of braided bullion and threw back her shoulders once more. Without a word, she resumed her march.

Again, the guards looked to one another for an instant.

When they reached the massive double doors leading into the throne room, Shahrzad realized her heart was racing at twice its normal speed. The doors swung open with a distended groan, and she focused on her target, ignoring all else around her.

At the very end of the immense space stood Khalid Ibn al-Rashid, the Caliph of Khorasan.

The King of Kings.

The monster from my nightmares.

With every step she took, Shahrzad felt the hate rise in her blood, along with the clarity of purpose. She stared at him, her eyes never wavering. His proud carriage stood out amongst the men in his retinue, and details began to emerge the closer she drew to his side.

He was tall and trim, with the build of a young man proficient in warfare. His dark hair was straight and styled in a manner suggesting a desire for order in all things.

As she strode onto the dais, she looked up at him, refusing to balk, even in the face of her king.

His thick eyebrows raised a fraction. They framed eyes so pale a shade of brown they appeared amber in certain flashes of light, like those of a tiger. His profile was an artist's study in angles, and he remained motionless as he returned her watchful scrutiny.

A face that cut; a gaze that pierced.

He reached a hand out to her.

Just as she extended her palm to grasp it, she remembered to bow.

The wrath seethed below the surface, bringing a flush to her cheeks.

When she met his eyes again, he blinked once.

"Wife." He nodded.

"My king."

I will live to see tomorrow's sunset. Make no mistake. I swear I will live to see as many sunsets as it takes.

And I will kill you.

With my own hands.

ONLY ONE

THE FALCON DRIFTED THROUGH THE BLEARING MID-afternoon sky, its wings held aloft on a passing sigh of wind and its eyes scanning the underbrush below.

At fleeting signs of movement, the raptor tucked its wings against its body and hurtled toward the dirt in a blur of blue-grey feathers and flashing talons.

The mass of fur, screeching and scurrying through the underbrush, had no chance of escape. Soon, the sound of clattering hooves drew near, a swirl of sand curling in its wake.

The two riders paused a respectful distance from the falcon and her kill.

With the sun at his back, the first rider, sitting astride a gleaming, dark bay al-Khamsa stallion, extended his left arm and whistled, low and soft.

The falcon twisted his way, her yellow-rimmed eyes narrowing. Then she took to the air once more and landed with her talons firmly embedded in the leather *mankalah* cuff bound from the rider's wrist to his elbow.

"Curse you, Zoraya. I lost another bet," the second rider groaned to the bird.

The falconer grinned at Rahim, his friend since childhood. "Stop complaining. It's not her fault you're incapable of learning a single lesson."

"You're lucky I'm such a fool. Who else would stomach your company for so long, Tariq?"

Tariq laughed under his breath. "In that case, perhaps I should stop lying to your mother about how smart you've become."

"Of course. Have I ever lied to yours?"

"Ingrate. Get down and collect her kill."

"I'm not your servant. You do it."

"Fine. Hold this." Tariq stretched out his forearm, with Zoraya still waiting patiently on her perch. When the falcon realized she was being passed along to Rahim, she ruffled her feathers and screeched in protest.

Rahim reared back with alarm. "That godforsaken bird hates me."

"Because she's a good judge of character." Tariq smiled.

"With a temper for the ages," Rahim grumbled. "Honestly, she's worse than Shazi."

"Another girl with excellent taste."

Rahim rolled his eyes. "A bit self-serving in that assessment, don't you think? Considering the one thing they have in common is you."

"Reducing Shahrzad al-Khayzuran to such a notion might be the reason you're always on the receiving end of her temper. I assure you, Zoraya and Shazi have a great deal more in common than me. Now, stop wasting time and get down from that blasted roan so we can go home."

Under continued grumblings, Rahim dismounted from his grey Akhal-Teke—her mane shining like polished pewter in the desert sun.

Tariq's eyes skimmed the stretch of sand and dry brushwood along the horizon. Blistering waves of heat rose from a sea of umber and adobe, rippling into patches of blue and white across the sky.

With Zoraya's catch now stowed in the leather pouch affixed to his saddle, Rahim swung back onto his horse, employing the grace of a young nobleman trained in the art since boyhood.

"As to the earlier bet regarding the bird . . ." Rahim trailed off.

Tariq groaned when he saw the determined look on Rahim's face. "No."

"Because you know you'll lose."

"You're a better rider than I am."

"You have a better horse. Your father is an emir. Plus, I already lost one bet today. Give me a chance to even the field," Rahim insisted.

"How long are we going to play these games?"

"Until I beat you. At every one of them."

"Then we'll be playing forever," Tariq joked.

"Bastard." Rahim suppressed a grin as he gripped his reins. "For that, I won't even try to play fair." He dug his heels into the mare before taking off in the opposite direction.

"Fool." Tariq laughed as he released Zoraya into the clouds and leaned over the neck of his stallion. At the click of his tongue, the horse shook out its mane and snorted. Tariq pulled on the reins, and the Arabian reared onto its massive hooves before launching across the sand, its powerful legs kicking up a vortex of dust and debris.

Tariq's white *rida'* billowed behind him, the hood threatening to blow back in spite of the leather band holding it in place.

As they rounded the final dune, a walled fortress of tan stone and grey mortar rose from the sands, its vaulted turrets capped in spirals of copper tinged by the turquoise patina of age.

"The emir's son approaches!" a sentry cried out as Rahim and Tariq neared the back gates, which swung open with barely a moment to spare. Servants and laborers scrambled out of their path as Rahim barreled past the still-screeching iron with Tariq on his heels. A basket of persimmons crashed to the ground, its contents rolling across the expanse before a grousing old man bent forward, struggling to collect the wayward orange fruit.

Oblivious to the chaos they had wrought, the two young noblemen reined in their horses near the center of the sprawling courtyard.

"How does it feel—being bested by a fool?" Rahim taunted, his dark blue eyes bright.

One side of Tariq's mouth rose with amusement before he swung down from the saddle and knocked back the hood of his *rida'*. He ran a hand through his unruly tangle of wavy hair. Grains of sand fell into his face, and he blinked hard to fend off their attack.

The sound of Rahim's choked laughter rang out from behind him.

Tariq opened his eyes.

The servant girl standing before Tariq looked away in haste, her cheeks blooming with color. The tray she held with two silver tumblers of water began to shake.

"Thank you." Tariq smiled as he reached for one.

Her blush deepened, and the rattling grew worse.

Rahim lumbered closer. He took his own tumbler and nodded to the girl before she twisted around and ran as fast as her legs could carry her.

Tariq shoved him. Hard. "You oaf."

"I believe that poor girl is half in love with you. After another wretched display of horsemanship, you should be extra grateful to the hand of fate that dealt you those looks."

Tariq ignored him and swiveled to take in the sights of the courtyard. To his right, he noticed the elderly servant stooping above a gaggle of persimmons scattered across the granite at his feet. Tariq glided forward and bent on one knee to help the old man place the fruit in a basket.

"Thank you, *sahib.*" The man bowed his head and touched the fingertips of his right hand to his forehead in a gesture of respect.

Tariq's eyes softened, their colors flickering in the shade. Their bright silver centers blended into rings of darkest ash, with black lashes that fanned against the soft skin of his eyelids. His brow had an air of severity that faded with the ready appearance of his smile. A day-old beard shadowed the square line of his jaw, further accentuating its finely wrought symmetry.

Tariq nodded at the elderly man and returned the customary gesture.

Above them, Zoraya's cry resounded from the sky, demanding immediate attention. Tariq shook his head in mock irritation and whistled for her. She swooped down with a wild shriek that cleared another portion of the courtyard. Again, she landed on Tariq's outstretched *mankalah* and preened as he carried her to her mews to feed her.

"Do you not find the bird a bit . . . spoiled?" Rahim studied the falcon as she guzzled an entire strip of dried meat without pausing for breath.

"She's the best hunter in the kingdom."

"Nevertheless, I'm convinced that accursed bird could get away with murder. Is that your intent?"

Before Tariq could retort, one of his father's closest advisors appeared in the nearby archway to the vestibule.

"*Sahib*? The emir requests your presence."

Tariq's eyebrows drew together. "Is something wrong?"

"A messenger arrived from Rey not long ago."

"Is that all?" Rahim harrumphed. "A letter from Shazi? Hardly worthy of a formal audience."

Tariq continued studying the advisor, taking in the deep lines marring his forehead and the tight weave of his interlaced fingers. "What happened?"

The advisor hedged. "Please, *sahib*. Come with me."

Rahim followed Tariq and the advisor into the columned marble vestibule and past the open-air gallery, with its tiled fountain of mosaic glass. Sparkling water fell in a steady stream from the mouth of a lion constructed of gilt bronze.

They entered the main hall to find Nasir al-Ziyad, emir of the

17

fourth-richest stronghold in Khorasan, sitting with his wife at a low table. Their dinner lay before them, untouched.

It was obvious Tariq's mother had been crying.

He stopped short at the sight. "Father?"

The emir exhaled and raised his troubled eyes to meet his son.

"Tariq, we received a letter from Rey this afternoon. From Shahrzad."

"Give it to me." The request was soft. Sharp.

"It was addressed to me. There is a portion of it that was meant for you, but the—"

Tariq's mother burst into tears. "How could this happen?"

"What happened?" Tariq demanded, his voice rising. "Give me the letter."

"It's too late. There's nothing you can do," the emir sighed.

"First Shiva. Then, lost in her grief, my sister took her own—" She shuddered. "And now Shahrzad? How could this happen? *Why?*" Tariq's mother wept.

Tariq froze.

"You know why," the emir rasped in a low tone. "It's because of Shiva that she did this. For Shiva. For all of us."

At that, Tariq's mother rose from the table and fled, her sobs growing louder with every footstep.

"Oh, God. Shazi. What did you do?" Rahim whispered.

Tariq remained motionless, his expression blank and inscrutable.

The emir stood and moved toward his son. "Son, you—"

"Give me the letter," Tariq repeated.

With grim resignation, the emir relinquished the scroll.

Shahrzad's familiar scrawl swam across the page, just as imperious and heavy-handed as usual. Tariq stopped reading when she began addressing him directly. The apology. The words of regret for her betrayal. The gratitude for his understanding.

No more. He couldn't stand it. Not from her.

The edge of the scroll crumpled in his fist.

"There is nothing you can do," the emir reiterated. "The wedding—it's today. If she succeeds . . . if she—"

"Don't say it, Father. I beg you."

"It must be said. These truths, no matter how harsh, must be said. We must deal with this, as a family. Your aunt and uncle never dealt with the loss of Shiva, and look what came of their daughter's death."

Tariq's eyes closed.

"Even if Shahrzad survives, there is nothing we can do. It is finished. We must accept this, however difficult it may seem. I know how you feel about her; I fully understand. It will take time. But you will realize you can find happiness with someone else— that there are other young women in the world. In time, you will see," the emir said.

"There's no need."

"Excuse me?"

"I already understand. Fully."

The emir eyed his son with surprise.

"I understand your points. All of them. Now I need you to understand mine. I know there are other women in the world. I know it's possible for me to find a measure of happiness with another girl. Given time, I suppose anything may happen."

The emir nodded. "Good. It's for the best, Tariq."

Rahim stared, dumbfounded.

Tariq continued, the silver in his eyes flashing. "But understand this: no matter how many perfect young women you put in my path, there is only one Shahrzad." At that, he cast the scroll to the floor and whirled on his heel, slamming his palms into the doors to thrust them aside.

Rahim exchanged a thoughtful look with the emir before following Tariq. They retraced their steps into the courtyard, and Tariq signaled for the horses. Rahim did not speak until both mounts were brought before them.

"What's the plan?" he asked gently. "Do you even have one?"

Tariq paused. "You don't have to come with me."

"And now who's the fool? Are you the only one who loves Shazi? Who loved Shiva? I may not be blood, but they will always be my family."

Tariq turned to his friend. "Thank you, Rahim-*jan*."

The taller, lankier boy smiled down at Tariq. "Don't thank me yet. We still need a plan. Tell me, what are you going to do?" Rahim hesitated. "*Is* there anything you can do?"

Tariq's jaw tightened. "As long as the ruler of Khorasan draws breath, there is always something I can do . . ." His left hand dropped to the hilt of the elegantly curved sword at his hip.

"What I do best."

THE VEIL BETWEEN

SHAHRZAD SAT ALONE IN HER CHAMBER, IN THE CENTER of a platformed cushion piled high with pillows covered in vibrant fabrics. Surrounding the bed was a thin veil of spider-silk, blowing with eerie leisure at the slightest disturbance. Her knees were drawn to her chest; her fingers were laced across her ankles.

And her hazel eyes were trained on the doors.

She had stayed in this position for the better part of the night. Each time she tried to venture from the spot, her nerves threatened to overcome her.

Where is he?

She exhaled loudly and clasped her hands even tighter above her feet.

Soon, the panic she had been fighting for the last hour began to bear down on her like a hammer on an ironsmith's anvil.

What if he doesn't come to see me tonight?

"Oh, God," she murmured, breaking through the stillness.

Then I lied to everyone. I broke every last promise.

Shahrzad shook her head. Her heartbeat rose in her ears as each breath became more labored.

I don't want to die.

These macabre thoughts rubbed at the edges of her composure, pushing her down into the fathomless realms of terror—a terror she'd managed to keep at bay, thus far.

How will Baba survive if I'm killed? And Irsa?

Tariq.

"Stop it!" Her words echoed into the yawning darkness. Foolish, but she needed something—anything—to fill the torturous silence with sound, if but for an instant.

She pressed her hands to her temples and willed the terror back . . .

Back inside the steel-encased enclosure of her heart.

And then the doors swung open with a low creak.

Shahrzad dropped her palms to the soft cushion at her sides.

A servant stepped through, clutching tapers of aloewood and ambergris, which gave off a faint perfume and a delicate light; after a beat, a girl bearing a tray of food and wine followed. The servants placed their wares throughout the room and left without a glance in Shahrzad's direction.

A moment later, the Caliph of Khorasan appeared at the threshold.

He waited, as if considering something, before entering the chamber and pushing the doors shut.

In the pale glow emitting from the candles, his tiger-eyes seemed even more calculating and remote. The lines of his face fell into shadow as he turned from the light, sharpening the bladed hollows of his features.

An immovable countenance. Cold and forbidding.

Shahrzad threaded her fingers beneath her knees.

"I'm told your father served under mine as one of his viziers." His voice was low and unassuming. Almost . . . kind.

"Yes, *sayyidi*. He was an advisor to your father."

"And he works as a custodian now."

"Yes, *sayyidi*. Of ancient texts."

He faced her. "Quite a change in position."

Shahrzad bit back irritation. "Perhaps. He wasn't a very high-ranking vizier."

"I see."

You see nothing.

She returned his gaze, hoping the mosaic of color in her eyes hid the thoughts running rampant behind them.

"Why did you volunteer, Shahrzad al-Khayzuran?"

She did not answer.

He continued. "What compelled you to do something so foolish?"

"Excuse me?"

"Perhaps it was the lure of marrying a king. Or the vain hope you might be the one to stay the course and win the heart of a monster." He spoke without emotion, watching her intently.

Shahrzad's pulse jumped to a martial beat. "I don't suffer those delusions, *sayyidi*."

"Then why did you volunteer? Why are you willing to throw away your life at seventeen?"

"I'm sixteen." She cut her eyes. "And I don't see why it matters."

"Answer me."

"No."

He paused. "You realize you could die for that."

The grip of her fingers tightened almost painfully. "I'm not surprised to hear that, *sayyidi*. But, if you truly want answers, killing me won't help in the endeavor."

A spark of something flashed across his face, lingering at the edges of his lips. It was gone too quickly to offer anything of significance.

"I suppose not." He stopped, again in seeming consideration. She could see him withdrawing, a veil falling over the harsh angles of his profile.

No.

Shahrzad rose from the bed and took a step toward him.

When he glanced back at her, she moved closer.

"I told you. Do not think you will be the one to break the cycle."

Shahrzad gritted her teeth. "And I told you. I don't suffer delusions. On any account."

She continued advancing until she stood but an arm's length from him, her resolve unwavering.

He locked upon her face. "Your life is already forfeit. I do not expect . . . more than that."

In response, Shahrzad reached up and began to unfasten the bejeweled necklace still hanging about her throat.

"No." He caught her hand. "Leave it."

He hesitated before shifting his fingers to the nape of her neck.

At this disturbingly familiar touch, Shahrzad fought the urge to pull back in disgust and strike out at him with all the pain and rage she possessed.

Don't be foolish. There will only be one chance. Don't waste it.

This boy-king, this murderer . . . she would not permit him to destroy another family. To rob another girl of her best friend—of a lifetime filled with memories that had been and never would be.

She raised her chin and swallowed the rising bile, the bitter taste remaining on her tongue.

"Why are you here?" he whispered, his tiger-eyes ever searching.

A corner of her mouth rose in sardonic reply.

She brought her palm to his hand.

Carefully.

Then she lifted the heavy mantle from her shoulders and let it slide to the floor.

Irsa sat astride her dappled mare in the alley closest to the structure housing Rey's most ancient and obscure texts. The city's library was once a grand edifice, columned and swathed in judiciously hewn stones quarried from the finest pits in Tirazis. Over the years, its façade had darkened, and deep cracks marred its surface, the worst filled with slipshod efforts at repair. Every visible edge was worn, and the glorious lustre of yesteryear had faded to a mottling of greys and browns.

When the team of horses behind her stirred in the dense silence before dawn, Irsa glanced over her shoulder apologetically. She opened her mouth to reassure the young driver, but the brittleness in her voice forced her to clear her throat before speaking.

"I'm sorry," she whispered to the boy, after a discreet cough. "I

don't know what's taking so long. I'm sure he'll be back shortly."
Her mare's left ear twitched as Irsa shifted around in her seat.

"No concern of mine, miss. As long as I'm paid in full. But if your father wishes to clear the gates of the city before dawn, we should leave soon."

She nodded, another knot forming in her stomach at the boy's words.

Soon, she would be leaving the city of her childhood—the city she had lived in for fourteen years. So, under the haven of night, with barely a moment's notice, she had thrown everything of value into the covered cart behind her, knowing her life would never be the same.

Odd that none of this mattered to her. At least, not yet.

The only thing she could think about—the reason for her scratched throat and knotted stomach—was Shahrzad.

Her stubborn tyrant of an older sister.

Her brave and loyal friend.

Again, hot tears welled in her eyes, even after she'd sworn not to shed a single drop more. Frustrated, she swiped at her already raw cheeks with the back of her hand.

"Is something wrong, miss?" the driver asked, his tone approaching sympathetic.

Of course something was wrong. But if they were to remain safe from prying eyes, he could never learn what it was. Shahrzad had been specific on this point. "No. Nothing's wrong. Thank you for asking."

The boy nodded before resuming his posture of disinterest.

Irsa thought instead of the journey before them. It would

take three days of hard traveling before they reached Taleqan, the stronghold of Tariq's family. She shook her head in bemusement; after all that had transpired, only Shahrzad would have the audacity to send them to the home of her childhood sweetheart. Every time Irsa stopped to think of Tariq and his family, her gamine features constricted with worry . . .

And remorse.

She heaved a weary sigh and stared down at the reins. Her spotted white horse flipped its mane as a gust of wind whipped through the alley.

"What's taking him so long?" Irsa said to no one in particular.

As if on cue, the heavy wooden door to the side entrance of the library scraped open, and her father's hooded figure stumbled into the night.

He was clutching something in his arms, pulled tight against his chest.

"Baba? Is everything all right?"

"I'm so sorry, dear. Everything's fine. We can leave now," Jahandar murmured. "I just . . . had to make sure all the doors were secure."

"What is that?" Irsa asked.

"Hmm?" Jahandar made his way to his horse and reached for his satchel.

"What are you holding?"

"Oh, it's nothing. Just a tome I particularly enjoyed." He waved his hand dismissively.

"Did we come all the way here for a book, Baba?"

"Just one, my child. Just one."

"It must be a special book."

"All books are special, dear."

"What kind of book is it?"

Jahandar tucked the aging, leather-bound volume into the satchel with great care and swung into his saddle with infinitely less consideration. Then he motioned for the driver to proceed.

The small caravan made its way down the still slumbering streets of Rey.

Irsa directed her mount to walk alongside her father's black stallion. When Jahandar gazed down at her with a kind smile, she reached for his hand, seeking the same reassurance she offered.

"All will be well, dearest girl," he said, almost absentmindedly.

She nodded.

It did not escape Irsa's notice that he had failed to answer her question.

THE MOUNTAIN OF ADAMANT

THE INSTANT SHAHRZAD BROUGHT HER PALM TO HIS, she felt a cool wash of dispassion take over. As though she had floated beyond her person and was now a mere witness to everything around her.

Thankfully, he did not try to kiss her.

Nor did the pain last; it was but a fleeting moment, lost in the welcome distraction of her thoughts. He did not appear to enjoy himself, either. Whatever pleasure he derived was brief and perfunctory, and Shahrzad felt a stab of satisfaction at this realization.

When it was done, he rose from the bed without a word and pushed aside the whisper-silk enclosing the platform.

She watched him dress with neat, almost militaristic precision, noting the light sheen of sweat on his back and the lean muscles that coiled and flexed with the slightest of movements.

He was stronger than she was. Of that, there was no doubt. She could not best him physically.

But I'm not here to fight. I'm here to win.

She sat up and reached for the beautiful *shamla* draped on a stool nearby. Shahrzad slid her arms into the lustrous brocade and tied the silver laces before moving to join him. As she rounded the edge of the bed, the robe's delicately embroidered hem twirled about her like a dervish in the midst of *sama*.

The caliph strode to the low table in the corner of the chamber, surrounded by even more sumptuous cushions and plump pillows covered in an array of jewel tones.

He poured himself some wine, still standing in silence. Shahrzad stepped past him and sank onto the cushions encircling the table.

The tray was laden with pistachios, figs, almonds, grapes, quince chutney, small cucumbers, and an assortment of fresh herbs. A basket of flatbread lay wrapped in linen off to the side.

Taking pains to return his subtle disregard, Shahrzad plucked a grape from the tray and began to eat.

The caliph studied her for a torturous instant before lowering to the cushions. He sat and drank while Shahrzad dipped pieces of bread into the tartly sweet chutney.

When she could stomach the quiet no longer, she lifted a slender brow at him. "Aren't you going to eat, *sayyidi*?"

He inhaled through his nose, the corners of his eyes tightening in thought.

"The chutney is delicious," she remarked in an offhand manner.

"Aren't you scared, Shahrzad?" he asked, so quietly she almost missed it.

She put down the bread. "Do you want me to be scared, *sayyidi*?"

"No. I want you to be honest."

Shahrzad smiled. "But how would you know if I were lying, *sayyidi*?"

"Because you are not a gifted liar. You only think yourself to be." He leaned forward and took a handful of almonds from the tray.

Her smile widened. Dangerously. "And you are not that good at reading people. You only think yourself to be."

He angled his head, a muscle ticking along his jaw. "What do you want?" Again, the words were so soft, Shahrzad strained to make them out.

She dusted the crumbs off her hands, biding time to construct the next trap.

"I'm to die at sunrise. Correct?"

He nodded once.

"And you wish to know why I volunteered for this?" she continued. "Well, I'd be willing to—"

"No. I won't play games with you. I despise manipulation."

Shahrzad snapped her lips shut, swallowing her nerve-riddled fury. "Perhaps you should spend less time despising the game and more time building the patience necessary to win."

She held her breath as his upper body froze. The knuckles in his hands stretched white for a harrowing instant before he released his grip.

Shahrzad watched the tension leave him, a swirl of emotions colliding in her chest, wreaking havoc on her mind.

"Brave words for a girl with hours left to live." His tone was edged in ice.

She sat up straight and twisted her fall of dark hair so that it

31

hung over one shoulder. "Are you interested in the rules of the game or not, *sayyidi*?"

At his silence, she chose to barrel ahead, concealing her trembling hands in the folds of her *shamla*. "I'm willing to answer your question, *sayyidi*. But before I do so, I wonder if you would be willing to grant me a small request . . ." She trailed off.

A hint of callous amusement darkened his countenance. "Are you trying to barter for your life with trivia?"

She laughed, the sound dancing around the room with the airy quality of chimes. "My life is forfeit. You've made that clear. Perhaps we should move past that issue and get to the matter at hand."

"By all means."

She took a moment to steady herself. "I want to tell you a story."

"Excuse me?" For the first time, she saw a distinct emotion ripple across his features.

Are you surprised? Rest assured, it won't be the last time, Khalid Ibn al-Rashid.

"I tell you a story. You sit and listen. When I'm finished with the tale, I'll answer your question." She waited for his response.

"A story?"

"Yes. Do you agree to the terms, *sayyidi*?"

He leaned back on an elbow, with an unfathomable expression.

"Fine. I agree. You may begin." He pronounced the words like a challenge.

And I accept it, you monster. Willingly.

"This is the tale of Agib, a poor sailor who lost everything he possessed only to gain the knowledge of self-discovery."

"A tale of morality? So you are trying to teach me a lesson."

"No, *sayyidi*. I am trying to entice you. I've been told a good storyteller can trap an audience with a single sentence."

"Then you have failed."

"Only because you are being unnecessarily difficult. And also because you did not let me finish. You see, Agib was a thief—the best thief in all of Baghdad. He could steal a solid gold dinar from your hand, right before your eyes, and pick the pocket of the wariest traveler with the stealth of a shadow."

The caliph inclined his head in consideration.

"But he was arrogant. And, as his escapades grew ever more daring, so did his arrogance. Until one day, he was caught stealing from a wealthy emir and barely managed to escape with his life. In a panic, he tore through the streets of Baghdad, seeking refuge. Near the docks, he happened upon a small ship about to leave port. The captain was in dire need of a final crewmember. Certain the emir's soldiers would find him if he remained in the city, Agib volunteered for the journey."

"Better." A trace of a smile graced the caliph's lips.

"I'm glad you approve, *sayyidi*. May I continue?" She shot him a pointed grin, warring with the urge to splash the remainder of his drink in his face.

He nodded.

"The first few days on board the ship were difficult for Agib. He was not a seafaring man and had very little experience traveling in this manner; consequently, he was sick for long stretches of time. The other crewmembers mocked him openly and gave him the most menial tasks to accomplish, solidifying his status as all but useless. The respect Agib had amassed as the best thief in Baghdad was meaningless in this world; after all, he could not steal from his shipmates. There was no place to run and hide."

"Truly a conundrum," the caliph remarked.

Shahrzad ignored his quiet jab. "One week out to sea, there was a terrible storm. The ship was lashed about on immense waves that threw it far off course. Alas, this wasn't the worst calamity to befall them: when the waters finally stilled two days later, the captain was nowhere to be found. The sea had swallowed him in its salty midst."

Shahrzad paused. As she leaned forward to select a grape, she shot a furtive glance over the caliph's shoulder to the decorative screens leading to the terrace. They were still shaded in the cloak of night.

"The crew began to panic. They were stranded in the middle of the sea and had no way of guiding the ship back on course. Arguments arose as to which sailor would assume the role of captain. Consumed in this struggle over power, the crew failed to realize a speck of land had appeared on the horizon. Agib was the first to point it out. It looked like a tiny island with a mountain at its center. At first, the crew rejoiced at the sight. But then an older sailor muttered something that ignited the panic anew."

The caliph listened, his amber eyes focused squarely on Shahrzad.

"He said, 'God be with us. It is the Mountain of Adamant.' When a general outcry ran through the others at the truth behind these words, Agib asked what made this mountain so terrifying that grown men quailed at its sight. The old sailor explained that the Mountain of Adamant possessed a dark magic that pulled ships toward it by virtue of the iron in their hulls, and once a ship was fully within its grasp, the Adamant had such power that all the nails would be drawn out of the vessel, thereby sinking it to the bottom of the sea and sentencing all its occupants to a watery grave."

"Instead of wasting time lamenting their predicament, perhaps they should try to sail in the opposite direction," the caliph suggested drily.

"And this is exactly what Agib advised. Every oar was manned, and immediate action was taken to foil the mountain's nefarious plot, but it was too late. For once the great blackness looms in the distance, there is little that can be done. By then the mountain already has you in its grip. Sure enough, in spite of all their efforts, the ship drifted closer and closer, faster and faster, into the shadow of Adamant. Soon, a terrible groaning could be heard from the depths of the ship's hull. It began to shudder and shake as though the weight of the world were perched on its bow. In horror, the crew watched as nails ripped and spun from the wood around them. The ship started to break apart and collapse in on itself like a child's plaything underfoot. Agib joined in the shrieking and the sorrowful wails of his fellow crewmen as they were thrown into the sea and left to fend for themselves."

Shahrzad lifted her glass and reached for the wine. She hid her surprise when the caliph filled her cup without a word.

The very edge of the screen behind him was beginning to lighten.

"Agib scrambled onto the stern of the ship—the last part of the boat still intact. In the melee, he noticed a heavy iron pot sliding past him in the direction of the mountain. Using the deft hands of a master thief, Agib snatched the pot and clung to it for dear life as he was pitched over the side and into the vast waters of the sea. The pot weighed him down terribly, and he fought to stay afloat, searching for something to cling to. The sound of his fellow sailors drowning around him only made his search all the more desperate. When he found a broken piece of the main mast, he flung his free arm around it, still clutching the pot with a frantic kind of fierceness."

The caliph's sharp features softened in understanding. "It's quick thinking on Agib's part. He is hoping the pot will direct him to the island."

Shahrzad smiled. "Precisely. After many hours, Agib's instincts led him to land. He stumbled onto the shining black coastline of Adamant, exhausted and trembling with fear. He passed out in the shadow of the mountain and did not awaken for many hours. When dawn broke, he stirred and began the search for food and water before realizing this was truly a place of death and destruction—no life stirred anywhere around him, and water was as scarce as hope on this desolate wasteland. He collapsed against a pile of rocks in despair, realizing his demise was, once again, upon him. As the rocks behind him shifted, a small metal chalice slid out from between the cracks. It was old and worn, beaten around the edges."

A faint blue light crept higher up the screen, sliding between its beautifully carved slats, bringing the designs from haunting silhouette to life.

"Agib studied the chalice. It was caked with sand and mud. He staggered to the water's edge to clean it. When the dirt floated away beneath the surf, he realized the cup was covered in markings, the like of which he had never seen. He raised it into the sunrise, but drops of water still marred the surface, so he swiped his sleeve across the cup to dry it . . ."

Now the very edges of the screen were tinged in the glowing white of dawn. The rays of light streamed through the slats onto the marble floor like veins of raw gold stretched thin in the heat of the early morning sun.

Shahrzad's heart threatened to burst from her throat.

"And the chalice started to tremble. From its hollow depths, a smoke the color of a clear midday sky began to swirl and grow until it became a flameless plume. In terror, Agib dropped the chalice and fell backward against the hard black pebbles of Adamant's shore. The smoke grew in size and density until a shadow formed in its center."

The caliph bent forward.

"The shadow solidified . . . and began to laugh."

Shahrzad stopped.

Dawn had arrived behind the caliph, in all its horrifying glory.

"Why did you stop?" he asked.

She twisted her eyes in the direction of the terrace. The caliph followed her gaze.

"You may finish the story," he stated.

Shahrzad inhaled with care. "I'm afraid that's not possible, *sayyidi.*"

"Excuse me?"

"I have only just begun the tale."

His eyes narrowed to ochre slits. "Finish the story, Shahrzad."

"No."

He unfolded to his feet in a ripple of grace. "So was this your plan all along?"

"What plan would that be, *sayyidi*?"

"A trick. A tactic to stay your execution . . . to begin a tale you had no intention of finishing." His voice was deathly low.

"I have every intention of finishing it—tomorrow night. Whether or not that happens is entirely up to you." She stared up at him, clenching her fists within her *shamla.*

"You said you understood; your life is forfeit. That was clear from the very beginning."

Shahrzad rose to her full height. She pulled back her shoulders and lifted her elfin chin.

When she spoke, she matched the biting softness in his tone.

"All our lives are forfeit, *sayyidi.* It is just a question of when. And I would like one more day."

He glared at her, the sharp cut of his profile even more menacing with the haze of anger coloring its surface.

A single knock struck the door of the chamber.

"Just one," she whispered.

The tiger-eyes raked up and down her, gauging their adversary, weighing their options.

A heart-stopping minute passed.

I will not beg.

Another quiet knock at the door.

Shahrzad paced forward, her hazel orbs trained on the caliph.

He took a slow step back before striding to the doors.

No. Please. Stop!

As he reached for the handle, he paused without turning to look at her.

"One." He pronounced the word like a soundless epithet before he stalked through the doors.

When they thudded shut behind him, Shahrzad sank to the floor and pressed her flaming cheek against the cool marble.

Even the release of tears involved too much effort.

DESPINA AND THE RAJPUT

THE TRAY SLAMMED ONTO THE TABLE WITH A CLATTER and a bang.

Shahrzad bolted upright, sleep caking the corners of her eyelids. She swiped at them with her hand. Traces of liquid gold and black powder dotted her palm when she was finished.

"You're very small to have caused such a big fuss," a musical voice intoned.

"What?" Shahrzad focused her bleary attention on its owner.

"I said, you're very small to have caused such a big fuss." A plump girl near her age strode to the foot of the bed and yanked aside the gossamer curtains. She had fair skin and thick honey-walnut hair, piled atop her crown in typical Grecian fashion. Her eyes were the sparkling blue of the Aegean and were lined in kohl with the practiced hand of an expert. Her lips were puckered into a perfect moue, stained pink with carmine and beeswax. The white linen garment clung to her rounded frame in all the right places. A thick silver band was looped around her upper left arm.

Shahrzad pushed aside her drowsiness and attempted to conjure a semblance of dignity. "I heard you the first time."

"Then why did you ask me to repeat myself?"

"Because I don't know who you are, and I have no idea why you're banging around making ridiculous pronouncements first thing in the morning," Shahrzad shot back.

The girl laughed. It was a loud and robust sound.

"I think I'm beginning to understand why there's such a fuss. Also, it's hardly first thing in the morning. It's noon." The girl marched to the screens and threw them open to reveal a midday sun sitting high in a clear cerulean sky.

Shahrzad cringed away from the harsh stream of light.

"I brought you some food. You should eat something. You're so small," the girl reiterated.

"I fail to understand why my size is of import."

"Because a waif of a girl can't manage a sustained fight, much less succeed in one. And I'd like to see you succeed."

Instantly wary, Shahrzad pulled her knees against her chest and shuttered her expression. "Succeed?"

"By Zeus, you're a strange thing. Yes, my lady, I'd like to see you succeed. Meaning, I'd like to see you live. I'm not fond of watching young girls die at the whim of our enigmatic ruler. Are you?"

Shahrzad studied her for a breath before placing her bare feet on the cold marble and rising from the bed.

Be careful.

"No. I'm not," she replied.

The girl grinned. "You're taller than I thought. Still too skinny, but not the worst I've seen. There's a curve or two where there should be. I'm sure you're stunning when you're done up well."

"I'm sorry, who are you?" Shahrzad demanded.

"Despina. Your handmaiden . . . as long as you're succeeding."

"I don't need a handmaiden."

"I'm afraid that's not your choice." Despina's grin widened, and her blue-fire eyes sparked at Shahrzad, daring her to rise to the challenge of such impertinence.

Shahrzad paused in consideration. "So he sent you here to spy on me?"

Despina's white teeth flashed in her face. "Yes."

"Are you a good spy?"

"The best."

"A good spy would hide her identity."

"The best spies don't have to."

Shahrzad smiled at this, in spite of herself. "You're arrogant."

"As are you, my lady Shahrzad. But I do not see this as a shortcoming. For without a measure of arrogance, how can one attempt the impossible?"

Shahrzad stepped down from the platform to stand before Despina.

The girl stood half a head taller, and everything about her radiated confidence and a sense of surety as to her place in the world. From her artfully draped dress to her impeccably enhanced features, it was clear Despina was a force to be reckoned with.

But her eyes caught Shahrzad's attention more than anything else.

They were the watchful eyes of a hunter.

And they mirrored her own.

She warned me she was a spy. Why did she warn me?

"Would you like to eat something? Or do you plan to go on a hunger strike? If that's the case, do your worst, for I believe a hunger strike will kill a pretty little imp like you long before our caliph does."

Shahrzad laughed wryly. "That's the best worst compliment anyone has ever paid me."

"You're welcome." Despina spun around in a whirl of white linen, the scent of jessamine saturating the air about her. Shahrzad followed her to the table in the corner. The tray atop it was covered with *lavash* bread, a round of goat cheese enfolded in sweet preserves, a tureen of soup, and a halved pomegranate, its seeds glistening like garnets in the warm light spilling from the terrace. An ornate silver pot of cardamom tea sat over a low burning flame.

Despina removed the lid from the tureen and began to prepare the tea, placing a sparkling crystal of rock sugar in the bottom of a small etched-glass cup.

As she sat on the cushions, Shahrzad reached for a piece of *lavash*.

The handmaiden peered through her eyelashes at Shahrzad while she poured the tea in a slender stream from high above the glass. "I meant what I said; I do hope you succeed, my lady." Her tone was filled with quiet circumspection.

"Please call me Shahrzad."

"Shahrzad." Despina grinned at her.

Shahrzad could not prevent herself from returning the gesture.

Be very careful.

An hour later, with Despina's help, Shahrzad had bathed and dressed in another elaborate ensemble of silk and damask. A slim circlet of silver, spangled with pearls and tiny blue sapphires, adorned her brow. Around her neck was another fetter, made to match. Thin diamond bangles clinked together on her left wrist with every movement.

"Am I allowed to leave?" she asked, once Despina had put the final flourish on the kohl lining her eyelids.

Despina nodded. "You can roam most of the palace, as long as you're with the Rajput."

"The Rajput?"

The corners of Despina's eyes crinkled with a mixture of dry humor and pity. "The caliph is apparently so enamored, he has gifted you a member of his personal bodyguard."

Shahrzad balled her hands into fists. "So I necessitate a spy *and* a ready executioner?"

"More or less."

Hate *is not the right word for such a man.*

"Who is the Rajput?" Shahrzad spat.

"At one point, he was known as the Scourge of Hindustan. He's the best swordsman in Rey, perhaps in all of Khorasan. A devotee of the *talwar*. There's only one other swordsman in Rey who comes close, but even he has never bested the Rajput."

Well, this information might be beneficial in the future.

"Who is the second-best swordsman in Rey?"

Despina's brow furrowed. "I expected better of you."

"What?"

"I thought you would make it a point to be informed."

"Forgive me for neglecting to carry around a list of the ten best swordsmen in Khorasan," Shahrzad shot back.

"I suppose this information wouldn't be readily available to a young girl with a librarian for a father. It isn't exactly posted on walls for public viewing."

"My father is a curator of ancient texts and the smartest man I know. He was a vizier for the former caliph." Shahrzad cut her eyes.

"And after his wife's death, I heard he lost his mind and was subsequently demoted. Now he's a librarian."

I can't lose my temper. She's clearly trying to bait me. But why?

Shahrzad replied instead with a measured silence intended to reestablish control. She fiddled with the heavy silver at her throat, despising its weight.

"So, do you still want to know who the second-best swordsman in Rey is?" Despina asked, changing tack.

"Never mind. It doesn't matter."

Despina smiled knowingly. "The second-best swordsman in Rey is Khalid Ibn al-Rashid. Our illustrious King of Kings."

Shahrzad's heart sank. Gifted swordsmen tended to be stalwart strategists. Quick to spot signs of subterfuge.

And this presented yet another obstacle. If he ever suspected her of treachery, it would be even more difficult to plot his death and catch him unawares.

She swallowed carefully. "Again, it doesn't matter."

"I guess it shouldn't matter to you. But I thought you might want to know, nevertheless."

What kind of game is she playing?

"You thought wrong." Shahrzad walked to the doors of the chamber and tugged on the handles. As soon as she crossed the threshold, a hulking figure stepped into view. His skin was the color of burnished copper, and he towered over Shahrzad, with his head bound in an intricately wrapped turban. His exposed arms were thick with corded muscle, and his black beard was neatly trimmed to a point just below his chin. Eyes the color of a moonless night gleamed down at her, stark and merciless.

"Uh, yes. You must be . . . I'm sorry, what is your name?" Shahrzad stammered.

"I told you; he's the Rajput," Despina replied from behind her.

"But he must have a name," Shahrzad rasped over her shoulder.

"If he does, I don't know it."

With an irritated sigh, Shahrzad faced forward and braved the sight of her potential executioner once more.

"I'm Shahrzad." She met his black gaze.

He glowered at her before moving aside to let her pass.

As she slipped by him, she noticed the long *talwar* sword hanging from his hip, shining with menace in the midday sun.

So this silent brute is the only swordsman who can best my enemy . . .

How am I to find any weakness in Khalid Ibn al-Rashid with his spies all around me, watching my every move?

She exhaled protractedly.

I might have a serious problem.

DRAW WEIGHT

T HE ORIGINAL STRUCTURE OF THE PALACE HAD BEEN built nearly three hundred years ago, by a king with a flair for extravagance. In the years since, many wings had been added to augment the base of marble and limestone. They branched off like tributaries, winding toward an unseen destination far in the distance.

It would be easy to get lost in such a place.

"How do I get to the courtyards?" Shahrzad asked Despina, after they had wandered the shining halls for half an hour.

Despina canted her head to the side in thought. "I suppose that would be fine. No one expressly forbade you from going outdoors."

Shahrzad resisted the urge to retort as Despina backtracked down a corridor to the right. The Rajput stalked alongside Shahrzad, his posture as rigid and implacable as his expression. After several minutes of traversing in silence, they came to an open-air gallery with a series of arched double doors leading outside.

An attendant pushed through one set of doors to allow them passage, and Shahrzad walked into a terraced courtyard arranged like colossal steps in a descending staircase. The first of these terraces was filled with flowering trees and an elaborate aviary enclosed on all sides by carefully wrought trelliswork. The sturdy acacia wood was covered with a thin layer of white paint and anchored by bolts of polished bronze. Lush blue-green grass flourished between pavestones of coarse granite.

Shahrzad strode past the aviary, glancing at the colorful trove of songbirds flittering within: nightingales, goldfinches, larks, canaries . . .

A loud squawk blasted from behind her. She twisted around to find a peacock strutting across the lawn, his plumage of malachite and gold fanning in the sun, catching errant beams of light.

Shahrzad glided closer. The peacock stopped to glare at her before lowering his fan and scurrying away.

She laughed to herself. "So quick to strut. So quick to flee."

"What are you talking about?" Despina asked.

Shahrzad shook her head.

"Are you talking about men?" Despina snorted.

Choosing not to reply, Shahrzad paced the length of the top terrace and took the stone stairs leading down to the next tree-lined expanse. This garden was bursting with white citrus blossoms and green figs hanging heavy on their boughs, still awaiting their moment to ripen.

She passed through this tier, pausing only to breathe in the scent.

Despina regarded her thoughtfully. "What are you trying to do?" she asked with a trace of suspicion.

Shahrzad lifted her hand to shield her eyes as she focused on signs of movement in an expanse of sand and stone below them.

"If you'll tell me what it is you're planning, I can take you there," Despina offered.

"I'm not planning anything. I'm looking for something."

"What are you looking for?"

"A handmaiden who doesn't ask so many questions."

Despina snickered.

Shahrzad quickened her pace as she flew down the last series of stairs, making her way to the intended destination of sand and stone.

The Rajput grunted his disapproval as they neared the entrance.

So he's not mute, after all.

Despina huffed audibly. "I'm pretty sure you're not supposed to be here."

"You said I could go anywhere, as long as the Rajput is with me," Shahrzad reminded her.

"I don't think anyone expected you to come to the training grounds."

Shahrzad's keen eyes ran over the sea of male faces lost in the art of swordplay, training with spears and perfecting their deadly aim with the axe-like *tabarzin*.

He's not here.

"Are you looking for the caliph?" Despina demanded.

"No."

But I assume the second-best swordsman in Rey will practice at some point today . . . if he intends to maintain his title.

And I need to learn his weakness, so that I may destroy him with it.

"Liar." Despina smirked.

"Actually, I came here because I wanted to—" Shahrzad glanced around until her eyes fell on something she recognized well. "I wanted to learn how to use a bow and arrow."

"What?" Despina exclaimed.

Feigning ignorance, Shahrzad moved toward the rack of weapons.

The Rajput raised his arm to block her path, a note of warning in his onyx gaze.

Shahrzad steeled herself before returning his belligerent stare. "Would you teach me how to shoot? I've always wanted to learn."

He shook his head.

She affected a pout. "Nothing will happen to me. Anyway, I won't be your concern after tomorrow. Please grant me this small request."

"Maybe he's not worried about you," Despina stated caustically.

Shahrzad attempted to sidestep his mammoth forearm. When he thwarted her again, she pursed her lips.

"Must you be so difficult?" she said in harsh undertone.

"He's not being difficult. That's how he normally is," a rich male voice remarked from behind them.

Both Despina and Shahrzad swiveled to meet the amused

scrutiny of a young man with a curly mop of mahogany hair and a warm, affable expression.

The Rajput stiffened.

"Perhaps I can be of assistance?" the newcomer offered with a grin.

Shahrzad shot him a winsome smile. "I hope so. I'm—"

"I know who you are, my lady. By now, everyone in the palace knows who you are." His brown eyes sparkled with mischief as he winked at Despina. She averted her gaze, her cheeks coloring.

He's quite the flirt.

"Then you have a decided advantage over me, sir," Shahrzad said.

"I'm Jalal." He bowed his head, his fingertips brushing his brow.

"He's captain of the guard and the son of General Aref al-Khoury . . . the *Shahrban* of Rey," Despina clarified in a rote tone.

"Don't let the title fool you, my lady. I'm no one of consequence, even if my father is the highest-ranking general in Khorasan."

"Well, we share a portion of that lamentable status, for I am also no one of consequence," Shahrzad said.

"I doubt that, my lady Shahrzad. I highly doubt that." Jalal grinned, bringing further light to an already easygoing demeanor.

The Rajput grunted again. His lingering ire brought Shahrzad back to the matter at hand.

"Would you be willing to teach me how to use a bow and arrow, Captain al-Khoury?" she asked.

"That depends on a few things. The first being that you dispense with the formalities and just call me Jalal. The second being that Khalid never discover my part in this transgression."

Khalid? He calls him by his first name?

"I can meet those terms. Gladly. If you'll return the gesture, on both parts."

Jalal leaned forward conspiratorially. "Then follow me, Jalal."

Shahrzad laughed. Despina looped her arms over her ample chest. "This is a bad idea," she cautioned, her blue eyes flitting to Jalal's puckish face.

"For whom? For you, or for me?" Shahrzad retorted. "Because it seems like a very good idea for me to spend the last day of my life doing the things I've always wanted to do."

Despina sighed with resignation and trudged behind Shahrzad and Jalal. The Rajput stomped in their shadows, his distaste as plain as his irritation, despite the sharp look of rebuke from the captain of the guard.

Jalal led Shahrzad to the rack of bows. Several quivers hung from a steel bar, their goose-feathered fletchings dyed in bright colors for easy recognition. Shahrzad pulled out an arrow from one of the quivers. Its tip was blunted for target practice. Taking special pains to appear nonchalant, she bent the back end of the arrow, ever so slightly, to determine the weight of its spine.

Not that flexible.

"You've shot a bow and arrow before?" Jalal inquired, observing her with a surprising amount of keenness for someone so seemingly blithe.

"Not really." She attempted to sound dismissive.

"So can I ask what you're doing with the arrow, then?"

"I'm merely curious." She shrugged and put the arrow back in its quiver. Then she reached for another arrow with different-colored fletchings. She performed the same test.

Much better.

She removed the quiver of arrows from the bar.

"It appears you might not need my tutelage, after all," Jalal commented in an airy tone.

"No, no—" Her mind scrambled to conceal her misstep. "My . . . cousin once told me it's easier to fire arrows with less spine when you don't have a lot of upper body strength."

"I see," Jalal stated dubiously. "And what did your . . . cousin have to say about bows?"

"Nothing. The comment on arrows was merely in passing."

His expression turned even more doubtful. "Of course. In passing." He made a quick study of the different bows leaning within the weapons rack. When his hand paused on a tall, straight-backed bow, he glanced over his shoulder at Shahrzad.

She smiled at him.

Still watching her, he shifted his hand to a much smaller bow with ends that curved away from the archer when strung.

The recurve bow.

Shahrzad held her smile, refusing to fall prey to his attempt to bait her with the weapon of her choice.

"Do you have a preference?" he asked.

"Whatever you think is best."

He nodded. "I think this will work for our purposes." With a knowing grin, he took the recurve bow from the rack and strode in line with the targets positioned fifty paces away.

As she followed him, Shahrzad grimaced at her thoughtlessness in disclosing an aptitude for archery.

What's done is done. But in the future, do better.

She reached up and coiled her wavy black hair into a knot on the nape of her neck. Then she shrugged off her cumbersome mantle and handed it to Despina. A faint desert breeze cooled the bare skin at her arms and stomach. Her fitted silver top had a square neckline and tiny, capped sleeves. A silk sash of cobalt blue hung low across her hips, its pearl-embroidered ends trailing against the ground. Silver slippers kicked up tufts of sand with each step she took.

Shahrzad slung the quiver onto her shoulder, and Jalal handed her the recurve bow.

A crowd of curious onlookers had begun to gather off to the side. Despina and the Rajput stood out front, still sporting their respective looks of unease and disgust.

Shahrzad placed her feet close together as she tugged an arrow from the quiver and struggled to position it on the sinewed string.

Jalal was markedly unconvinced.

When Shahrzad nocked the arrow back, the thin strip of wood struck against the handle of the bow as it trembled in her purportedly ignorant grasp.

"Is this right?" she asked Jalal.

"No. It's not." He snorted. "But you know that, don't you?"

"Of course not."

"Are you sure?"

"Are you going to teach me, or not?" she demanded.

He laughed. "Put your left foot forward so that your stance is shoulder-width apart."

She did as she was told.

"Now relax your grip and lower your elbows. Use the sights positioned on the bow grip to aim."

Shahrzad almost sneered. She hadn't needed sights since she was thirteen. Tariq had seen to that.

"Once you've settled your sights, pull the arrow back as far as you can and release it."

When she loosed the arrow, it spun in the general direction of the target before it floated to the ground, twenty paces shy of its destination.

Shahrzad looked over at Jalal. He remained dubious.

"Did your 'cousin' explain draw weight to you?"

She shook her head.

He exhaled before stepping closer to her. "I chose this bow because it has a lower draw weight. I suspect this is the reason you chose that particular quiver of arrows. Meaning this bow and this arrow will work in tandem to help you draw back without having to use a great deal of upper body strength. Which is especially beneficial for smaller archers, like you."

"So draw weight is about size?"

"I think it's more about speed and accuracy. If you don't have to expend a lot of energy firing a single arrow, it makes it easier to nock another one into position quickly. You also tend to be more accurate when you're not straining yourself."

"It makes sense," Shahrzad agreed.

"I'm sure it does." He grinned.

She ignored his meaningful tone as she reached back for another arrow. After she fitted it into position on the sinewed bowstring, her eyes darted to his face.

"You must know the caliph well," she began.

His amusement faded slightly. "I've known Khalid since he was a little boy."

"Are you good friends?"

"No."

"I see." She drew back the arrow farther and released it. This time, it sailed much closer to its target, but still managed to land buried in the sand.

"I'm older than he is, by two years. His brother, Hassan, and I grew up together; we were very close. When Hassan died, I tried to extend a hand to Khalid, but . . ." He shrugged. "He never took it."

Shahrzad turned to face him. "I'm sorry."

"Why are you sorry?"

"It isn't easy to lose your best friend. At least, I can't imagine it would be."

"Thank you for saying so. But Khalid lost his older brother. His father died the following year. And because of that terrible incident with his mother . . . he was only fourteen when he took the throne. Fourteen and alone. I'm sure you have an idea of what came after."

I don't care. There is no excuse for the monster he's become. He's had four years to grow accustomed to being king. And as for what came after . . .

When Jalal saw the look on Shahrzad's face, he took a step in her direction.

"Please understand; I'm not making . . . excuses." His voice was very soft.

Shahrzad twisted away from him and snatched another arrow from the quiver at her back. She stopped herself when she realized she had fitted the arrow and nocked it in a seamless motion ill-befitting a novice.

Jalal laughed. "I'm sorry, but I'm now convinced I've earned the right to ask for a favor, Shahrzad."

"And why do you think that?" she said under her breath.

"Because my silence has a price."

She blinked. "Excuse me?"

He edged closer. "I don't know what you're trying to do to Khalid, but you are the first person to rattle him in years. And he needs to be rattled."

Shahrzad met his steady gaze, the arrow still pressed tight against her neck.

"Is there a favor in there somewhere?"

"Khalid is not my friend. He is not my enemy, either. He *is* my king. I remember the boy he was quite fondly . . . kind, with a bright and inquisitive mind. A wandering soul. The broken creature he is now—I'm tired of it. Will you help me fix it, Shahrzad?"

Shahrzad stared back in morose silence, wondering where

such blind faith came from. Such misplaced faith in a boy with a murderous past and a girl with treacherous intent.

Jalal studied her, his sun-bronzed face a hairsbreadth from her own.

At that moment, Despina burst from the shadows, her features alight with horror. When Shahrzad traced the terror to its source, she felt the air leave her chest in a single, sharp gasp.

Across the courtyard, the Caliph of Khorasan stood watching them, his expression cool and composed.

Like the calm before a storm.

BY THE LIGHT
OF A SINGLE CANDLE

At THE SOUND OF SHAHRZAD'S WORDLESS EX-clamation, Jalal glanced over his shoulder. Humor washed across his features, mixed with a hint of defiance. "I guess neither of us will be able to meet our earlier terms."

"I guess not." Her hazel eyes were locked on her amber-eyed nemesis.

"But I hope we can continue this discussion at a later time." Jalal stepped away from her with a mocking bow.

The caliph crossed the expanse. He was wearing a *qamis* of the finest white linen and grey *sirwal* trowsers. A tapered sword in a style Shahrzad did not recognize hung from the black *tikka* sash looped about his hips. As always, he embodied the antithesis of everything she found warm and good in the world.

All motion within the courtyard had ceased at his arrival. To his right was an older gentleman whose carriage and countenance were distinctly reminiscent of Jalal's. At his left was a nervous-looking man, clutching an armful of scrolls. Flanking him was a retinue of soldiers and bodyguards.

For a perilous beat, Shahrzad considered turning her arrow

on him. At this distance, she knew she could hit him. But the arrow's tip was blunted—meant only for target practice.

It might not kill him.

She lowered the weapon.

It's not worth the risk.

As he drew near, she willed her heart to cease its irrational pounding. If she intended to conquer this monster, she had to first quell all fears of him. Quickly.

He stopped several paces before her.

And turned to Jalal.

"Captain al-Khoury." His voice was deathly quiet.

"*Sayyidi.*" Jalal dipped his head, touching his fingertips to his brow. "I was just showing the queen how to use a bow and arrow."

"I can see that. The question is why."

"Because I asked him," Shahrzad interrupted, much too loudly.

His eyes shifted to her with dispassion. Shahrzad watched him take in her appearance—the lack of a mantle, the haphazard knot of hair . . . and the quiver of arrows dangling from her shoulder.

"Then I redirect the question to you," he said.

She set her jaw, drawing on a sudden reserve of impudence. "Do I need a reason?"

"I asked for an explanation. Not a reason."

"They're the same thing."

"Not necessarily."

"Actually, they are. Regardless of your perspective on the matter, I simply wanted to learn, and Jalal agreed to teach me." As she spoke, wisps of hair began to uncoil from the knot at her nape.

"Jalal?" His eyebrows rose at this informality, the only sign of a reaction to her bold display.

"Yes. Jalal." A lock fell forward into her face, and she shoved it behind her ear.

"And what have you learned from Jalal?"

"What?" she exclaimed, unable to conceal her surprise at his interest.

"If he's been teaching you how to shoot a bow and arrow, you must have something to show for it. Unless he's an abysmal tutor."

Jalal started to laugh. "If you'll recall, *sayyidi,* I believe I had a hand in teaching you when you were a boy."

"Jalal-*jan,*" the *shahrban* rasped at his son, the lines of consternation further weathering his face.

"Though archery has never been my strong suit," the caliph continued.

"Your words, *sayyidi.* Not mine." Jalal grinned.

"Jalal! That's enough," the *shahrban* said sharply. "He is your king!"

Jalal bowed, his obedience still tinged by ridicule.

"Well?" The caliph looked again to Shahrzad.

She returned his expectant gaze. Then, without a word, Shahrzad refitted the arrow to the sinew, keeping the bow at her side for a moment.

She desperately wanted to show him how well she could shoot, to demonstrate to the entire contingent of onlookers that she was no one to trifle with. She also wanted to do justice to the many years of patient instruction she'd received at Tariq's side.

When she'd first asked him, as a young girl of eleven, to teach her how to use a bow and arrow, she'd fully expected the twelve-year-old son of a powerful emir to ignore a silly child's request. Yet, it was that summer in the desert, clutching a makeshift bow and arrow, that she first fell in love with Tariq Imran al-Ziyad. With his refreshing candor and his ready humor. With the charm of his beautifully devious smile. Granted, it had been nothing more than a starry-eyed infatuation at the time, but it was from those precious memories that she drew her strength whenever she felt darkness descend upon her.

For the wonder of a first love can never be matched.

She closed her eyes.

Tariq.

No. Today is not the day to make a point.

She drew in a breath.

But it is also not a day to appear weak.

With her eyes still shut, she raised the bow and drew back the arrow.

She did not need to aim. She knew precisely where she wanted the arrow to fly.

From the age of thirteen, she had aimed purely on instinct, relying on her ability to gauge her surroundings at a glance.

She exhaled slowly.

As soon as she opened her eyes, she loosed the arrow. It flew toward the target in a perfect spiral.

And struck exactly where she intended.

"Amazing. Despite never taking care to aim, you actually hit the target that time," Jalal intoned drily. "In a fashion."

"It's because you're such a good teacher," she replied in a blithe manner.

The shadows from a passing cloud seemed to cast a small smile across the caliph's lips.

"Is it?" Jalal murmured.

"In a fashion." She grinned. "Nevertheless, I did hit the target . . . rather, I hit one of its legs."

"Which would have been a remarkable shot, had it been intentional."

"But we've already established that I didn't aim. Regardless, I think I did fairly well, don't you?"

"What do you think, *sayyidi*?" Jalal asked. "Does the queen pass your test of merit?"

It was a brazen question on his part. Shahrzad felt a hint of color rise in her neck as she faced the caliph.

He was merely watching them interact in detached silence.

"She missed the target," he stated simply.

Shahrzad's eyes narrowed. When the wayward lock of hair fell forward yet again, she stabbed it behind her ear with undue vehemence.

"Perhaps my king would care to demonstrate the proper technique?" she asked in a cool tone. Reaching back, she extracted an arrow and offered it, alongside the bow, to the caliph.

That same incomprehensible flash of emotion flitted across his sharp profile.

And Shahrzad found herself growing ever more curious as to the thoughts behind it.

It doesn't matter what he's thinking. It will never matter.

It should never matter.

He strode forward and extricated the weapons from her hands. When his fingers grazed hers, he hesitated before pulling away. Then his tiger-eyes clouded over and he drew back, his expression unreadable. Without a word, he nocked the arrow into position on the string.

Shahrzad watched him assume his stance. His lean form struck unnervingly precise lines as he pulled the arrow far back, bending the recurve bow until the arches at each end became all but unnoticeable.

He exhaled while he took aim.

Shahrzad resisted the urge to smile.

He uses the sights.

The arrow flew in a tight spiral toward the target, striking near the center, but not within the bull's-eye.

He lowered the bow.

"Not bad, *sayyidi,*" Jalal said with a smile.

"It's acceptable," he replied under his breath. "Nothing to boast about."

The caliph extended his left arm to return the bow to Shahrzad. He refused to meet her eyes, and then he turned to leave.

"*Sayyidi*?" she attempted.

He halted, but did not face her.

"Perhaps you wouldn't mind—"

"Jalal can teach you. He is far more proficient than I."

Irritation flared in Shahrzad at the assumption she desired anything from him. Beyond his death.

"Fine," she bit out.

He took a few steps before he stopped again. "Shahrzad?"

"Yes?"

"I'll see you tonight."

She snatched an arrow from the quiver and fitted it to the string.

I despise him. As if he could truly teach me anything about a bow and arrow . . . a boy who still uses sights! Tariq could tear him apart. Second-best swordsman in Rey—ha!

She tried to ignore the flutter of uncertainty in her stomach.

Jahandar studied the wall of the tent as it flapped in the cool night air.

He lay on his side, listening. Waiting.

Once he was certain Irsa's soft breaths had deepened into a restful sleep, he turned with great care and lifted his blankets.

She stirred on the other side of the tent, and he froze. When she rotated in place so that her back faced him, he exhaled and rose to his feet. With a careful stretch, he warded away the weariness of a full day's travel.

One foot in front of the other, Jahandar padded his way to his satchel.

As soundlessly as possible, he raised the fold and eased the worn leather volume from between the sleeves. His heart pounded when he felt the warmth of the tome settle against his chest.

The raw power of the pages now within his grasp . . .

He shuffled to a corner of the tent and placed the ancient manuscript atop a trunk of clothes. Then he lit a single candle.

And took a deep breath.

The cover of the tome was tattered and illegible. The edges were degraded, and a rusted lock bound its center.

He stared at the blackened, aged book before him.

If he started down this path . . .

He closed his eyes and swallowed. He thought of his wife in her final days, as she lay gasping for breath, begging for a moment more with her children.

Pleading for Jahandar to save her from the wasting disease.

He thought of the instant he failed her, of the helplessness he felt holding her lifeless form in his arms.

And of the crippling powerlessness as he watched his elder daughter march toward a monster only two sunsets ago.

Whatever the cost, he would fix it. If Shahrzad had managed to survive the dawn, he would work to be worthy of such a daughter. And if she had not . . .

He clenched the spine of the book tight between his fingers.

No. He would not let himself cower in the darkness of doubt again.

Jahandar reached into his nightshirt and pulled out the long silver chain hanging from his throat. Dangling on its end was a black key. He bent over the ancient tome and inserted the key into the lock. When the volume sprang open, a faint silver light emanated from the pages. Jahandar reached for the first page . . .

And stifled a cry.

It burned his hand.

No matter.

He dragged his sleeve onto his fingertips and tried again.

The text was an early form of Chagatai. Translating it would be a painstaking process, even for a man as learned as Jahandar. And especially with such pressing time constraints.

Again, no matter.

His heart thundered as he drew the single candle closer to begin his work.

For his children, he would move mountains.

He would not fail again.

ALADDIN
AND THE WONDERFUL LAMP

T HIS TIME, SHAHRZAD KNEW BETTER THAN TO WAIT for him.

So it was no surprise when he failed to make an appearance until well into the night.

The servants who delivered the food and wine found no trace of Shahrzad anywhere within the chamber. It was the caliph who discovered her standing on the terrace, overlooking a side entryway flanked by fountains.

She did not turn around when he arrived. Instead, she leaned over the railing and smiled to herself.

He paused for a moment and then joined her.

A crescent moon hung high in the sky, reflecting back into the shimmering pools of water below.

"You can't see them, but I love how you can smell the citrus blossoms from here . . . the suggestion of something beautiful and alive," she began.

He didn't respond immediately. "You're partial to citrus blossoms?"

"Yes. But I prefer roses above all. My father has a beautiful rose garden."

He turned to her, studying her profile in the moonlight. "I think a father who tends to flowers must have objected to . . . this."

Shahrzad continued to stare ahead. "I think a king who hopes to be beloved by his people shouldn't execute their daughters at dawn."

"Who said I hoped to be beloved by my people?" the caliph replied in a staid monotone.

At this, Shahrzad twisted to meet his gaze. "And all this time, I could have sworn you were a smart man." She mimicked his quietly aloof tone as she pronounced this judgment, and the effect of her subtle mockery was not lost on him.

A corner of his lips twitched. "And all this time . . . I could have sworn you didn't want to die."

Shahrzad blinked.

And then decided to laugh.

The sound carried over the terrace, bubbling out into the night, filling the sky with the tinkling music of bells.

The caliph watched her, his spark of surprise quickly masked by somber reflectiveness.

"You're very strange," Shahrzad commented, once her laughter had subsided.

"So are you, Shahrzad al-Khayzuran."

"At least I know it."

"I'm aware of it as well."

"But I don't punish people for it."

He sighed. "I envy people who see the world as you do."

"Are you insinuating I'm simpleminded?" Anger seeped into her words.

"No. You see things the way you live your life. Without fear."

"That's not true. I'm afraid of a lot of things."

He cast her a searching glance. "What are you afraid of?"

Just then, as if the night had foretold the moment, a vicious breeze raked across the terrace, whipping through Shahrzad's long black hair. Tendrils flew into her face, obscuring her features.

"I'm afraid of dying," she announced over the wind.

And I'm afraid of losing to you.

He stared at her as the gust died down . . . as it finished toying with Shahrzad's tresses, winding them to and fro.

When the last vestiges disappeared, that same errant lock from earlier in the day still hung in her eyes. She started to reach for it—

But he caught her hand in one of his own and brushed the curl behind her ear, gently.

The fluttering in her stomach returned with a vengeance.

"Tell me why you're here." It sounded entreating in his low voice.

I'm here to win.

"Promise me you won't kill me," she breathed back.

"I can't do that."

"Then there's nothing more to say."

As with the first night, Shahrzad was amazed by her ability to detach from reality.

And again, she remained strangely grateful he never once tried to kiss her.

Grateful . . . yet somewhat perplexed.

She had kissed Tariq before—stolen embraces in the shadows of vaulted turrets. The illicit nature of these encounters had always thrilled her. At any time, a servant could have found them; or worse, Rahim could have caught them kissing . . . and he would have needled Shahrzad mercilessly, as he'd done from the moment he'd crowned himself the brother she'd never had.

So, while she appreciated not having to kiss a murderer, it did appear odd for her new husband to refrain from this particular act, especially when it seemed a great deal less intimate than . . . other things.

Shahrzad found herself wanting to ask why. And her curiosity grew by the hour.

Stop it. It doesn't matter.

Instead of rising to dress as he did, Shahrzad lingered on the bed and grabbed a large cushion the color of bright carnelian. She pulled it against her chest and wrapped her slender arms around its center.

He turned to face her when she did not join him by the table.

"I'm not hungry," she stated.

He inhaled, and she watched his shoulders move in time with his breath.

Then he returned to the foot of the bed so that they were positioned on opposite ends, as far from each other as possible.

So strange.

Shahrzad rolled on her side and burrowed into the mass of silken pillows. Her bronze ankles dangled off the bed.

The edges of the caliph's amber eyes tightened, ever so slightly.

"Would you like me to continue the story?" she said. "*Sayyidi?*"

"I almost thought you were above the use of honorifics now."

"Pardon?"

"Have you forgotten who I am, Shahrzad?"

She blinked. "No . . . *sayyidi.*"

"So then a lack of decorum just comes with your sense of comfort."

"Inasmuch as bitter apathy does yours."

Again, his shoulders rose and fell. "Tell me, why do you find it permissible to talk to me like this?"

"Because someone has to," she replied without hesitation.

"And you think it should be you?"

"I think it should be someone who isn't afraid of you. And, though I do feel . . . anxious in your presence, the more I see of everything around me, the less I have reason to fear you."

As soon as she said the words aloud, she was startled to realize their truth. In the single day she'd been his wife, she'd seen remarkably little of the bloodthirsty monster she'd expected.

This time, it was much more than a mere flash of surprise that etched its way across his face. His astonishment burgeoned into dismay before it melted back into the landscape of emptiness that forever shrouded his features.

"You know nothing," he countered.

Shahrzad almost laughed at this. "You're right. I know nothing. Would you care to educate me, *sayyidi?*"

It was a quiet taunt . . . a poisoned glass of wine, meant to intoxicate and exsanguinate.

Meant to compel him into exposing his weakness.

Please. Give me the rope from which to hang you.

"Finish the story of Agib, Shahrzad."

The moment was lost.

For now.

She smiled at him from across the bed. "The shadow forming within the blue plume of smoke solidified . . . and began to laugh."

The caliph's shoulders relaxed. He eased forward.

"Agib scrambled back farther, his terror mounting. The laughter grew until it echoed across the black sand of Adamant's shore. Agib covered his face with trembling hands. And, from the depths of the shadow, a figure emerged. He was bald, with sharply tapered ears adorned in gold. His skin was blanched white and covered with raised markings in a language Agib did not recognize. When the figure opened his mouth to speak, Agib saw that every one of his teeth was filed to a razor-sharp point."

Shahrzad bunched a pillow below her neck and crossed her ankles. When the caliph's gaze flickered down her bare legs, her eyes widened in awareness, and he glanced away.

Ignoring the rising warmth in her neck, she continued. "Agib was sure he was about to die. He clasped his hands before him and closed his eyes, offering a silent plea for a quick and painless end to a worthless life. So when the creature spoke to Agib in a voice that shook the very ground they stood upon, his words were the last things Agib expected to hear, for a multitude of reasons. The creature said, 'What question does my master wish to ask of me?' And Agib just sat there, speechless. The creature repeated himself. Agib sputtered, almost inaudibly, 'Question? What kind of questions do you speak of, O creature of the cup?' The creature laughed again and replied, 'That was the first of my master's three questions. He is permitted three, and only three. After this, he has two questions remaining. The questions I speak of are the questions the master of the Bronze Chalice may pose to the All-Knowing Genie of the Bronze Chalice. I possess the answers to questions—past, present, and future. Choose them wisely, for once you ask three, you are a master no more.'"

At this, the caliph smiled to himself.

"Agib pitched to his feet, still reeling in disbelief. But the sharp mind of a thief was beginning to take control, and he quickly realized his foolishness had already cost him one precious question. So he stopped himself from speaking out of turn and succumbing to yet another trick by the clever genie before him. He formulated his next question carefully in his mind before posing it. Then he asked, 'Genie of the Bronze Chalice, your master wishes to know the exact way to escape this island so as to reach his homeland without any further harm befalling his person.' The genie grinned wickedly before bowing before Agib. With a nod toward the mountain, the genie said, 'Buried at the top of Adamant lies a boat with bolts of brass. Drag it to the shore and sail in the direction of the third brightest star in the night sky. After twenty days and nights, you will reach your homeland.' His eyes wary, Agib prodded further. 'My question demanded that no further harm befall my person for the duration of this journey. Nowhere in your answer did you address food or water.' The genie cackled once more. 'My master learns faster than most. I shall direct you to a hidden spring near the westernmost point of the island. And, as for food, I suggest you dry enough fish for the journey.'"

"That seems rather convenient," the caliph interjected. "The genie cannot be trusted."

"They rarely can be, in my opinion, *sayyidi.*" Shahrzad grinned. "Over the next few days, Agib followed the genie's instructions. He brought the boat to the shore and filled it with supplies for the journey. On the third night, by the light of a full moon, he set sail, with the Bronze Chalice safely stowed in a pouch at his feet. For ten days, he traveled without event. He began to believe his journey might end well . . . that luck might be on his side, after all. Hoping against hope, he started to dream of what to ask as his final question. Where could he obtain all the riches in the world? How could he win the love of the most beautiful woman in Baghdad?"

Shahrzad paused for effect.

"And then . . . the boat started to creak. Briny water began seeping into the seams. Aghast, Agib discovered the brass bolts were cracking at the edges, allowing the sea to flow in through the joints. In a panic, he tried to bail the water out of the boat with his bare hands. When he realized the futility of his efforts, he grabbed the chalice and rubbed its surface. The genie appeared and sat calmly on the boat's listing bow. 'We are sinking!' Agib shouted at the genie. 'You assured me I would reach my home-land without any harm befalling my person!' The genie merely stared at Agib, without a seeming care in the world. 'You may ask me a question, Master,' he replied. Agib glanced about frantically, wondering if now was the time to use his last, and most precious, question. Just then on the horizon, Agib saw the mast of another boat—a much larger vessel. He stood up and waved his hands, shouting for its attention. When it shifted in his direction, Agib yelled with triumph, and the genie smirked before vanishing back into his chalice. Agib boarded the vessel, trembling with gratitude, his clothes tattered and his sun-stained face hidden beneath a scraggly beard. But, lo . . ."

The caliph's eyebrows lifted.

"When the owner of the vessel emerged from belowdecks, Agib was horrified to discover it was none other than the emir . . . the very man whose soldiers had chased him out of Baghdad and driven him to take this wretched voyage in the first place. For an instant, Agib considered plunging headfirst into the sea, but, when the emir smiled warmly at him and welcomed him aboard the ship, Agib realized his disheveled appearance made him all but unrecognizable. So he broke bread at the emir's table, sharing in his food and drink as though he were unaware of his patron's identity. The elder gentleman was a consummate host, refilling Agib's cup with his own hand and regaling him with tales of his many seafaring adventures. As the evening wore on, Agib learned the emir had set sail several weeks ago in search of an island with a mysterious mountain at its center. Hidden on this island was a chalice with the mystical power to answer any question in the world—past, present, and future."

The caliph leaned back on his elbow, his eyes warm.

"At this news, Agib stilled. For, of course, the emir could be speaking of none other than the very chalice lying in Agib's pouch. Feigning complete ignorance, Agib asked the emir why he had decided to take on such a dangerous mission, especially in the twilight years of his life. The emir's eyes saddened. He confessed there was one reason, and one reason alone, for him to take to the sea in search of the black mountain and its hidden chalice. Several weeks ago, something very precious had been stolen from him—a ring that had belonged to his dead wife. It was all that remained of her, and he considered it his most prized possession. In the streets of Baghdad, a gifted thief had slipped the trinket from the emir's own hand and disappeared into the crowd with the stealth of a shadow. Ever since that afternoon, the emir had been haunted at night by the ghost of his dead wife, and he knew he had to recover that ring, whatever the cost. If he could ask the chalice where it was, he could appease his wife's spirit and restore honor to the memory of their love."

"So his question to an all-knowing genie would be about a mere trinket of love?" the caliph interjected.

"A mere trinket? Love is a force unto itself, *sayyidi*. For love, people consider the unthinkable . . . and often achieve the impossible. I would not sneer at its power."

The caliph held her gaze. "I am not sneering at its power. I am lamenting its role in this story."

"You are saddened by love's importance in the emir's life?"

He paused. "I am frustrated by its importance in all our lives."

Shahrzad's lips formed a sad smile. "That's understandable. If a bit predictable."

He inclined his head. "Again, you presume to know a great deal for a day and two nights, my queen."

Shahrzad averted her eyes and toyed with the corner of the red pillow in her arms. She felt a flush in her cheeks.

My queen?

At her silence, he stirred with discomfort.

"You're right," Shahrzad murmured. "I should not have said that."

He inhaled through his nose.

An odd stillness seemed to stretch over the room.

"And I should not have interrupted you. I'm sorry," he whispered.

Shahrzad wound the scarlet fringe of the pillow tight between her fingers.

"Please continue," he said.

She looked up at him and nodded.

"Agib listened to this tale with a growing sense of unease. Obviously, he was the perpetrator of the theft. The ring in question had been discarded in his panicked attempt to flee the emir's soldiers. He had no intention of turning over the chalice before he had a chance to determine what his all-important final question would be. And if the emir discovered Agib had the chalice, he would likely kill him to procure it. Even more imminent was the danger that someone would recognize the thief responsible for the emir's heartache. Agib resolved to stay close by the man's side for the remainder of the journey and use every means available to conceal his identity."

Shahrzad sat up carefully when she noticed a faint light streaming through the edge of the screens leading to the terrace.

And it begins again.

"For the next few months, the ship sailed the waters in search of the Mountain of Adamant, with Agib managing to keep them safely off course. In that time, he learned a great deal from the emir about his many experiences and, ultimately, about his life. He grew to admire the emir, and the emir soon saw in Agib an intelligent young man with a wide aptitude for knowledge and a courageous heart. Agib became a capable sailor. He realized men could respect him for being more than just a thief—they could respect him for being a man of honor upon whom they could rely. Alas, time did not stand on their side. The aging emir grew sick, and they were forced to turn back to port. Soon, it became clear he was dying. Every day became that much more precious. Agib watched in horror as his mentor, as his friend, began wasting away before his very eyes. He thought about asking the genie if there was a way to save him, but he knew it was beyond the realm of possibility."

The dawn crept up the screen with a haunting pallor.

"As soon as the boat docked, Agib knew what he had to do. He fled from the boat with nothing but the chalice in hand. Once he cleared the docks, he scrubbed at the chalice's edge and demanded the genie tell him where he could find the ring. The genie laughed uproariously when he realized Agib was wasting his final wish on such a question, but told Agib the ring was on the pinky finger of one of the most notorious mercenaries in Baghdad. Agib wasted no time seeking him out. The fight that ensued over the ring was bloody and brutal. Agib was forced to turn over his entire trove of spoils in exchange for safe passage through the den of cutthroats. His eyes blackened and his body bruised, he returned to the ship with nothing but the ring in hand."

Dawn had arrived, in all its white-gold splendor.

And Shahrzad was certain the caliph was aware of it.

She blazed ahead, undeterred. "The emir lay gasping for breath. When he saw Agib, he reached for him. Agib knelt at his bedside and placed the ring on his finger. Through blood-shot eyes, the emir took in Agib's bruises. 'My son,' he rasped, 'I thank you. From the bottom of my heart.' Agib began to weep. He started to confess his identity, but the emir stopped him. 'I knew who you were the moment you came aboard my ship. Promise me that, for the rest of your life, you will not steal from your fellow man. But that you will work alongside him to better the lives of those around you.' Agib nodded and wept harder. And then, clutching Agib's hand, the emir died with a peaceful smile on his face. Afterward, Agib discovered the emir had willed his entire estate to him, passing along his title as though Agib were truly his son. Agib soon chose a wife, and the wedding of the new emir was a celebration the like of which Baghdad had not seen in many years."

Shahrzad stopped, her eyes flitting to the sunlight streaming from the terrace.

"Are you finished?" the caliph asked softly.

She shook her head.

"At the wedding of the new emir was a guest from a faraway land—a magician from Africa in search of a magic lamp. But in truth, he was not really looking for the lamp. He was looking for a young boy. A young boy named Aladdin."

A muscle rippled along the caliph's jaw. "This is a new story."

"No, it's not. It's part of the same story."

A knock sounded at the door.

Shahrzad rose from the bed and grabbed her *shamla.* With shaking hands, she tied it about her waist.

"Shahrzad—"

"You see, Aladdin was an excellent gambler . . . a trickster of the highest pedigree. His father before him was—"

"Shahrzad."

"It's not a different story, *sayyidi,*" she said in a calm, quiet tone, fisting her hands against the fabric of her robe to hide their treachery.

He unfurled to his feet as another knock struck at the door, this one more insistent than the last.

"Come in," the caliph instructed.

When four soldiers and the *Shahrban* of Rey entered her bedchamber, Shahrzad felt the floor beneath her begin to sway. She locked her knees and stood ramrod straight to prevent her body from betraying any sign of weakness.

Why is Jalal's father here?

"General al-Khoury. Is something wrong?" the caliph asked.

The *shahrban* bowed before his king, a hand to his brow. "No, *sayyidi.*" He hesitated. "But . . . it is morning." His eyes darted in Shahrzad's direction. He paled, refusing to meet her gaze.

He can't . . . he . . . does he want to kill me? Why would he want me to die?

When the caliph made no move to stop him, the *shahrban* motioned to the guards with his head.

They strode to Shahrzad's side.

And her heart . . . her heart flew into her throat.

No!

A guard reached for her arm. When his hand closed around her wrist, Shahrzad saw the caliph's features tighten. She yanked her arm from the guard's grasp, as though it were a flame held too near her flesh.

"Don't touch me!" she yelled.

When another guard seized her shoulder, she slapped his hand out of the way.

"Are you deaf? How dare you touch me? Do you know who I am?" A note of panic entered her voice.

Not knowing what else to do, she locked upon her enemy.

The tiger-eyes were . . . torn.

Wary.

And then?

Calm.

"General al-Khoury?"

"Yes, *sayyidi.*"

"I'd like to introduce you to the Mountain of Adamant."

The *shahrban* stared back and forth between the caliph and Shahrzad.

"But, *sayyidi* . . . I don't understand. You cannot—"

The caliph swiveled to face the *shahrban.* "You're right, General. You do not understand. And you may never understand. Regardless, I'd like to introduce you to the Mountain of Adamant . . ."

The caliph glanced back at Shahrzad, a ghost of a smile playing across his lips.

"My queen."

THE BEGINNING IS THE END

Tariq's *RIDA'* WAS COVERED IN A THICK LAYER OF dust. Sand clung to every exposed part of his skin. His dark bay stallion was sleek with sweat, and white foam was beginning to collect around the iron bit at its mouth.

Rahim's grumblings grew louder with each passing hour.

But Tariq could see the city gates of Rey looming on the horizon.

And he refused to stop.

"By all that is holy, can we ease our pace for a spell?" Rahim yelled for the fifth time in as many minutes.

"Go ahead. Ease your pace. And then tumble from your saddle. You should be quite a feast for the crows," Tariq shot back.

"We've been riding with fire at our backs for two days straight!"

"And, as a result, we're nearly there."

Rahim slowed his horse to a canter, rubbing the sweat from his brow. "Don't misunderstand me; I'm just as concerned about Shazi as you are. But what use will you be to anyone, half starved and near dead?"

"We can sleep under a cloud of perfume once we reach Uncle Reza's house," Tariq replied. "We just have to get to Rey. I have to—" He spurred his horse faster.

"It will do you no good to worry so. If anyone can beat the odds, it's Shazi."

Tariq reined in his Arabian to match pace with Rahim. "She never should have had to try."

"This is not your fault."

"Do you think this is about guilt?" Tariq exploded.

"I don't know. All I know is that you feel a responsibility to fix it. And I feel a responsibility to you. And to Shazi."

"I'm sorry," Tariq said. "I have no right to yell at you. But I would have done anything to prevent this. The thought of her—"

"Stop. Don't punish yourself."

They rode in silence for a few minutes.

"I do feel guilty," Tariq admitted.

"I know."

"I felt guilty when Shiva died, too."

"Why?"

"Because I didn't know what to say to Shazi after the death of her best friend. After the death of my cousin. I didn't know what to say to anyone. My mother was a complete disaster. My aunt—well, I don't think there was anything anyone could have done to prevent her death, in the end. And Shahrzad . . . was just so quiet."

"That alone unnerved me," Rahim recalled in a rueful tone.

"I should have known then. I should have seen."

"Would that you were a seer of the future, Tariq Imran

al-Ziyad," Rahim sighed. "Would that we all were. Instead of being a useless third son, I'd be a rich man in the arms of a beautiful wife . . . with curves for days and legs for leagues."

"I'm not joking, Rahim. I should have realized she would do something like this."

"I'm not joking, either." Rahim frowned. "You can't foresee the future. And there's nothing you can do about the past."

"You're wrong. I can learn from it . . ." Tariq dug his heels into his stallion's flanks, and the horse shot forward, painting a dark smudge across the sand. "And I can make sure it never happens again!"

It was midmorning when Tariq and Rahim dismounted from their horses in the middle of Reza bin-Latief's elegant compound, deep in the heart of Rey. A gleaming oval fountain of mazarine-glazed tile graced the center of the courtyard, and terra-cotta stones cut in an elaborate hexagonal fashion lined the surroundings. Green vines crept up each of the columned arches. At the base of every arch were small flowerbeds filled with violets, hyacinths, daffodils, and lilies. Torches of smelted bronze and iron adorned the walls, awaiting nightfall for the chance to showcase their faceted grandeur.

And yet, for all the home's beauty, there was an aura of sadness to the space.

A sense of tremendous loss no amount of splendor could ever fill.

Tariq placed Zoraya on her makeshift mews in the far corner of the courtyard. She squawked with discomfort at her new surroundings and the unfamiliar perch, but quieted as soon as Tariq began to feed her.

Rahim crossed his arms, and a cloud of dust puffed out around him. "The damned bird is fed before I am? Where is the justice in this?"

"Ah, Rahim-*jan* . . . I can see little has changed over the past few years."

Tariq turned at the sound of this familiar voice.

Standing beneath the curtain of vines in a nearby archway was his uncle.

Both young men stepped forward and lowered their heads, pressing their fingertips to their brows in a sign of respect.

Reza bin-Latief walked into the sun with a sad smile on his face. The dark hair on his head had thinned out even more since the last time Tariq had seen him, and his neatly trimmed mustache was peppered with a good deal more grey as well. The lines at his eyes and mouth that Tariq had always associated with humor had deepened to reflect something decidedly incongruous—

The smile of a soul haunted by specters.

All a part of the masquerade put on by a grief-stricken man whose cherished seventeen-year-old daughter had died one morning . . . only to be followed by his wife, three days later.

A wife who couldn't bear to live in a world without her only child.

"Uncle." Tariq put out his hand.

Reza grasped it warmly. "You made it here quite quickly, Tariq-*jan*. I was not expecting you until tomorrow."

"What happened to Shazi? Is she . . . alive?"

Reza nodded.

"Then—"

Reza's sad smile turned faintly proud. "By now, the whole city knows about our Shahrzad . . ."

Rahim paced closer, and Tariq's empty fist clenched at his side.

"The only young queen to survive not one, but two sunrises in the palace," Reza continued.

"I knew it," Rahim said. "Only Shazi."

Tariq's shoulders relaxed for the first time in two days. "How?"

"No one knows," Reza replied. "The city is rife with speculation. Namely, that the caliph must be in love with his new bride. But I am not of the same mind. A murderer such as this is not capable of—" He stopped short, his mouth drawn in sudden fury.

Tariq leaned over, clasping his uncle's hand tighter. "I have to get her out of there," he said. "Will you help me?"

Reza stared back at his handsome nephew. At the determined lines and the set jaw. "What are you planning to do?"

"I'm going to rip out his heart."

Reza gripped Tariq's palm hard enough to hurt it. "What you're suggesting—it's treason."

"I know."

"And, to succeed, you'd have to break into the palace or . . . or start a war."

"Yes."

"You can't do this alone, Tariq-*jan*."

Tariq held Reza's gaze in silence.

"Are you prepared to start a war for her? Regardless of whether or not she . . . continues to survive?" Reza asked in a gentle tone.

Tariq grimaced. "He deserves to die for what he's done to our family. I won't permit him to take anything else from me . . . or from anyone else, for that matter. It's time for us to take something from him. And if it means seizing his kingdom in order to do it—" Tariq took a deep breath. "Will you help me, Uncle?"

Reza bin-Latief looked around at his beautiful courtyard. Ghosts tormented him in every corner. His daughter's laughter lilted into the sky. His wife's touch slipped through his fingers like a handful of sand.

He could never let them go. Their memories, no matter how faded and broken, were the only things he had left. The only things worth fighting for.

Reza glanced back at the Emir Nasir al-Ziyad's son—the successor to the fourth-largest stronghold in Khorasan. With a lineage of royalty.

Tariq Imran al-Ziyad—a chance to right a wrong . . .

And make his memories whole again.

"Come with me."

THE *SHAMSHIR*

"Get up."

Shahrzad moaned and drew the pillow over her face in response.

"Get up. Now."

"Go away," Shahrzad grumbled.

At that, the pillow was unceremoniously snatched from her grasp and slammed against her cheek with a force that shocked her.

She sat upright, sheer outrage eclipsing her exhaustion.

"Are you deranged?" she shouted.

"I told you to get up," Despina replied in a matter-of-fact tone.

Not knowing what else to do, she pelted the pillow back at Despina's head.

Despina caught it with a laugh. "Get up, Shahrzad, Brat Calipha of Khorasan, Queen of Queens. I've been waiting all morning for you, and we have someplace to go."

When Shahrzad finally rose from the bed, she saw yet again that Despina was flawlessly garbed in another draped garment and polished until every facet of her pale skin was artfully rendered in the light flowing from the terrace.

"Where did you learn—that?" Shahrzad asked with begrudging admiration.

Despina positioned her hands on her hips and peaked an eyebrow.

"The clothes, the hair, the—*that.*" Shahrzad raked her fingers through her tangled mane as she clarified.

"At home in the city of Thebes. My mother taught me. She was one of the most famous beauties in all of Cadmeia. Perhaps in all of the Greek Isles."

"Oh." Shahrzad studied Despina's glossy curls and then proceeded to toss back the snarled mess in her hands.

"I wouldn't." Despina smirked.

"Wouldn't what?"

"Attempt to bait me into complimenting you."

"Excuse me?" Shahrzad sputtered.

"I've encountered your kind many times before—the effortlessly lovely ones; the green sylphs of the world. They flail about, without concern for their charms, but they suffer the same desire to be liked that we all do. Just because you don't know how to make the best of your many gifts does not mean they go unnoticed, Shahrzad. But I could teach you, if you like. Although it seems you don't need my help." Despina winked. "Obviously, the caliph appreciates your charms as they are."

"Well, he's not a very particular man. How many wives has he had in the past three months alone? Sixty? Seventy-five?" Shahrzad retorted.

Despina quirked her mouth. "But he hasn't gone to see them at night."

"What?"

"Usually, they're chosen at random, he marries them, and . . . well, you know what happens the next morning."

"Don't lie to me, Despina."

"I'm not. You were the first bride he sought out after the wedding."

I don't believe her.

"In case you were wondering, I wasn't supposed to tell you that," Despina admitted.

"Then why did you?"

"I don't know." She shrugged. "Maybe I just want you to like me."

Shahrzad gave her a long, hard look. "If you want me to like you, help me figure out what to wear. Also, where's the food? I'm starving."

Despina grinned. "I already laid out a long *qamis* and matching trowsers. Get dressed, and we can leave."

"But I haven't bathed! Where are you taking me?"

"Do you have to spoil everything?"

"Where are we going?" Shahrzad insisted. "Tell me now."

"Fine!" Despina exhaled. "I'll tell you while you're getting dressed." She shoved the clothing at Shahrzad and directed her behind the privacy screens.

"So," Despina began, "last winter, the caliph went to Damascus to visit the Malik of Assyria and, while he was there, he saw the malik's new bathhouse . . . it's this huge pool of water they keep warm with these special heated stones. The steam is supposed to do wonders for your skin. Anyway, the caliph had one built here, in the palace! They just finished it!"

"And?"

"Obviously, I'm taking you there." Despina rolled her eyes.

"Obviously. I just don't understand why this is such cause for excitement."

"Because it's amazing. And new. And you will be one of the first ones to try it."

"So he wants to boil me to death?" Shahrzad said acerbically.

Despina snickered.

"I'm ready." Shahrzad emerged from behind the screens clad in simple pale green linen with matching jade earrings and pointed gold slippers. She plaited her hair in a single braid down her back and strode to the door of the chamber.

The Rajput was nowhere to be found.

"Where is he?" Shahrzad asked.

"Oh. He was dismissed for the day."

"What? Why?"

"Because we're going to the bathhouse. He can't very well accompany us there, can he?"

Shahrzad pursed her lips. "No. But . . ."

As Despina pulled the doors shut, Shahrzad saw her chew on her carmine-stained lower lip.

As though she were concealing something.

"Despina. Where is the Rajput?"

"I told you. Dismissed."

"That's fine. But where does he go when he's dismissed?"

"How should I know?"

"You know everything."

"I don't know this, Shahrzad."

Why is she lying to me? I thought I wasn't allowed to go anywhere without the Rajput. Where is she really taking me?

"I'm not going anywhere until you tell me where my bodyguard is."

"By Zeus, you are a nuisance, Shahrzad al-Khayzuran!" Despina cried.

"It's good you know that. It will save you time. Now, answer my question."

"No."

"Answer me, you wretched Theban!"

"No, you horse's ass!"

Shahrzad's mouth fell agape. "Listen to me: we can either stand in the hallways of the palace and shout at each other, or you can let me have my way now and spare yourself the trouble. When I was twelve, my best friend and I were falsely accused of stealing a necklace. The shopkeeper's fourteen-year-old son said he would let us go for a kiss each. I broke his nose, and my best friend shoved him in a trough of water. When we were confronted by his father, we denied the entire incident, and I had to sit outside our door for a whole night. It was the best sleep of my life."

"And your point is?"

"I never lose, nor am I afraid to spill blood."

Despina stared down at her. "Fine! The Rajput is—he's in a tournament. The men are having a swordsmanship tournament this afternoon."

A calculating gleam entered Shahrzad's hazel eyes.

"See! This is precisely why I didn't want to tell you!" Despina groaned. "And you can't go, anyway. If the caliph sees you there, he'll—"

"Is he fighting in the tournament?"

"Of course."

Then there is no way you're going to stop me.

"He won't do anything to me," Shahrzad announced, though her voice was laced with uncertainty.

"I can't say the same for myself," Despina retorted.

"Fine. Is there a way to watch it so no one knows we're there?"

"Can we please just go to the bathhouse?" Despina pleaded.

"Of course. After the tournament."

"Holy Hera. I'm going to die as your handmaiden."

"This is, by far, the most asinine thing I've ever done in the six years I've lived at the palace," Despina said quietly, as they crouched behind a wall of tan stone. The latticework at its top afforded them a vantage point from which to see the sand-filled expanse below.

"You can blame me," Shahrzad breathed back.

"Oh, I will. Make no mistake."

"Have you ever seen one of these tournaments?"

"No. They're not meant for an audience."

"Why is that?"

"I'm not sure. Maybe because—" Despina gasped as the first soldier stepped onto the sand.

"That might be the reason," Shahrzad joked with a slight hitch in her voice.

He was clad in nothing but *sirwal* trowsers and a burgundy *tikka* sash. Barefoot. No *qamis*. No *rida'*. His bare chest glowed with sweat in the hot afternoon sun. In silence, he withdrew a large scimitar from his left hip. Its blade was narrow at the hilt and widened as it curved outward before tapering to a lethal point.

The soldier raised the scimitar high.

"Where is his opponent?" Shahrzad asked.

"How should I know?"

The soldier began swinging his blade in the air, performing an extended drill. He danced across the sand, the silver sword cutting arc after arc through the bright blue sky.

When he was finished, cheers and whistles of approval emanated from the sidelines.

"They must start with drills before they launch into fighting," Despina decided.

"Ever the smart Theban."

"If I push you over, you'll look decidedly unqueenlike."

Several more soldiers showcased their drilling techniques before a hulking form materialized in the sand. His shoulders were immense, and every muscle appeared to strain beneath his copper skin.

"My God," Shahrzad said. "He could crush my skull with his bare hands."

Despina snickered.

When the Rajput drew his *talwar* into the sun, he paused for an eerie moment, the sword poised above his head.

Let's see what it means to be the best swordsman in Rey.

The second he brought the blade down was the last time Shahrzad remembered seeing it for the entire duration of the Rajput's demonstration. The slender *talwar* whipped through the breeze, curling over its master's arm as the Rajput stretched and dove into the sand.

Then, near the end of the drill, he lifted his free hand to his mouth . . .

And blew over his open palm.

A stream of fire extended onto the sword.

The *talwar* was ablaze.

He whirled it over his head, slicing the screaming dragon of a weapon downward. With a final thrust into the sand, he extinguished the flames.

The soldiers raised an earsplitting chorus on the sidelines.

Shahrzad and Despina stared at one another in shared amazement.

"I—I . . ." Shahrzad attempted.

"I know," Despina finished.

Lost in their wordless conversation, it took both girls some time to recognize the next figure striding onto the sand. When Shahrzad looked down, she was dismayed by the instant tightening sensation in her chest. She knitted her brow and pressed her lips into a line.

The caliph's shoulders were tan and lean; each of the muscles in his trim torso shone, defined and well articulated in the afternoon sun.

Despina sighed. "Despite everything, I have to admit I've always found him quite handsome. Such a shame."

Again, Shahrzad felt the strange reaction spike within her core.

"Yes. It is a shame," she spat.

"There's no need to be angry at me for admiring him. Trust that he's the last man I'd ever have designs on. I don't enjoy gambling with my own life."

"I wasn't angry at you!" Shahrzad protested. "I don't care if you or anyone else admires him!"

Despina's eyes danced with amusement.

And then the caliph drew his sword.

It was a unique weapon. Not as wide as a scimitar, nor as sharply curved. The blade was thin, and its point tapered to a more severe angle than all the other swords Shahrzad had seen so far.

"Do you know the name of that weapon?" she asked.

"It's called a *shamshir.*"

As the caliph began his drill, Shahrzad found herself gripping the top of the wall, seeking a better vantage point.

Like the Rajput, he slashed and arced so quickly it was almost impossible to discern the location of the blade. But where the Rajput's superior strength granted him the ability to radiate menace without shifting a muscle, the caliph's far more agile form underscored the subtle grace—the cunning instincts—behind every motion.

Halfway through the drill, he placed both hands on the hilt of his *shamshir* and twisted the handle apart.

The sword split in two, and he began swinging one in either hand. The blades tore through the air like a dust devil in the desert, whistling about his head as he made his way across the sand.

Shahrzad heard Despina catch her breath.

The twin *shamshirs* rained a shower of sparks as he struck them against each other and brought the drill to an end with a sword positioned in each hand at his sides.

Again, a riotous cheer rang through the throng of soldiers standing witness to the spectacle. Whatever one's personal feelings about the caliph, it could not be denied he was a masterful swordsman.

Nor was he a king solely reliant on the protection of others.

He would not be an easy man to kill.

And this presents a serious challenge.

"Well, does that satisfy your curiosity?" Despina asked.

"Yes, my lady. Does it?" A gruff voice announced its presence behind them.

Both girls scrambled to their feet, still trying to remain unseen by the soldiers below.

The color drained from Shahrzad's face.

The *Shahrban* of Rey was standing across the way, his face a mask of false composure, and his eyes filled with . . . frustration.

"General al-Khoury." Shahrzad brushed the debris from her hands and her clothes.

He continued studying her, some kind of war raging behind his eyes.

When the battle was over, it was obvious Shahrzad had lost.

"What are you doing here, my lady?"

"I was . . . curious."

"I see. And may I ask who gave you permission to be here, my lady?"

At this, Shahrzad's indignation rose. He might be the *Shahrban* of Rey and a good deal older than she, but she had done nothing to warrant such disrespect. She was his queen, after all—not a child to be scolded for misbehaving.

She strode forward. "I did not seek permission from anyone, General al-Khoury. Nor shall I seek permission from anyone in the future. For anything."

He inhaled carefully, his brown eyes, so like Jalal's and yet so dissimilar, narrowing invectively. "I'm afraid we can't allow you to behave thus, my lady. You see, it is my job to protect the king and this kingdom. And you—you conflict with my job. I'm sorry. I can't let you continue to do this."

Does he—does he know?

"I thank you, General al-Khoury."

"Excuse me, my lady?"

"It's never been a question of who is going to let me behave a certain way; it's always been a question of who is going to stop me. I thank you for answering it."

The older gentleman leaned back onto his heels for a moment, staring down at the impudent girl with the flashing colors in her hazel eyes and the small hands positioned on her hips.

"I am sorry, my lady. Sorrier than you will ever know. But threats against the caliph . . . must be eliminated."

"I am not a threat, General al-Khoury."

"And I intend to make sure it stays that way."

Oh, God. How does he know?

A SILK CORD
AND A SUNRISE

T HE SHAHRBAN OF REY SUSPECTS I MIGHT HARM
the king.

Shahrzad listened to Despina's incessant chatter as they spent the rest of the afternoon lounging in the warm waters of the palace's newest addition, commenting where it was appropriate and jesting where it was not.

But her mind refused to allow her a moment's respite.

What if he says something to the caliph?

How much does he know? How did he find out?

Now, many hours later, she sat on her bed in a darkened chamber . . .

Back at the beginning.

Staring at doors and fending away demons.

She was dressed in wide silk trowsers and a fitted top stained a deep violet color, with thick straps that banded over each shoulder. The necklace and thin chain at her waist contained amethysts surrounded by tiny, pale pink diamonds. At her ears and along her brow were large teardrops of purple and gold. Her waist-length hair hung in shining waves down her back.

Shahrzad willed the doors to open with the force of her unflinching stare. Met by the same stoic silence as always, she rose from the bed and began pacing.

He's usually here by now.

Unwilling and incapable of leaving her fate in the hands of others, she walked to the doors and pulled one open.

The Rajput turned in place, his hand resting on the hilt of his *talwar*.

Shahrzad felt the fear leech its way onto her heart . . . felt it tug at the corners of her eyes and mouth.

"Do you—do you know if . . ." she tried.

She gritted her teeth.

"Is he coming?" she asked.

The Rajput merely stared down at her, a lethal statue of muscle and menace.

"Can you tell me where he is?" she demanded, the tenor of her voice clearly trying to compensate for her waning courage.

At this, Shahrzad saw the tiniest flicker of a response in his dark-as-night gaze.

Pity?

He . . . pities me?

She slammed the door shut and leaned against it, her chest starting to heave.

No.

She stifled a sob.

Enough. That's enough.

Shahrzad stood upright and walked, with her head high, to the bed. She fell back onto the silken pillows, her eyes still trained on the doors.

"He'll come," she said into the darkness.

I know it.

As she clung to this last thread of hope, two words kept resonating in her mind, taunting her . . . plaguing her with a meaning she should not see.

These two words from a boy who was less than nothing.

These two words that gave her the will to fight off the demons:

My queen.

The groan of the doors opening brought Shahrzad out of a restless half sleep.

And the light of pure dawn streaming through the wooden screens shot her to her feet.

Standing at the threshold were four soldiers.

Shahrzad straightened her rumpled clothing and cleared her throat.

"Is it not customary to knock first?"

They all looked past her without answering. Their eyes bore an air of grim detachment.

Shahrzad clasped her hands behind her back, forcing herself to stand up straight. "What are you doing here?"

Without a word, the soldier in front stepped into the room and moved toward Shahrzad, still looking to a spot beyond her . . .

As though she had ceased to exist.

Her heart. Her heart.

"I asked you a question!"

The soldier took hold of her shoulder. When Shahrzad reached up to smack his hand away, he trapped her wrist and grasped tightly.

"Don't—touch me!"

The soldier nodded to his subordinates, and another grim-faced dragoon seized her by the arm.

The blood flew through her body, soaring on a mixture of terror and rage.

"Stop!"

They began to drag her from the room.

When she tried to wrench free and kick at them, they merely lifted her off the floor as though she were trussed-up game, caught for sport.

"Where is the caliph?" she cried.

Stop! Do not beg.

"I want to speak to the caliph!"

Not a single one of the soldiers even paused to glance at her.

"Listen to me!" she screamed. "Please!"

They continued half carrying, half dragging her struggling form down the marble halls of the palace.

The servants they passed averted their gazes.

They all knew. Just as the soldiers knew.

There was nothing to see.

It was then Shahrzad realized the inescapable truth.

She was nothing. She meant nothing.

To the soldiers. To the servants.

She stopped struggling. She raised her head.

And pressed her lips tightly together.

Baba and Irsa.

Shiva . . . and Tariq.

She meant something to them. And she would not disgrace their memory of her by making a scene.

Her failure was disgrace enough.

As the soldiers pushed open the doors into the dawn and Shahrzad saw her death before her, it was this last thought that thrust its final weight upon her, breaking the dam.

Shiva.

Silent tears streamed down her face, unchecked.

"Let go of me," she rasped. "I won't run."

The three soldiers looked to the first. After a wordless conversation, they placed Shahrzad on her bare feet.

The grey granite pavestones felt cool to the touch, the warm rays not having seeped into their gritty surface yet. The grass on either side was blue from the silver light of an early morning sun.

For a moment, Shahrzad considered stooping to run her hands through it.

One last time.

They filed to a covered alcove, where another soldier and an older woman stood waiting. In the woman's hand was a long piece of white linen, fluttering in an all-but-dead breeze.

A shroud.

And in the soldier's hand . . .

A single stretch of silk cord.

The tears continued their final trek down her face, but

Shahrzad refused to utter a sound. She stepped to the soldier. His arms were thick and burly.

I hope it will be quick.

Without a word, she turned around.

"I'm sorry." He whispered so softly it might have been the wind.

Startled by his kindness, she almost looked back at her would-be murderer.

"Thank you." An absolution.

He lifted her hair, gently, and brought the dark waves over her head—a veil, shielding her from the nameless witnesses.

The ones who already refused to see her.

The silk cord felt so soft at her throat, at first. Such an elegant way to die.

Shiva died this way.

The thought that Shiva died like this, surrounded by people who saw nothing, made the tears flow harder. Shahrzad gasped, and the cord tightened.

"Baba," she breathed.

It cinched tighter . . . and she couldn't stop her hands from flying to her throat.

Irsa. I'm so sorry. Please forgive me.

As her fingers battled against her pride's directive, the soldier lifted her from the ground by her neck, pulling the cord as he did.

"Tariq," she choked.

Her chest was falling in on itself. Silver stars ringed the edges of her vision.

The pain in her chest grew. The silver stars were rimmed in black now.

And her neck was on fire.

Shiva.

The tears and the pain all but blinding her, she forced open her eyes one more time, to a curtain of dark hair; to a waterfall of black ink spilling across the last page of her life.

No.

I'm not nothing.

I was loved.

Then, from the distant reaches of her mind, she heard a commotion . . .

And the cord was released.

She fell to the ground, her body striking the granite, hard.

Sheer will to live forced air down her throat, despite the burning agony of each breath.

And someone grasped her by the shoulders and took her into his arms.

As her vision struggled to clear, the only things she saw were the amber eyes of her enemy, close to her own.

Then, with the last dram of strength she possessed—

She struck him across the face.

Another man's hand seized her forearm, yanking it back so hard she felt something pop.

Shahrzad screamed, a harsh and anguished cry.

For the first time, she heard the caliph raise his voice.

It was followed by the sound of a fist against flesh.

"Shahrzad." Jalal grabbed her, enveloping her in his embrace. She collapsed against him, her eyes swollen shut by tears, and the burning sensations in her arm and throat almost unbearable.

"Jalal," she gasped.

"*Delam.*" He stroked the hair out of her eyes, comforting her, bringing her back from a place of nothingness.

Then he glanced behind him, to the sound of continuing commotion.

To a chorus of whimpers and fury.

"Stop it, Khalid!" he yelled. "It's done. We have to get her inside."

"Khalid?" Shahrzad murmured.

Jalal smiled ruefully. "Don't hate him too much, *delam* . . ."

Shahrzad buried her face in Jalal's shirt as he lifted her from the ground.

"After all, every story has a story."

Hours later, Shahrzad sat on the edge of her bed with Despina.

At her throat was a ring of purple bruises. Her arm had been pushed back into place with a sickening sound that made her cringe in remembrance. Afterward, with Despina's assistance, she'd bathed carefully and changed into comfortable clothes.

The entire time, Shahrzad had not uttered a single word.

Despina lifted an ivory comb to untangle Shahrzad's still-damp hair. "Please say something."

Shahrzad closed her eyes.

"I'm sorry I wasn't in my room." Despina's gaze flicked toward the small door by the entrance, leading to her chamber. "I'm sorry

I didn't know . . . they were coming for you. You have every right not to trust me, but please talk to me."

"There's nothing to say."

"Obviously, there is. You might feel better if you talked about it."

"I won't."

"You don't know that."

Yes, I do.

Shahrzad did not want to talk to Despina. She wanted her sister's soothing voice and her father's volume of poetry. She wanted Shiva's bright smile and infectious laugh.

She wanted her own bed and a night when she could sleep without the fear of dawn.

And she wanted Tariq. She wanted to fall into his arms and feel the laughter rumble in his chest when she said something very wrong that sounded exactly right. Perhaps it was weakness, but she needed someone to take the weight off her shoulders for a moment. To ease the burden, as Tariq had done the day her mother died, when he'd found her sitting alone in the rose garden behind her house, crying.

That day, he'd held both her hands in his and said nothing. Just drawn her pain away, with the simple strength of his touch.

Tariq could do that again. He would gladly do that.

For her.

Despina was a stranger. A stranger she couldn't trust in a world that just tried to kill her.

"I don't want to talk about it, Despina."

Despina nodded slowly and dragged the comb through

Shahrzad's hair. The tension against her neck hurt, but Shahrzad said nothing.

There was a knock at the door.

"May I open it?" Despina asked.

Shahrzad raised an indifferent shoulder, and Despina placed the comb in Shahrzad's lap before she made her way to the double doors.

What can they do to me now?

When she looked past the threshold, her heart crashed into her stomach.

The Caliph of Khorasan shadowed her doorway.

Without a word, Despina exited the room, pulling the doors shut behind her.

Shahrzad stayed at the edge of the bed, fidgeting with the comb in her lap, staring down her king.

As he drew closer, she saw the mark across his face where she'd struck him. It colored his skin a deeper bronze, with a tinge of purple at his jawbone. His eyes were drawn and tired, as though he had not slept in a long while. The knuckles along his right fist were red and raw.

He returned her scrutiny, taking in the bruises at her neck, the hollows beneath her eyes, and the wary posture of her spine.

"How is your arm?" His voice was even and characteristically low.

"It hurts."

"A great deal?"

"I'm sure it won't kill me."

It was a pointed jab, and Shahrzad saw it strike a chord, his careful composure falling for an instant. He strode to the foot of the bed and sat beside her. She shifted uncomfortably at his proximity.

"Shahrzad—"

"What do you want?"

He paused. "To make amends for what I've done."

Shahrzad expelled a caustic breath and looked him in the eye.

"You will never be able to make amends for what you've done."

He studied her. "That may be the first truly honest thing you've ever said to me."

She laughed bitterly. "I told you, you aren't that gifted at reading people. I may have lied once or twice in my day, but I have never lied to you."

It was the truth.

His chest rose and fell in steady consideration. Then he reached up and brushed aside her hair. With great care, he touched the slender column of her throat.

Unnerved by the obvious concern on his face, Shahrzad drew back.

"That hurts, too." She pushed his hands away.

Flustered, she snatched the comb from her lap so she could finish untangling her hair—

And grimaced with pain.

Her arm.

"Do you need help?" he asked.

"No. I do not."

He sighed. "I—"

"If I need help, I'll wait for Despina. In any case, I do not need your help." When she moved to stand, he caught her waist and pulled her back against him.

"Please, Shahrzad." He spoke into her still-damp hair. "Let me make amends."

The hammering in her chest grew as he wrapped his other arm around her, holding her close.

Don't.

"There are no excuses for what happened this morning. I want you to—"

"Where were you?" Shahrzad tried to control the tremor in her voice.

"Not where I should have been."

"This morning and last night."

His breath fanned on her skin as he bent toward her ear. "This morning, I was not where I should have been. Last night, I was not where I wanted to be."

Shahrzad tilted her face upward, and her eyes grew wide at what she saw.

His hands tightened at her waist. He lowered his head and pressed his brow to hers, his touch as soft and gentle as a whisper.

"My Mountain of Adamant."

She felt herself leaning into him, bowing into his caress. He smelled of sandalwood and sunlight. Strange that she'd never noticed before—that in her desire to distance herself from him, she had not detected something so simple and yet so marked as a scent.

She inhaled, letting the clean fragrance clear her thoughts.

As he placed his palm against the side of her face, Shahrzad realized something horrifying.

She wanted to kiss him.

No.

It was one thing to return his kiss; she'd been prepared for that. But it was another thing entirely to *want* his kiss . . . another thing entirely to desire his affections. To melt into the arms of Shiva's killer at the first sign of adversity.

Weak.

She sat up in disgust, destroying the moment in a single action. "If you want to make amends, I will think of a way."

And it will not involve you touching me.

He withdrew his hands. "Good."

"Are there any rules?"

"Does everything have to be a game?" he said in the barest shred of a whisper.

"Are there rules, *sayyidi*?"

"The only rule is that I have to be able to grant your request."

"You're the Caliph of Khorasan. The King of Kings. Is there a request you cannot grant?"

His face darkened. "I am just a man, Shahrzad."

She stood up and faced him. "Then be a man who makes amends. You tried to have me killed this morning. Consider yourself lucky I have not tried to return the favor."

Yet.

He rose to his feet, more than a head taller than Shahrzad. The veil of dispassion had returned, and it deepened the lines, as always.

"I'm sorry."

"Pitiful. But a start, nevertheless."

His tiger-eyes softened, almost imperceptibly. He bowed his head. Then he made his way to the door.

"Shahrzad?"

"Yes, *sayyidi*?"

"I'm leaving for Amardha this afternoon."

Shahrzad waited.

"I'll be gone for a week. No one will bother you. Jalal will be in charge of your security. Should you need anything, go to him."

She nodded.

He stopped himself once more. "I meant what I said to General al-Khoury the day I introduced you."

The day he called me his queen.

"You have a strange way of showing it."

He paused. "It won't happen again."

"See that it doesn't."

"My queen." He bowed again before he left, his fingertips to his brow.

Shahrzad closed her eyes tight, falling against the bed as soon as the doors shut behind him.

Shiva, what do I do now?

A RIGHTEOUS BLAZE
AND A RESTLESS SPIRIT

T HE HALF-MOON OVER REY WAS A MILKY COLOR, framed by a thin haze of clouds.

Along the border of Reza bin-Latief's elegant courtyard, the torches blazed in their sconces, throwing off shadows that danced with abandon against the walls of tan stone. The musky scent of smoke and ambergris hung heavy in the air.

"I feel human again," Rahim announced as he crossed the courtyard and took a seat at the low table before him.

Reza smiled warmly. "You look a great deal more rested, Rahim-*jan*."

"I was promised a cloud of perfume, and I was not disappointed, Reza-*effendi*."

Tariq joined them a moment later, sitting across from Rahim in the open-air gallery.

Soon, platters of food were brought before them—steaming, buttery basmati rice with bright orange saffron staining its center, surrounded by lamb in a savory sauce of dates, caramelized onions, and tangy barberries; skewers of marinated chicken and roasted tomatoes, served alongside chilled yogurt and cucumbers;

fresh herbs and *lavash* bread, with rounds of goat cheese and sliced red radishes splashing brilliant colors against a polished wood backdrop.

The aroma of the food mingled with the fragrance of the tapers, saturating the senses with spices and decadence.

"This almost makes me forget the last three days," Rahim said. "Almost."

"Did you sleep well, Tariq-*jan*?" Reza asked.

"As well as can be expected, Uncle."

"Don't sound so frustrated," Rahim grumbled. "You've barely rested a moment since receiving Shazi's letter. Do you think you're invincible? That you live off nothing but fresh dew and cold fury?"

Tariq glared at his friend before grabbing a skewer of chicken.

"He's right. I know you are eager to discuss our plans, but it's important to take care of yourself first." Reza glanced over his shoulder. "Thank you. Please leave us," he directed his servants. Once they were gone, he served himself a portion of basmati rice and lamb stew.

"While you were resting this afternoon, I made a few inquiries," Reza began in a low voice. "First, I will sell everything I have here. We will need money and mobility. Following this, we will need the support of others with money and mobility. Am I correct in assuming your father does not share our point of view?"

"My father will not want to be a part of this," Tariq replied with resignation. "It is likely he will forswear all involvement, if put to question."

Reza nodded, seemingly unfazed. "Then this presents us with our next problem. If your father does not wish to be linked to this endeavor, you cannot brandish your family's name about freely without risking their lives and, possibly, the lives of Shahrzad's family as well. The same goes for you, Rahim; the al-Din Walad name is an old one, and your elder brothers will not take kindly to you jeopardizing their families. You must conceal your identities."

Tariq considered this. "You're right, Uncle."

"I am of the same mind, but how are we to garner support if no one knows who we are?" Rahim interjected. "What will inspire them to follow?"

"Leave that to me," Reza continued. "I was one of the foremost merchants of Rey for decades, and I understand the notion of a commodity. Something is rare and desirable when it is made to seem so."

"I'm not sure I understand what you mean, Uncle," Tariq said.

The light from the torches blazed in Reza's eyes. "I will make you what they want to see. You need only be what you already are—strong young men and gifted warriors."

Tariq's forehead creased, his gaze uncertain. "But that still doesn't explain how we intend to persuade others to follow a leaderless cause."

"It will not be leaderless. You will be its leader, Tariq-*jan*. You will give this cause a voice. The lack of a voice is the reason the riots in the city streets are quelled time and again. Your voice must be one that resonates, that demands we see what truly lies at the heart of our kingdom: a boy-king who does not deserve to rule Khorasan. A boy-king who must be destroyed, at all cost."

Rahim pounded his palm against the table in approval.

"So we mean to organize a force and storm the city? That is my greatest hope, but is such a feat even possible?" Tariq asked.

Reza took a sip of wine. "It will work if we build on our beliefs and make them a reality. Your hope will be our tinder, and my righteousness, our blaze."

Tariq looked to his uncle once more. "Where do we begin?"

Reza pushed his plate aside. "Return home. I need time to clear my affairs in Rey and determine who might be willing to assist with our cause. The Emir of Karaj will likely provide some form of aid . . . his wife's cousin suffered the same fate as Shiva a few weeks ago. Once I am in the position to do so, I will send for you."

"What about Shazi? I won't leave Rey until—"

"The caliph left for the city of Amardha this afternoon. He does not—" Traces of hidden rage settled around Reza's mouth. "He does not murder his brides unless he's in Rey, presumably to witness the spectacle. She will be safe for at least a week."

Tariq paused for a beat before nodding. "Then, after we collect Irsa and Jahandar-*effendi*, Rahim and I will return home and await your missive."

"Jahandar and Irsa? Did you not know? They left Rey the night of the wedding. No one has seen or heard from them since."

"Gone? But where could they—"

"I assumed they were going to you, Tariq-*jan*. Did you not receive a letter from them?"

"Shazi's letter. Did she not make mention of her family in it?" Rahim asked.

"I don't know. I never finished reading it."

"Of course not." Rahim harrumphed.

Reza gazed thoughtfully at his nephew. "In the future, you must be more deliberate in your actions. Take time before making decisions. It will be of great benefit to you."

Tariq inhaled through his nose. "Yes. I'll do better, Uncle."

"You've always done better, Tariq-*jan*. Which is why I know we will succeed."

"Thank you. For taking on such a task so willingly."

"I am the one who should be grateful to both of you. It has been a long time since I've felt hope spark within me."

The three men rose from the table and moved farther into the courtyard, where Zoraya remained perched on her makeshift mews, patiently awaiting Tariq. He donned his *mankalah* cuff and whistled for her. She soared to his outstretched arm, reveling in his attention. Then, with a flick of his right hand, Tariq directed Zoraya into the sky so she could hunt. She shrieked once, her cry filling the courtyard, before she ascended into the hazy darkness.

The shadow of her body in flight drew across Tariq's face, masking his features from the torchlight for an instant.

Reza smiled to himself.

Something to fight for.

And something to use.

✾○✾○✾

The following morning, Rahim was jarred awake by the sound of metal thumping into the wood just outside his open window. He rolled from his bed and lumbered to the sill.

"What the hell are you doing?" he grumbled to Tariq.

"What does it look like?" Tariq lifted the recurve bow and nocked an arrow to the sinew. "We need to leave."

Rahim glanced up at the sky. The sun had yet to crest above the horizon; it was nothing but a jagged ribbon of light along the eastern rooftops of Rey.

"Did you even sleep?" Rahim yawned.

Tariq let the arrow fly. It thudded into the wood beside Rahim's head.

Rahim did not flinch. "Was that truly necessary?"

"Get your things. Before my uncle returns and insists we eat with him."

"Where did he go?"

"I don't know. He left while it was still dark outside." Tariq fitted another arrow to the string and took aim.

"Why are we vanishing like thieves in the night?"

Tariq shot him a look to skewer a stone. "Because I don't want him to know what we're doing."

"Oh? What are we doing?"

"You and your infernal questions!" Tariq loosed the arrow. It coiled in a tight spiral and thunked into the wood, perfectly grouped alongside seven other arrows with matching fletchings.

"All hail Tariq, son of Nasir, Emir of Taleqan. Congratulations. You can shoot an arrow," Rahim said in a flat tone.

Tariq swore under his breath and started for the window. "I knew I never should have—"

"Calm down." Rahim scratched at his scalp. "I'll get my things. But can you tell me the reason for such secrecy?"

Tariq stopped near the open window and took a steadying breath.

"You're starting to worry me," Rahim continued. "I know you're concerned about Shazi, but Reza-*effendi* said we should wait until—"

"No. I won't wait. I can't wait."

Rahim pinched the bridge of his nose. "What are you planning to do?"

"Something. Anything."

"We still don't have a plan. And Reza-*effendi* said to wait. We should wait."

Tariq leaned a shoulder into the tan stone wall. "I've been thinking."

"I'm listening," Rahim sighed. "Despite my wiser inclinations."

"The Badawi tribes along the border of Khorasan and Parthia . . . they've notoriously claimed no allegiance to either kingdom. What if we offered them a reason to change their position?"

"What kind of reason?"

"The reason any man fights for a cause. Purpose."

"Sounds vaguely poetic," Rahim rejoined. "You're going to need more than that."

"Land. The rights to land. The organization they need to demand those rights."

Rahim shifted his lips to one side in contemplation.

"Interesting. But they're nomadic by nature. Why would they have any interest in land?"

"Some of them may not. But they've fought against each other over the centuries, and save an influx of gold, land is the quickest way to gain power and influence. Perhaps one of their leaders might take an interest in fighting alongside us. They may be notoriously ruthless, but they're also some of the best horsemen I've ever encountered. I see nothing but an advantage for both parties."

Rahim hedged. "It sounds dangerous."

"It's worth speaking to them. The worst that can happen is a refusal."

"Actually, the worst that can happen is that they slit your throat."

"Yes." A series of vertical lines formed along the bridge of Tariq's nose. "There is that. But it was not on my agenda to insult them, in the process."

"Well, if anyone can talk their way out of a beheading, it's you."

"I thank you, Rahim. As always, your abiding confidence in me casts any possibility of doubt astray."

Rahim countered with a lopsided grin. "Actually, if anyone can talk their way out of a beheading, it's Shazi. Thankfully, some of that charisma managed to rub off on you."

"It was never charisma. It was unmatched nerve," Tariq said in amused remembrance.

"Perhaps you're right. I could see her daring a cobra to strike, swearing her venom would kill first."

Tariq smiled. "And she would win."

"Of that, there is no doubt. In fact, I'm almost certain she terrorized the mighty Caliph of Khorasan until he was nothing but a mewling kitten, cowering in the corner. Who knows—we might be deposing her one day."

Tariq sombered immediately at the mention of their king. "No. He is not a man to rescind any kind of power with ease."

"And how would you know this?"

"I just know it," Tariq snapped. "He murdered my cousin. And now he has Shahrzad. This is a man with nothing but evil in his blood. The only thing to consider when it comes to Khalid Ibn al-Rashid is how many times I wish he could die at my hands. And how unfortunate it is that the answer is only once."

"I despise him, too. With the fire of a thousand suns, I despise him. But it is always a good idea to know your enemy, Tariq."

"Don't mistake my vehemence for foolishness. I intend to learn everything I can about him. But that will never happen locked in the walls of my family's fortress. With that in mind, I'm going into the desert to seek out the Badawi." Tariq's face was set with determination. "Alone."

"Alone?"

"Yes. Alone. I need you to go to Taleqan in case my uncle sends word. I'll dispatch Zoraya every two days with my location."

"You'd leave me with your parents?"

"You could always go home."

"To my brothers and their screaming children?" Rahim scoffed. "To the constant attempts to marry me off to a cousin's friend's ugly sister? I think not. Besides, I owe you this much for all these years of friendship. And I owe Shazi even more."

Tariq laughed softly. "I thank you, Rahim-*jan*. As I always should, yet seldom do."

"You're welcome, you selfish bastard. In any case, I can look forward to one good thing coming from all this secret plotting."

"And that would be?"

"A full night of sleep . . . without being shot at for it."

The first morning Shahrzad awoke in the palace without fearing the dawn was a strange one.

Her heart clenched reflexively at the light, and then relaxed when she heard the sound of Despina bustling about the room. She breathed deeply and settled back into the pillows, allowing her body to bask in this newfound ease.

"Maybe he should just stay in Amardha," Shahrzad mumbled to no one.

"I was about to wake you up," Despina replied. "Your food is getting cold."

Shahrzad paused. Then made a decision.

Honey catches more flies than vinegar.

"Thank you for using your better judgment. And not resorting to your usual churlishness," Shahrzad teased.

"Churlishness? You're not exactly pleasant in the morning."

Shahrzad grinned before rising to her feet. She pushed aside the thin silk surrounding the bed and strode to the table, where her customary tray of food sat waiting. When she glanced over at Despina, she was surprised to see her handmaiden's face was not as glowing and perfect as usual. Her skin was wan, and her forehead appeared strained.

"What's wrong?" Shahrzad asked.

Despina shook her head. "I'm fine. Just a bit piqued."

"Piqued? You look ill."

"No. I'll be fine."

"Do you need to rest?"

"I'm fine, Shahrzad. Truly." Despina raised the lid from the tureen of soup and dropped a crystal of rock sugar into the bottom of a small etched-glass cup. Then she lifted the ornate silver pot from its resting place above a low-burning candle. As she raised it high above the glass cup and began to pour, her hand trembled, and the stream of tea splashed back from inside the cup before hitting the teapot.

"I'm sorry," Despina mumbled.

"You're permitted to make mistakes, on occasion." Shahrzad smiled impishly.

"All evidence to the contrary," she shot back under her breath.

"When did I ever make such outrageous demands?"

The lines on Despina's brow deepened.

"Despina. What's wrong?"

"Nothing!"

She's lying. Again.

Shahrzad cut her eyes and tore a piece of *lavash* in half.

"I'm sorry." Despina finished pouring the tea. "What were you saying about Amardha?"

"I was just commenting on the caliph's recent journey. Do you know why he went there?"

"He's most likely visiting the Sultan of Parthia—his uncle."

"I see. Does he visit him often?" Shahrzad began eating her soup.

Despina shook her head. "No. They are not exactly . . . friendly. The sultan is not his uncle by blood. He's the brother of the former caliph's first wife. And he despised our caliph's mother."

Interesting.

"Why?"

Despina shrugged. "I suppose it's for the logical reason any man would hate his dead sister's replacement. In addition, our caliph's mother was beautiful, smart, and vivacious. By all accounts, the first wife was . . . not."

"Then why would the caliph visit the sultan?"

"I'm not sure. I suppose it's for diplomatic reasons. You should ask him when he returns."

"He won't tell me."

Despina gave her a half grin. "I'm glad you're talking to me again."

"Staying silent isn't a good option for someone like me."

"A wise decision. For someone like you."

"I just said that."

"I know."

Shahrzad snorted. She reached for her glass of tea. Just then she noticed an unusual smattering of small, dark spots on the side of the silver teapot. She grasped the handle and drew it closer, her eyebrows tufting together. With a linen napkin, she rubbed at one of the areas of discoloration.

It did not clear away.

Shahrzad pursed her lips.

She lifted her cup of tea and poured a drop of its contents onto the pot. As soon as the liquid hit the shining surface, the silver changed color.

Black.

Like death.

"Despina?" Shahrzad began in an even tone.

"Yes?"

"I think there's something wrong with my tea."

WHERE YOUR HEART LONGS TO BE

SOMEONE HAD TRIED TO POISON HER.

And it was not the tea, as Shahrzad had first suspected.

It was the sugar.

Jalal was furious.

When he confronted all those with access to her food, each person staunchly proclaimed innocence. As was customary when serving any member of the royal family, the cook had tasted all the items on Shahrzad's tray before sending it to her room, and numerous individuals had attested to this fact.

Though no one had thought to taste the sugar.

Unsurprisingly, Shahrzad did not eat anything else the rest of the day.

And now a young servant girl accompanied every tray of food brought to Shahrzad's room. A girl whose sole purpose in life was to taste the queen's food and drink one last time before it entered her mouth.

A young girl who must mean something to someone.

It disgusted Shahrzad.

As did the knowledge that her time feeling safe—those fleeting moments without the weight of her impending doom hovering about her like a dark specter—had been taken away from her before she'd had a true chance to enjoy it.

But the worst part was that she knew now, beyond the shadow of a doubt, that she could not trust her handmaiden.

After all, Despina was the last person who had handled her tray of food.

The one who had prepared that fatal cup of tea.

For some reason, this fact disheartened Shahrzad more than anything else. She had not trusted Despina before, but some part of her had wanted to. Had hoped that, one day, she could be a real friend, despite everything.

That hope was shattered.

And it made Shahrzad angry.

Three nights of mostly uninterrupted sleep had not dulled the anger.

This afternoon, Shahrzad had elected to wander one of the many terraced courtyards in search of a perfect rose. The banality of this task added a feeling of uselessness to her already irritated disposition.

She wandered past another flowering hedge, her eyes squinted against the sun, and her forehead creased with frustration.

"If you'll tell me what you're looking for, I can help," Despina offered.

"No. You can't."

"My, but you're in a mood."

"You really can't help me. There's an art to a perfect rose. The scent. The color. The arrangement of the petals. My father even argues that one too many petals can ruin the entire flower . . . can disturb the way it grows."

"And I would argue the prettiest flowers are the ones that seem a little imperfect."

"See? You can't help me," Shahrzad groused.

Just then she felt Despina stiffen by her side.

"What's wrong?" Shahrzad asked.

"Cap—Captain al-Khoury is coming down the stairs." Her flush spread from throat to hairline.

"So? Why are you nervous?"

Despina hesitated. "Ever since the incident with the tea, I've felt uncomfortable around him."

"I see." Shahrzad pursed her lips, fighting to contain the accusations.

As Jalal stepped into view, Despina took special pains to scramble behind the Rajput, out of sight. Jalal curved a languid eyebrow in her direction and then turned to Shahrzad.

"How are you this afternoon, Shahrzad?" He bowed with an easy grin, his gold-trimmed cloak spilling over one shoulder and a hand resting casually on the hilt of his scimitar.

"Alive."

He threw back his head and laughed. "I'm glad to see it. Are you in the midst of something important?"

"Of course. I have a possible coup in the works. Then I intend to draw up plans for a new form of trade involving elephants at sea and sails of spun silk. Would you care to join me?"

He smiled. "Only in the coup. The rest sounds a bit common-place, if you ask me."

Shahrzad laughed. "No, of course I'm not doing anything important. I'm firmly entrenched in the mundane. Please rescue me."

"Actually, I was wondering if you could do something . . . queenly for me."

"Queenly? What do you mean?"

"We have an unexpected visitor. I was wondering if you could receive him, in the caliph's absence."

"Who is it?"

"He's—a scholar, so to speak. He was Khalid's first tutor, as well as the lifelong tutor of Khalid's mother. He has not seen Khalid since he was a little boy. I know he meant a great deal to his mother, and I would *hate* to send him along without receiving him formally." He winked.

Shahrzad could not help but smile.

"Additionally, I assume the visit may satisfy some . . . lingering curiosities." Jalal grinned knowingly.

"Why, Captain al-Khoury, you make it sound so . . . intriguing."

He laughed. "So are you coming, Shahrzad?"

She nodded, her hazel eyes sparkling.

"I have to warn you, he's a bit—odd," Jalal stated as he began retracing his steps, with Shahrzad and her tiny retinue in tow.

"How so?"

"He's a relic of days past. Very devoted to the ancient arts. But I think you'll like him, and I know he'll be very pleased to meet you."

"What's his name?"

"Musa Zaragoza."

"That's a very unusual name," Shahrzad said.

"He's Moorish."

"Ah, I see. Well, I'll do my best."

"I know you will."

They continued up the numerous flights of stairs and into the cool marble hallways. Jalal led them to a large room with a domed ceiling five times the height of a man. Its walls were tiled and covered with painstakingly carved reliefs, depicting battle scenes long forgotten of warriors brandishing their weapons and vanquishing their foes.

In the corner stood a very tall man draped in garments of vibrant fabric. His deep blue *rida'* fell to the floor, and its hood was wound about his head, secured by a circlet of leather and gold. Thick *mankalah* cuffs were wrapped around both wrists, and his beautiful dark skin reminded Shahrzad of the finest Medjool date.

When he turned to face her, he smiled so widely his teeth seemed to glow white, like pearls set against ebony.

Jalal and Despina left her at the door, and the Rajput stood inside nearby, his sword at the ready.

Shahrzad returned her guest's smile and walked toward him.

What do I say?

"Welcome!" she began. "I am—Shahrzad."

He glided to her in a swirl of colors, his hands outstretched.

"And I am Musa. What a privilege to meet you." It was an intense voice, like honey and smoke.

Shahrzad took his hands. Standing so close to him, she realized he was actually a great deal older than he appeared. His eyebrows were peppered with white, and the fine lines etched about his face indicated a propensity for deep thought and a predilection for amusement. As he grasped her hands, Shahrzad saw something register in his rich brown eyes, but it came and went in a flash.

"Thank you so much, Musa-*effendi*. I am so sorry my—the caliph is not here to greet you."

He shook his head. "It is my fault for coming here unannounced. I was hoping to see him as I was passing through, but, alas, it appears I must save our reunion for another journey."

"Please sit." Shahrzad gestured toward the cushions surrounding the low table to her right, and they took their places across from each other. "Would you care for something to eat?"

"No, no. I cannot stay. Again, this was not meant to be anything but a short visit. I do not wish to impose on anyone."

"It is not an imposition, in any way. I would not have such an esteemed guest leave the palace hungry." Shahrzad grinned.

He laughed. The sound seemed to leap from wall to wall.

"And how do you know I am esteemed? Were you not told the truth?" His mouth twitched with humor.

"And what is the truth, Musa-*effendi*?"

"That the last time I was in this palace, I was thrown out on my heels, with nothing but the clothes on my back."

Shahrzad controlled her expression. She took a deep breath and folded her hands in her lap. "Well, it seems we owe you at least a meal, then, sir."

His laughter burst from his mouth once more, even bolder than before.

"Thank the stars for you, my lovely child. What light you must bring to my poor Khalid."

Light *may not be the appropriate word.*

She offered him a small smile in response.

"As I feared, this is not a harmonious marriage," Musa said gently. "Is there any hope for one?"

"In truth, it is too soon to tell. We have only been married a few days. And marriage to the caliph is—somewhat difficult."

"So I've heard." His voice was knowing and sad. "And do you wish for a harmonious marriage with him?"

Shahrzad shifted uncomfortably in her seat. For some reason, lying to this strangely garbed man with the rich laugh and the probing eyes seemed . . . wrong.

"I long for a marriage based on love and mutual respect, Musa-*effendi*. Whether it is possible with the caliph remains to be seen."

"Ah, so honest. Khalid values such honesty above all else. He craves it. Even as a small child, he sought the truth with a kind of fervor I've rarely encountered in any individual. Do you know this about him?"

"I know very little about his past."

He nodded. "Tell me, beyond the rumors, what kind of man has Leila's son become?"

Shahrzad paused and studied the kind face of the stranger across from her.

If I answer his questions, will he answer mine?

"A quiet one. A smart one."

"These things I could find out on the streets of Rey. I want

134

to know the things you know. The things a clever young girl has deduced, even in such a short time."

Shahrzad chewed on her lower lip for a moment.

"A joyless one. A calculating one. A bitter one . . ." she whispered.

She thought of his raw fist and the punishing fury.

"An angry one."

"It was not always thus." Musa sighed. "He was such a kind boy."

"I've been told. But it is difficult to believe."

"Understandably." He paused. "Will you permit me to share a story with you, my lovely Shahrzad? About the night I was thrown out on my heels?"

"Of course, Musa-*effendi.*"

"It is a sad story."

"I imagine any story that ends in such a manner would be."

Musa sat back in remembrance before he began.

"I was the tutor for Khalid's mother, Leila. And Leila was a joy. Beautiful and talented. A lover of books and poetry. When she married Khalid's father and became his second wife, she was young—only fifteen years old. I came along with her to Rey, at her insistence. She was very headstrong. Unfortunately, it was not an easy marriage. Her husband was a good deal older than she, and he had clearly loved his first wife very much. Leila did not appreciate the constant comparisons. I tried hard to rein in her tantrums and bouts of despair, but the disparity between them in age and interests was oftentimes too difficult to breach. It was no one's fault, really. Khalid's father was quite set in his ways. And Leila was a spirited young woman."

He stopped, his features growing sad.

"After Khalid was born, I hoped everything would change. I had never seen a more devoted mother. Leila kissed his feet and sang to him as an infant. When he was older, she told him stories every night before he went to sleep. And Khalid loved her more than anything."

Musa closed his eyes for a moment, and Shahrzad took a careful breath.

His mother told him stories at night.

"I was there the night Khalid's father learned of Leila's betrayal . . . when he discovered she had been carrying on an affair with a member of the palace guard."

His tenor became low and grave.

"He dragged Leila through the halls of the palace by her hair. She was screaming at him, calling him horrible names. I tried to help her, but his soldiers prevented me from doing so. In the atrium, he called for Khalid. Leila kept telling Khalid everything would be fine. That she loved him. That he was her world."

Shahrzad's hands curled into fists.

"And there, in front of her six-year-old son, Khalid's father slit Leila's throat. When Khalid started to cry, his father yelled at him. I will never forget what he said. 'A woman is faithful, or she is dead. There is no in-between.' After that, I was thrown out of the palace, with nothing but the clothes on my back. I should have fought harder. For Leila's sake. For Khalid's sake. But I was weak. Afraid. Later, I heard what had become of Leila's son. And I always regretted it. From the bottom of my soul, I regretted it."

Something had risen in Shahrzad's chest, forming a barrier

that prevented her from speaking. She swallowed hard. Not knowing what else to do, she reached across the table and took Musa's hand. He wrapped her small hands in both of his, and they sat in this manner for a time.

And then, with careful respect, Shahrzad attempted to break the silence.

"Musa-*effendi* . . . I feel certain you should not hold yourself responsible for anything that transpired, not that night or any of the nights after. I am young, and, therefore, I know my words only carry a certain weight with the world, but I do know enough to realize you cannot control the actions of others. You can only control what you do with yourself afterward."

His grip on her hand tightened. "Such wise words. Does Khalid know what a treasure you are, my dearest star?"

Shahrzad's eyes furnished him with the smile her lips could not.

Musa shook his head. "He has suffered a great deal. It troubles me immensely to know he inflicts suffering on others as a result. And it vexes me because these are not the actions of the boy I knew. But as you are young, I am old, and in my age, wisdom becomes less of a birthright and more of an expectation. In my life, the one thing I have learned above all is that no individual can reach the height of their potential without the love of others. We are not meant to be alone, Shahrzad. The more a person pushes others away, the clearer it becomes he is in need of love the most."

I could never love such a man . . . such a monster.

Shahrzad started to withdraw her hand from his.

But he held on to it.

"Tell me," he pressed. "How long have you possessed the gift?"

Taken aback, Shahrzad merely stared at him, her hazel eyes blank.

Musa returned her gaze, his warm eyes searching.

"Then you are unaware. It lies dormant in your blood," he said to himself.

"What are you talking about?" she demanded.

"Perhaps a parent?" he continued. "Does your mother or father possess any . . . unique abilities?"

Realization dawned on Shahrzad. "My father. He can do certain things. Very small things. But he's never been adept at controlling it."

Musa nodded. "If ever you wish to learn about these abilities, send word to me. I would be happy to share my knowledge with you. I am not extremely proficient, but I've learned to . . . control it." He grinned slowly. As he spoke, Shahrzad saw the flame dancing in the nearby lamp flicker out and spark back to life, unbidden.

"And I could learn to do this?" she whispered.

"In truth, I do not know. It is impossible to gauge an individual's abilities. I only know what I knew the moment I first held your hands in my grasp: that you and I share a common bond. And now that bond extends beyond this mere twist of fate. I beseech you, my star . . . please see past the darkness. There is potential for boundless good in the boy I knew. Trust that the man you see now is a shadow of what lies beneath. If you would, give him the love that will enable him to see it for himself. To a lost soul, such a treasure is worth its weight in gold. Worth its weight in dreams." As he spoke, Musa leaned over their still-clasped hands, a bright smile of affection lighting his features.

"Thank you, Musa-*effendi*. For the wisdom, the story, and so much more."

"Thank *you*, my star." He released her hand and stood from the table.

"Will you not stay for a meal?" Shahrzad asked again.

He shook his head. "I must be on my way. But I promise to visit again very soon. I shall not let so many years pass by this time. And I will cling to the hope that, when I see you next, it will be with Khalid at your side. At your side and the better for it."

A strange twinge of guilt knifed through Shahrzad's stomach.

Musa made his way to the satchel of belongings he had left in the corner. He lifted the pack from the floor and paused, as if in consideration. Then he reached inside and withdrew a thread-bare, moth-eaten rug rolled tightly in a bundle and bound by a hemp cord.

"A gift for you, dearest Shahrzad."

"Thank you, Musa-*effendi*."

What an odd gift.

"Keep it with you always. It is a very special carpet. When you are lost, it will help you find your way," he said, with a knowing glint in his eyes.

Shahrzad took the parcel and held it against her chest.

Musa reached over and placed his warm palm on her cheek.

"Let it take you where your heart longs to be."

THE OLD MAN AND THE WELL

THE DESERT SUN BORE DOWN ON TARIQ WITH THE heat of a brazen fire. It rippled off the dunes, distorting his vision and searing the sky.

He wrapped the hood of his *rida'* tight across his face, securing the leather band low on his brow. Whorls of sand curled around the legs of his stallion, trailing a glittering haze with the rise and fall of each massive hoof.

Zoraya circled above, her cries growing louder with each passing hour.

As the sun started to set, they approached the border of Khorasan and Parthia, and Tariq began searching for a place to rest. He knew the Badawi tribes were nearby, but he did not want to run the risk of encroaching on their territory without a full night's rest, as he had not slept well since leaving Rey almost four days ago. In the morning, he would devise a way to speak with a local so as to determine the current state of affairs in the region.

In the distance, he spotted a small settlement of sun-weathered buildings situated around a decrepit stone well. The horseshoe of cracked mud houses was capped by caving roofs and appeared all but abandoned. An elderly man stood at the well's edge, removing animal skins from across the backs of two aging camels.

Tariq spurred his dark bay Arabian forward, tugging once more on the hood of his white *rida'*.

When he neared the well, the elderly man glanced over his shoulder.

Then he grinned up at Tariq.

He was dressed in simple clothes of spun brown linen, and his thick beard was stippled with silver. A prominent gap separated his two front teeth, and his hooked nose was broken across the bridge. His hands were gnarled from age and use.

"A fine horse." He nodded, still grinning.

Tariq nodded in return.

The elderly man reached a shaking hand for the bucket above the well . . .

And promptly knocked it down.

The bucket struck the murky caverns of the hollow, ricocheting with each hit, until it splashed into the water with a taunting sound.

Tariq exhaled loudly.

The elderly man groaned, ripping his *rida'* from his head and stomping his feet in the dirt. He began wringing his hands, the dismay on his face as plain as the day.

Tariq observed this melodramatic performance until he could stomach it no longer, and then dismounted from his stallion with a moribund sigh.

"Do you have some rope?" he asked the elderly man as he removed the hood from his face.

"Yes, *sahib.*" The man bowed, over and over.

"That is not necessary; I am not your *sahib.*"

"The *sahib* has a fine horse. A fine sword. He is most definitely a *sahib.*"

Tariq sighed again. "Give me the rope, and I will climb down for the bucket."

"Oh, thank you, *sahib.* You are most generous."

"Not generous. Just thirsty." Tariq smiled wryly. He took the rope from the man and secured it to the post over the well. Then he paused in consideration. "Don't try to steal my horse. He's a temperamental beast, and you won't get far."

The elderly man shook his head with such fervor that Tariq thought it might cause him injury. "I would not do such a thing, *sahib!*"

His intensity put to question his intent.

Tariq studied the man before extending his left arm and whistling to the skies. Zoraya came hurtling from the clouds in a mass of feathers and wicked talons. The elderly man lifted a trembling forearm to his face, warding away the raptor's piercing menace.

"She likes to start with the eyes," Tariq said in a flat tone, as Zoraya spread her wings above his leather *mankalah* and glared at the man.

"I will not do anything disgraceful, *sahib!*"

"Good. Do you live around here?"

"I am Omar of the Badawi."

Tariq considered the man once more. "Omar of the Badawi, I'd like to make a deal with you."

"A deal, *sahib?*"

"Yes. I'll retrieve the bucket from the well and assist you in filling the skins with water. In return, I'd like some information on your tribe and its sheikh."

Omar scratched at his beard. "Why does the nameless *sahib* want information on my tribe?"

"Don't worry; I do not wish them ill. I have a great deal of respect for the Badawi. My father purchased this horse from a tribesman several years ago, and he always said the desert wanderers are among the best horsemen in the world."

"Among?" Omar smiled widely. "We are the best, *sahib*. Without a doubt."

Tariq offered him a tentative grin. "Do we have a deal?"

"I believe so, *sahib*; however, may I ask one last question?"

Tariq nodded.

"What is the purpose behind you seeking out the Badawi?"

Tariq thought for a moment. This elderly man was, at best, a servant. Most likely, a relic sent to collect water on a daily basis so as to maintain an appearance of usefulness in his old age. Giving him information seemed rather harmless.

"I have a business proposition to make."

"Business?" Omar cackled. "With the Badawi? Why would a rich young *sahib* need a desert wanderer's help?"

"I answered your question. Do we have a deal?"

Omar's dark eyes twinkled. "Yes, yes, *sahib*. We do."

Tariq directed Zoraya to a perch atop the well, and then turned to his horse to remove his recurve bow. He lashed the quiver to his back and slung the sinew across his chest, for he was not fool enough to leave behind a weapon. Finally, he tugged on the rope to make sure it was solidly rooted before positioning himself on the stone and mortar brim.

The well was as wide as a man and two times his height, so it was not an especially difficult task to ease his way down and grab the wooden bucket floating on the water's surface. In short order, Tariq climbed back up the stone hollow and out into the orange dusk of a desert sunset.

He passed the bucket to Omar. "I suggest tying a rope to the handle, for the sake of future ease."

Omar laughed. "A wise suggestion!"

The two men began the process of filling the animal skins with water and securing them to the camels waiting nearby.

"So," Tariq commenced, "which Badawi tribe do you ride with?"

Omar grinned. "I ride with the al-Sadiq family."

"I've heard that name before."

"Many say it is a great family. From a long line of powerful desert wanderers."

"Who is your sheikh?"

"A sixth-generation son of the al-Sadiq line. Some would argue he's a bit strange. He studied in Damascus for a time before returning to the desert."

"And what did he study in Damascus?"

"Sword making. He mastered the craft of iron and steel, *sahib.*"

"What possessed him to learn this trade?"

Omar shrugged. "He believes such knowledge gives him an edge over his enemies."

Tariq nodded pensively. "He sounds like an interesting man."

"As are you, *sahib*. But I am most curious; what is the nature of your business with the Badawi?"

Tariq hedged. "It is personal."

"Personal?" Omar laughed. "Then you are trying to overthrow a family member or . . . win the heart of a woman."

"What?"

"Why else would a rich young *sahib* have business of a personal nature with the Badawi? So which is it? Is your father a despicable despot of lore? Are you the hero your people long to serve?"

Tariq glared down at Omar.

"Ah! So then you are trying to win the heart of a beautiful young woman."

Tariq turned to his horse.

"She must be very beautiful," Omar mused. "To bring a handsome *sahib* with a falcon and a fine al-Khamsa this far into the Sea of Sand."

"It has nothing to do with that," Tariq muttered.

"Then she is not beautiful?"

Tariq whirled around. "It has nothing to do with her beauty."

"So it *is* about a girl!" Omar crowed.

Glowering, Tariq grabbed the reins of his stallion and swung into the saddle.

"Do not be offended by old Omar, *sahib*! I did not mean to press the issue. I am just curious at heart, and my curious heart has quite a fondness for love stories. Please! If you follow me, I would be happy to introduce you to the sheikh."

"And why would you do that?"

"For the sake of my curious heart," Omar replied with a ridiculous smile that emphasized the dark gap between his crooked teeth.

Tariq paused in deliberation. The old servant could be lying to him, but this could also be his best chance to meet with a sheikh from one of the most celebrated of the Badawi tribes.

It was worth the risk.

"I will follow you to your camp." Tariq adjusted the quiver of arrows on his back, for good measure.

Omar nodded, straightening his *rida'*. "I will be sure to tell the sheikh of your helpfulness at the well today."

"Thank you."

"Of course, *sahib*! I am nothing if not honorable."

Tariq followed Omar at a wary distance as Omar guided the two camels back into the desert. Omar rode the smaller camel at a steady pace, looking over his shoulder every so often to give Tariq a reassuring grin.

The sky darkened to blue-black, and the brightest stars began to flicker above, winking white at the edges. After riding for half an hour, a large enclave of tents surrounded by a ring of torches materialized in the sea of rising dunes.

Omar led the camels directly into the center, whistling cheerfully to himself. As he passed, several men stopped to nod at him, and Omar bowed back, with a hand to his brow. He dismounted from the camel before a large, patchworked tent in the middle of the encampment. The instant his sandaled feet hit the ground, a pattering of footsteps burst from the shadows to the side.

Tiny burnished arms grabbed at his legs and battled for his embrace.

"Baba Aziz! Why are you so late?" several children cried in discordant harmony.

Tariq's eyes narrowed.

The flap of the tent opened, and an elderly woman with a beautiful braid of muted copper strode into the moonlight. "Omar-*jan,* where have you been? Your grandchildren are hungry, and your daughters are irritated, as a result."

Omar smiled indulgently. "I've brought a guest. Can we make room for one more?"

She shot her eyes heavenward before shifting to Tariq. "And who are you, young man?"

"He is our nameless *sahib.* And my curious heart longs to hear his story. I believe it is a good one, Aisha. About love and its many struggles," Omar answered with a wink.

She shook her head. "Well, bring him inside."

Tariq continued staring at Omar, his suspicions rapidly reaching a logical conclusion. He dismounted from his horse.

"You are not a servant," he said.

Omar turned back to Tariq. Again, his gap-toothed grin took over his weathered face. "Did I say I was?"

Tariq held Omar's gaze. The guise of a silly old man had vanished in the lambent torchlight. In its place was a look of wisdom and mirth.

A look of cunning intelligence.

"Forgive the misunderstanding," Omar continued.

Tariq snorted in disbelief. "There was no misunderstanding. I saw precisely what you wanted me to see."

Omar laughed loudly. "Or perhaps you saw exactly what *you* wanted to see."

Tariq knocked back his *rida'* and stepped forward. "My name is Tariq."

Omar's bushy eyebrows rose in approval.

"And I am Omar al-Sadiq, the sixth sheikh of my line . . ."

He put his wrinkled palm out before him, and Tariq grasped it.

"Welcome to my home."

THE PROMISE OF TOMORROW

Two days after the Caliph returned from Amardha, Shahrzad was ready to put her plan to action.

Enough was enough.

It did not matter that Musa-*effendi* had hinted about a tragic past.

It did not matter that this world was far from as simple as she might have thought.

And it absolutely did not matter that her heart was . . . misbehaving.

She had come to the palace with a clear purpose.

The Caliph of Khorasan had to die.

And she knew just how to do it.

She sat across from him in her chamber that night, eating grapes while he drank wine.

Biding time for the moment to strike.

"You're very quiet," he remarked.

"And you look very tired."

"The journey from Amardha was not an easy one."

She peered across the table into his tiger-eyes. The hollows beneath them were pronounced, and his bladed features seemed even more severe with such clear lines of fatigue at their edges. "But you came back over two days ago."

"I haven't slept well since I returned."

"Would you rather not continue Aladdin's tale? Perhaps you should sleep," Shahrzad suggested.

"No. That's not what I want. At all."

She looked away, unable to hold his piercing gaze. "May I ask you something, *sayyidi*?"

"You may do as you please. And I will behave in a similar fashion."

"Why did you go to Amardha?"

His eyebrows drew together. "I heard Jalal arranged for you to meet Musa Zaragoza. Undoubtedly, you learned interesting facts about my childhood while he was here. I assume you know about my mother now?"

"He told me about her, yes."

"The Sultan of Parthia and I have a tacit agreement. Every six months or so, I go to see him and make veiled threats, posturing like a peacock in a show of force meant to dissuade him from suggesting I am not the rightful heir to the Caliphate of Khorasan."

"Excuse me?" Shahrzad sputtered.

The caliph continued. "It's logical, really. He openly calls my mother a whore. And everyone questions my parentage. Then he's able to rally support and wage war for the caliphate. Only, he lacks the strength and the numbers to take a stand. And I intend to keep it that way."

"He—would call your mother a whore?"

"It shouldn't shock you. My father said as much to me. Many times."

Shahrzad took a careful breath. "Did your father also question whether or not you were his son?"

The caliph raised the cup of wine to his lips and took a long sip.

"Again, it shouldn't shock you."

She almost wished she had misheard his words.

What kind of loveless childhood did he have?

"And this is normal to you?"

He set his cup down on the table. "I suppose I have a skewed understanding of the word."

"Do you want me to pity you, *sayyidi*?"

"Do you want to pity me, Shahrzad?"

"No. I do not."

"Then don't."

Frustrated, she snatched his cup from the table and drank what remained of its contents.

A corner of his lips rose ever so slightly.

The wine burned; she cleared her throat and set the goblet before her. "By the way, I've decided how you can make amends. If you're still willing, of course."

He leaned back into the cushions, waiting.

She took a deep breath, preparing to spring her trap. "Remember last night, when Aladdin saw the princess in disguise, roaming the city streets?"

The caliph nodded.

"You told me you envied the freedom the princess experienced in her city, without the mantle of royalty about her shoulders. I want to do that. With you," she finished.

He stilled, his eyes scanning her face. "You want me to go out into Rey without bodyguards?"

"Yes."

"With just you?"

"Yes."

He paused. "When?"

"Tomorrow night."

"Why?"

He didn't refuse outright.

"For the adventure," she goaded him.

He cut his gaze.

Calculating.

"And you are indebted to me," she pressed.

Please. Don't deny me this chance.

"I agree. I am indebted to you. I accept."

Shahrzad beamed.

His eyes widened at the brightness of her smile.

And, to her great surprise, he offered her one in return.

It looked foreign on his usually cold and angular face.

Foreign, yet wondrously striking.

The tightening in her chest . . . would have to be ignored.

At all cost.

They stood in a small alley next to the entrance of the souk. The sky above was purpled by dusk, and the mixture of spices, sweat, and livestock filled the spring air with the heady perfume of life, in all its abundance.

Shahrzad pulled her dark grey cloak tight about her. The crystal of poisoned sugar she had stolen away in her pocket felt like it would catch flame at a thought.

The caliph's keen ochre eyes took in the scene around them. His black *rida'* was bound across his brow by a slim circlet of matching leather.

"Have you been to Rey's souk before?" she whispered.

"No."

"Stay close. It's very much like a labyrinth. Each year it grows bigger, its corridors snaking about without rhyme or reason."

"And here I had every intention of leaving you behind to explore on my own," he murmured.

"Are you trying to be funny, *sayyidi*?"

His brow furrowed. "You can't use that word here, Shahrzad."

A fair point. Especially considering the riots against him in the city streets.

"You're right . . . Khalid."

He expelled a quick breath. "And what should I call you?"

"Excuse me?"

"What do your friends call you?"

She hesitated.

Why am I trying to protect a silly nickname Rahim gave me when I was ten?

"Shazi."

A suggestion of a smile played across his lips.

"Shazi. It suits you."

She rolled her eyes. "Come with me."

With that, Shahrzad left the safety of the shadows and darted out into the bustling crowds of Rey's most active outdoor market. The Caliph of Khorasan followed closely behind as they passed under the archway and into the sweltering maze of people and goods.

To their right were vendors plying food wares—sugared dates and other dried fruits, an assortment of nuts in water-stained wood barrels, mountains of spices piled high in vivid hues—and to their left were vendors of spun cloth, dyed fabric, and skeins of yarn idling in a faint breeze, their colors like a banner cut from a rainbow. Many salesmen pounced on the couple, trying to coax them to taste a pistachio or sample a delicious dried apricot. At first, Khalid tensed at every one who approached them, but soon he fell into the leisurely gait of an ordinary patron wandering around the souk on a warm spring evening.

Until a young man leapt from behind a post to wrap Shahrzad in a bolt of bright orange silk. "So beautiful!" he sighed. "You must buy this. It suits you so."

"I think not." She shook her head, pushing his hands away.

He pulled her closer against him. "Have I seen you before, miss? I would not forget such beauty."

"No, you have not," Khalid said in a low tone.

The young man smirked back at him. "I am not having a conversation with you. I am having a conversation with the most beautiful girl I have seen in a long time."

"No. You are having a conversation with my wife. And you are quite close to having the last conversation of your life." His voice was as cold as the edge of a dagger.

Shahrzad glared at the young man. "And if you want to sell me fabric, being a lecherous bastard is not the way to go about doing it." She shoved against his chest, hard.

"Daughter of a whore," he muttered.

Khalid froze, his knuckles turning a perilous shade of white.

Shahrzad grabbed his arm and dragged him away. She could see the muscles ticking along his jaw.

"You know, you have quite a temper," she remarked after they had cleared some distance.

He said nothing.

"Khalid?"

"Is that kind of disrespect . . . normal?"

Shahrzad lifted a shoulder. "It's not normal. But it's not unexpected. It's the curse of being a woman," she joked in a morose manner.

"It's obscene. He deserves to be flogged."

Says the king who murders a bride every morning.

They continued strolling through the souk, and Shahrzad was surprised to note that Khalid now walked firmly in her shadow, with his hand grazing her lower back. His eyes, which were usually vigilant, appeared even more watchful than before.

She sighed to herself.

He notices everything. This will be even more difficult than I thought.

Shahrzad led him through a maze of small alleyways, past

vendors of oil and imported vinegar, rugs and fine lamps, perfumes and other cosmetics, until she came to a thoroughfare filled with purveyors of food and drink. She directed him to a small, crowded establishment with outdoor seating.

"What are we doing here?" Khalid demanded quietly as she pushed him into a chair by an available table near the front.

"I'll be right back." She smiled at his irritation as she weaved her way through the crowd.

When she returned a short time later with two cups and a pitcher of wine, the corners of his eyes constricted.

"They are famous for their sweet wine," Shahrzad explained.

He crossed his arms.

Shahrzad grinned knowingly. "You don't trust me?" She poured some wine into a cup and drank from it first before handing it to him.

"Where did you get the money?" He took the cup from her.

She rolled her eyes. "I stole it. From the perfidious Sultan of Parthia." As he raised the cup to his lips, she saw him smile. "Do you like it?"

He tilted his head in consideration. "It's different." Then he reached over and filled the other cup for her.

They sat for a time in comfortable silence, taking in the sights and sounds of the souk, drinking wine and enjoying the raucous conversations of those in various states of inebriation around them.

"So," she interjected in a conversational tone. "Why are you having difficulty sleeping?"

Her question seemed to catch him off guard.

He stared at her over the rim of his cup.

"Do you have nightmares?" she probed.

He inhaled carefully. "No."

"What was your last dream?"

"I don't remember."

"How come you don't remember?"

"Do you remember your last dream?"

Shahrzad canted her lips to the side in thought. "Yes."

"Tell me what it was about."

"It's a bit a strange."

"Most dreams are."

"I was in a grassy field with . . . my best friend. We were twirling. I was holding her hands. We were spinning slowly, at first. And then faster and faster. So fast it felt like we were flying. But it didn't seem dangerous at all. It's strange now that it didn't seem dangerous, but I guess that's the way of dreams. I remember hearing her laughter. She has the most beautiful laugh. Like a lark on a crisp morning." Shahrzad smiled to herself in memory.

Khalid stayed silent for a moment.

"You have a beautiful laugh. Like the promise of tomorrow." He said it gently, with the poise of an afterthought.

And Shahrzad's heart hurtled about in response, roaring for attention.

Shiva, I swear to you, I will ignore the fickle little beast.

She refused to look at him as she drank from her cup and remained proud of herself for this display of fortitude, until she felt his entire body go rigid across from her.

A sandaled foot came crashing to a stop on the empty seat nearby.

"If it isn't the beautiful girl with the barbed tongue," a voice slurred from above.

When she gazed upward, her eyes thinned in disgust.

"Apparently, this is too popular a venue," Khalid said, the tension banding across his features.

"For lecherous bastards and kings of old alike," Shahrzad retorted under her breath.

"What?" the young man drawled, the wine clearly impairing his comprehension.

"Never mind. What do you want?" Shahrzad asked with a spark of annoyance.

The young man leered down at her. "Perhaps I may have been a bit forward earlier. But I'd like to share a recent observation. This one here?" He gestured toward Khalid with his thumb. "He seems entirely too grumpy for a girl like you. I think you're much better suited for a man with charm. Such as myself."

At this, Khalid made a motion to stand. Shahrzad placed her palm against his chest, her flashing eyes never wavering from the young man's glazed stare.

"You seem to have forgotten—in a rather short time, I might add—that you called my mother a whore. In what world do you think I would prefer you to any man, grumpy or not?"

He grinned at her, his friends behind him laughing at her temerity.

"Don't take it to heart, beautiful girl. What if I told you my mother really was a whore? Would that make it better? In any case, I happen to have a great appreciation for women of that ilk." He winked at her.

The laughter behind him grew louder.

Again, Shahrzad felt the fury beneath her palm as she pressed against Khalid, keeping him in his seat with nothing more than the force of her will.

She nodded. "I can't say I'm surprised. As for me? I believe I'll leave this set of goods on the rack, as well. I have no interest in . . . tiny cucumbers."

At this, Khalid's head twisted to hers, his eyes registering shock. And the edge of his lips twitching.

The silence around them was deafening for a painful beat.

Then a wild chorus of amusement filled the air.

The young man's friends slapped their knees and pounded one another's backs as they guffawed at his expense. His face turned several shades of red once he comprehended the full breadth of Shahrzad's insult.

"You—" He lunged for her.

Shahrzad bolted out of the way.

Khalid grabbed the man by the front of his *qamis* and hurled him into his passel of friends.

"Khalid!" Shahrzad shouted.

Once the young man managed to scramble to his feet, Khalid reared back and struck him in the jaw so hard he staggered into a table of dangerous-looking men, heavily engrossed in their dice match, with the betting at an all-time high. The coins and the *astragali* dice crashed to the ground as the table shuddered under the young man's weight.

The gamblers roared with rage as they shot to their feet, everything around them falling to shambles.

And their precious game destroyed beyond repair.

All eyes turned on Khalid.

"Holy Hera," Shahrzad moaned.

With grim resignation, he reached for his *shamshir.*

"No, you idiot!" Shahrzad gasped. "Run!" She grabbed his hand and spun in the opposite direction, the blood pummeling through her body.

"Get out of the way!" she cried as they dodged past a vendor's cart, her sandaled feet flying above the dirt. The sound of their pursuers only spurred her faster, especially with Khalid's broader strides propelling them along the narrow thoroughfare of the souk.

When he yanked her down a small side alleyway, she pulled him back.

"Do you even know where you're going?" she demanded.

"For once in your life, stop talking and listen."

"How dare—"

He wrapped his right arm around her and pressed their bodies together in between a shadowed alcove. Then he shoved his index finger onto her lips.

Shahrzad listened as their pursuers ran past the alleyway, still shouting and carrying on in a drunken haze. When the sounds faded away, he removed his finger from her lips.

But it was too late.

Because Shahrzad could feel his heart beating faster.

Just like hers.

"You were saying?" He was so close, his words were more breath than sound.

160

"How—how dare you say that to me?" she whispered.

His eyes glittered with something akin to amusement.

"How dare I imply you caused this mess?"

"Me? This is not my fault! This is your fault!"

"Mine?"

"You and your temper, Khalid!"

"No. You and your mouth, Shazi."

"Wrong, you wretched lout!"

"See? That mouth." He reached up and grazed his thumb across her lips. "That—magnificent mouth."

Her traitor heart thudded against his, and when she peered up at him through her eyelashes, his hand at the small of her back pulled her impossibly closer.

Don't kiss me, Khalid. Please . . . don't.

"They're here! I've found them!"

Khalid grasped her hand in his, and they took off down the alleyway once again.

"We can't keep running," he said over his shoulder. "We might have to stand and fight, eventually."

"I know," she huffed back.

I need a weapon. I need a bow.

She began scanning everyone in sight for a quiver or a possible bow left strewn against the side of a building, but all she saw was the occasional shimmer of a sword. In the distance, she noticed a burly man with a huge, straightbacked bow across his body, but she knew there was little chance of getting it from him quickly. And it was even less likely that she could draw an arrow on such a large bow.

It seemed a futile exercise.

Until she finally saw a young boy playing with his friends in a back alley.

With a makeshift bow and a quiver of exactly three arrows lashed to his shoulder.

Shahrzad tugged on Khalid's arm, yanking him farther into the alleyway. She crouched before the boy, lifting the hood of her cloak.

"Can you give me your bow and arrows?" she asked breathlessly.

"What?" he replied in surprise.

"Here." Shahrzad offered him the five gold dinars in her cloak. A veritable fortune in the eyes of the boy.

"Are you crazy, lady?" the boy said, his mouth agape.

"Will you give them to me?" Shahrzad pleaded.

He passed the weapons to her without a word. She placed the money in his dirty hands and threw the quiver over her shoulder.

Khalid observed this exchange, his eyes tight and his mouth drawn.

"Do you know them, miss?" The boy glanced behind Shahrzad.

Khalid whirled around, unsheathing his *shamshir* in a single metallic rasp and knocking the black *rida'* from his brow.

"Get out of here," Shahrzad said to the boy and his friends.

The boy nodded and took off, his friends scampering alongside him.

Somehow, the group of men Shahrzad and Khalid had managed to offend numbered seven. Of this seven, three showed signs of obvious injury, while the other four appeared at a loss of pride more than anything else. Not counting money, of course.

And money counted for a lot.

At the sight of Khalid with his sword at the ready, several of them withdrew their own piecemeal weapons.

Without a word, Khalid advanced.

"Gentlemen!" Shahrzad cut him off. "This seems a bit—premature. I believe this whole situation can be attributed to a misunderstanding. Please accept my sincere apologies for our part in the matter. In truth, this is between myself and the . . . gentleman with the questionable manners from earlier."

"*My* questionable manners? Why, you shrewish bitch!" The young man stepped forward.

"That's enough!" Khalid raised his *shamshir* into the moonlight, its silver edge glistening with menace.

Poised to kill.

"Stop!" Shahrzad's tone verged on desperation.

"I said, that's enough, Shazi. I've heard enough," Khalid said with deadly inflection.

"Yes. Let him do as he pleases, *Shazi*. Seven to one? I like our odds," the imbecile continued.

You have no idea what you're saying. The second-best swordsman in Rey will cut you down, one by one. Without hesitation.

Then the imbecile lifted his rusted scimitar from its sheath.

At that, Shahrzad nocked an arrow to the sinew and loosed it, all in one swift motion. It flew in a perfect spiral, despite the bow's humble origins and the arrow's mud-stained fletchings.

And it pierced clean through the imbecile's wrist.

He howled in agony, dropping the scimitar to the ground with a resounding clang.

Before anyone had a chance to react, Shahrzad had fitted and nocked another arrow onto the string. As she pulled it tight, she felt something give in the sinew.

Oh, God.

Nevertheless, she stalked past Khalid, the arrow held in position against the side of her neck.

"This is where all of you were sorely mistaken. It was never seven to one. And I strongly suggest the seven of you take to your heels and return home. Because the next one who draws a weapon—the next one who takes a single step forward—will find an arrow through his eye. And I can assure you my friend is even less forgiving."

At the sight of movement to her left, Shahrzad swiveled quickly, her grip on the bow tightening. Again, the sinew unraveled by her ear.

"Don't test me. You mean nothing to me."

Her knees shook, but her voice was as cool as a stone beneath the water.

"This is not worth it," one of the gamblers muttered. He sheathed his weapon and left the alley. Soon, others took his lead, until the only ones remaining were the original troublemaker and his trio of miscreants.

"I believe you've had enough, sir." Shahrzad's fingers were still wrapped around the bow and arrow.

He grasped his arrow-skewered wrist as his friends exited the alley. His face was contorted with fury and the anguish of a man bested in all ways. Tears of pain trickled down his cheeks, and a glimmer of crimson stained his forearm.

Gritting his teeth against the sting, he snarled, "Have a care, grumpy. Before she ruins you, too." He left, choking on his wounds.

Shahrzad did not lower the bow until the alley was completely clear.

When she turned around, Khalid was standing there with his *shamshir* at his side—

His expression devoid of emotion.

"That day in the courtyard," he began. "You didn't miss the target."

Shahrzad took a deep breath. "No. I didn't."

He nodded.

Then he sheathed his sword.

Do it now. He's unarmed. This is perfect. Even better than your original plan to ply him with wine and eventually poison him.

"Shazi."

Do it. Get justice for Shiva—justice for all those girls who died as nothing, without cause or explanation.

"Yes?"

Loose the arrow.

He took a step toward her. His gaze swept down her body, searing wherever it touched.

End this. End this and go to Baba. To Irsa.

To Tariq.

Shahrzad tensed her grip on the weapon still nocked at her side. She inhaled, preparing to fire . . . and the frayed sinew came undone at one end.

Such a worthless coward.

"You are—remarkable. Every day, I think I am going to be surprised by how remarkable you are, but I am not. Because this is what it means to be you. It means knowing no bounds. Being limitless in all that you do."

With each word, he broke past every barrier, every wall. And Shahrzad's will fought him, screamed a silent scream, while her heart welcomed the intrusion as a songbird welcomes the dawn.

As the dying find grace in an answered prayer.

She closed her eyes, clenching the useless bow and arrow.

Shiva.

When she opened them again, he was standing before her.

"I didn't like it when you called me your friend," he said, a light in his amber eyes.

He raised both palms to either side of her face, angling her chin upward.

"Do you prefer 'my king' or '*sayyidi*'?" she choked in dry disgust.

He leaned forward, his brow almost brushing against hers.

"I prefer Khalid."

Shahrzad swallowed.

"What are you doing to me, you plague of a girl?" he whispered.

"If I'm a plague, then you should keep your distance, unless you plan on being destroyed." The weapons still in her grasp, she shoved against his chest.

"No." His hands dropped to her waist. "Destroy me."

The bow and arrow clattered to the ground as he brought his mouth to hers.

And there was no turning back.

She was drowning in sandalwood and sunlight. Time ceased to be more than a notion. Her lips were hers one moment. And then they were his. The taste of him on her tongue was like sun-warmed honey. Like cool water sliding down her parched throat. Like the promise of all her tomorrows in a single sigh. When she wound her fingers in his hair to draw her body against his, he stilled for breath, and she knew, as he knew, that they were lost. Lost forever.

In this kiss.

This kiss that would change everything.

MISBEGOTTEN OATHS

SHE WANTED TO LET GO OF HIS HAND. BUT SHE didn't.

His touch burned her skin.

The shame. The betrayal.

The desire.

How could I waste such a perfect opportunity? Why did I hesitate?

She knew she was not to blame for the useless bow. Nonetheless, the self-recriminations could not be silenced.

The moment they stepped into the palace courtyard, Shahrzad tried to pull away.

Khalid merely tightened his grip.

A contingent of guards stood at the ready, prepared to receive the caliph upon his arrival. The *Shahrban* of Rey stared down at their interlaced fingers and turned his brown eyes to Shahrzad in pained accusation.

She returned nothing but defiance.

"*Sayyidi.*" He gave Khalid a mincing bow.

"General al-Khoury. It is late. I did not expect to see you until morning."

The *shahrban* frowned. "My king's whereabouts remained uncertain. As such, I cannot stand about idly, waiting for the dawn."

Shahrzad almost laughed.

"Your vigilance is appreciated," Khalid replied.

He grunted in response as his gaze shifted again to Shahrzad. "I'm sure it has been a taxing evening, *sayyidi*. I would be happy to escort the queen to her chamber."

"That is not necessary. I will take her there myself. Then I would like to speak to you in the antechamber."

The *shahrban* nodded. "I will await your arrival, *sayyidi*."

Khalid continued down the darkened hallways with Shahrzad at his side, surrounded by their retinue of bodyguards. Here, in the palace's coolly foreboding passages of marble and stone, she witnessed his features retreat to a place far in the distance. A place no one was permitted to follow.

The only inkling she had—the only hint she was still part of his reality—was her hand wound in his.

And she did not care for it at all.

It should not matter. He should not matter.

Again, she slackened her grasp. Once more, he simply reinforced his.

The Rajput was waiting outside her chamber. He nodded to Khalid with the brusqueness of a friend as one of the guards held open the doors.

As soon as they shut behind them, Khalid released her hand.

Shahrzad turned to him, uncertain. "Why does General al-Khoury dislike me?" she asked, point-blank.

Khalid's gaze leveled to hers. "He sees a threat."

"Why does he see a threat?"

"Because he doesn't understand you."

"Does he need to understand me? Because I don't understand him."

Khalid inhaled through his nose. "So are you ready to answer my questions, then?"

Very well. I, too, have questions.

"What questions?"

"I'll answer your questions when you're ready to answer mine."

"Khalid—"

He leaned forward and pressed a kiss to her brow. "Sleep well, Shazi." His hand skimmed to her waist, as if seeking permission.

Shahrzad drew a quick breath.

This is madness. He makes me weak. He makes me forget.

I should push him away.

Yet she wanted so much to curve against him. To lose herself in honey and sunlight, and forget everything but the way it felt to be held in such a tantalizing trap of her own making.

"Thank you—for the adventure," he said.

"You're welcome."

He toyed with a smile. An invitation.

But the yoke of betrayal hung about her, weighing on her every action. Shaming her for even considering a moment in his arms, and insisting she not succumb once more to the wishes of a fickle heart.

How can I desire him? After he killed Shiva? After he killed so many young girls, without explanation?

What's wrong with me?

As she stared up at him in obvious deliberation, he took away the choice, as quickly as he had offered it.

"Good night, Shahrzad."

She exhaled, with the worst kind of relief.

"Good night, Khalid."

Shahrzad watched the doors as they shut behind him.

If given another chance, would I take the shot? Can I do what needs to be done?

Her fists curled at her sides.

I may not be able to kill him outright, but I must do what needs to be done.

I will learn why he killed all his brides.

And I will punish him for it.

He stood outside her doors.

Torn.

It was a familiar stance for him of late.

He despised it.

Khalid ignored the Rajput's knowing grin as he began his trek toward his chamber. As usual, the bodyguard's sense of humor was ill-timed and ill-bred.

Each step Khalid took echoed down the corridors of shadow and stone. The callous granite and blue-veined agate of his palace had provided little but a refuge for the screams of ghosts.

A haven for nightmares . . .

Until Shahrzad.

A true plague of a girl. And yet a queen in every sense of the word.

His queen.

He left the soldiers outside the antechamber leading into his private rooms.

General al-Khoury was waiting for him, sitting before an ebony table with two bronze lamps casting halos of gold and a silver pot of tea glistening atop a low-burning flame.

The *shahrban* rose to his feet as Khalid entered the antechamber. "*Sayyidi.*"

"Please sit." Khalid took position on the cushions directly opposite. "I apologize for the hour, but I have an important matter to discuss with you. As such, I'll dispense with the formalities."

"Of course, *sayyidi.*"

"The standing order regarding the queen—was I not clear before I left last week?"

The *shahrban's* harried features grew even more agitated. "*Sayyidi*—"

"There will be no further attempts on her life."

"But, *sayyidi*—"

"No. No more underhanded schemes. No more poisoned sugar. Furthermore, I will treat any effort to subvert this order as a direct attempt on my own life. Do you understand, General?"

"*Sayyidi!*"

"I asked you a question, General al-Khoury."

The *shahrban* bristled for an instant. "And I cannot answer it."

"Uncle Aref!"

Khalid's uncharacteristic outburst hung about the space, lingering with the tension of many unspoken things.

"She will be your undoing."

"That is my decision."

"And so you would undermine all that has been done? No matter how unconscionable our actions have been, we are nearly at an end now. Please. I implore you. Reconsider this. She is just one girl. What is she to you? We cannot trust her, Khalid-*jan*. Has she told you why she volunteered? Has she confessed her motivations? Who is this child? I beg of you. You cannot withstand this. Do not allow this brazen young girl to become a source of ruination."

Khalid gazed across the table at his uncle. "I've made my decision."

The *shahrban*'s face faltered. "Please. If you—do you love her? Tell me you do not love this child, Khalid-*jan*."

"It is not about love."

"Then why? You do not have to take part in the matter. Merely step aside. Cease all contact with her, as you did that night, and I will handle the sunrise."

"No. I tried, Uncle Aref. That morning . . ." Khalid winced in remembrance.

The *shahrban*'s eyes narrowed. "Yet you do not love her?"

"You're aware of my thoughts on the matter."

"Then what do you want from this insolent young girl, Khalid-*jan*?"

"Something more."

"And what if the rains cease again?"

Khalid paused. "I will do what is right for the people of Rey."

The *shahrban* heaved a world-weary sigh. "You will not be able to withstand it. Even now, I can see the toll it is taking on you."

"Again. My decision."

"And your enemies will celebrate as it destroys you from within, as well as from without."

Khalid leaned forward and braced his forehead on his palms. "Then I trust you will see to it they never find out." He spoke to the floor, his faith in his uncle implicit.

The *shahrban* nodded before placing his hands on the marble and pushing to his feet. As he looked back at the exhausted figure of his king, the *shahrban*'s features saddened once more.

"*Sayyidi*? Please forgive this last question. But I must know—is she worth this risk?"

Khalid raised his head, his eyes reflecting a fiery orange in the flickering lamplight. "In truth? I don't know . . ."

The *shahrban*'s shoulders sagged.

"But I do know I can't remember the last time I wanted something so much," he finished in a quiet voice.

It was the careful smile Khalid offered his uncle that finally convinced the *shahrban*—the first real smile he had seen on his nephew's face in years.

"Khalid-*jan*. I will protect your queen. For as long as I can."

"Thank you."

"*Sayyidi*." The *shahrban* started to bow.

"General al-Khoury?"

"Yes?"

"Please send in the *faqir* after you leave."

"Yes, *sayyidi*."

"And, if I could ask one last thing . . ."

"Of course."

"Have you made any progress in determining the whereabouts of the queen's family?"

"No, *sayyidi*. We are still searching."

Khalid raked his fingers through his black hair, tousling its smooth surface. "Continue the search. Be tireless in your efforts."

"Yes, *sayyidi*." With a hand to his brow, the *shahrban* exited the antechamber.

Khalid removed the dark *rida'* from his shoulders and placed it in his lap. He knew it was likely Shahrzad had sent her family away or that they had fled voluntarily, leaving behind a store of unanswered questions. And he found the timing too coincidental for it to be unrelated to their marriage.

If he could find her family, perhaps he could obtain the answers he so desired.

But would he want these answers once they were within his grasp?

So many issues already plagued him.

He could ask her.

Ask her where she had sent her family. What she was hiding from him.

Why she insisted on tormenting him.

But the thought that she might lie to him—that those eyes, with their unpredictable onslaught of colors, flashing blue one instant and green the next, only to paint his world gold with the bright sound of her laughter—that those eyes might endeavor to conceal the truth, pained him more than he cared to admit.

Because he had lied to her only once.

He balled an edge of the dusty cloak in his fist and heaved it into the corner. His eyelids felt heavy, and his vision was starting to blur. Now the longer he gazed at things, the harder it was to focus. The pounding in his forehead was growing worse.

A knock at the door to the antechamber stirred him from his thoughts.

"Come in."

A ghostly figure, garbed solely in white, cut through the darkness into the lamplight. His long beard trailed down his chest.

"*Sayyidi.*"

Khalid sighed.

"It is worse?" the *faqir* asked as he took in Khalid's haggard mien.

"The same."

"It appears worse, *sayyidi.*"

"Then it is good you are here." Khalid's eyes flashed in warning.

The *faqir* exhaled slowly. "I've told you. I cannot stave off the effects forever. I can only ensure it will not kill you. Eventually, the madness will ensue, *sayyidi.* You cannot fight it."

"I understand."

"*Sayyidi,* I must implore you. No matter how repugnant, stay the prior course. This option . . . will not end well."

"Your counsel is noted. And appreciated," Khalid said in a low tone.

The *faqir* nodded.

Khalid bowed his head. The *faqir* raised both his palms to Khalid's temples, leaving just enough space for silk to pass, then closed his eyes. The air in the antechamber stilled. The flames in

176

the lamps grew tall and lean. When the *faqir*'s eyes opened once more, they glowed with the light of a full moon. Between his hands, a warm red-orange fireburst spread up and around the entirety of Khalid's brow. The circle pulsed yellow, then white, spiraling upward all the while, before it retracted back into the *faqir*'s clawed hands.

Once the magic had faded back to the realm of its origins, the *faqir* dropped his hands.

Khalid raised his head. The pounding was less profound, if still present, and his eyelids were not as heavy as before. "Thank you."

"Soon there will come a time when I will not deserve such words, *sayyidi*."

"You will always deserve such words, no matter what happens."

The *faqir*'s frustration further marred his features. "Would that all of Khorasan could see the king I see, *sayyidi*."

"They would not be much impressed. For I did bring all of this upon myself, did I not? And, as a consequence, they have had to endure the unthinkable."

The *faqir* bowed with his fingertips to his brow, then floated to the door.

Before exiting, he turned. "How long should a man pay for his mistakes, *sayyidi*?"

Khalid did not hesitate.

"Until all debts are forgiven."

THE HONOR OF BETRAYAL

W HEN SHAHRZAD AWOKE THE NEXT MORNING, sunlight streamed through the opened screens leading to the terrace. A fresh arrangement of citrus blossoms lay on a small stool next to the raised platform.

At the sight of the white flowers by her bed, her first thought was of Khalid. She stretched her arms, trying her best to ignore the pang of guilt that ensued.

"Do you like them?" Despina asked. "I thought you might."

Shahrzad raised her head from the pillow. "What?"

"You have a rather strange preoccupation with flowers, so I asked them to bring some to your room."

"Oh. Thank you."

Despina snorted. "You don't sound grateful. You sound disappointed."

Shahrzad rolled over. She rose from the bed and slipped into her *shamla*.

I hate that she notices everything. Almost as much as I hate her for being right.

As Shahrzad stepped from the platform, Despina removed the lid from the tureen of soup.

And Shahrzad heard her stifle a gasp in the process.

"What's wrong?" Shahrzad took a seat on the cushions before the low table.

"Nothing," Despina squeaked.

Shahrzad gazed at her handmaiden, and her heart lurched.

Despina's brow was beaded with sweat. Her usually flawless coloring of delicate ivory and blushing coral was decidedly green and sallow. Tension darkened every crease. Her graceful fingers trembled next to her beautifully draped dress of lilac linen.

She looked exactly as she had the day Shahrzad's tea had been poisoned.

"Where is the servant who tastes my food?" Shahrzad's voice wavered at the end of her question.

"She just left." It was a terse response, pushed forth from unwilling lips.

Shahrzad nodded. "Fine. I'll ask you once more, Despina. What's wrong?"

Despina shook her head, backing away from the table.

"Nothing. Nothing's wrong, Shahrzad."

Shahrzad stood up, jangling the edge of the tray. "Don't make me do this!"

"Do what?"

"Why do you look scared?"

"I'm not scared!"

"Come here."

Despina hesitated before striding back to the table. As she stood alongside Shahrzad, her trembling worsened, and she pressed her mouth into a single, bright pink line.

Shahrzad's heartbreak began anew. "Sit down."

"What?" The word passed through clenched teeth.

"Sit down, Despina!"

"I—no."

"No?"

"I—can't, Shahrzad!" She shuffled away from the table, raising a hand to her lips.

"How could you?" Shahrzad whispered.

"What?" Despina gasped.

"Stop lying to me!" She seized Despina by the wrist and dragged her closer. "Why?"

The flat of Despina's hand remained clamped over her mouth as she glanced at the tray of food below.

"Answer me!" Shahrzad wailed. "How could you do this?"

Despina shook her head, the beads of sweat dripping from her brow.

"Despina!"

Then, with a retching sound, Despina snatched the lid of the soup tureen and began vomiting into it.

Shahrzad stood there in shock, her eyes huge as she watched her handmaiden sink to the floor in a miserable heap, clutching the silver lid in both hands.

Once Despina's suffering had lessened to dry heaving, she peered up at Shahrzad through tear-stained lashes.

"You—are a miserable brat, Shahrzad al-Khayzuran," she choked.

At first, Shahrzad could think of no way to string together a coherent response. "I—you're—Despina, are you . . ." Shahrzad trailed off. Then she cleared her throat. "Well, are you?"

Despina rose to her knees, blotting her forehead on her arm. She sighed in defeat. "I truly despise you right now."

"Hate me or don't hate me. But answer my failed attempt at a question."

Despina expelled a pained breath. "Yes."

Shahrzad fell back against the cushions in disbelief.

"Holy Hera."

Despina laughed hoarsely. "I must say, you donning the guise of a friend is quite the heartwarming sight. Especially in light of the fact you thought I was trying to poison you."

"Well, what else was I supposed to think? Especially after last week's incident with the tea. I suppose you were sick that day, too?"

The handmaiden sighed again.

"Despina," Shahrzad said, "who is the father?"

"Now, that question I won't answer."

"What? Why not?"

"Because you share a bed with the Caliph of Khorasan."

"Ah, the web of secrets grows thicker every day!" Shahrzad retorted. "So is he the father?"

"No!"

"Then why does that matter?"

Despina sat back on her heels. "Because I can't trust that you won't tell him."

"What? I don't tell him anything."

"You don't need to. Your eyes search for him the moment they leave this room."

"They do not!" Shahrzad screeched.

"By Zeus, my ears." Despina clutched the side of her head. "Don't yell. I beg of you."

"I won't tell Khalid. I swear."

"Khalid?" The edges of Despina's lips curved upward. "I know you're tenacious in your endeavors, Brat Calipha, but I would give up on this one. You're bound to be disappointed when your attempts at persuasion prove futile on me . . ."

Shahrzad frowned.

"After all, I am not the King of Kings."

"Enough!" Shahrzad flushed. "Tell me who it is."

"I'm very sorry, Shahrzad, but I am not telling you. I simply can't."

"You *can't*?" Shahrzad mulled over the word. "Then he must be someone of import."

"Don't push the matter." Despina's voice was tight.

"I wonder . . ." Shahrzad disregarded Despina's look of warning and drummed her fingers along her chin. "It can't be the Rajput or any of the other palace guards. There would be no reason for someone as bold as you to conceal that."

"Shahrzad—"

"So," Shahrzad continued, "it must be either the *Shahrban* of

182

Rey, which is preposterous, or . . ." Her expression smoothed in sudden understanding. "Jalal."

Despina burst into laughter. "The captain of the guard? Even I'm not that bold. What makes you—"

"Actually, you are that bold." Shahrzad pushed back the tray of food and rested her elbows on the beveled ledge of the low table. "And this explains your odd behavior whenever you're around him."

"You're being ridiculous." Despina laughed again, the sound trilling ever higher, her eyes burning with a blue light.

Shahrzad grinned slowly. "I know I'm right."

Despina glowered at her in sullen silence.

"You needn't worry." Shahrzad propped her chin on the heel of her palm. "Your secret is safe. You can trust me."

"Trust you?" Despina sputtered. "I'd sooner trust a sieve."

"That's—rather unfair."

"Is it? You don't trust me."

"Of course I don't trust you. You're a self-admitted spy, and I've nearly died twice on your watch." Shahrzad stared at her pointedly.

Despina blinked. "Don't be dramatic."

"Dramatic? Need I remind you about the tea?"

"You still think that was *me*?"

"Then who was it?" Shahrzad demanded. "If you want me to trust you, tell me who was responsible."

"It wasn't the caliph, if that's why you're asking. He was . . . quite furious when he found out about it."

"Was it the *shahrban*?"

Despina said nothing, but failed to conceal a cringe of affirmation.

"I'm not surprised," Shahrzad continued. "I suspected as much."

"Did you? Perhaps *you* should be the spy and I the calipha."

"Perhaps. But I believe your pregnancy by another man may present a hindrance to that," Shahrzad said in a droll tone. "Does Jalal know about the baby? If so, he should marry you. Or face my fury. The choice is his."

"He doesn't know. And I don't intend to tell him." Despina stood up and straightened the folds of her dress. "Because I don't think he needs to know."

"Well, that is simply ridiculous."

Despina hooked a strand of golden brown hair behind an ear. "Maybe it is. But, for now, I choose to believe it is not."

Shahrzad watched in pained silence while her handmaiden began cleaning up the mess as if nothing had occurred. As if a world of chaos had not been unleashed only moments before.

Like a canary in a gilded cage, Despina flitted about, stunning and resilient.

Trapped.

"You should rest," Shahrzad directed.

Despina faltered, midstep. "What?"

"You're pregnant. You don't have to hide it from me anymore. Sit. Rest."

Despina's eyes swam crystalline for an instant before they flashed back to blue. "I don't need to rest."

"I insist."

"Truly, it's not—"

"Rest this morning. I'll go with the Rajput to practice shooting in the training grounds. Come there when you feel better." Shahrzad began preparing a cup of tea. "Do you think some tea would help your stomach?"

"I can make the tea," Despina whispered.

"So can I."

Despina paused, staring down at the figure of the small girl with the long mane of sleep-rifled hair. "Shahrzad?"

"Yes?"

"You are not at all what one would expect."

"Is that supposed to be a compliment?" Shahrzad grinned over her shoulder.

"Absolutely. I think it's kept you alive."

"Then I'm very grateful for it."

"As am I." Despina smiled. "Most grateful."

A wild cheer rang out from the sidelines as the arrow struck the eave on the opposite side of the courtyard with a solid thud. The shouts of the soldiers rolled into a chorus of laughter that rose into a cloud-filled sky.

A sky tinged with the scent of impending rain.

Shahrzad smiled at Jalal.

His shoulders shook with soundless mirth. He ran his free hand through his curly brown hair and shrugged at his men.

"You cannot dispute that, Captain al-Khoury," Shahrzad announced.

"Indeed. I cannot, my lady." He bowed, his fingertips to his forehead. "Your arrow struck the target. Mine . . . did not. Name your price."

Shahrzad thought for a moment. Her question had to be a good one. It had to be worth discarding any attempt to conceal her skill with a bow. It also had to be worded in a judicious manner. He was gifted at deflecting responses and offering eloquent nonanswers.

"Why are you permitted to call the caliph by his first name?"

Jalal shifted the yew of his longbow from palm to palm. Ever careful. Ever calculating. "Khalid is my cousin. My father married his father's sister."

Shahrzad had difficulty suppressing her reaction. This was the most information she had obtained the entire morning.

Jalal grinned with a dangerous gleam in his light brown gaze. "Choose the next target, Shahrzad."

She scanned the courtyard. "The topmost branch of the tree to the right, beyond the roofline."

He wagged his eyebrows, appreciating the challenge, as he pulled an arrow from his quiver and nocked it to the string. When he drew it back, the edges of the unyielding longbow barely shifted.

Jalal was an excellent archer. Not as gifted as Tariq, but precise and sharp in his movements. He loosed the arrow. It flew in a spiral and sailed above the roofline before it struck the topmost branch, causing the entire tree to shudder from the force of its impact.

The men began to cheer in approval.

Shahrzad fitted an arrow to the recurve bow. She closed her eyes as she nocked it tight against the sinew. Exhaling, she pulled the arrow back.

The instant she opened her eyes, she released the string. The arrow soared through the air, whistling past the branches . . .

Embedding just below her intended target.

Shahrzad frowned.

The soldiers raised another cry of triumph. Again, Jalal bowed, this time with his hands outstretched at his sides.

"Oh, don't gloat," Shahrzad scolded. "It's quite unbecoming."

"I have never gloated. Not a day in my life."

"I find that rather difficult to believe."

"Gloating is for weaker men."

"Then stop smiling like such a fool."

Jalal laughed, raising his arms to the sky. "But it's going to rain, Shahrzad. And I'm a fool for the rain."

"Just collect your prize, Captain al-Khoury," Shahrzad grumbled, folding her arms across her chest, letting her recurve bow dangle by her feet.

"Don't be so frustrated with me. I've been quite fair in my questions."

She rolled her eyes.

"In fact," he continued, "this will be my first truly unfair question of the day."

Shahrzad's posture reacted to his words before her features did.

Jalal took a step forward, balancing his longbow across his shoulders. "Where is your family, my lady?" he said in a low voice.

They're looking for my family . . . as I expected.

She smiled up at him. "Safe."

"That's not an answer."

"In a place of sand and stone."

"That's also not an answer. Everything is made of sand and stone."

"You cannot force a better answer out of me, Jalal. These are my answers. If you dislike them, we can cease with our game."

His eyes moved across her face with an odd mixture of ready discernment and playful diversion. Yet, in that instant, she saw more of his father in him than she had ever seen thus far. And she understood.

This was not merely his occupation. Jalal al-Khoury was protecting his family. To him, family always came first.

And she was not family.

"No," he countered, "but I would like to ask another question in lieu of the last. Since your answer was quite unsatisfactory, I feel it only appropriate I be permitted another question."

"Excuse me?"

"I promise to grant you the same right, should the occasion arise on your end."

"Jalal—"

"Why do you always close your eyes before you aim?"

"Because . . ." Shahrzad hesitated. "I—"

What is the harm?

"I learned to shoot in a place where the sun played tricks on the mind. You could not rely on it if you wanted to aim well. So you had to practice until you were good enough that you only needed its light for the blink of an eye."

Jalal braced both palms on the yew of his longbow. A slow grin spread across his sun-drenched face.

It unnerved Shahrzad. And made her want to provoke him.

"That was much better," he said loudly. "You know, not everything has to be so difficult, Shahrzad."

"What are you talking about?"

"Exactly what I said. Next time, just answer the question."

"We shall see. Choose the next target, Jalal."

His grin grew even wider. "Yes, my lady." He studied the courtyard. Then he pointed to a slender pillar with a *tabarzin* axe embedded in its side. "The winner is the archer with the arrow closest to the axe blade."

It was by far the most difficult shot. The *tabarzin*'s wooden handle was quite narrow by the blade, and it was wedged into the pillar at an odd angle that all but obscured it from view. To make matters worse, the impending storm had now added a wind factor that would put to rout even the most gifted of archers.

As the winner of the last match, Jalal was given the first shot. He waited for the gusts to calm as much as possible before he positioned the arrow to the string and let it fly. It spiraled toward the *tabarzin* and managed to strike the wood of the handle.

An impressive achievement.

Shahrzad pulled an arrow from the quiver at her back. She fitted it to the sinew and nocked it tight. Closing her eyes, she let the breeze blow against her face, calculating its trajectory. Her fingers curled around the white-feathered fletchings.

She opened her eyes and pinpointed the small stretch of wood fixed before the gleaming axe blade.

Then she loosed the arrow.

It sailed through the wind, over the sand . . . and thudded into the handle, a mere hairsbreadth from the metal.

The soldiers shouted in collective disbelief.

Jalal began laughing. "My God. Perhaps I should try my hand at not aiming."

Shahrzad mimicked his previous bow, her arms outstretched at her sides.

His laughter grew. "Well, you've earned this next question, my lady. Do your worst."

Yes. I believe I will.

It's time I learned the truth.

She strode forward. "What is the real reason all of Khalid's brides must die?"

It was posited in a ghost of a whisper. Only Jalal could have heard it.

But it was as though she had shouted it from the rooftops.

Jalal's amusement vanished, doused by an urgent gravity she had never seen on his face before. "This game is over."

Shahrzad pursed her lips. "Why is it you get to decide the rules on all fronts?"

"It's over, Shahrzad," he said, confiscating the recurve bow from her grasp.

"At least give me the right to ask another question."

"No."

"You promised me that right!"

"I'm sorry, but I cannot honor that promise."

"Excuse me?"

"I'm sorry." He stalked to the weapons rack and restored both the longbow and the recurve bow to their respective places.

"Jalal!" Shahrzad raced in his footsteps. "You can't—"

He nodded to the Rajput, who began making his way over to Shahrzad.

Outraged, Shahrzad snatched a scimitar from a nearby weapons rack.

"Jalal al-Khoury!"

When he still refused to acknowledge her, Shahrzad raised the sword into the light with both hands, and the Rajput shifted closer.

"How dare you dismiss me, you horse's ass!" she yelled.

At that, Jalal turned around, his stride off-kilter. She swung the heavy blade in a sloppy arc meant to goad him into taking her seriously.

He dodged her and reached reflexively for the scimitar at his hip. "What the hell are you doing, Shahrzad?"

"Do you think you can get away with treating me in such a manner?"

"Put down the sword," he said in an uncharacteristically stern tone.

"No."

"You have no business handling a blade like that. Put it down."

"No!"

When she swung it again in another haphazard slice, Jalal was forced to deflect it with his own blade. The Rajput grunted loudly and withdrew his *talwar,* shoving Jalal away from her with a single push of his palm.

"Stop it!" Shahrzad said to the Rajput. "I don't need your help."

The Rajput sneered down at her with obvious disdain.

"Are you, is he—laughing at me?" Shahrzad asked incredulously.

"I imagine so," Jalal replied.

"Unbelievable. What's funny?"

"I would assume it's both the sight of you wielding a sword in such an abysmal manner and the presumption you wouldn't need his help when doing so."

Shahrzad spun to face the Rajput. "Well, sir, if you're really in the business of helping me, then, instead of laughing at my ineptitude, do something about it!"

The Rajput merely continued sneering at her.

"He's not going to help you, Shahrzad," Jalal said, seamlessly resurrecting his smug façade. "I'd venture a guess that not many soldiers out here, save myself, would take the risk of getting within an arm's length of you."

"And why is that?"

"Well, by now every soldier in Rey knows what happened to the last guard who dared to put his hands on the queen. So if I were you, I'd give up on cajoling the Rajput into giving you lessons on swordplay. Even though you did ask him so nicely," Jalal joked drily.

"Did . . ." Shahrzad frowned. "What happened to the guard?"

Jalal shrugged. "A bevy of broken bones. Your husband is not a forgiving man."

Wonderful. Yet another attribute of note.

"So please put down the sword and go back to the palace, my lady," Jalal finished in a firm tone.

"Don't you dare dismiss me, Jalal al—" And Shahrzad's rant died on her lips, before it even started.

She wanted to turn around.

Because she knew, instinctively, that he was there. There was no logical explanation for it, but she felt his presence behind her, like the subtle change in the seasons. A shift in the wind. This was not necessarily a welcome change. She did not suffer that kind of delusion. Not yet.

But even the moment when the leaves fall from their boughs— even that moment—has a beauty to it. A glory of its own.

And this change? This change made her shoulders tense and her stomach spin.

It was real . . . and terrifying.

"This moment could not be any more perfect," Jalal muttered, glancing to his left.

Still Shahrzad did not turn around. She clenched the scimitar tight in both hands, and the Rajput stepped even closer, his *talwar* glinting with a silent warning.

"By Zeus, Shahrzad!" Despina cried. "Is this what happens when I leave you alone? You get into a sword fight with the captain of the guard?"

At that, Shahrzad twisted her head to the right.

Despina stood by Khalid with a look of worry and dismay on her pretty face.

Khalid was as inscrutable as ever.

As cold as always.

Shahrzad wished she could end it here and now, with the slash of a sword. She wished she could grab Khalid by the shoulders and shake a semblance of life onto his frozen countenance.

Instead, Shahrzad continued with the pretense—the one she gave to the world, and the one she gave to herself.

"Well?" Despina said.

Khalid's eyes flicked to the handmaiden.

"I apologize, *sayyidi*. I did not mean to address the queen so informally." Despina bowed in haste, her hand to her brow.

"You don't have to apologize, Despina. I did not get into a fight with Jalal. We're merely trading a few . . . lessons. Apparently, I am not that gifted with a sword. There are, in fact, limitations to my greatness," Shahrzad jested.

"Thank the gods," Despina mumbled.

"Limitations plague us all, Shahrzad." Jalal grinned, seizing upon this opportunity for levity. "Don't take it to heart."

She wrinkled her nose at him, plunking the scimitar to the ground.

"What limitations?" Khalid asked quietly.

The sound of his voice slid down her back, bringing to mind cool water and sun-warmed honey. She gritted her teeth. "For one, I can't seem to wield a sword. And that seems to be a basic premise of swordsmanship."

Khalid watched her as she spoke.

"Pick it up," he directed.

Shahrzad looked at him. He blinked, and his features softened.

She raised the scimitar in both hands. Then, to her surprise, Khalid backed away and unsheathed his *shamshir*.

"Try to hit me," he said.

"Are you serious?"

He waited in patient silence.

She swung the sword in a clumsy swipe.

Khalid parried it with ease and grabbed her wrist. "That was awful," he said, pulling her into him. "Again."

"Can you offer some direction?" she demanded.

"Widen your stance. Don't throw your entire body into the movement. Only your upper body."

She sunk into a lower stance, her brow lined with irritation. Once more, she curved the scimitar at him, and he blocked it, grasping her by the waist and bringing the flat of the *shamshir* against her throat.

In her ear, he whispered, "Do better than this, Shazi. My queen is without limitations. Boundless in all that she does. Show them."

Her pulse raced at his warmth. In the words and the actions. The nearness of him.

She broke away and raised the scimitar.

"Smaller movements. Quicker. Lighter," Khalid commanded. "I don't want to see you act before you do."

Shahrzad lashed out with the sword. Khalid parried the blow.

The Rajput grunted, crossing his mammoth arms.

After Shahrzad cut the scimitar in Khalid's direction a few more times, she was shocked when the Rajput stepped forward and kicked at her back foot, nudging it into a new alignment. Then he lifted his bearded chin with a jerk.

He . . . wants me to keep my head up?

Khalid stood by, watching.

"Like—this?" Shahrzad asked the Rajput.

He cleared his throat and moved back.

When Shahrzad looked at Khalid again, his eyes were alight with an emotion she recognized.

Pride.

And the moment felt so terrifyingly real that the thought of anything destroying it cinched the air from her body . . .

Like a silk cord around her neck.

TO INFLICT A DARK WOUND

SHAHRZAD PICKED UP THE VIAL OF SCENTED ROSE-water and pulled out the glass stopper. The perfume smelled heady and sweet—like a bouquet of aging blossoms alongside a vat of slowly melting sugar. Intoxicating and mysterious.

Perhaps too much so.

It didn't smell like her.

She sighed and put down the vial.

Following her impromptu sword lesson, Shahrzad and Despina had returned to her chamber for dinner. Then her handmaiden had retired to her small room by Shahrzad's chamber, mistakenly leaving behind a few cosmetics near the mirror in the corner. Shahrzad had wandered past this arrangement several times over the course of the last few hours.

Considering.

Situated by the vial was a tiny pot of polished ivory. Shahrzad twisted open the lid to discover a mixture of carmine and beeswax. She dipped her index finger into the shining paste and daubed it onto her lower lip. It felt sticky and strange on her skin as she attempted to mimic the alluring pout she always admired on her handmaiden. She stared back at her reflection.

I look ridiculous.

Shahrzad rubbed away the stickiness with her palm. It stained her hand pink.

What am I doing?

She paced toward the raised platform of her bed.

None of this was right.

She was not here to spend time troubling about her appearance. Such childishness was beneath her. She had come to the palace with a singleminded purpose: to discover her enemy's weakness and destroy him with it.

How could she lose sight of everything over a mere kiss? Over a mere moment in a dark alley by the souk.

A moment that replayed in her mind with staggering frequency.

Shahrzad inhaled and tightened the silver laces of her *shamla*. She could not—*would* not—stray from her purpose.

How had this even happened?

It's because he's not the monster I thought he was.

There was so much more below the surface, and she had to know what lay at the root of it all.

Why did General al-Khoury try to poison her?

And *why* did Shiva have to die?

Shahrzad no longer believed the tales running through the streets of Rey. Khalid Ibn al-Rashid was not a madman from a line of murdering madmen, hell-bent on senseless brutality.

He was a boy with secrets.

Secrets Shahrzad had to know. It was no longer enough for her to stand at his side and play along with the dance of ice and stone. To watch him fade into the distance, barricaded in a room no one was permitted to enter.

She was going to break down the door. And steal all of his secrets.

Shahrzad walked to the pile of cushions on top of her bed and coiled into its center.

The least she could do was pretend she was not waiting for him.

That she was worthy of better.

Did she really care about him? For this acknowledgment would mean giving teeth to the most dangerous realization of all—

Caring about him meant he had real power over her. That he held sway over her heart.

Shahrzad sighed, hating her weak heart more with each passing breath. If she had to fail so abominably in her task at the souk, then at the very least, her heart should not have been so complicit in her failure. Where was the resolute, steel-encased enclosure she had constructed for herself, not so long ago?

Her mind drifted back to the night before the soldiers had come for Shiva.

They had stayed up together, just the two of them, huddled in the blue darkness with a single candle. Instead of crying over what would never be or wailing to the stars for what was to come,

Shiva had insisted they laugh for what they still had. So they'd sat in her courtyard under a slivered moon, giggling at years of shared memories.

This is what Shahrzad had done for Shiva.

What Shiva had done for Shahrzad.

That morning, when Shahrzad had left her so that Shiva could spend her last day with her family, Shiva had smiled at Shahrzad and said, with a simple hug, "I will see you one day, my dearest love. And we will smile and laugh again."

Such strength.

For such betrayal.

Shahrzad seized a pillow and curled her fists into the silk.

Shiva. What do I do? I—can't find the hate anymore. Help me find it. When I see his face . . . when I hear his voice. How can I do this to you? How can I love you so much and—

The doors to the chamber opened with a creak. Shahrzad sat up, expecting to see the usual servants with their nightly wares.

Khalid stood at the threshold.

Alone.

"Were you sleeping?" he asked.

"No."

He stepped inside and pulled the doors shut behind him. "Are you tired?"

"No." Shahrzad's fingers tightened against the silk.

He remained by the doors.

She rose from the cushions and straightened her *shamla*. It spun about her as she moved past the gossamer veil at the foot of the bed.

"Do you want me to finish the tale of Aladdin?"

"No." Khalid strode from the doors to stand before her.

He looked . . . exhausted.

"Did you not sleep?" she asked. "You should sleep."

"I should."

The air between them swirled with the intensity of the unsaid.

"Khalid—"

"It rained today."

"Yes. For a little while."

He nodded, his amber eyes catching fire on a thought.

Shahrzad blinked. "Are you a fool for the rain, like Jalal?"

"No. I'm—just a fool."

Why? Tell me why.

She lifted her right hand, slowly, to his face.

He closed his eyes.

When he opened them again, he placed his palms on either side of her neck.

How could a boy with legions of secrets behind walls of ice and stone burn her with nothing more than his touch?

He trailed his right hand through her hair, over her shoulder, and down her back. His left thumb lingered on her neck, brushing across the hollow at its base.

I—I won't stop fighting, Shiva. I will discover the truth and seek justice for you.

She stared up at Khalid. Waiting.

"What are you doing?" she whispered.

"Exercising restraint."

"Why?"

"Because I failed to do so in the souk."

"Does that matter?"

"Yes, it does," he said quietly. "Do you want this?"

Shahrzad paused. "We've done this before."

"It's not the same. It won't be the same."

The blood flew through her body, ignited by his words.

He pressed his lips beneath her earlobe. His tongue lingered for an instant on her skin. "Do you want this?" he repeated in her ear.

Shahrzad steeled herself, fighting back an onset of trembling limbs.

"Why do you think I'm standing here, you idiot?"

Then she seized his chin in her hands and slanted her mouth to his.

What began as a playful kiss soon changed into something more in keeping with the prurient thoughts that had filled the space only moments before.

Shahrzad's fingers curled into Khalid's soft hair as his lips curved over hers. He enveloped her in an embrace that took her bare feet from the marble. The veil tore from its mooring as they fell back onto the cushions with complete disregard for such trappings as gossamer.

Her hands dragged the hem of his *qamis* over his head. The muscles of his torso coiled at her touch, and the air in the room grew ever more stifling, ever more tangible. When his lips moved to her neck and his palms slid across her stomach to the laces of her *shamla,* she knew he was right.

This would not be the same.

For this was untrammeled need; this was a body of water and a soul of ash.

The laces of her *shamla* were free. If this progressed much further, it would be pointless to even consider such a thing as thought. She had to ask now, before the flames consumed her.

"Tell me," she gasped, her fingers gripping his shoulders.

"Anything."

Her heart soared, and the guilt clutched at it. "Why did they have to die?"

He stilled in her arms for an interminable beat.

Then Khalid lifted himself from her and stared down at Shahrzad, his face frozen in horror.

He saw the conflict in her eyes.

She saw the terror in his.

Without a word, he rose from the bed and made his way to the doors.

As his fingers grasped the handle, he paused.

"Never do that to me again." It was low and harsh.

Filled with unmitigated pain.

He slammed the door shut behind him.

The deprivation of him was palpable. A part of her almost reveled in it—the reminder that this was all a result of vast suffering at his hands. The other part longed to chase after him. For she knew it was possible to conquer him if she did.

Shahrzad buried her face in the cushions and began to sob.

At last, she had discovered a real weakness.

It was her.

And I will use it; I will find out why Shiva had to die.

Even if it kills me.

The corridors of Taleqan were as silent as the grave.

As dark as the most sinister of intentions.

Jahandar climbed the stairs, clutching the bundle in his left arm tight. The torch in his right hand wavered with every cautious step, casting shadows along the uneven stone walls.

His heart pounding, he pushed the wooden door to his room ajar and leaned into it until it shuddered closed with an echoing thud.

When he was certain no one had heard him moving about, he breathed a sigh of relief before setting the bundle atop his desk and barring the door.

Then he removed the dagger from beneath his cloak.

It was a simple blade. Insignificant at first glance. A wooden handle with commonplace carvings. Slightly hooked and forged of dark iron.

Quite unremarkable, really.

Jahandar closed his eyes and clenched the dagger in his palm.

It was time. After more than two weeks of painstaking study and tedious translation, the moment was upon him.

Tonight, he would learn if the book had chosen him.

Tonight, he would discover if he was worthy of its power.

Again, he walked to the bundle on his desk. He unwrapped the linen.

Nestled in its center was a sleeping hare of soft tan fur.

His first test.

Jahandar swallowed.

He did not want the creature to suffer. It seemed wholly unfair to take the life of such a helpless thing in such a gruesome manner.

But it could not be helped.

He had to do what was necessary. For his children. For himself.

He raised the dagger in his right hand and drew it across his left palm in a single, quick motion. A line of blood appeared in its wake. He dripped the crimson liquid onto the dark blade.

As soon as his blood coated the dagger's edge, the metal began to glow a white-hot blue.

Jahandar's eyes gleamed.

Now the cycle had to be completed.

He inhaled through his nose, silently beseeching the sleeping hare for forgiveness. Then he drew the luminous blade across its throat.

Jahandar watched the small creature's bright blood spill onto the dagger, and the metal turned from a glowing blue to a fiery red.

The magic rose from the blade into the air, filling the chamber with an eerie rubicund light.

Finally, he touched the dagger to his palm.

Power flowed into the open wound, raw and frightening. It seared as it pummeled through his body, heating him to his very bones. His eyes flashed once, and the dark blade fell to the floor.

When his vision cleared, everything around him appeared sharper than before. The fatigue of only a moment ago was but a distant memory. He stood taller. Breathed deeper.

Felt invincible.

He bent to the floor and retrieved the dagger, wiping its surface on the bundle of linen next to the motionless body of the tiny hare.

Jahandar paused in thought.

Then he waved his hand over the bloody carcass.

And it disappeared in a burst of cool light.

A BRUTAL TRUTH

SHAHRZAD DID NOT SLEEP WELL THAT NIGHT.

Her dreams were filled with visions of Shiva's smiling face and the sound of doors slamming shut in a black void. Voices filled with pain and betrayal echoed in her ears.

Once she pried open her eyes to the morning light, she rolled over and shoved her face into a cushion, feeling the bitter exhaustion settle between her shoulders.

Despina's merry laughter lilted around her, clear as a bell and just as annoying.

Shahrzad groaned.

"Do you want to sleep more?"

"No," Shahrzad said into her pillow. "That won't help."

"Are you sure? Because it looks as though you had a rather . . . unrestrained evening."

"What?" Shahrzad lifted her head from the silk in confusion.

Despina's highly amused gaze was fixed on the gossamer veil torn from its mooring, lying in a forgotten pile beside the platform.

A flush bloomed on Shahrzad's cheeks.

"Well done," Despina teased.

"It's not what it looks like."

"Are you quite certain? Because if the *qamis* on your bed belongs to another man, you have just become even more interesting than you already were."

"That's enough, Despina." Shahrzad's voice was filled with warning.

Despina stood akimbo, her perfect eyebrows high on her forehead. "What happened?"

"Nothing."

"I'm sorry, but this situation and that response do not follow." Collecting the folds of her skirt in one hand, Despina marched to the platform and plopped onto the edge of the bed. "What's wrong? Tell me."

Shahrzad sighed at her handmaiden's cursed persistence. "Everything."

"Can you be more specific? After all, secrets are infinitely more useful when they're shared," Despina said in a teasing tone.

"Tell that to Khalid," Shahrzad grumbled. "As his supposed spy, he might actually listen to you."

Despina's expression softened in understanding. "The Caliph of Khorasan hasn't listened to anyone for a very long time."

"Nor will he be likely to. Not after last night."

Despina kicked off her sandals and sat cross-legged on the bed. "We women are a sad lot, aren't we?"

"What do you mean?"

"Strong enough to take on the world with our bare hands, yet we permit ridiculous boys to make fools of us."

"I am not a fool."

"No, you're not. Not yet." Despina grinned. "But it's inevitable. When you meet the one who makes you smile as you've never smiled before, cry as you've never cried before . . . there is nothing to do but fall."

"I—" Shahrzad chewed on her lower lip.

"You can speak freely, Shahrzad. What you say will not pass these walls."

Shahrzad remained silent.

Despina edged closer. "When I was a little girl in Thebes, I remember asking my mother what heaven was. She replied, 'A heart where love dwells.' Of course, I then demanded to know what constituted hell. She looked me straight in the eye and said, 'A heart absent love.'" Despina studied Shahrzad as she spoke.

Shahrzad returned Despina's scrutiny while toying with the silver laces of her *shamla*. "Your mother sounds quite wise."

"She was."

Shahrzad chose her next words with care. "May I ask what happened to her?"

"She fell in love with the wrong man. He promised her the world and then left her with nothing but the child in her belly."

"I'm truly sorry, Despina."

"I'm not. She died young, but she died happy, and a man like that is incapable of making a woman happy. Rich men don't know how to sacrifice for love, because they've never had to." Despina's last statement was marked in its harshness.

"Is that it?" Shahrzad said gently. "Are you worried Jalal will do the same?"

"I don't know. He's unfailingly loyal to his family, but I have yet to see him espouse such loyalty to the many young women who've lost their hearts to him." Despina's blue eyes tightened at the corners. "I've always believed a man is what he does, not what others say. But Jalal al-Khoury does very little to refute what others say."

"Such behavior appears to be a family trait."

"Yes. It does."

"I don't—" Shahrzad caught herself before turning a pleading eye to her handmaiden. "Do you know, Despina? If you do, please tell me. Why is Khalid killing all of his brides?"

Despina stared down at the discarded skein of spider-silk by the bed. "I don't know."

"Then what *do* you know? Please tell me."

"I've lived in this palace for six years, and I've always found Khalid Ibn al-Rashid quite aloof, yet strangely honorable. Until the events of these past few months, he has never given me occasion to question his character."

"But how can you continue to serve a king who kills young women without explanation?"

"I came to this kingdom as a slave; I don't have the luxury of choosing whom I serve," Despina retorted drily. "The Caliph of Khorasan may very well be a monster, but to me he's always been a troubled king with good intentions."

"*Good intentions?*" Shahrzad spat. "Tell that to the families of the girls he murdered. Tell that to those who loved them."

Despina flinched, and Shahrzad looked away, rising from the bed in a rush to conceal her pain.

"Shahrzad—"

"Leave me alone."

Despina grabbed her wrist. "If you care about him at—"

"I don't."

"Stop lying, you miserable brat."

Shahrzad wrenched her arm free, glaring at Despina before turning to leave in a swirl of lustrous brocade.

"You care about him," Despina insisted. "And since secrets matter so much to you, I'll divulge one."

Shahrzad halted in her tracks.

"You are safe, Shahrzad al-Khayzuran. Nothing will happen to you. For I have it on high authority that any attempt to harm you will be treated as a direct attempt on the life of our king."

Shahrzad's stomach clenched.

"Do you understand, Brat Calipha?" Despina continued.

Shahrzad glanced over her shoulder at her handmaiden, in stalwart silence.

Despina sighed. "On pain of death . . . you are as important to him as his own life."

LILACS AND
A RAGING SANDSTORM

JALAL SLID THE REPORT ACROSS THE TABLE AND drummed his fingers against the edge of the stained wood.

"Do you have someplace you need to be, Captain al-Khoury?" Khalid did not look up from his work.

"No. Not at the moment."

Jalal continued tapping his right hand on the carved mahogany, staring intently at Khalid's face.

"It appears—"

"I wish you would confide in me, Khalid."

Khalid's gaze flickered to Jalal, giving away less than nothing.

"And what brought on this sudden desire for closeness?"

"It rained yesterday. You must have a great deal on your mind."

Khalid studied Jalal with deliberate composure. "There is usually a great deal on my mind."

"And what of the rain?"

Khalid put down the scroll in his hand. "Rain is merely one element of a storm—generally a hint of things to come."

"As always, you are the perfect portrait of bleak."

"As always, you are the perfect portrait of nothing."

Jalal smiled in a slow arc. "Regarding Shahrzad—"

"I am not discussing Shahrzad with you." The tiger-eyes fired once in an otherwise cool countenance.

"She must have rattled you last night, with a vengeance. Well done, my lady."

"That's enough, Jalal."

"Don't be unduly vexed, cousin. It rained yesterday. You don't have to feel guilty anymore, on top of everything else. The people of Rey are not suffering unnecessarily on your account. Or Shahrzad's, for that matter."

"Enough!"

At that, all traces of Jalal's smugness vanished. Lines of consternation appeared across his forehead. "See? I wish you would confide in me. You are clearly troubled. Perhaps even afraid. Do not live in fear, Khalid-*jan,* for that is not a life."

"I am not afraid. I am tired, and you are presumptuous. There is quite a difference." Khalid turned back to the stack of scrolls before him. "It appears the riots in the city square have completely ceased?"

"Of course they've ceased. We are no longer executing their daughters without explanation," Jalal muttered offhand.

When Khalid failed to respond, Jalal glanced over and saw Khalid glaring at him, with his left hand clenched in a white-knuckled fist.

"Must you always be such an unapologetic bastard?" Khalid exacted in a deathly whisper.

"Be fair. I'm only like that when it suits a purpose. I *have* been known to apologize when the situation warrants it."

"I doubt you grasp the notion."

"You are not the only one who suffers in this. Admittedly, you bear the brunt, but you are not alone. And you take on far more than necessary. Let me help. I would gladly assume some of your burden. That is what I've been trying to tell you."

Khalid shoved aside the scrolls and strode to the window to his right. A marbled arch framed a midday sky above. In the garden below, lilacs bloomed, and their clean scent mingled on the breeze, blowing back into the alcove, rustling the pages strewn on his desk.

Taunting him.

He shuttered his gaze. The sight of shining black tresses across jewel-toned silk and half-lidded hazel eyes flashed back at him. Khalid latched the screens shut, but the aroma of the pale purple blossoms lingered, much to his chagrin.

Jalal took note of Khalid's irritation. "So you have an aversion to sunlight and flowers now?"

"Just that particular flower."

"And what has that flower done to you?"

Khalid remained resolutely silent, and Jalal's eyes widened in understanding.

"Tell the gardeners to remove it," Jalal suggested after a time, leaning back against the cushions.

"No."

Smiling to himself, Jalal laced his fingers across his stomach and stared at the mosaicked alcove above. "Khalid?"

"Are you still here?"

"I'm waiting for you to confide in me."

Khalid twisted his head to Jalal and expelled a frustrated breath.

"I can wait all day. As you so cheerfully noted, the city riots have ceased . . . for the time being." Jalal crossed his feet at the ankles.

"Fine. I'll leave." Khalid walked to the doors and thrust them aside.

Jalal followed in his footsteps, like a shadow with a dubious agenda. When Jalal began whistling to the domed ceiling of blue-veined agate, the muscles in Khalid's jaw flexed.

"We're blood, *sayyidi*. I am every bit as stubborn as you. It would behoove you to confide in me because, sooner or later, you'll feel compelled to rid yourself of my enduring nuisance."

After they strode a few more paces down the polished corridors, Khalid glanced at Jalal. "Salim . . . wishes to visit Rey on his way back to Amardha in two weeks' time."

Jalal froze midstep. "That—*jahkesh*?" he swore. "Why?"

"It should be obvious."

"To you. Would you care to elaborate?"

"Shahrzad."

Jalal paused and then laughed with palpable scorn. "Of course. The *Jahkesh* of Parthia wants to meet Khorasan's new calipha."

"And he will undoubtedly bring Yasmine."

"*Marg-bahr* Salim Ali el-Sharif." Jalal drew his index finger across his throat as a warning to their impending guest. "What are you going to do?"

"Your father thinks I should send Shahrzad away while Salim is here."

Jalal snorted.

"You disagree?" Khalid asked.

"Yes. Very much."

Khalid stopped walking. "Why?"

Jalal swiveled to face him. "Because, if the *jahkesh* wants to see the future of Khorasan, I can think of nothing better than the sight of you with Shahrzad al-Khayzuran. The strength she instills in you. The utter rightness of it all."

Khalid studied Jalal's fiery expression. "You seem quite convinced."

"I am. As you should be, *sayyidi*. Trust me. And trust in this."

"In the rightness of it all?" A look of acerbic amusement settled across Khalid's face.

"Yes. In her and in you."

"Two rather unreliable people, Jalal."

"I disagree. Shahrzad is a remarkably reliable girl. Brash and unpredictable, yes, but steadfast in her convictions. It's true you are taxing and rather bleak, but you've always been reliably so." Jalal grinned.

"So you would have me throw Shazi to the wolves?"

"Shazi?" Jalal's grin widened. "Honestly, I pity the wolves."

"Be serious for once."

"I am. In fact, I would take the enterprise a step further. Invite all your bannermen to Rey—every last emir. Let them see that you are not your father. You are not the rumors that have been plaguing you of late. You are a king worthy of their allegiance . . . with a queen full of fire and promise."

The edges of Khalid's mouth turned upward, ever so slightly.

"My God. Are you smiling, Khalid-*jan*?" Jalal teased in an incredulous voice.

"Perhaps."

The two young men continued making their way down the hallways until they passed into the main corridor, where they were joined by Khalid's normal retinue of bodyguards. As they entered the open-air gallery, Khalid stopped short, his features darkening at the prospect before him.

Shahrzad was crossing toward the series of double doors leading to the gardens, with Despina at her side and the Rajput trailing behind her.

When she saw Khalid, she paused and pivoted on her slippered heel, gliding in his direction.

She captivated him in the way she always did, with unguarded beauty and unassuming grace. Her hair rippled behind her in shimmering waves of ebony, and her pointed chin was turned high and proud in the rays of sun streaming from above. The light gold of her mantle cloaked the deep emerald of the silk beneath it. Woven into the myriad colors of her eyes, Khalid saw the same mixture of reticence and defiance as always.

But now there was something else. A new emotion he could not place.

She wrinkled her nose at the Rajput's looming presence, and the power behind this simple gesture pulled Khalid to her side, like sweet wine and the sound of bright laughter.

As she drew closer, the memory of last night washed over him.

The feel of her in his arms. The scent of lilac in her hair.

The futility of all else, save his lips against hers.

Of his will . . . crumbling.

"*Tell me.*"

"*Anything.*"

She opened her mouth to say something, a strangely uncertain look marring her lovely features . . .

And Khalid blew past her, without a glance in her direction.

Jalal followed him, wordlessly. Once they were out of earshot, he grabbed his cousin's shoulder. "What are you doing?"

Khalid knocked his hand aside.

"Khalid!"

His gaze mutinous, Khalid continued striding down the corridor.

"Are you a fool?" Jalal persisted. "Did you not see her face? You wounded her!"

Khalid whirled around, seizing the front of Jalal's *qamis.*

"I told you once, Captain al-Khoury: I will not discuss Shahrzad with you."

"To hell with that, *sayyidi*! If you continue down this path, there won't be much to discuss. Have you not learned your lesson yet, cousin?"

Jalal bent toward Khalid, his brown eyes harboring a cold fury.

"Was Ava not enough?" he whispered in a cruel tone.

At that, Khalid shoved Jalal back and punched him once in the jaw. His bodyguards scrambled to Khalid's side as Jalal slid across the marble floor and wiped at his bloodied lower lip before sneering up at his king.

"Get out of my sight, Jalal," Khalid seethed.

"Such a wizened old man in so many ways. And such a little boy in so many others."

"You know nothing about me."

"I know very little, and I still know more than you, Khalid-*jan*. I know love is fragile. And loving someone like you is near impossible. Like holding something shattered through a raging sandstorm. If you want her to love you, shelter her from that storm . . ."

Jalal rose to his feet, straightening the insignia of the Royal Guard at his shoulder. "And make certain that storm isn't you."

MEHRDAD THE BLUEBEARDED

SHAHRZAD PACED BEFORE HER BED THAT NIGHT, wearing a path in the cool white stone beneath her feet. Every step was a war between wrath and resentment, between pain and petulance.

Between the unmitigated hurt at being summarily dismissed and the unadulterated fury that it mattered so greatly to her.

How dare he do that to me?

Her strides lengthened as she twisted her hair over one shoulder. She had not even bothered to change out of her clothes from earlier that day. Her mantle was strewn across the floor in a pile of discarded damask. The emerald *sirwal* trowsers and fitted top were not as comfortable as her nightclothes and *shamla,* but she could not be bothered with such things right now. Shahrzad yanked the band of brilliant green stones from her brow and heaved it across the room. Strands of hair tugged free along with the gems, and she swore a pained oath at her own stupidity before collapsing to the marble in a heap of irate misery.

Why did he treat me like that? He didn't have to hurt me.

I—didn't mean to hurt him.

All day, she had hidden these thoughts from Despina. Concealed these worries from the world. But now, alone in the desolate greys of her bedchamber, she could no longer hide these things from herself. Beyond the concerns she had for the way he had scorned her so coldly in front of everyone was the nagging truth he had done so because he felt betrayed. Because he felt wounded by her actions from the night before.

And she did not know how to fix it and return to his good graces.

She had tried today. Shahrzad had wanted to apologize. Had wanted to tell him she had not meant to take advantage of the situation. How, in hindsight, it appeared worse than she intended.

He must have thought she was in control.

Shahrzad laughed to herself bitterly as she leaned her forehead against the green silk on her knee.

Control?

The mere thought was ludicrous. How could he not know as much? And now he was punishing her for it. Like an angry boy denied access to a plaything.

How dare he?

In front of Despina. In front of Jalal. He had embarrassed her.

Treated her as though she were nothing.

As though she merited a silk cord at sunrise.

Her throat tightened in memory.

Shiva.

"How dare you!" she cried out to the darkness.

Two could play at this game. She, too, could rage at him like a small child deprived of sweets. And then, maybe, she would not feel quite as miserable and alone as she had all day. As broken.

As lost to him as she was.

Shahrzad pushed to her feet and adjusted the thin chain of gold around her waist. Dangling from its center was a series of emeralds and diamonds that matched the necklace at her throat and the bangles on her left wrist. She shook out her hair and made her way to the low table in the corner.

She lifted the lid from the tray and began eating some jewel rice and saffron chicken. In between bites of fresh herbs and cool yogurt, she drank tea and nibbled on pistachio cakes sweetened with honey. Everything was cold, and she chewed from habit rather than enjoyment, but she knew she would regret it later if she went to bed hungry as well as angry.

Halfway through her halfhearted meal, the doors to her chambers opened.

Shahrzad paused but did not turn around. Instead, she resumed eating. She poured herself another cup of lukewarm tea with the steady hand of feigned indifference.

Again, she felt his presence behind her. The same shift in the wind.

The same maddening glory.

Shahrzad tore into a piece of flatbread with vicious precision.

"Shahrzad?"

She ignored him, despite her heart's sudden clamoring.

Khalid strode to the other side of the table and sat down on the cushions with soundless grace.

Still, Shahrzad did not look up from her tray. She was tearing the piece of flatbread into tiny bits she proceeded to pile in a heap before her.

"Shazi."

"Don't."

He remained still, awaiting clarification.

"Don't pretend with me."

"I'm not pretending," Khalid said quietly.

Shahrzad threw down the rest of the flatbread and met his gaze with stinging circumspection. His eyes were ringed in deep lines of fatigue. His jaw was set, and his posture was rigid.

He doesn't look sorry for hurting me.

Something knifed in Shahrzad's chest, behind her heart.

But he will be.

"Shahrzad—"

"You once lamented the fact that the characters in my stories place so much value on love."

Khalid returned her penetrating stare in silence.

"Why is that?" she continued. "What is your aversion to the sentiment?"

His eyes flicked across her face before responding. "It's not an aversion. It's merely an observation. That word is used too often for my taste. So I attribute it to things, rather than to people."

"Excuse me?"

Khalid exhaled carefully. "People fall in and out of love with the rising and setting of the sun. Rather like a boy who loves the color green one day, only to discover on the morrow that he truly prefers blue."

Shahrzad laughed, and the sound was lemon to her wound. "So you intend to go through life never loving anyone? Just . . . things?"

"No. I'm looking for something more."

"More than love?"

"Yes."

"Is it not arrogant to think you deserve more, Khalid Ibn al-Rashid?"

"Is it so arrogant to want something that doesn't change with the wind? That doesn't crumble at the first sign of adversity?"

"You want something that doesn't exist. A figment of your imagination."

"No. I want someone who sees beneath the surface—someone who completes the balance. An equal."

"And how will you know when you've found this elusive someone?" Shahrzad retorted.

"I suspect she will be like air. Like knowing how to breathe." He regarded her with the stillness of a hawk as he said these words, and Shahrzad's throat went dry.

"Poetry," she whispered. "Not reality."

"My mother used to say that a man who can't appreciate po-etry lacks a soul."

"In that respect, I'm inclined to agree."

"She was referring to my father," he intoned drily. "A soulless man, if ever there was one. I'm told I resemble him greatly."

Shahrzad studied the tiny mountain of bread before her.

I will not feel sorry for you. You do not deserve my pity.

Guarding herself against a rising tide of emotion, she looked up again, resolute in her next course of action. "I—"

"I hurt you today." He spoke softly, in a voice of soothing water over scorched steel.

"It doesn't matter." Her cheeks flushed.

"It matters to me."

Shahrzad exhaled in a huff of derision. "Then you shouldn't have done it."

"Yes."

Shahrzad stared at the cut-glass angles of his profile. Even now, his handsome face gave no hint that her pain affected him in any way.

The boy of ice and stone . . .

Who dashed her heart against a jagged shore, only to walk away without so much as a glance.

I will not let him win. For Shiva's sake.

For my sake.

I will *learn the truth. Even if I have to destroy him to get it.*

"Are you done?" she asked under her breath.

He paused. "Yes."

"I have a story for you."

"A new one?"

She nodded. "Would you like to hear it?"

Khalid inhaled cautiously and then leaned an elbow onto the cushions.

Shahrzad took another sip of cardamom tea and eased back against the pile of vibrant silk on her side.

"There was once a young girl named Tala. She was the daughter of a wealthy man who lost everything in a slew of poor business decisions, followed by the tragic death of a most-beloved wife. Mired in his grief, Tala's father found solace in music and art and could often be found whiling away the hours with a paintbrush in one hand and his favorite *santur* in the other."

Shahrzad brushed a curl of black hair off her face.

"At first, Tala tried to understand his need to distract himself from the heartbreak of his losses, but it became increasingly difficult to ignore what it all meant for their family. What it meant for Tala. Because, even though she loved her father dearly and believed in his goodness with every fiber of her being, she knew that he could not provide for them. That she could not trust him to sustain a life for Tala and her little brother."

Khalid's forehead creased at Shahrzad's somber expression.

"So Tala began searching for a husband. She knew she could not hope to make a great match, given her family's unfortunate circumstances, but soon she heard tell of a wealthy merchant in need of a bride. He was older and had been married several times before, but no one was sure what had become of his earlier wives. And this made young women rather wary of making a match with him. Additionally, he had a very long beard of indigo black . . . so black that, in the light, it gave off a worrisome tinge of blue. This had afforded him a rather unfortunate moniker. He was known as Mehrdad the Bluebearded."

Shahrzad sat up and removed her emerald necklace, placing it alongside the silver pot of tea. Khalid observed her in silence.

"Even with these reservations, Tala set about arranging the

match with Mehrdad. She was sixteen and rather pretty. Intelligent and vivacious. Mehrdad was pleased, even though she had little to offer, besides herself. Her only stipulation was that he care for her family. He agreed without hesitation, and they were promptly married. She left her home and moved into his impressive walled residence on the other side of the city. At first, everything seemed normal, perhaps even ideal. Mehrdad was respectful and felicitous as a husband. And he appeared quite content with Tala. He gave her ready access to the many rooms in his home and showered her with gifts of new clothes and jewelry, perfume and art—beautiful things Tala had only dreamed of seeing, let alone owning."

Shahrzad locked eyes with Khalid, clenching her hands in the fine silk of her trowsers.

"After a time, Mehrdad made plans to travel for his work. He handed Tala a ring of keys to their home and bade her take charge of the residence in his absence. He entrusted her with the daily tasks and gave her free access to all that was his, save one thing, and one thing alone. On the ring of keys, he designated the smallest and held it before her. He told her it was the key to a locked room in the cellar, and barred her from entering that room for any reason. He made her swear, on pain of death, that she would obey this directive. Tala promised she would not go near this room, and after she made it clear she understood the gravity of the situation, Mehrdad handed her the keys and took leave, promising to return in one month."

Shahrzad drained the remnants of the cold tea from the bottom of the etched glass cup. The dregs were oversweet, mixed with the last of the rock sugar. It swirled in her mouth—the grit of bitter cardamom and crystallized mettle.

Her hand trembled with nerves as she set down the tiny cup.

"For a time, Tala relished this opportunity to have free rein over such a magnificent home. The servants treated her with deference, and she hosted friends and family members for wonderful meals prepared with a delicate hand, served under a starry sky. Each room of her husband's home enchanted her. In his travels, he had amassed things of beauty and wonder that brought her imagination to new worlds. And yet, with each passing day, that room in the cellar . . . began to gnaw at her. Plague her. Call to her."

Khalid shifted forward in his seat, his features tightening.

"One day, against her better judgment, she strode by it. She swore she heard a voice inside, crying out. She tried to ignore it. But it cried out again: 'Tala!' Tala's heart pounded. She reached for the ring of keys in a panic. Then she remembered Mehrdad's directive and fled up the stairs. That night, she could not sleep. The next day, Tala went back down to the cellar. Again, she heard a voice beseeching her from within that room. 'Tala!' it cried. 'Please!' This time, she knew, beyond the shadow of a doubt. It was the voice of a young girl. Tala could not ignore it. She fumbled for the ring of keys at her waist. They fell once to the stone floor at her feet. When she finally managed to select the right key, her fingers shook so badly she struggled to fit it into the lock."

Shahrzad swallowed, her throat parched. Khalid watched her closely, every muscle strained with heightened awareness.

"Your husband is not a forgiving man."

Her pulse thundered, but Shahrzad forged ahead. Unwavering.

You will not treat me like this. You will not dash my heart against a shore.

And walk away.

"The tumblers clicked with a sound that made Tala jump in her skin . . . and she stepped forward into utter darkness. The first thing she noticed was the smell—iron and old metal, like a rusted sword. The cellar was warm and humid. Then her foot slid in something, and a rush of rot and decay sailed back at her."

"Shahrzad," Khalid warned in a low tone.

Shahrzad barreled forward, heedless. "When Tala's eyes adjusted to the darkness and she looked down, she saw her foot was caked in blood. Hanging around her . . . were bodies. The bodies of young women. They were Mehrdad's—"

"Shahrzad!"

Shahrzad's heartbeat resounded in her ears as Khalid shot to his feet, his face a mask of anguished fury. He towered over her, his chest heaving. Then he turned to the door.

No!

Shahrzad raced behind Khalid, struggling to keep up with his powerful gait. As he reached for the handle, she launched herself at him, wrapping her arms around his waist.

"Please!" she cried.

He did not respond.

She pressed her face into his back and the tears began to flow, embarrassing and unbidden. "Give me the key," she gasped. "Let me see behind the door. You are not Mehrdad. Show me."

When he put his hands on her wrists to free himself, she merely clasped tighter, refusing to let go.

"Give me the key, Khalid-*jan*." Her voice broke.

She felt his body tense at the term of endearment. Then, after an endless moment of racked silence, Khalid exhaled and his shoulders sagged in defeat.

Shahrzad laced her fingers to his chest.

"You hurt me last night, Shahrzad," he said quietly.

"I know."

"A great deal."

She nodded against the linen of his *qamis*.

"Yet you have said nothing about it," he continued.

"I wanted to. I meant to. But then you were so hateful."

"There is a vast difference between meaning to do something and actually doing it."

She nodded again.

He sighed and swiveled in her arms to look at her.

"You're right. I was hateful to you."

He raised his palms to her face and wiped away her tears.

"I'm sorry I hurt you," Shahrzad said, her eyes luminous.

Khalid slid a hand behind her neck and rested his chin atop her head.

"As am I, *joonam*," he whispered. "So very sorry."

THE DIE IS CAST

J AHANDAR STOOD BENEATH THE SHADE OF THE marbled vestibule at Taleqan with his thumbs looped through his wrinkled *tikka* sash. He watched Rahim al-Din Walad dismount from his gleaming Akhal-Teke and nod at several laborers carrying bushels of grain toward the kitchens. The workers returned smiles and exchanged a few pleasantries with the young nobleman before parting ways.

As soon as Rahim turned to walk in his direction, Jahandar scrambled from behind the polished stone pillar and into Rahim's path.

"Rahim-*jan!*" Jahandar cleared his throat with a cough and a gasp.

Rahim took a startled step back. "Jahandar-*effendi.* It's good to see you."

"Is it?" Jahandar offered him a mangled attempt at a grin. "Thank you for not saying what you must be thinking about me."

Rahim forced his mouth into a patient half smile. "This cannot be easy for you."

"It is not. But I am doing much better now."

Rahim nodded. "I'm glad to hear it. And I'm sure Irsa will be happy as well."

Jahandar cleared his throat again, looking away.

Rahim's eyes cast a sudden chill of judgment. "Since you arrived from Rey, Irsa has spent most days in the far corner by the fountain, painting or reading from a book. I believe it's one you gave her."

"Of course. The book on tea," Jahandar remarked absentmindedly.

Rahim bowed his head in a curt gesture. When he began striding down the vestibule once more, Jahandar held up his palms to stall him.

"Why are your hands burned?" Rahim asked with alarm, glancing at Jahandar's blistered fingers.

Jahandar shook his head, flicking away Rahim's distress like a bothersome gnat. "I mishandled a lamp while I was translating a text. Don't worry yourself, Rahim-*jan*. I already prepared a salve in my room."

Rahim frowned. "Please be careful, Jahandar-*effendi*. Shazi will rail at me if something happens to you while you're here at Taleqan. And if Shahrzad is unhappy, Tariq will be furious. Dealing with hellions of their ilk falls rather low on my list of things to enjoy. Like scorpions and quicksand."

Jahandar sighed piteously, scuffing his feet. "You must find me quite pathetic as a father, do you not?"

"You love your children. That is obvious. But I cannot speak to what it means to be a good father."

"You've always been so good, Rahim-*jan*. Such a wonderful

friend to Tariq and to my Shahrzad." Jahandar studied Rahim in an unusually intense manner.

Rahim's features stiffened, discomfort settling between the lines. "Thank you."

An awkward silence fell between the two men.

And Jahandar knew it was time to take action. For a new kind of test was at hand. The kind he had always dreaded, ever since he was a boy. So he forced back the needling part of him that wanted to shuffle away to the safety of the shadows. Those last remaining traces that babbled from lofty corners reminded him he was not a fighter.

Just an old man with a book.

Jahandar's jaw squared under his wispy beard. "I know I have very little right to ask anything of anyone, Rahim al-Din Walad. But as a father, I have no choice."

Rahim waited, drawing in a careful breath.

"I know Tariq left Taleqan because of Shahrzad," Jahandar continued. "There is no way for me to know what he has planned, but I will not sit in a darkened room while others take charge of rescuing my child. I did not do as a father should have at the onset; I did not stop her. But whatever needs to be done now, trust that I will do it. I cannot fight as you can. I am not fearless and strong. I am not Tariq. But I *am* Shahrzad's father, and I would do anything for her. Please do not dismiss me. Please allow me to be part of your plans. Find a place for me in them."

Rahim listened to Jahandar with quiet consideration. "I'm sorry, but this is not my decision to make, Jahandar-*effendi*."

"I—I understand."

"But I will take you to see Tariq when the time comes."

Jahandar nodded, a peculiar, martial light entering his gaze. "Thank you. Thank you, Rahim-*jan*."

Now Rahim's smile was genuine. He put a hand on Jahandar's shoulder. Then he bowed his head and lifted his fingertips to his brow.

Jahandar remained in the archway of the vestibule, pleased by his success—the passing of this test.

He looked down at his palms. The newest blisters formed over the scars of the last, and they smarted at the slightest touch. Seared with the promise of pain to come. His skin was hard and crusted beneath his nails, and he could no longer sacrifice the sleeves of his remaining garments to this endeavor.

It was time.

Jahandar stared across the courtyard at the entrance to the kitchens.

A mere hare would not do. Not *this* time.

He needed more.

Always more.

THE FALCON AND THE TIGER

SHAHRZAD STOOD AT THE MARBLE RAILING OF HER balcony, overlooking the pools of water below. A midday sun reflected back in their glistening surfaces, rippling with each passing breeze.

But this was not of particular interest to Shahrzad.

The arriving guests were far more fascinating.

It was a veritable menagerie of the absurd.

One nervous-looking young man entered the courtyard with a bevy of attendants, each waiting to remove a particular article of his clothing. First one leather *mankalah*. Then another. Then his *rida'*. Then his boots, which were quickly replaced by a pair of pristine sandals. Each of the servants stashed away the garments in methodical order before the young man ventured a single step from his steed.

Another man—the size of three men put together—swayed atop an elephant sporting hooked tusks, its grey trunk trailing across the gritty granite pavestones below. This man had an oiled mustache with ends that twitched at the slightest movement, and each of his fingers displayed immense rings of a different gemstone, glittering with abandon in the rays of the sun.

Shahrzad rested her chin in her palm and stifled a giggle.

Another nobleman galloped through the entrance on a creature Shahrzad had never seen before. It resembled a horse in size and build, yet its coat was covered in the strangest pattern of black and white stripes. The animal stomped its hooves and snorted, flinging its neck to and fro. As soon as Shahrzad saw it, she gasped and called Despina to her side.

Despina shook her head as she stood next to Shahrzad. "You really shouldn't be out here."

"Why not?" Shahrzad waved a flippant hand. "It's perfectly safe. All weapons are surrendered at the palace gate."

"I wish I could make you understand. You're not a girl on a lark, watching an amusing display. You're their queen."

"They came here because of that wretched sultan from Parthia, not because of me." Shahrzad leaned farther over the railing. "Despina, did you see that imbecile on the camel? The one with the brass bells and the finger in his nose?"

Despina's eyes clouded over.

And Shahrzad ignored the lines creasing her handmaiden's forehead.

Ignored them because she needed a lighthearted moment. Needed it enough to appear foolish, just for an instant, so she would not have to deal with the reality of her life in a palace of polished marble, with flashing gems at her throat and a shimmering pool of water at her feet.

In a marriage rife with growing tension . . .

With a husband who would not touch her. Nor venture near her, much less share his secrets.

Shahrzad clenched her teeth.

Ever since that night two weeks ago, when she'd told the tale of Tala and Mehrdad, Khalid had come to have dinner with her each evening and hear a new story. He would listen at a distance, engage her in stilted conversation, and share pithy observations he'd made throughout the day.

Then he would depart, and she would not see him until the following night.

"Your husband is not a forgiving man."

Shahrzad gripped the stone railing in both hands, the blood leaching from her fingertips. "Who are all these fools, anyway?" She tried to smile at Despina.

Despina's lips puckered into a moue. "Most of them are the caliph's bannermen. A general invitation was issued to every emir of Khorasan."

A bubble of air caught at the top of Shahrzad's throat. She twisted away from the railing to look at her handmaiden.

"What?" she whispered.

Despina canted her head to one side. "I told you. You never listen. This gathering is not just for the Sultan of Parthia. The caliph wants to introduce you as his queen. He invited every nobleman in the kingdom to share in the spectacle. To meet you."

A knot of panic started to gather in the pit of Shahrzad's stomach.

Tariq wouldn't. He may be a nobleman, but he's not an emir. Not yet.

He wouldn't dare.

Despina's ongoing lecture dissolved into a muted din in Shahrzad's ears.

Until a familiar, screaming cry echoed from above.

Shahrzad balled her hands into fists and spun back to the railing, pleading to the heavens that—

No.

Clattering across the granite pavestones on a dark bay al-Khamsa was her first love.

Tariq Imran al-Ziyad.

"My, my, my," Despina breathed.

Had Tariq not reined in his stallion at that moment and whistled to the skies, he still would have drawn attention. Even dust-worn and bedraggled, he cut an imposing figure. Broad-shouldered, with skin of the desert and eyes of silver and ash, he was the kind of boy who turned heads and never noticed. The faint shadow of hair that darkened his jaw served only to accentuate features hewn from stone by the hand of a master sculptor.

When Zoraya came plummeting from the clouds to land on his outstretched *mankalah,* Tariq glanced up.

And saw Shahrzad.

His look was a touch.

Shahrzad's heart began to pound, the fear rising. Taking hold. But it was nothing compared to the panic that gripped her, that screamed a soundless scream at the scene unfolding before her . . .

When Khalid rode into the courtyard atop a black Arabian—

A stone's throw from her first love.

Shahrzad had disappeared from the balcony.

It was just as well.

For, as much as Tariq wanted to drink in the sight of her, now was not the time for distraction, even one as welcome as she.

His target had arrived.

Khalid Ibn al-Rashid.

Murderer of Shiva. Husband of Shahrzad.

Tariq gripped the reins in his free hand.

The monster rode past Tariq on a magnificent black Arabian. His dark *rida'* billowed in his wake. A visceral hatred coiled in Tariq's chest. When the monster stopped in the middle of the courtyard and pulled back the hood of his cloak, Tariq's wrath flowed to his fists.

And he envisioned them smashing against the monster's chilly regalness until nothing remained but blood and bits of bone.

To the right of the monster was a young man with an arrogant grin, curly brown hair, and a cuirass with the standard of the Royal Guard embossed on its breastplate. To his left was an older man with a golden griffin stitched on his cloak, signifying his status as the *Shahrban* of Rey.

As the noise in the courtyard died down, the monster began to speak.

"Welcome to Rey."

His voice was surprisingly unassuming.

"I trust your journeys were safe and uneventful. It is an honor to host you on this occasion, and I thank you for always striving to embody—in all the days past, present, and future—the greatness of Khorasan to those who would take notice."

A polite cheer rose from the edges of the courtyard.

"Again, I welcome you to my home. I have the fervent hope that when you leave it, you will have come to care for it as much as I do. It is the city of my childhood." The monster paused. "And the city of my queen."

At this, the chorus of approval grew, mingled with a clear tenor of curiosity. The arrogant boy to the monster's right smirked appreciatively, while the *shahrban* sighed with seeming resignation.

It took all Tariq's willpower to look away and not draw undue attention. The hate was too palpable. It roiled off him in murderous waves.

Death was too easy for this monster.

He *dared* to flaunt Shahrzad, as if she were a prize he had won?

Zoraya flapped her wings from her perch on his *mankalah*, aware of his fury. Tariq raised a hand to soothe her while he observed the monster exiting the courtyard, his gold-clad retinue clamoring in his shadow.

Tariq was not impressed by the show.

Rahim was a far better rider. The Caliph of Khorasan was an above-average horseman, at best. For all his dour black and stern expressions, all the whispered rumors of trick swords and cold brutality, he did not appear worthy of genuine fear. He appeared bored with life. Bored and in need of a nap.

Tariq sneered to himself, his loathing mingled with a new-found distaste.

Monster? Hardly. Merely a boy-king.

And a dead one, at that.

TWO CROSSED SWORDS

Aₙₒₜₕₑᵣ ₘₒₘₑₙₜ ₒf ₜₕᵢₛ, ₐₙd ₛₕₐₕᵣzₐd would scream.

Sitting here, idling about in her room, while somewhere in the palace, a reckless boy with a falcon and a quick-tempered king with two swords—

"Hold still!" Despina commanded. She clutched Shahrzad's chin in her left hand. Then she lifted the tiny, three-haired brush to Shahrzad's eyelid once more.

Shahrzad gritted her teeth.

"You are an utter nightmare," Despina grumbled. When she was finished, she pulled back and nodded with satisfaction at her work.

"Can I leave now?" Shahrzad blew a lock of glossy black hair out of her face.

"Such a brat. Would you at least do me the courtesy of feigning a dram of appreciation for all my efforts?" Despina grabbed Shahrzad's wrist and hauled her before the mirror in the far corner of the chamber.

"Despina, I'm going to be late for—"

"Just have a look, Shahrzad al-Khayzuran."

When Shahrzad glanced into the polished silver, her hazel eyes nearly doubled in size.

Nothing about her appearance seemed normal.

Despina had turned tradition on itself. She had dressed Shahrzad in *sirwal* trowsers of luminous black silk with a matching fitted top, and chosen to eschew the typical mantle of muted gold or silver. Tonight, Shahrzad's sleeveless mantle was the same cerulean blue as Despina's eyes. It matched the glittering sapphires swinging from her earlobes. Instead of placing a band of stones across Shahrzad's brow, Despina had woven tiny strands of obsidian beads throughout her hair. They caught at wayward beams of light, making each curl flash like shadow incarnate.

For the final touch, Despina had painted a thick line of black kohl above the top portion of Shahrzad's eyelashes. She had flicked the lines far past each outer corner, giving the illusion of cat's eyes.

The entire effect was . . . arresting, to say the least.

"No—necklace?" Shahrzad stuttered.

"No. You don't like them. Or you do a good job of pretending you don't."

"My arms are bare."

"Yes."

Shahrzad ran her fingers across the shining blue fabric of her mantle. Black diamond bangles clinked together on her left wrist.

"Tonight is a night to turn heads. Make them remember you.

Make sure they never forget. You are the Calipha of Khorasan, and you have the ear of a king." Despina put her hand on Shahrzad's shoulder and grinned at their shared reflection. "More important, you have his heart." She bent forward and lowered her voice. "And, most important, you are a fearsome thing to behold in your own right."

Shahrzad smiled, but it came from a place of unexpected despondency.

For once, you're wrong about several things.

She reached up and clasped Despina's hand. "Thank you. I'm sorry I was so distracted on the balcony earlier. I didn't realize the . . . importance of the gathering until that moment. It's not an excuse for being so wretched all afternoon, but—"

Despina laughed, and it was a balm to Shahrzad's nerves. "I'm used to it. Just handle yourself with aplomb tonight, and all is forgiven."

Shahrzad nodded and walked to the door of her chamber. The Rajput was waiting beyond the threshold to escort her through the vaulted marble corridors. When he looked down at her, his moonless eyes constricted for an instant, and she thought she saw something resembling amity in their depths. Then he directed her down the labyrinthine hallways.

As they rounded the final corner, Shahrzad paused midstep.

Khalid stood before a set of massive, gilt-framed double doors three times his height. They were guarded on either side by creatures carved from stone, with the body of a bull, the wings of an eagle, and the head of a man.

He turned when he heard their footsteps, and Shahrzad's breath was gone before she could catch it.

The linen of his off-white *qamis* was so finely spun that it reflected a faint sheen from the torches lining the corridor. Their fires gave life to the carved hollows of his features. The hilt of his sword was looped through the crimson *tikka* sash wound across his hips. His mantle was a rich brown that enhanced the amber of his eyes, making them appear even more intense, even more fluid. Even more illusory.

And these eyes were hers. From the moment he turned and saw her.

Shahrzad slowed her pace as she neared him, her fear fading into a strange sort of calm.

She attempted a smile.

He reached out his hand.

When she took it, she noticed a thick band of muted gold on the third finger of his right hand. Embossed on its surface were two crossed swords. Shahrzad ran her thumb over it.

"It's my standard," Khalid explained. "They're—"

"Twin *shamshirs*."

"Yes."

She looked up, worried he would wonder how she knew.

But he was unfazed.

"The general told you I saw the tournament?" she asked flatly.

"Of course." A corner of his lips twitched.

Shahrzad exhaled in a huff. "Of course."

He laced his fingers through hers. "You look beautiful."

"So do you."

"Are you ready?"

"Are you?"

At this, Khalid smiled. He raised her hand to his lips and kissed it.

"Thank you, Shazi. For standing at my side."

She nodded, words failing her.

Then Khalid strode forward and the Rajput pushed open one of the huge doors. The warmth of Khalid's hand led Shahrzad onto the upper landing of an immense two-way staircase shaped like open arms. For an instant, she hesitated, thinking they were supposed to go their separate ways, but Khalid grasped her palm tight and started down the stairs with Shahrzad beside him. Over her shoulder, she caught a glimpse of blue damask trailing behind her like gently rolling waves across a sea of hewn marble.

When they paused at the base of the staircase, Shahrzad gasped in wonder for the second time that evening.

The royal audience hall of the palace at Rey was undoubtedly the largest room she had ever seen in her life. The floor was immense, alternating stones of black and white, patterned diagonally as far as the eye could see. Beautiful reliefs depicting human bulls charging into battle and winged women with long tresses flowing in the wind adorned the walls, which stretched high into the air. So high that Shahrzad had to lengthen her neck to see the very tops of the carved columns bearing the ponderous weight of the ceiling. Fashioned near the base of each of these columns were two-headed lions with iron torches protruding from their roaring mouths.

In the center of this vast space was a three-sided, raised dais with a series of low tables situated upon its surface. Sumptuous fabric and richly appointed cushions littered the dais with vibrant color and lush texture. Fresh rose petals and dried jessamine were strewn across the silk and fringed damask, perfuming the air with a sweetly intoxicating scent that beckoned to anyone who wandered by.

Their guests were milling about, awaiting their arrival.

Tariq.

The fear returned in a rush.

She could sense Khalid watching her. He squeezed her hand, offering his gentle reassurance in one simple gesture.

Shahrzad glanced back at him with a wavering smile.

"If it pleases our esteemed guests . . ." a sonorous voice echoed from above.

Every head in the room swiveled their way.

"The Caliph of Khorasan, Khalid Ibn al-Rashid . . . and the Calipha of Khorasan, Shahrzad al-Khayzuran."

All eyes turned toward her, bodies twisting, necks craning for a better vantage point. From the edge of her gaze, she finally saw a pair of silver eyes flash to her face, glide over her resplendent form . . . then back to her hand, still interwoven in Khalid's steady warmth.

Then the silver eyes vanished into the crowd.

Leaving behind panic.

Please. Not here. Do nothing. Say nothing.

She briefly recalled the skirmish in the souk a few weeks ago.

The drunken men with their piecemeal arms . . .

And the cloaked caliph with his deadly *shamshir*.

If you threaten Khalid, he'll kill you, Tariq. Without a second thought.

Khalid strode onto the dais and took his place before the center stretch of tables. Shahrzad released his palm and sat to his right, her mind a jumbled mass of thoughts.

I can't look for Tariq. I can't do anything. It will only make matters worse.

What could he be planning?

"Is this seat available?" Jalal grinned down at Shahrzad.

She looked up, blinking hard. "That depends. Is it for you?"

He sat down next to her.

"I did not give you per—"

"Good evening, *sayyidi*," Jalal said in a loud tone.

Shahrzad wrinkled her nose at Jalal.

"Don't do that, my lady. You ruin your face when you do that," he teased.

"Good evening, Jalal. And I disagree," Khalid retorted under his breath.

Jalal laughed heartily. "My apologies, then. If you would permit me this indulgence in its place, *sayyidi*: I do believe every man here is currently reassessing his notion of beauty."

Despina was right. He is such a consummate flirt.

"Stop it." Shahrzad flushed, glaring at Jalal's arrogant mien.

"Now, *that* . . . ruins nothing," Jalal said.

"At last, we agree on something." Khalid spoke to Jalal, though his eyes lingered on Shahrzad.

And Jalal leaned back into the cushions with a satisfied smile, his hands laced across his stomach.

"If it pleases our esteemed guests . . ." the announcer intoned once more.

Again, all heads turned to the set of open-armed staircases.

"The Sultan of Parthia, Salim Ali el-Sharif."

When Jalal rose to his feet with a grumbled oath, Shahrzad placed her palms on the dais to follow suit.

But Khalid immediately reached his hand out to stop her.

Shahrzad met his gaze, and he shook his head very slightly, his eyes narrowing at the edges. His thumb trailed along the underside of her forearm, and the knot in her stomach pulled tight. Then he let go, his features blank once more.

As the sea of faces parted before them, Shahrzad took her first glimpse of the man who wished to lord over Khalid with accusations of illegitimacy. The uncle who had treated Khalid's mother with such disdain.

The sultan who would do anything for the chance to gain a kingdom.

Salim Ali el-Sharif was an attractive man with a strong jaw, nicely greying hair, and a meticulous mustache. He was trim and appeared in good health, with a deceptively warm set of dark brown eyes. His charcoal-colored mantle was exquisitely embroidered at its collar and hem, and the scimitar at his hip had a burnished hilt of solid gold with an emerald the size of a child's fist embedded in its base.

He strode onto the dais with the confidence of a man absent worry and took a seat in the empty space by Khalid.

At Salim's arrival, the rest of the guests began filtering to the tables. Shahrzad finally dared to run her eyes across the room and was distressed to discover that Tariq was seated quite close, well within earshot. When their glances met, his handsome face eased into perilous familiarity—awash in the memory of stolen embraces—and Shahrzad immediately looked away.

Stop it! Please don't do this, Tariq. If Khalid sees you looking at me . . . you don't understand.

He notices everything.

And you are risking your life.

"Khalid-*jan*!" the Sultan of Parthia began in a spuriously pleasant voice, putting his wolfish white teeth on full display. "Are you not going to introduce me to your new wife?"

As Salim spoke, the *shahrban* sat down next to him, shielded by his usual armor of circumspection.

Khalid's piercing gaze turned to Salim. Then he smiled slowly, with such patent falseness that its chill blew back like an icy gale on a mountaintop.

"Of course, Uncle Salim. It would be a privilege to introduce you." Khalid shifted to one side. "Shahrzad, this is my uncle by marriage, Salim Ali el-Sharif. Uncle Salim, this is my wife, Shahrzad."

Salim regarded her with an eager friendliness Shahrzad found disarming. He beamed at her with no small amount of charisma.

"It's a pleasure to meet you, my lord." Shahrzad offered him a ready smile. She bowed her head and touched her fingertips to her brow.

"By all that is holy, Khalid-*jan*—she is a vision." Though Salim looked at her, he addressed Khalid, treating Shahrzad as little more than a tapestry hanging on his nephew's wall. It rankled her.

Shahrzad held firm to her smile. "A vision with eyes and ears, my lord."

Khalid continued staring ahead, but the ice set around his features thawed at her retort.

Salim's eyes widened, and something flared for an instant in their pools of contrived warmth. He laughed, and the sound was just as charming as his voice. Just as overdone. "Stunning *and* silver-tongued. What an interesting combination! I can see I will have quite a time getting to know you, my lady Shahrzad."

"Quite a time," Shahrzad agreed. "I look forward to it, my lord."

Though his smile wavered for less than an instant, there was no mistaking it; she was irritating him.

"As do I," he replied. Each word was like a spear soaked in sweet water.

"If it pleases our esteemed guests," the announcer boomed from above, "dinner is served!"

Two rows of servants descended the open-armed staircases, bearing steaming trays above their heads. They marched in unison until they arrived before the dais, setting plates of food in front of each guest—aromatic rice with fresh dill and split fava beans, lamb simmered in a sauce of turmeric and caramelized onions, skewers of chicken and roasted tomatoes, fresh vegetables garnished with mint and chopped parsley, olives marinated in fine oil, *lavash* bread with rounds of goat cheese and seemingly endless sweet preserves . . .

Shahrzad had never seen so much food.

The air filled with the aroma of spices and the clamor of conversation. Shahrzad began with some *lavash* bread and quince chutney, which had quickly become a favorite of hers since she arrived at the palace. As she ate, she chanced another perusal of the room. Tariq was speaking with an older gentleman seated to his left. When he felt her eyes on him, Tariq turned his head, and Shahrzad was forced, yet again, to look away.

Khalid poured himself a cup of wine and eased back onto the cushions, leaving his plate of food untouched.

"Have you no appetite, nephew?" Salim raised an eyebrow at Khalid. "Perhaps it has mysteriously disappeared. That can happen when one is—troubled."

Khalid ignored Salim's attempt to bait him, choosing instead to take a sip of wine.

"Or . . . is it possible you are concerned your food seeks to lash out at you in response to some inexplicable offense?" Salim laughed at his own joke, winking at Shahrzad.

Hateful man.

Shahrzad reached over and snared an olive from Khalid's plate. Holding Salim's gaze, she popped the olive in her mouth and ate it. "His food seems fine to me, my lord. I'm not certain which inexplicable offense you might be referencing, but rest assured, his food is quite safe," Shahrzad replied with a wink of her own. "Would you like me to taste your food as well, Uncle?"

At that, Jalal began barking with laughter, and even the *shahrban* was forced to lower his grizzled chin.

The suggestion of a smile tugged at Khalid's lips.

Across the way, a cup was set down on the table with unwarranted vehemence.

Please, Tariq. Don't make a scene. Don't do anything.

Salim grinned at Shahrzad. "Truly silver-tongued, my lady Shahrzad. I'd ask where you found her, Khalid-*jan*, but . . ."

Khalid's right hand clenched, and Shahrzad held back the desire to stab Salim in the eye with a utensil.

"Why would you be curious as to where he found me, my lord? Are you in the market?" Shahrzad asked in a nonchalant manner.

Salim's brown eyes glittered. "Perhaps I should be. Have you any relatives, my lady? Maybe a sister?"

He knows I have a sister. Is he . . . threatening my family?

Shahrzad tilted her head to one side, tamping down a flare of concern. "I do have a sister, my lord."

Salim propped his elbows onto the table, studying Shahrzad with an amused yet predatory gleam.

Khalid's full attention was fixed on the Sultan of Parthia, and a taut band of muscle flexed in his forearm. His hand shifted in Shahrzad's direction. Conversation around them had all but ceased in recognition of the growing tension in the air.

"Am I not dangerous enough, Shahrzad?" Salim asked in a

chillingly thoughtful tone. "Perhaps too *forgiving* of the women in my past? Too willing to let them *live*?"

Several gasps emanated from around them, rippling across the hall like a rumor being passed through a square. Jalal released a pent-up breath followed by a low oath that garnered a look of warning from his father.

Shahrzad swallowed her fury and then smiled with the brightness of the sun.

"No, Uncle Salim. You are simply too old."

The room was as silent as a tomb.

And then the huge man with the collection of rings on his fingers began to laugh, his oiled mustache twitching all the while. Followed by the nobleman who had arrived on the black-and-white-striped steed. Soon, others started to join in until a chorus of amusement echoed throughout the space.

Salim's robust laughter rose above the rest. Only those closest to him saw the venomous gaze he shot at the young Calipha of Khorasan. Only those who knew him well understood he was beyond enraged by the recent turn of events.

And only those watching very carefully saw the Caliph of Khorasan lean back against the cushions and toy with the bangles on his wife's arm.

The boy with the silver eyes was one of them.

A DANCE ON A BALCONY

As the meal drew to a close, an assemblage of musicians gathered in the corner by the raised dais. A heavily bearded man with a *kamancheh* slid the hair of his bow across his instrument, checking to see if it was in tune by tightening its ivory pegs, while a young woman adjusted the reed of her *ney* one last time. An elderly man settled the base of his *tombak* against his left hip and struck the drum's taut surface . . . slow, then quick, quick. He began pounding out a driving rhythm, and the dulcimer melody of the *santur* joined in before all four musicians were lost to their music. Lost to the beat.

Then, from the opposite side of the dais, a young girl appeared.

A collective murmuring arose from the tables. A communal sigh of disbelief.

Jalal groaned. Khalid looked away.

For she was undoubtedly the most beautiful girl Shahrzad had ever beheld.

She was dressed in a fitted top of fiery red silk that left little to the imagination and a matching flowing skirt with intricate embroidery along the hem. Her hair fell past her waist in spiraling curls of mahogany, with hints of auburn set aflame by the torchlight. Her face would have brought a painter to his knees—high cheekbones, flawless skin, arched brows, and a fringe of black lashes that fanned over obscenely large eyes.

Of course, the girl began to dance.

She moved like a snake, writhing across the black and white stones to the rising strains of the music. The curves of her body seemed inspired by the moon itself. Her hands and hips beckoned, beseeched . . . befuddled. She twisted and swayed in a manner that was altogether otherworldly.

Altogether unfair.

As the girl made her mesmeric way to the center of the tables, Shahrzad tensed in awareness.

She's—dancing for Khalid.

It was obvious. The girl's eyes were locked on the Caliph of Khorasan, her dark irises a host of the forbidden. With each slow spin, her rich mane of hair coiled about her shoulders, and the gems at her stomach flashed in wild abandon.

When she smiled at Khalid as though they shared a lifetime of secrets, an ugly series of images flickered through Shahrzad's mind—most of them beginning and ending with mahogany curls being torn by their roots from the beautiful girl's head.

How could I be so childish? She's just dancing.

It doesn't matter. None of this matters.

Shahrzad took a deep breath and averted her gaze. When Jalal started to laugh, she glowered at him, the heat rising in her neck.

The brazen girl ended the dance a stone's throw from the dais, her hands positioned above her head and her endless curls thrown into an alluring mass over one shoulder.

Wonderful. Now go home.

Instead, the girl sashayed toward them, her slender hips continuing to sway, even without music. She stopped right in front of Shahrzad.

Then she grinned.

"Hello, Khalid," she said in a voice of silken sin.

Khalid exhaled carefully before lifting his tiger-eyes.

"Hello, Yasmine."

Irritated would not be an apt word.

Distressed?

No. That wouldn't be quite right, either.

Furious?

Shahrzad shook her head and smiled at the chattering nobleman before her, struggling to clear her mind so she could focus on their conversation.

Yasmine el-Sharif. The daughter of that hateful man.

As soon as Shahrzad had learned the beautiful girl's identity— from Jalal, no less—she had smiled patiently through their formal introduction. Through the painfully obvious, *lifelong* connection between Khalid and the otherworldly Princess of Parthia. Then Shahrzad had risen from the table, stone-faced, to begin greeting all the noblemen in attendance.

Without Khalid.

She had been determined to carry on for a time without the Caliph of Khorasan at her side.

Without the so-called King of Kings and his many, many secrets.

And she had. But now she was . . . foundering.

He should have told me about Yasmine. I looked like a fool.

"Hello, Shahrzad. May I call you that?"

"What?" Shahrzad said, shaken from her trance.

Yasmine smiled, and it was so perfect that Shahrzad wanted to smear soot on her teeth.

"Of course," Shahrzad responded, cursing her internal pettiness.

The nobleman whose name she had already forgotten beamed at Yasmine, his eyes nearly bulging from their sockets.

"Would you mind if I borrowed the calipha for a moment?" Yasmine fluttered her eyelashes at him with a skill Shahrzad could never hope to espouse.

He nodded vigorously, spittle flying from his lips in place of an actual response.

Yasmine took Shahrzad's hand, pulling her into the shadows behind an immense stone column.

"You looked like you needed to be saved."

"Thank you." Shahrzad hid her suspicion under a warm smile.

Yasmine studied Shahrzad in the torchlight emanating from the roaring lion nearby.

"You are frustratingly pretty," she pronounced.

"What?" The comment drew Shahrzad's brows together.

"I wasn't expecting you to be so beautiful."

Shahrzad held firm to her smile. "Well, I wasn't expecting you at all."

Yasmine laughed airily, leaning against the polished marble with her hands behind her back. "You're honest. It makes sense now. He adores honesty."

"Forgive me, but I'm a bit dense. You're going to have to be more specific."

"It makes sense why he chose you." Yasmine's long-lashed eyes were trained on Shahrzad.

Is she trying to be funny?

"I'm quite certain you know he didn't choose me."

"You're wrong. He did choose you. And he does not make such decisions lightly." Yasmine pushed off the pillar and took a step toward Shahrzad. "Especially when he could have chosen a girl who wants nothing more than to love him."

Shahrzad's baser instincts drove her to strike back at Yasmine for the slight, but she refused to argue with the beautiful girl over a mercurial boy.

Especially a boy who kept his secrets closer than he kept his confidences.

"While I do appreciate you saving me from a rather tedious conversation, I think it's time for me to rejoin my guests." Shahrzad started to turn away.

"Do you love him?"

The question stopped Shahrzad in her tracks. "I believe that's none of your business."

"I disagree. You see, I've loved Khalid since we were children. And he deserves to be loved by someone who understands him." Yasmine paused for a breath. "Even if it's not me."

Of all the things Shahrzad expected Yasmine to say, it was not this. She'd expected the girl to threaten her or engage in other such pettiness. But this admission proved Yasmine was not just a spoiled princess, denied her heart's desire.

She actually cares about him.

Even though he'd shown her the same icy welcome he'd granted her father.

A strange feeling of pity began eclipsing Shahrzad's irritation.

"You understand Khalid?" Shahrzad laughed in an effort to mask her growing unease. "If so, please enlighten me. I'd be most grateful."

Yasmine smiled with an almost mincing kind of sympathy. "That depends. How willing are you to assist your enemy, Shahrzad?"

"Alas, your great failure of the evening is that I do not see an enemy, Princess of Parthia." Shahrzad inclined her head in a brisk bow. "If you'll excuse me."

"What *do* you see, then?" Yasmine stepped into Shahrzad's path, her dark eyes sparkling with amusement.

"I see a beautiful manipulator. A weaver of words."

Yasmine nodded, her half smile swooping in a lazy arc. "It must be like looking in a mirror."

She's quick. And fearless.

"How very fortunate." Shahrzad grinned back. "We should all be so lucky as to share a reflection with you."

Yasmine laughed, and for the first time, it sounded genuine. "What a shame, Shahrzad al-Khayzuran. A part of me thinks I could like you, were we to meet under a different sky, at a different time."

"I'm surprisingly inclined to agree, Yasmine el-Sharif." Shahrzad bowed deep, her fingertips brushing her forehead in a flourishing gesture. Then she turned on her heel to round the column . . .

And ran smack into the broad chest of a man.

She stumbled and almost fell to the floor, but a steadying hand reached for hers, saving her from certain humiliation. When Shahrzad faced her erstwhile rescuer, a pair of familiar silver-and-ash eyes stared down at her, shining with a fierce light.

Unmatched in their love.

Tariq. No. You can't . . .

She tried to withdraw her hand, but he pressed something in her grasp.

A scrap of parchment.

Shahrzad wrapped her palm around it and pulled away.

"Thank you," she said.

"You're welcome, my lady." He smiled politely.

Concerned that others might see this strange interaction, Shahrzad stepped back and smoothed the fabric of her mantle, tucking the scrap of parchment beneath her thumb.

"I don't believe we've met," she said casually, though her heart tripped in her chest with worry.

He shook his head, taking her lead. "I am Tariq Imran al-Ziyad of Taleqan, my lady." Tariq bowed, touching his hand to his brow.

The Rajput emerged from the shadows behind Tariq, scowling all the while at the young nobleman's impressive height.

"Is this your first visit to Rey?" she continued, determined to appear at ease.

"No, my lady. I used to have relatives in the city."

"Used to?"

Tariq grinned with ready charm, though his eyes continued to betray their depth of feeling. "Yes. But I hope to change that soon." He lowered his voice. "When I marry."

The sentiment behind his words was clear. She felt the warmth in his gaze, and for a moment, Shahrzad allowed herself to really look at him. To look up into the perfect face of the brash boy she fell in love with, and remember . . .

The scrawny girl whose eyes followed his every move.

And the tall boy who followed her with all of his senses.

"Shahrzad."

At the sound of Khalid's voice, Tariq took a protective step toward her. Shahrzad's hazel eyes sparked in warning as she warded off a sharp current of fear.

Khalid will see everything. Because Tariq . . . can't hide anything.

Khalid strode to her without so much as a glance at Tariq.

"Shahrzad," he repeated.

"Yes?"

"I've been looking for you," he said in an even tone.

Shahrzad twisted his way, not even bothering to hide her anger. "A thousand apologies, *sayyidi*. I was talking to Yasmine and lost track of what truly matters." Her words were a carefully aimed strike.

Khalid took the blow without flinching, his amber eyes cool.

"I see."

Do you?

Shahrzad held his gaze, her mind a muddle of thoughts and emotions.

Now was not the time or the place to share them.

After all, Khalid had his secrets.

He did not deserve to know hers.

Baba and Irsa.

Tariq.

She had to keep those she loved safe. Safe from this boy with a cruel past and an untenable future.

Safe from the sway he held over her heart.

"Have you met Tariq Imran al-Ziyad, *sayyidi*?" she asked Khalid, determined to have control over the situation.

Khalid blinked once. Finally, he turned to acknowledge Tariq's presence.

Tariq's entire demeanor hardened. His mouth flattened into a line.

Oh, God. Please do better than that.

Then he relaxed and smiled at Khalid.

"*Sayyidi*." He bowed low with a hand to his brow. "I am Tariq Imran al-Ziyad, son of Nasir al-Ziyad, Emir of Taleqan."

Khalid returned a crisp nod. "I hope you enjoy your stay in the city."

Tariq's smile widened. "With such hospitality, *sayyidi,* I'm certain I will."

Is he insane?

Shahrzad paced in the shadows on her balcony, her heart pounding in time with her steps.

The sliver of parchment in her hand was now mingled with the sweat from her palm. A dash of ink had managed to bleed onto her skin, making a black-and-blue mess of the whole thing. She unfurled the ruin once more to read the outlandish missive scrawled across its surface in Tariq's bold script:

> *Your balcony. When the moon is
> at its highest point in the night.
> I'll wait until dawn, if I must.
> Do not test me.*

At least he'd had the sense not to sign it.

Utterly mad!

She crumpled it in her fist for the fifth time.

He was risking everything with his foolhardiness. With his arrogance. With his—

"Shazi?" A form materialized in the darkness at the edge of the balcony.

"Come here," she seethed.

Tariq glided closer, hunching low. Shahrzad grabbed him by the hood of his *rida'* and hauled him against the deepest shade along the wall.

"Are you completely insane?" she demanded. "Do you realize how dangerous—"

Tariq pulled Shahrzad into his chest. "God, I've missed you."

When Shahrzad tried to speak again, he pressed her face tight against him, laughing at her protests. "Just stop. For the space of a moment, let me hold you."

"You are mad, Tariq Imran al-Ziyad. Utterly mad," she grumbled, smacking his shoulder. "How did you even manage an invitation?"

He shrugged. "I intercepted the one sent to my father at Taleqan. Or, to be more precise, Rahim intercepted it."

"You idiot! Coming here was beyond foolish, and—"

"Foolish though it may be, I am here to finish what you started." Tariq ran his fingers through her hair. "Tell me how you plan to kill the boy-king."

Shahrzad was oddly silent.

"Shazi?"

"I—" she hedged.

"Have you not made plans yet?"

Shahrzad pushed away from his chest, unwilling to give voice to her uncertainty.

"Fine. What have you learned?" he continued.

She frowned and glanced from the shadows to the stone railing beyond.

"Shahrzad. You've been here for weeks. What have you learned? What are the boy-king's habits? His weaknesses?"

Tell him what you know.

"I—don't know. He's difficult to read."

Why can't I tell him?

"Difficult? He has the personality of an aging camel. Just as surly and just as useless."

A strange pang cut through Shahrzad at this assessment. "What do you mean?"

"He picks at his food, lounges in sullen silence, and lets his wife fight his battles for him."

"What? No. You misunderstood the situation."

"Please tell me you're not defending him. He barely acknowledged your presence the entire evening, except to parade you before everyone like a prize he had won . . . and then that irritating moment when he fidgeted with your jewelry. I could have done without that."

"I'm not defending him. I'm saying that it's—complicated." Even through the layers of darkness, Shahrzad could see Tariq's thick eyebrows gather at the bridge of his nose.

"Complicated? There's nothing complicated about it. As far as I'm concerned, all I need is ready access to a weapon and a clear shot."

No!

Shahrzad heard a sound in her room.

Her heart stopped. She pressed a hand to Tariq's lips and shoved him into the shadows. Then she strode into her chamber, sighing with relief to find no one there.

Tariq was leaning against the wall when Shahrzad returned.

"Are you expecting someone?" he asked in a cool tone.

"You have to leave."

"Why?" There was a note of warning to his voice.

"Tariq, please."

His eyes narrowed to silver slits. "Will he come to see you tonight?"

"You need to leave. Now." Shahrzad tugged at his wrist, but he refused to budge from the wall.

"Good. Let him come. That will solve the matter on all fronts."

"Do you have a death wish?" she cried in muted despair.

Tariq laughed, and the sound was full of heedless arrogance. "From the boy-king? That aging camel?"

"You idiot! He'll kill you!"

"Are you sure? You don't think he'll ask his mother to do it for him?"

Shahrzad sucked in a breath. Before she could stop herself, she launched into a whispered tirade.

"You know nothing about him, and your ignorance will be your downfall. Get out of here, Tariq, because if Khalid walks through that door, he will cut you to ribbons before you have a chance to open your mouth, and it will destroy me. Beyond words. Beyond time. If you love me, do not force me to watch such a sight."

Shahrzad clutched the front of his *rida'* as she spoke. Her features twisted in deep distress.

Tariq's initial shock melted away at the prospect of her pain. "Shazi—I'm sorry."

"Don't be sorry. Just . . . go."

Tariq took a slow step from the wall. Then he swiveled around to grab Shahrzad by the waist and press her back against the stone. He ran his palms along her arms.

"I love you, Shahrzad al-Khayzuran. There is nothing I would not do for you. Nothing I would not consider if it meant keeping you safe. The world itself should fear me if it stands between us."

"I—I love you too, Tariq."

He smiled. Then, without warning, he caught her lips in his. Shahrzad's jaw slackened in surprise, and Tariq deepened the kiss, tilting her chin upward with a gentle caress of his thumb.

Shahrzad's mouth responded automatically. Her lips curved over his as they had on many occasions before. But . . . why did it feel wrong this time? Where was that breathless, weightless thrill? That thoughtless moment of incandescence?

Where was that feeling of falling?

It's here. I know it's here. I can get it back.

I have to get it back.

REALIZATIONS
UPON EXPLANATIONS

A DAY OF HUNTING FOR SPORT SHOULD PROVE interesting, indeed.

Tariq strode down another never-ending corridor with a guard at his side. As he walked, he glanced around him at the splendor of the palace at Rey. The walls and domed ceilings above were polished beyond reason, and each portico was delineated at its center by a golden sunburst, supported by swooping beams and columned arches of blue-veined agate.

It was beautiful, without a doubt. If a bit cold and imposing.

Soon, he joined a gathering of noblemen taking part in today's hunting excursion. In truth, Tariq was glad for the distraction and glad for the opportunity to spend time in the company of his target; his interaction with Shahrzad the night before had troubled him greatly.

It was unlike her to be so cagey and distant. It was also unlike her to be so concerned with safety. Usually, she was the first one to throw herself into the fray, heedless of the consequences.

When they were younger, Shahrzad had wanted to learn how to climb trees. Bored with the prospect in short order, she'd then insisted on breaching the walls of Taleqan. Both he and Rahim had begged her to cease in this foolishness, but, if anything, it had only spurred her onward. While watching her climb one afternoon, with her black hair streaming behind her in a tangled mess, he had caught sight of the mortar easing from the wall in a cloud of white dust by her foot. He had known, in that instant, that the brick was about to come loose. Tariq had shouted an all-too-late warning. He had heard Shiva's scream from behind him when Shahrzad fell. His heart had left his chest as her small body plummeted to the sand. Tariq was the one who had reached her first, who had clutched her to him, demanding she respond. And he was the one who had cursed loudly when she laughed at him, saying she was fine, even if her head did hurt a little.

That was the day he first told her he loved her.

Tariq inhaled through his nose.

It was also unlike Shahrzad to hesitate. About anything.

And she had hesitated last night.

When he said he loved her on the balcony, she hesitated in her response. Then, when he kissed her, something was wrong. He could feel her thinking. Feel her questioning. Feel her wanting . . . something else.

Or someone else.

It was driving him mad.

"I don't believe we've been introduced. I'm Captain al-Khoury."

Standing next to him was the arrogant boy with the curly hair and the omnipresent smirk.

Tariq returned a polite smile. "Tariq Imran al-Ziyad."

"Yes. I know."

270

"Does my reputation precede me?"

"I should hope not, if I were you." The boy grinned in jest. "You brought your own falcon, correct? Rather fortuitous, considering today's event."

"Are you this well informed in all matters?"

"It's a hazard of my occupation. Speaking of such things, I was surprised to learn that you arrived with your father's invitation in hand; I was looking forward to meeting him."

Tariq crossed his arms to conceal his sudden discomfort. "He was ill and asked me to come to Rey in his stead."

"A pity. Please convey my wishes for a speedy recovery." Captain al-Khoury's gaze roved to an archway in the corner, and his features leveled, retaining a semblance of their former amusement.

The boy-king had arrived. This time, Tariq took care to note the sword at the caliph's left hip. The blade was an unusual one, to be sure—longer and more slender than a scimitar, with a sharply tapered edge.

"It's called a *shamshir,*" Captain al-Khoury offered, watching Tariq with unabashed curiosity.

"I'm not familiar with that particular weapon."

Captain al-Khoury nodded. "It's unusual. But then, so is Khalid."

"Khalid?"

"He's my cousin."

Tariq's lips flattened. "I see."

Captain al-Khoury laughed. "Don't worry. We have very little in common, beyond blood."

"Meaning?"

"Meaning I won't break *every* bone in your body for a single misstep." Though he continued smiling, his tone hovered on the verge of threatening, and Tariq chose to ignore it.

"That sounds unduly harsh." And appropriately fitting.

Captain al-Khoury grinned again, this time a bit wider. "I told you. Khalid is unusual."

Tariq swiveled back toward the boy-king, a series of lines creasing his sun-drenched forehead. "He seems very quiet."

"He is quiet. But a man much wiser than I once said that the smartest men are the silent ones . . ."

Tariq waited, barely managing to conceal his growing contempt.

Captain al-Khoury leaned closer. "Because they hear everything."

"It's an interesting notion," Tariq mused. "Who said it?"

Captain al-Khoury smirked with cool deliberation. "Khalid." Then he strode to the boy-king's side.

When the Sultan of Parthia arrived, the group of men began making their way down the corridors toward an open-air gallery ten times the size of the one at Taleqan. On one end of the gallery was a series of arched double doors leading to the beginnings of a lush, tree-lined garden.

As the men traversed this course, they crossed paths with Shahrzad. She was walking through another set of double doors with an attractive young handmaiden and the same menacing brute of a bodyguard from last night.

Tariq's chest hollowed at the sight of her.

She grew more beautiful with each passing moment, as though

life in this palace of cold, polished stone suited her. Today, her garments of silver and rose made her black hair and bronze skin appear even more stunning than usual. He much preferred this to her showy garb of last night, even though she'd dazzled every man in the room with her blue sapphires and black silk.

But then, she dazzled Tariq always.

The assemblage of men paused to greet the calipha, and the bastard from Parthia stepped forward to make his own particular effort.

Tariq fought back the urge to react. To lash out.

Thankfully, Captain al-Khoury moved in Shahrzad's direction, and Tariq disliked him a little less for it.

Until the boy-king stopped his cousin, with a single motion of his hand.

Infuriated, Tariq's eyes shot to his target.

A hint of emotion flashed across the boy-king's face.

Pride?

The Sultan of Parthia glided before Shahrzad, charm oozing from him like a wasting disease. "Good morning, my lady! I trust you had a nice evening."

Shahrzad bowed. "I did, my lord. And you?"

He nodded. "A very nice evening. My daughter tells me she had a lovely conversation with you and was glad to have made your acquaintance."

"I did enjoy my conversation with Yasmine, my lord. It was— enlightening."

"I believe she used the very same word, my lady."

"I find that rather appropriate, my lord. Given our exchange."

"As silver-tongued as a viper." He laughed. "Tell me, my lady, do you ever miss a moment to strike?"

Shahrzad smiled, and it was brilliant and biting, all at once. "I fear that would be unwise, my lord. Especially in a den of snakes."

The sultan shook his head, his amusement too lasting to be real.

"You must visit us in Parthia, for our snakes have far less occasion to strike. Yasmine and I insist upon it. The next time Khalid comes to Amardha, you must join him so we can return your hospitality."

"It would be an honor, my lord." Shahrzad dipped her head, her fingertips grazing her brow.

The sultan turned back to the boy-king, a disconcerting gleam in his eye.

"Truly, nephew. She is a treasure. See that you keep her safe." Only a fool would have missed the implied threat dripping from his every word.

Yet the weak boy-king said nothing—did nothing—even though Tariq longed to assail the bastard from Parthia with both fists. And an axe.

Silent men are the wisest?

Tariq fumed to himself and folded his arms across his chest.

The boy-king strode to Shahrzad. He stopped an arm's length in front of her and, yet again, said nothing. He regarded her in silence with his strange orange-gold eyes. After a moment, he started to smile, and Shahrzad nodded once, almost indiscernibly.

The hollow in Tariq's chest deepened further.

Shahrzad and the boy-king shared an understanding that did not require words.

The boy-king bowed low before his calipha, with a hand to his forehead. As he straightened, he shifted his palm over his heart and walked away. The group trailed behind him, paying their respects to Shahrzad as they passed. When Tariq paused before her, she averted her eyes, her cheeks pink and her fists clenched in the folds of her silver cloak.

It was in that instant Tariq remembered his uncle's words the first night he and Rahim had arrived in Rey, covered in dust and exhausted from two days of hard traveling:

The city is rife with speculation. Namely, that the caliph must be in love with his new bride.

Tariq quickened his pace as the assemblage gathered in the first portion of a multitiered garden full of flowering trees and an elaborate aviary of colorful songbirds.

The boy-king kept glancing over his shoulder at his palace as they descended into each subsequent tier.

Finally, Captain al-Khoury announced, in a voice far beyond the scope of normal conversation, "*Sayyidi,* I do believe you left something rather important in the Grand Portico."

The boy-king narrowed his strange eyes at his cousin.

"Perhaps you should attend to it and join us later for the hunt." Captain al-Khoury's obnoxious grin grew even wider.

The boy-king glanced over his shoulder once more. Then he pivoted in a faultless motion, offering murmured apologies as he cut through the crowd.

Tariq knew, without a doubt, that he was on his way to Shahrzad. As did all the noblemen remaining. Their caliph had barely disappeared from view before the conversation turned raucous. The less scrupulous began taking bets as to how long it would be before Khorasan had a new heir to the throne.

The Sultan of Parthia listened with a ready ear . . . and a disparaging eye.

Tariq grinned—through waves of rage and torment. After a time, he could no longer abide it. He turned on his heel.

"Where are you going?" Captain al-Khoury asked.

Tariq thought quickly. "I left my *mankalah* in my chamber."

"I believe we can find one for you."

Tariq shook his head with an apologetic smile. "Zoraya is a temperamental bird—a creature of habit. Tell me where to meet you, and the guard can show me the way."

Captain al-Khoury's gaze darted across Tariq's face. "The horses will be saddled and waiting at the promenade by the royal stables."

Tariq nodded and motioned to a guard off to the side.

"Tariq Imran al-Ziyad?"

"Yes, Captain al-Khoury?"

"Is that particular *mankalah* really of such import?"

Tariq grinned, his silver eyes bright. "It is if I intend to win."

Shahrzad paused before the calligraphy, studying the intricate dips and delicate flourishes in each of the artist's brushstrokes. The many colors of the ink swirled across the parchment, giving life to the words on the page.

Above her, streams of gauzy light spilled through the dome of the Grand Portico from windows around a sunburst of silver and gold. The gilded rays stretched across the dome to nine cornices forming a halo of shelves that connected columns of sienna marble from the ceiling to the floor.

"This one is completely unreadable," Despina complained, staring over Shahrzad's shoulder.

"I think it's another love poem." Shahrzad smiled.

"What is the purpose behind learning to write so beautifully if no one can decipher your words?"

"It's an expression of feeling. I suppose this is how the poem made the artist feel."

"So this poem rendered him illiterate?"

Shahrzad laughed, and the lyrical sound carried up into the dome, bouncing from the cornices back to the stone at their feet.

"You laugh very loud—as if you are the only one in the world," Despina commented.

Shahrzad wrinkled her nose. "That's funny. My sister says something very similar."

"I assume it makes little difference to you."

"Why? You'd prefer I stop?" she teased.

"No," Khalid said, as he strode into the Grand Portico. "I would not."

"*Sayyidi.*" Despina bowed.

He nodded at her. "I cannot speak for Despina. But you do laugh too loud. And I hope you never stop."

Despina tucked her chin to her chest and smiled as she hurried out of the Grand Portico without a word.

Shahrzad stared up at Khalid, warring with a resurgence of emotions. Her throat tightened, and the anger threatened to pour from her in a storm of words he did not deserve to hear.

Because he did not deserve to know her deepest thoughts. Her truest desires.

How much she cared for him. And how little it should matter.

May your secrets give you solace, Khalid Ibn al-Rashid.

For I won't.

Shahrzad lifted her chin and turned to leave.

Khalid snared her elbow as she passed him.

"I knocked at your door last night," he began.

Her heart shuddered to a stop. "I was tired." She refused to look his way.

"And angry with me," he said softly.

Shahrzad glared at him over her shoulder.

He studied her features. "No. Irate."

"Let go of me."

Khalid released her arm. "I understand why. I was remiss in not telling you about Yasmine. I apologize. It won't happen again."

"Remiss?" Shahrzad faced him with a caustic laugh. "*Remiss?*"

"I—"

"Do you know how foolish I looked? How foolish I felt?"

Khalid sighed. "She wanted to hurt you, and it troubles me to see how successful she was."

"How successful *she* was? You miserable, unfeeling ass! You think I'm angry because of what she did? Because she *danced* for you? My God, Khalid, how can you be so intelligent and so inexcusably dense in the same instant?"

He flinched. "Shahrzad—"

"This has nothing to do with her. *You* hurt me, Khalid Ibn al-Rashid. The secrets—the locked doors I will never be given keys to—they wound me," she shouted. "Time and again, you wound me and walk away!"

Her pain followed the same course as her laughter, striking against the cornices above and back to the marble at their feet.

Khalid listened to its echo and closed his eyes with a grimace. When he opened them again, he reached for Shahrzad.

She drew back.

I will not cry. Not for you.

Undeterred, Khalid grasped her wrists in each of his hands and lifted her palms to his face. "Strike out at me if you wish, Shazi. Do whatever you will. But don't inflict the selfsame wound; don't leave."

He placed her hands on either side of his jaw, skimming his fingertips down her arms while awaiting her judgment.

Shahrzad stood frozen, a mask of ice and stone between her palms.

When she did nothing, Khalid brushed back the hair from her face with a touch that soothed and burned all at once.

"I'm sorry, *joonam*. For the secrets. For the locked doors. For everything. I promise to tell you one day. But not yet. Trust that some secrets are safer behind lock and key," he said quietly.

Joonam. He'd called her that before. *My everything.*

As on the night she'd told the tale of Tala and Mehrdad, why did it have such a ring of truth to it?

"I—" She bit her lower lip in an effort to keep it still. To stop the fount of words longing to spring forth.

Longing to confess the yearnings of a capricious heart.

"Forgive me, a thousand times over, for wounding you." He leaned in and pressed a soft kiss to her forehead.

I'm lost to him. I can't ignore it any longer.

Shahrzad closed her eyes in defeat and slid her palms to his chest. Then she reached behind him in an embrace of sandalwood and sun. Khalid wrapped both his arms around Shahrzad, and they stood together under the dome of the Grand Portico, with the indecipherable art of love poems giving silent testament.

The hollow in his chest was nothing now.

He would gladly go back to that, if it meant never having to witness this sight again.

When Tariq first entered the vestibule leading into the Grand Portico, he thought he was in the wrong place. It was so quiet. There was no way Shahrzad could be here.

Then, when he rounded the corner, he saw the reason for the silence.

It stopped him like a dagger hurled through the air.

The boy-king was holding Shahrzad in his arms. Placing a gentle kiss on her brow.

And Shahrzad was leaning into his embrace.

Tariq watched as she shifted her slender fingers to the boy-king's back and drew him closer, resting her cheek against his chest as a weary traveler to the bole of a tree.

The worst part of it all—the part that took the very breath from Tariq's body—was the unguarded look of peace on her face.

As though this was right. As though she wanted nothing more.

Shahrzad was in love with Shiva's murderer.

The guard behind him deliberately made noise. Apparently, he did not care to learn the consequences of eavesdropping on the Caliph of Khorasan.

From the distant shadows to Tariq's right, Shahrzad's mammoth bodyguard twisted into view, flashing a silver blade and a guise of punishing promise.

But the thing that truly gave Tariq pause was the reaction of the boy-king.

The supposed aging camel.

At the first hint of an unforeseen threat, he pulled Shahrzad behind him. He shielded her in a menacing stance augmented by the metallic rasp of his *shamshir*, which he held steady in his right hand, with the blade pointed to the floor—

Poised to attack.

The boy-king's usually expressionless face was drawn and tight, with signs of barely leashed fury rippling along his jaw. His eyes blazed like molten rock, livid and single-minded in their purpose.

Shahrzad grabbed the boy-king's shoulder.

"Khalid!" she cried. "What are you doing?"

He did not waver.

Now Tariq understood Shahrzad's plea from last night.

This was not a bored, dispassionate king who sent his wife to fight his battles.

This was definitely something more.

Something Tariq needed time to consider.

And time . . . to rip out his heart, in kind.

Tariq grinned, running his fingers through his hair.

"Are we not meeting here for the hunt?" he asked.

Khalid regarded Nasir al-Ziyad's son with mounting irritation.

The boy's explanation for his intrusion into the Grand Portico was absurd. His stupidity had nearly cost him his life.

Under normal circumstances, Khalid would not have reacted in such a manner, but Salim Ali el-Sharif was in Rey. Just this morning, he had stood in the open-air gallery of Khalid's palace and made veiled threats against Shahrzad. Khalid had expected as much, but it did not affect him any less to bear witness to it.

Ignoring any threat from the Sultan of Parthia, no matter how inconsequential, had always proved to be unwise.

Khalid did not know who this foolish boy was or where his allegiances might lie. Yesterday, such matters were not of pressing import. Yesterday, the boy was but a mild nuisance. The only reason he had sparked Khalid's interest at all was because of the way he'd looked at Shahrzad today. It was not in the manner most men appreciate a beautiful woman. Most men appreciated beauty with an emphasis on form.

The vast majority of Khalid's guests were mindful of such behavior. The ones who didn't were of note, but they had reputations to match—morally reprehensible men with lascivious eyes that latched on to anything in their general vicinity.

Tariq Imran al-Ziyad did not linger on Shahrzad with the eye of man appreciating form.

What Shahrzad had to say mattered to the boy. As did the thoughts behind her words.

Khalid walked beside Nasir al-Ziyad's son down the stairs into the next tier of gardens as they made their way to the stables. His guards trailed close behind them.

"Please permit me to apologize again, *sayyidi*." The boy adjusted his *mankalah* with another sheepish grin.

Khalid continued through the garden, glancing sideways at the boy.

"Rest assured, I've noted the difference between a portico and a promenade, *sayyidi*."

"It would have served me better had you known that today," Khalid muttered.

The boy laughed, and the sound was rich. An easy laugh that inspired others to take part. "Thank you for not cutting me to ribbons, *sayyidi*."

"Thank the queen. Had I been alone, things might have gone differently."

The boy's assertive gait faltered a step. "May I congratulate you, *sayyidi*? The queen—you seem well suited to each other."

An ever-increasing nuisance. Khalid halted and faced the boy.

He was half a hand taller than Khalid and broad in the shoulder. It needled Khalid to look up at such a fool. "Shahrzad is a difficult girl, and I am a monster. I suppose that makes for a good match."

The boy's pale eyes flared at Khalid's words.

"You're offended." Khalid watched his features intently. "By which part?"

"By—all of it, *sayyidi*."

The boy was not a gifted liar. The mild nuisance was now a full-blown concern.

When the boy attempted to crack the awkward silence with another charming smile, Khalid proceeded down the path.

"Are you married, Tariq Imran al-Ziyad?"

"No, *sayyidi*. But I plan on marrying soon."

"Then you are engaged."

"Yes, *sayyidi*. To a girl I've loved for many years."

The boy appeared to be telling the truth.

"Which is why I congratulated you earlier. It is a great gift to find lasting love—one that gives for every bit it takes," the boy stated with unusual conviction.

It was the first interesting thing the boy had contributed to their conversation. And it did not sit well with Khalid.

After a time, they approached the stables, and Jalal wandered out to greet them. His head slanted with puzzlement when he saw the foolish boy. Then he nodded with welcome and the boy smiled back.

"Again, *sayyidi*, I apologize for earlier. Please thank the queen on my behalf. It appears I owe her my life." The boy bowed low before Khalid and sauntered toward the stables, his white *rida'* trailing behind him.

"What happened?" Jalal asked once he was out of earshot.

Khalid did not respond.

"All is well with you and Shazi?" Jalal pressed.

Khalid continued staring after Nasir al-Ziyad's son.

"Khalid?"

"Find out everything about Tariq Imran al-Ziyad. His family. Their associations. All of it."

Jalal started to laugh.

"What's so amusing?" Khalid demanded.

"Blood runs true. That boy has bothered me all day."

A FLOATING CARPET
AND A RISING TIDE

SHAHRZAD STOOD IN THE SMALL ROOM HOUSING all her garments. She watched Despina set aside parcel after parcel of wrapped silk in a wide assortment of colors.

"By Zeus, would you just pick one?" Shahrzad groaned, coiling her waves of black hair to one side.

"Be patient. I'm looking for something specific."

"Then be specific about it, and I can help."

Despina rose to her feet and stretched her arms above her head. She winced as she kneaded her left shoulder.

Shahrzad's forehead wrinkled in concern. "How do you feel?"

"I'm fine. I slept poorly last night."

"That's not what I meant."

Despina laughed with trilling dismissiveness. "I have many months before it will be an issue, Shahrzad."

"Have you told Jalal yet?"

"No."

"When will you tell him?"

"When I muster the courage or when I'm left with no choice—whichever comes first. And I won't discuss the matter further."

Despina twisted to the back corner of the room and stooped to rustle through more parcels of silk.

Shahrzad frowned at her handmaiden, wondering if Despina ever managed a decent night's rest with such worries wreaking their silent havoc.

Why won't she tell him?

When Despina resurfaced, her features were pinched by annoyance. "The garment may be in my room for mending. Come with me."

The two girls left behind the piles of silk and damask to cross Shahrzad's bedchamber. They paused before a single, polished wood door near the entrance. Despina pushed it open and walked down a narrow corridor before grasping the silver handle leading to another chamber at the end.

Shahrzad had never been in Despina's room before, even though it was so near her own. The chamber was small and tidy, with a neat arrangement of cushions on one side and a low table on the other. The wardrobe in the corner was made of the same honey-colored wood as the table, and the entire space was lightly perfumed in the floral scent of jessamine.

Despina walked to the wardrobe and opened one side to begin her search.

Shahrzad's eyes wandered past the wooden chest, and she noticed something wedged against the wall, tied in a bundle secured by hemp cord.

It was the rug gifted to her by Musa Zaragoza.

"Why is that in here?" Shahrzad nodded toward the bundle.

Despina glanced over her shoulder and sighed. "I kept meaning to ask you if I could throw it away."

"It was a gift!"

"It's old and threadbare, and it will likely attract vermin. I don't want such a thing amongst your garments."

Shahrzad rolled her eyes. "Give it to me."

Despina shrugged before passing along the bundle. "Why anyone would gift the Calipha of Khorasan a tiny, shabby carpet is beyond me."

Shahrzad held it in both hands as she recalled the day Musa-*effendi* had visited the palace.

"It is a very special carpet. When you are lost, it will help you find your way."

"I don't think it's a mere rug."

"Then what is it?"

"It could be a map of sorts," Shahrzad mused.

"If it's a map, it's outdated and, therefore, useless."

Shahrzad turned from Despina's room and strode down the narrow hall back to her bedchamber. She knelt on the floor and set the bundle down. Then she began tugging at the knot of hemp at its center. When her efforts proved futile, she remembered why her curiosity had failed to win out upon first receiving the gift.

"This knot is from hell itself," Shahrzad grumbled as Despina peered over her shoulder.

"Let me try." Her handmaiden crouched beside her and began pulling at the strings. Faced with similar results, she lifted the knot and studied it for a spell. Then she removed a silver pin from the crown of hair atop her head. A cascade of golden-walnut curls spilled onto her shoulder, and Despina started working the pin into the center of the knot.

"You shall not prevail, little hell-knot," she whispered, squinching her blue eyes over the bundle.

Moments later, the knot tugged free, and both girls shouted in triumph.

Shahrzad unwrapped the rug and spread it out on the floor.

It was indeed as worn and threadbare as it initially appeared—rust colored, with a border of dark blue and a center medallion of black-and-white scrollwork. Almost all the fringe of tassels had frayed away. The few that remained were dirty and yellowed with age, still clinging to misbegotten hope. Two corners boasted holes that resembled scorch marks.

As she ran her palms across it, an odd, tingling sensation began to form in her chest. She drew back in sudden alarm.

"What's wrong?" Despina asked.

The sensation was gone.

Shahrzad glanced down at her hands and ran her thumbs across her fingers.

"Nothing."

Both girls stood to inspect the small rug.

"Well . . . that's an ugly carpet," Despina pronounced.

Shahrzad laughed.

"May I please throw it away?" Despina pressed.

"I thought it might be a map. Musa-*effendi* told me it would help me find my way." Shahrzad's brow furrowed.

"You mean the magus from the Fire Temple?"

"Is that what Musa-*effendi* is?"

Despina pursed her lips and looked away.

"You weren't supposed to tell me that." Shahrzad smirked. "Were you?"

Despina glared at her.

"Interesting," Shahrzad continued. "Though I'm not surprised. Jalal does seem to be the talkative type. I wonder what he says in moments of—"

"Shahrzad!"

Shahrzad laughed as she dodged Despina's threatening shove. Her bare heel grazed the rug, and the strange tingling flared in her chest once more. Increasingly disturbed, she knelt before the carpet and placed her palm to its surface.

A prickly feeling, almost like losing sensation in a foot from sitting too long, began to warm around her heart. The warmth soon spread to her shoulders and down her arm. Then, when she ran her fingers along the edge of the rug—

It curled into her hand, as though it had a life of its own.

Shahrzad gasped in shock and fell on her side in a graceless heap.

"What happened?" Despina demanded, kneeling beside her.

"The rug—moved!"

"What?"

Shahrzad scrambled to her knees, her heart tripping about in her chest.

"Look!" She pushed her hand to the carpet until the prickly sensation filled her palm . . . and one corner of the rug rose from the floor.

Despina shrieked a curse and jumped back. "What's wrong with it?"

"How should I know?" Shahrzad yelled.

"Do—do it again."

Shahrzad repeated the process, and another corner of the carpet lifted from the floor with the ease of a rising cloud.

At this, Despina regarded her with wary circumspection. "Have you ever done that to anything before?"

"No! It's the carpet, not me."

Despina knelt and placed her own palms to the worn, rust-colored surface. She waited a beat. Nothing happened.

"It's not just the carpet, Shahrzad. It's you."

Shahrzad chewed on the inside of her cheek.

"Then you are unaware. It lies dormant in your blood."

Despina exhaled in a huff of exasperation. She held Shahrzad's hand to the carpet. When its edges curled off the floor and Shahrzad tried to pull away, Despina refused to let go.

Soon, the entire rug was floating in the air beside their shoulders—weightless, as though woven from a dream. When the girls withdrew their touch, the carpet drifted back to the marble with the grace of a petal to the earth.

"Well," Despina whispered in awe, "that certainly is a neat little trick."

Tariq dismounted in the desert before Omar al-Sadiq's large patchworked tent. He grabbed his stallion's bridle and led it to a trough of water nearby. As the horse drank, the mirrored surface rippled around its snout in concentric rings. Tariq ran his palm along the magnificent animal's neck.

The return journey had not been an easy one.

Despite her reassurances as to her safety, leaving the city of Rey—leaving Shahrzad—had been all but impossible. He'd acquiesced to her wishes, but it had been done with a heavy, bitter heart. For the past five days, Tariq had ridden through the blowing sands under a blazing sun, in constant war with his thoughts.

How had it come to this?

Nothing made sense. The girl he knew was not capable of such fickleness. The girl he loved was too smart, too resourceful . . . too *loyal* to be won over by a monster. Especially one who had murdered her best friend.

As this tempest raged about in his mind, Tariq found himself returning to its most salient point: none of this made sense.

Therefore, it required an explanation.

Tariq remembered hearing tales of captives losing their will to their captors. Prisoners falling in love with their vanquishers. While he'd never believed in such a possibility before, it was the only thing that made sense of Shahrzad's behavior.

She was not herself. That palace, that world . . . that monster had taken away the girl Tariq loved and driven her to forget all she held dear.

He had to get her out of there. Soon.

The sound of Zoraya's piercing cry tore him from his thoughts. Tariq whistled for her, and she landed on his outstretched *mankalah,* impatient for her evening meal. He was preoccupied, but he managed to smile at the falcon as he offered her a strip of dried meat.

"Our nameless *sahib* returns!" a familiar voice crowed from behind him. "Though, if the rumors are to be believed, he is nameless no more."

Tariq turned to the sun-weathered face of Omar al-Sadiq. "Rumors?"

Omar grinned, wide and gaptoothed. "Such is the way of rumors. We are often the last to know the ones in our honor."

Tariq closed his eyes for a spell. The eccentric sheikh was trying his last bit of patience. "There are rumors in my honor?"

"About the White Falcon. The savior of Khorasan."

"What are you talking about?" Tariq heaved a weary sigh.

"Have you not heard of him? They say he rides under a banner emblazoned by the standard of a white falcon. That he intends to storm the city of Rey and overthrow its evil king." Omar's eyes twinkled. "As it turns out, I believe you're quite familiar with the White Falcon. His friends call him Tariq."

"I'm sorry," Tariq said brusquely, knocking back the hood of his dusty white *rida'*. "But I'm in no mood for your games."

"Games? War is not a game, my friend. Games are for small children and old men like me. War is a young man's blighted delight."

"Cease with the word games, Omar! I can't stomach—"

"Would you like to see your banner, instead?" Omar winked. "It's quite—"

"Please!" The single word cracked against the desert sky, filling it with frustration and the lasting hint of pain.

Omar's keen eyes took in Tariq's aggrieved face. "What happened while you were in Rey, my friend?"

Tariq released Zoraya into the clouds and leaned back against the trough.

"Tell me what troubles you so," Omar pressed in a gentle voice.

"I—I have to get Shazi out of there. Away from that place. Away from that monster."

"You are worried for her safety." Omar nodded slowly. "Then why have you returned?" His concern eclipsed his bluntness.

Tariq cringed, unable to respond.

"Can you not tell me what happened, my friend?"

Tariq gazed into the settling dusk on the horizon. A trace of the sun's warmth lingered along the edge, fading into blues that bled their way to black.

"I suspected he might care for her. After all, he let her live when so many others . . ." Tariq's silver eyes chilled in thought. "But I did not expect this."

Omar scratched at his beard. "I see."

"What? What do you see?" Tariq turned toward the Badawi sheikh.

"You believe the young caliph . . ." Omar lifted a gnarled hand to Tariq's shoulder. "Is in love with your Shahrzad."

Tariq fixed his gaze on the coarse linen of Omar's sleeve.

"And what led you to believe this?" Omar continued in the same kind tone.

"The—it's the way he looks at her," Tariq whispered. "It's the only time I even begin to understand him."

Omar squeezed his shoulder. "Perhaps . . . it is for the best.

I've heard the young caliph has lived a life of profound loss. If Shahrzad can—"

"I will not leave Shazi in the arms of a murdering madman!"

Omar blinked hard. The heavy creases of his eyelids rose and fell with a purposeful weight. "Tariq, why are you doing this? Why are you fighting this battle?"

"Because I love her," Tariq said without hesitation.

"But . . . why do you love her?"

"What kind of a ridiculous question—"

"It is not a ridiculous question. It is a very simple one. The difficulty lies in the answer. Why do you love her?"

"Because—" Tariq rubbed at the back of his neck. "All of my most cherished memories are of her. I've suffered alongside her. And . . . we've laughed at nothing together."

Omar's hand fell from Tariq's shoulder. "A shared history does not entitle you to a future, my friend."

"How could I expect you to understand?" Tariq said. "No one ever tried to take Aisha from you. No one—"

"I do not have to lose my wife to understand the meaning of loss, Tariq. A child with a broken toy understands such things."

Anger coiled through Tariq's chest. "Are you likening my suffering to that of a child?"

Omar shook his head with a bemused smile. "Loss is loss. And the lesson is always the same."

"I am not in the mood for a lesson."

"Nor am I." Omar laughed. "So I will share a story instead."

"Please don't—"

"On a clear night, many years ago, I watched a thousand stars fall from the sky. I was only a small boy, but I possessed a very curious heart, so I decided to chase them into the desert, far beyond the horizon. You see, I wanted to know where stars went when they fell. I ran and ran until I could run no more. And still I could not see where the stars went."

"Your story is a lesson, Omar," Tariq said in a flat tone. "I am not that big a fool."

Omar grinned. "Did I ever tell you that, to this day, I still fight the urge to chase falling stars?"

"I can well understand it, as I'm currently fighting the urge to flee."

Omar threw his head back and laughed. "Not until our lesson concludes, my young friend! You cannot rob an old man of this well-deserved right."

"No. I cannot." Despite the heaviness around his heart, Tariq could not help but smile. "Conclude your lesson, my esteemed *effendi.*"

"Some things exist in our lives for but a brief moment. And we must let them go on to light another sky."

Tariq stared into the darkness beyond the enclave of tents. "You want me to leave things as they are. But I can't. I won't."

"And I will always respect your choice, Tariq-*jan.* Though we may disagree, I shall try to offer whatever support I can. Come with me. Your uncle is waiting for you."

"Uncle Reza is here?" Tariq looked over Omar's shoulder.

"He arrived two days ago with your friend Rahim and has been anxiously awaiting your return ever since." Omar led Tariq to the entrance of the largest tent in the desert enclave. He pushed aside the flap, and the two men stepped inside.

"Our prodigal hero has returned!" Omar announced as he strode to the back corner and took a seat beside Reza with a jocular flourish.

Tariq removed his shoes and discarded his cloak before pacing farther into the semidarkness. The patchwork of carpet at his feet was soft and worn. It mirrored the dark collage of woven fabric shaping the walls of the tent around him. A thin haze of smoke suffused the air about his head. It smelled of tobacco and molasses.

"Come, have some tea," Omar said with a smile. "I've been having the most wonderful time with your uncle these past few days, for he is quite fond of love stories as well."

Tariq sat on the woolen cushions around a knotted wood table with a silver pot of tea, several etched glasses, and a towering *ghalyan*. The *ghalyan* was made of deep green glass, with a long pipe wrapped in copper silk, snaking around the table to Reza bin-Latief's outstretched palm. The coal atop it burned bright orange as he puffed on the carved mouthpiece, and the water within its glass basin bubbled at a slow roil. The sweet smoke rose into the air, curling into tendrils of blue grey, mingling into the haze above.

"Uncle." Tariq extended his hand toward Reza, and Reza took it.

"You have been quite busy, Tariq-*jan*," Reza said quietly.

Tariq inhaled through his nose. "I know you asked me to wait at Taleqan for your missive."

Reza continued puffing on the *ghalyan* in silence.

"But I could not allow you to do all the work," Tariq finished.

"See? I told you. He is quite the hero already." Omar cackled.

"Part of being a hero is knowing when to be still," Reza countered.

In response, Tariq said nothing, and Omar laughed heartily.

"So what did you learn in this foolhardy excursion to Rey?" Reza asked.

"I learned I have a great deal to learn."

Reza passed Omar the pipe. "What else?"

"I learned the Caliph of Khorasan is dangerous, in addition to being a madman."

"How so?"

"He's smart, for a madman. Rather . . . surprising."

"Madmen tend to be." Omar's eyes glittered in the shadows as streams of smoke emitted from his nostrils.

"What else?" Reza asked.

Tariq leaned back into the cushions. "He's arrogant, and he has a quick temper."

"What of weaknesses?" Reza prodded.

Tariq hesitated.

"Tariq?"

Before Tariq could respond, the flap of the tent opened once more, and Rahim stepped beneath its wing, with Jahandar al-Khayzuran in tow. The three men seated around the *ghalyan* gazed their way. Rahim shot Tariq an apologetic glance, and Jahandar cleared his throat with a cough.

"May—may I join you?" Jahandar asked.

Omar smiled brightly. "Of course! You are most welcome."

Tariq rose from the table, trying his best to conceal his irritation as Jahandar crossed the carpets. He bowed his head with a hand to his brow. "Jahandar-*effendi*."

"Tariq-*jan*." Jahandar looked into the silver eyes, eager and hopeful. When he was met with nothing but steely judgment, his face fell to the soundless specter of shame.

Once everyone was seated again, Reza resumed his line of questioning. "You were speaking of the boy-king's weaknesses?"

Tariq inhaled protractedly. "Yes, Uncle."

Reza's frown deepened at Tariq's obvious discomfort. "Tariq-*jan*, what—"

"Shahrzad," Tariq ground out. "He cares about Shahrzad."

Reza's face was expressionless. "A great deal?"

"I don't know. I only know that he cares. And that I wish to take her out of there. Now."

At this, Reza's eyebrows arched. "Did something happen while you were there?"

"Every day she's in that palace, she's at risk. I cannot abide it any longer."

"Such a hero." Omar laughed softly.

Reza raised his glass of tea to his lips and took a sip. "I understand your concern, but—"

"Please, Uncle. Let me do this. Help me."

Reza stared back at his nephew, calm in his assessment. "I'm sorry, Tariq-*jan*, but we are just beginning to gather our strength;

we are nowhere near laying siege to a city like Rey. The Emir of Karaj has pledged seven hundred soldiers, as well as a large cache of weapons. They should be arriving soon. His friend from the north is sending two hundred more, and I am in contact with numerous other friends of mine—men of trade and means—who are weary of being ruled by a cruel tyrant. By a boy-king who kills without reason. They are willing to unite under the banner of the White Falcon. They are willing to fight for you."

"Then, if you would give me a few—"

"No. If all of these men are willing to fight, it must be for something more than your love, Tariq. You cannot march into the biggest city in Khorasan with a fledgling army just to save one girl. Be a true leader. Be still. You must wait. When the time comes, your patience will be manifestly rewarded. Trust me."

Tariq closed his eyes and clenched his fists, fighting to control a rising tide of emotions. "Omar—"

Omar sighed. "Ah, my friend. You do so prey upon my fondness for love stories. Alas, I am an old man without brothers or sons—the last of my line. I will not fight. It is too hard to wash away blood from an old sword. Know that I would gladly risk my lowly life for love. But the lives of my people and those who ride under my name? I cannot risk such a treasure. I'm very sorry, my friend."

Tariq drank his tea in silence as Omar and his uncle moved the discussion along to other matters. Their words drifted around him, echoing in his ears, filtering up into the smoke . . . meaningless. When the tea grew cold, Tariq took his leave. The anger continued roiling within him like the water in the *ghalyan,* and each time he thought of the boy-king, he saw eyes that burned like the coal atop its tower.

A madman with a temper and a penchant for death—

And Shahrzad's face at peace in his arms.

"Tariq-*jan*?" A meek voice called out from behind him.

"What?" Tariq whirled around.

Jahandar backed away, his mouth agape and the ends of his wispy beard curling in the balmy night breeze.

Tariq exhaled with care. "I'm sorry, Jahandar-*effendi*. Forgive me."

Jahandar shook his head. "No, no. I apologize for disturbing your thoughts."

"It's fine." Tariq gritted his teeth. "I should learn to control them better."

Jahandar nodded. He gathered his hands before him, fidgeting with the front of his *tikka* sash.

"Is there something you wish to discuss with me?" Tariq asked.

"Yes." Jahandar swallowed. "Yes, there is." He straightened his shoulders and clasped his hands still. "Are—are you willing to do whatever it takes to save my daughter?"

Tariq's gaze widened. He took a step forward. "You know I am."

Jahandar's eyes shone in the surrounding torchlight.

"Then let me help you."

SOMEONE WHO KNOWS

IT WAS THE MUTED GROAN OF THE DOOR THAT WOKE her. Shahrzad could recognize it, even in her sleep.

But this time, something was different.

Something was in her room. Something brash and unafraid.

Eyes watched her. Unwanted eyes. Tiny pinpricks ran down the back of her neck, and the blood coursed through her body, ignited by fear.

The hush of footfall nearby forced her to make a sudden decision.

Shahrzad opened her eyes and screamed, filling the darkness with sound and shock. Footsteps rushed at her, and she scrambled across the cushions in an effort to escape. She yanked the gossamer aside, cursing its pointless existence.

Her heart clamored in her chest at the sight of Despina's door cracking open across the chamber. "Shahrzad?"

Hulking shadows began to move about her room—shadows cloaked in more than night.

Oh, God. Despina!

Shahrzad grabbed the stool next to her bed and screamed

again, trying to draw them away from her handmaiden. If Despina could make it past the door of the chamber . . .

When a hand reached for Shahrzad, she swung the stool in its direction.

"Shahrzad!" Despina cried.

"Go!" Shahrzad yelled.

Despina rushed for the double doors as two shadows converged on her. She managed to yank one open and race into the marbled hallways of the palace. A single, terror-fueled word echoed in her wake:

"Jalal!"

The shadows descended on Shahrzad, and one seized her from behind. When it pulled her closer, a pair of angry male eyes glittered at her from above a black mask. She pitched the stool at his head. He caught it with a whispered oath and struck her across the cheek with the back of his hand.

Shahrzad reeled to the marble, her eyes tearing at the burgeoning sting. When another shadow tried to haul her to her feet, she reached out and snatched the cloth off his face. He lifted her by the throat and shoved her against the wall.

"Who are you? What do you want?" She kicked and scratched at him.

More footsteps pounded down the corridors outside her room.

Both doors were shoved aside in doleful protest, revealing a lone figure and the silhouette of a sword.

Khalid.

Her captor began to laugh, low and cruel, as he cinched his hold on her neck.

Khalid did not ask questions. He did not try to negotiate. His *shamshir* flashed in the darkness, and a shadow near the door fell with a gurgle and a series of sickening thuds. A moment later, Jalal burst across the threshold with the Rajput on his heels.

"Take Khalid out of here!" Jalal shouted to the Rajput.

With a dismissive shove, the Rajput pushed past Jalal and raised his *talwar.*

Khalid brandished his sword and moved forward. The shadows congregated in his path. There were at least eight of them, including the one pinning her to the wall.

The sound of blades being drawn from their sheaths rippled through the chamber, and the man grasping Shahrzad by the throat pulled her back against him, wrapping a forearm of corded muscle around her neck.

The Rajput engaged the vanguard of shadows, and Khalid and Jalal flanked him on either side. Weapons clashed against one another, metal to metal, and death sliced through the air, leaving behind blood and vengeful wrath.

The shadows were losing.

Shahrzad's captor began dragging her to the open screens leading to the terrace. His hold loosened, and she managed to twist an arm free. She swung a haphazard fist at his face. It caught him in the jaw, and she spun around to bolt. He lunged at her, snagging a shoulder in one hand and the back of her neck in the other.

"I'll kill you for that," he spat in her ear.

"Says a dead man," she rasped.

"Not just yet." He slid his hand from her neck into her hair and coiled his fingers through to the roots, positioning her as a shield before him. Shahrzad bit back a gasp as her eyes began to water.

"Khalid Ibn al-Rashid!" he bellowed.

When her vision cleared, Jalal and the Rajput stood a body's length away, with their weapons at the ready.

Khalid slashed his sword a final time, and the blood of his opponent spewed across his bare chest and face in lines of dark red. Then he crossed the room, his eyes awash with rage, and the silver of his sword dripping crimson.

The marauding shadows were silent and motionless now.

As Khalid stalked closer, the hand in her hair tightened its grasp. Her captor pulled up sharply, and it tore a cry from her lips.

Jalal swore an oath, and the blade of his scimitar gleamed white on a moonbeam.

Khalid halted in his tracks.

Her captor laughed, and it was like stone against metal. With his other hand, he positioned a small dagger to her throat.

"Not a single plea?" he whispered in Shahrzad's ear.

"I don't beg," Shahrzad retorted. "Especially to dead men."

"And the mighty Caliph of Khorasan?" her captor said into the night. "Does the King of Kings have any pleas?"

Again Khalid stalked toward them in brutal silence, raising his *shamshir* across his body.

"Don't move, you bastard son of a whore!" her captor exploded. "Or I'll slice a maggot hole across her throat. You can watch her die, just like your mother."

Khalid froze in time. Then Shahrzad watched his face shatter.

The eyes of molten amber faded to dull memory. Faded to ruin. His raw anguish seared her soul and robbed her of breath. The bloodstained *shamshir* fell to his side.

"I *will* kill you for that," Shahrzad choked over her shoulder.

His laughter was a vicious rumble against her back.

"What do you want?" Khalid asked quietly.

"Drop your weapon."

The *shamshir* struck the marble with a sharp clang. Without the slightest hesitation.

Her captor sneered in triumph. "Tell them to drop their weapons."

"Stop it!" Shahrzad cried.

Look at me, Khalid. Please! Do not listen to this animal.

Her captor withdrew his hand from the back of her head and seized Shahrzad's chin, angling her jaw higher. Pressing his dagger closer.

"Jalal. Vikram. Do as he says." Khalid's voice was heavy. Mired in acceptance.

"Khalid!" Shahrzad despaired. "Don't do this. Jalal, don't listen to him. You can't—"

"Say one more word, and I'll make certain it's your last." He shifted his hand from her chin to her mouth.

Shahrzad bit down on his flesh as hard as she could. The taste of salt and sweat rushed onto her tongue. Her captor bellowed, slackening his hold. She rammed her elbow into his midsection, and his dagger slid back across her throat, leaving behind a white-hot trail. Then a pair of strong arms yanked her aside, pulling her into a bloodstained chest.

Khalid's heart thudded around her, loud and fast. It raced against her cheek, each beat an unspoken promise.

And, for a breath of time, it was enough.

The Rajput slammed her captor to the floor. Jalal shoved a knee into his torso and smashed a jeweled hilt across his jaw.

"In what world did you think you could get away with this?" Jalal seethed. "To my cousin? To *my* family?" His gleaming hilt continued its punishing onslaught.

"Enough!" Khalid pronounced the word with such force, such unmitigated fury, that it stilled all sound within the chamber. He reached down for his *shamshir,* and the blade dragged across the marble in a threatening skirr.

Without further prompting, Jalal stepped back from the man and strode to Shahrzad's side. The Rajput melted into the shadows nearby, his huge hands wrapped around his *talwar,* and his bearded features coldly feral in the moonlight.

Khalid walked forward.

The man was lying on the floor, blood coursing from his mouth and his nose. When he saw Khalid looming above him, he began to laugh in a broken rasp.

Khalid positioned the end of the blade to the man's throat. "She was right. You are a dead man. But I'm willing to discuss degrees of pain."

The man's wheezing laughter grew louder.

"Who sent you?" Khalid continued in a savage whisper.

"Someone who wants to see you suffer."

"Tell me, and I will spare you a measure of the pain you greatly deserve."

The man coughed, and streaks of crimson spurted from his swollen mouth. "Do you think I fear you, boy?"

"I will ask one last time. Then the answer will be torn from your lips."

"You think to thwart the hands of fate? No matter how long you try to fight it, you will pay the price, Khalid Ibn al-Rashid." The man's eyes shot to Shahrzad with irrefutable significance.

"We are now past words." Khalid eased his sword into the man's neck, drawing a thin stream of blood. "In this, I am definitely my father's son."

The man's laughter turned maniacal. "You wish to know who sent me, mighty King of Kings? I'll tell you," he gasped, starting to choke. "*Someone who knows.*"

With that, he dragged his own throat across the edge of the blade.

Jalal grabbed Shahrzad and tucked her face into his shoulder. Her hands shook against him, and he pressed his palm to her cheek in an effort to soothe her.

The Rajput crouched beside her captor's body. He ran his depthless black eyes across the man's motionless form. Then he pulled back the dark sleeve covering the man's right forearm. In the pale light of the moon spilling from the terrace, Shahrzad saw a faint mark seared into his skin: the outline of a scarab.

"A Fida'i dog," the Rajput grumbled like distant thunder.

Khalid regarded the brand in silence before turning away. With a low curse, he heaved his *shamshir* across the room.

"What?" Shahrzad asked Jalal.

"The Fida'is. Hired mercenaries. Assassins."

Shahrzad inhaled sharply, the questions massing at the top of her throat.

Jalal peered at her neck. "My God. You're bleeding." He shoved aside her hair.

Before she had a chance to react, she was lifted off her feet. Khalid dismissed her protests as he carried her away from the carnage, with Jalal and the Rajput following close behind. When they crossed the threshold, the lifeless bodies of the two Royal Guards positioned outside her door stared up at her with glassy eyes. Their throats were slashed to gaping maws. She stifled a gasp.

"They're all dead," Khalid said without looking at her. "Every guard in this corridor is dead."

She tensed her grip around his neck as he continued down the hall. Once they rounded the corner, soldiers burst through the doors, led by General al-Khoury.

"Is she hurt?" the *shahrban* demanded in an urgent voice.

"I'm fine," she replied, momentarily taken aback by his concern. "Really, I am."

"She's wounded," Jalal clarified.

"It's not bad," Shahrzad countered. "Put me down. I can walk."

Khalid ignored her.

"I can walk, Khalid."

Again, he refused to look at her, much less respond.

They moved down the hallways with guards lighting their path, encircling them in a gleaming bastion of steel and torchfire. Deciding to cede this particular battle, Shahrzad leaned against

Khalid, closing her eyes to the glare for an instant, and his hold on her tightened.

They turned down another, smaller corridor Shahrzad had never seen before. It was lined in stone with an arched ceiling of smooth alabaster. Soon they halted before a set of double doors made of polished ebony, hinged in bronze and iron.

"Guards are to stand post here and at the doors leading to my chamber until further notice," Khalid commanded. "Be advised—if there is the slightest breach at either entrance, you will answer to me."

A guard nodded briskly before pulling on one of the bronze handles. Khalid walked through the huge, ebony doorway with Shahrzad in his arms. He did not put her down. Instead, he crossed a pitch-black antechamber to another set of doors identical to the first. Once they passed this threshold, they entered a vast room with a vaulted ceiling lit in its center by a single lamp of latticed gold. Khalid set Shahrzad on the edge of a platformed bed covered in dull silk. Then he strode to an immense ebony cabinet positioned against the back wall, where he removed strips of spun linen and a small, round container before collecting a pitcher from atop his desk.

He knelt before Shahrzad and brushed her hair over her shoulder to look at the wound.

"I told you," Shahrzad said. "It's not bad. It can't be much worse than a scratch."

Khalid poured water from the pitcher onto a strip of linen. He lifted it to her neck and began cleaning the wound.

Shahrzad studied his face as he worked. The dark circles

beneath his eyes were even more pronounced now. Lines of dried blood ran across his cheek and brow, marring his sun-bronzed skin. His features were set on edge, and he refused to meet her gaze. The angles of his profile remained obdurate. Unyielding. Like the edges of a rumpled scroll, demanding to be smoothed . . . or cast aside, once and for all.

When he dampened another piece of linen, Shahrzad placed her hand over his and removed the cloth from his grasp. She raised the strip to his face and wiped at the dark blood of his enemy.

Khalid's tiger-eyes finally fell to hers. They roved across her in poignant silence as she washed away the remnants of death with steady, graceful fingers. Then he leaned forward, pressing his brow to hers, catching her hands in his. Stilling them both.

"I want to send you away. To a place where none of this can touch you," he began.

Her heart shuddered, and she pulled back. "Send me away? As if I were a thing?"

"No. That's not what I meant."

"What did you mean, then?"

"I meant that I cannot keep you safe. From anything."

"And your answer to that is to send me away?" Shahrzad repeated in a dangerous whisper.

"My answer is not an answer. It is a willingness to do whatever it takes—even something as distasteful as sending you from my side."

"And you expect me to obey? To go wherever you command?"

"I expect you to trust me."

Shahrzad narrowed her eyes. "You should know I will not take kindly to you treating me like a possession."

"I have never treated you like a possession, Shahrzad."

"Until you spoke of sending me away."

Khalid shifted his hands to her sides. "You're my wife. They are hurting you because of me."

"They? Do you mean the Fida'is?" She hesitated. "Who are they? To whom do they pledge loyalty?"

"To whoever can pay their price. Loyalty ebbs and flows with the tide; gold does not. The men who hire them have little to offer beyond that."

"And you think it will help if you yield to such men?"

"I don't care what they think as long as you're safe."

"You should care. It's time to start caring. You cannot continue to rule this kingdom in such a callous manner."

He smiled, bitter and unamused. "You speak as though you understand. As though you know."

"You're right. I understand nothing. I know nothing. And whose fault is that?" Shahrzad pushed against his bare chest and stood from the bed, walking past him.

"I've told you why." Khalid rose to his feet. "It is not safe for you to know these things. To know—"

"To know what?" She spun around to face him. "To know you? As if I could ever hope to achieve such a thing. Yet, like a fool, I've wanted to learn. To understand what pains you, what brings you joy. But I remain ignorant of even the most trivial of things. I don't know your favorite color. What foods you detest.

What scent brings to mind a treasured memory. I know nothing, because you fight me every step of the way."

He watched her as she spoke, his features careful, his composure deliberate, though his eyes revealed a deeper conflict he no longer fought to conceal.

"I don't know what you want from me, Shahrzad. I only know I can't give it. Not now."

"It does not have to be so difficult, Khalid-*jan*. My favorite color is violet. The scent of roses makes me feel at home, wherever I am. I do not enjoy fish, but will eat it to make a loved one happy, suffering through my smiles."

He remained stone-faced, the conflict in his eyes warring on.

With a beleaguered sigh, she turned and strode to the entrance. "Good night."

Khalid was beside her in a few long strides, pressing his hand to the ebony door. Preventing her from leaving.

"What do you want me to do?" he said in a low voice.

She did not look up, though her heart thrummed in her throat. "Prove that a real man doesn't make a show of what's his. It just is."

"Is it? Are you mine?" Khalid asked with quiet solemnity.

Her conviction wavered further. "I told you; don't try to own me."

"I don't want to own you."

She swiveled her neck to meet his gaze. "Then never speak of sending me away again. I am not yours to do with as you will."

Khalid's features smoothed knowingly. "How right you are.

You are not mine." He dropped his palm from the door. "I am yours."

Shahrzad curled her fingers tight, forcing herself to recall a time when she meant nothing to him. A time when he meant less than nothing to her, and all that mattered was blood for blood.

Alas, she no longer saw the same boy before her. Just light amidst a sea of darkness, and the unerring promise of something more. But she never saw the things she should see. The pain, the anger, the betrayal. These things always faded, and she despised herself for it.

Before she could stop her hands, they reached for him, as though they existed for no other reason than to touch him. Her fingers brushed across his jaw with a feather's caress before pulling away, and he closed his eyes on a soft inhale. Like the poison toying with its remedy, Shahrzad's hands ignored her and took control, a mere taste of his skin not nearly enough. Never enough. They began at his brow and eased their way to his temples before sliding into his hair, smooth as silk, dark as night. She watched his eyes open and turn from liquid to fire under her fingers. Shahrzad ran her palms down to his neck, where she paused.

"Why won't you touch me?" she whispered.

It took him a moment to reply. "Because if I start, I won't stop."

"Who asked you to stop?" Her fingers traveled to his chest.

"What if I can't give you the answers you want?"

Again, she returned to nothing.

Yet there, in the warmth of his eyes, was everything.

"Then give me this." Shahrzad stood on her toes and brought

her mouth to his. When he did not respond, she curved her tongue against his lower lip, and his hands drew across her waist in a slow burn. She thought he would push her away, but he dragged her against him. Khalid kissed her, melding nothing to everything. Shahrzad wrapped both arms around his neck, and he backed her into the ebony door until she was braced up against it, each of their breaths matched, measure for measure, beat for beat.

"Khalid." She gripped his shoulders as his lips brushed the delicate skin beneath her chin. Her heart was pounding so loud that she did not at first recognize the noise at the door.

"*Sayyidi.*"

"Khalid," she repeated, catching his wrists.

He swore softly. Then he reached for the bronze handle.

"Yes." His reply was low and irascible.

The guard bowed through the crack in the door.

"The *shahrban* wishes to speak with you. Captain al-Khoury may have determined how the intruders gained entry into the palace."

Khalid nodded curtly as he shut the door. He ran his palm along the side of his jaw before turning to Shahrzad once more.

She was leaning against the ebony with her hands clasped behind her back.

"Go," she said softly.

He paused in thoughtful scrutiny. "I—"

"Don't worry. I'll stay here."

"Thank you." As he reached for the handle again, he lingered and smiled to himself.

Her brows drew together. "What is it?"

"It's a fitting punishment for a monster. To want something so much—to hold it in your arms—and know beyond a doubt you will never deserve it." Khalid pulled open the door and stepped over the threshold without waiting for a response.

Shahrzad slid to the floor. The hands that had appeared steady against him now shook before her face. Proof that she was being equally punished for her own transgressions. Punished for desiring a monster.

She offered silent thanks to the stars that dealt in fate—for her monster did not seem to know how all reason had left her for the space of a breath.

How the guilt crashed down around her.

And how the questions burdened her soul.

"Someone who knows."

A SHADE OF WHAT I FEEL

SHAHRZAD REMAINED IN THE WASTELAND OF HER thoughts, studying the prisms of light from the lamp of latticed gold. When she could no longer feel any sensation in the soles of her feet, she rose to a standing position. Her eyes wandered around the room, taking in her surroundings with the careful study of a predator to its prey.

The floor was constructed of black onyx, and the walls were hewn from the same smooth alabaster as the corridor leading to the entrance of the antechamber. All the furniture was built of ebony, crafted in harsh lines. Every surface was stark and unobstructed. The bed lacked the bold surfeit of cushions Shahrzad had grown accustomed to in her own bed—that familiar, lush vibrancy, yearning to be lounged upon.

Like its occupant, the room appeared cold and uninviting—unlikely to offer the slightest hint of clarity.

This chamber is like a prison, once removed.

She sighed to herself, and the sound susurrated back at her from the heights of the vaulted ceiling. Shahrzad paced around the perimeter of the room, her bare footsteps leaving imprints on the shining black onyx. Then, like a whisper of a suggestion, they vanished without a trace.

The single lamp in the chamber's center looked eerie and forlorn. It failed to provide enough light, rendering its flickering shadows more baleful than beautiful against the cool white alabaster.

It was a sad place to call a refuge, with just as unyielding an aspect as its master.

The more Shahrzad gazed at the chamber, the more she realized, and the less she understood. Everything had a specific place in this room—a designated order to its existence. The only things out of place were she and the bloodstained strips of linen at the edge of the platformed bed. Any evidence of life—or lingering emotions—did not belong.

Shahrzad strode to the bed and discarded the bloodied linen. Then she gathered the unused strips, along with the small container of salve Khalid had removed from the ebony chest upon their arrival. Its immense cabinet door was still ajar. Shahrzad walked toward it with the clean linen and the tub of salve in her arms. She tugged on one of the bronze rings and peered inside. As with the room, its shelves were meticulous in their construction and organization. Two were lined with books in descending height order, and another was stacked with scrolls bound by wax seals. A shelf at eye level contained an assortment of jars in various shapes and sizes. The empty space for the container of salve was evident, and Shahrzad replaced it, along with the strips of unused linen, in their clearly demarcated positions.

As she began to shut the door, her eyes fell on a leather sleeve

filled with sheets of parchment, wedged like an afterthought between two massive tomes on a shelf high above her.

It seemed out of place. Just like her.

A small part of her knew she should leave it be. This was not
her room. These were not her things.

But . . . it called to her. This collection of afterthoughts whispered her name, as if from behind a locked door with a forbidden
key. Shahrzad stared up at the sleeve of leather.

As with Tala and her bluebearded husband's ring of keys, the
parchment pleaded for attention.

And, like Tala, she could not ignore it.

She had to know.

Shahrzad stood on her toes and tugged on the leather sleeve
with both hands. It slid from between the tomes, and she
clutched it to her chest for a nervous beat before kneeling against
the black onyx. Cold fear skittered down her back as she raised
the fold. The sheaf of parchment was inverted and illegible, so she
grabbed the stack and upended it with care.

The first thing she noticed at the bottom was Khalid's formal
signature, composed in clear, neat script. When her eyes skimmed
across the rest of the page, she rapidly discerned it was a letter—

A letter of apology, addressed to a family in Rey.

Shahrzad turned to the next piece of parchment.

It was another letter of apology. Written to another family.

As she leafed through the stack of parchment, her eyes began
to swim in realization. In recognition.

These were letters of apology to the families of the girls murdered at dawn by a callous hand and a silk cord.

Each was dated. Each acknowledged Khalid's sole responsibility. None offered any justification for the death. No excuse.

He merely apologized. In a manner so open and full of feeling that it left her throat dry and her chest aching.

It was clear they were written with no intention of being delivered. Khalid's words were far too personal and introspective to indicate he ever meant for any eyes to see them apart from his own. But his unabashed self-loathing cut into Shahrzad with the effectiveness of a newly honed knife.

He wrote of staring into frightened faces and tearful eyes, with the abject knowledge he was robbing families of their joy. Stealing their hearts' blood from them, as though he had the right. As if anyone had the right.

Your child is not a notion or a whim. Your child is your greatest treasure. And you should never forgive me for what I've done. As I will never forgive myself.

Know that she was not afraid. When she gazed at the face of the monster sanctioning her death, she did not quail. Would that I had half her courage and a quarter of her spirit.

Last night, Roya asked for a santur. Her playing drew every guard in the corridor to her door, and I stood in the garden and listened, like the cold, unfeeling bastard I am. It was the most beautiful music I have ever heard in my life. A music that rendered all thereafter dull and colorless in its memory.

Tears began streaming down Shahrzad's face. She turned the pages faster.

Until she found the one addressed to the family of Reza bin-Latief.

How does one begin to apologize for robbing the world of light? Words seem strangely insufficient in such a case, and yet I fall to their uselessness in my own inadequacy. Please know I will never forget Shiva. For the brief moment she stared into the face of a monster, she deigned to smile and forgive. In that smile, I sensed a strength and a depth of understanding I could never hope to fathom. It tore at what professes to be my soul. I'm sorry, I'm sorry, I'm sorry. A thousand, thousand times. At your knees, and it will never be enough.

Shahrzad sobbed, and the sound rang out in the chamber. The parchment shook in her hands.

Khalid was responsible. Whatever the excuse, whatever the reason—he was the one. He had killed Shiva.

He had robbed Shahrzad of this light.

She had known it, all along. But now, clutching the undeniable truth between her fingers, she realized how much she had wanted it to be a lie. How much she had wanted there to be some kind of excuse. Some kind of ready scapegoat. That, somewhere along the line, she would discover it was not his fault.

Even now she knew how ridiculous it sounded.

But it was breaking her . . . slowly. The wall around her heart was crumbling, leaving behind scorched embers and bleeding wounds. Her sobs grew louder. Shahrzad wanted to hurl the leather sleeve across the room, shred its contents, and deny its pernicious truths, but she lifted the next page. And the next.

So many.

And not a single explanation.

She continued scanning the parchment, searching for a semblance of purpose behind such senseless death. Clinging to this thread of hope, she labored on.

Until finally, her eyes fell on the last page, and her heart faltered.

It was addressed to her, dated for that fateful sunrise with the silk cord.

Shahrzad,

I've failed you several times. But there was one moment I failed you beyond measure. It was the day we met. The moment I took your hand and you looked up at me, with the glory of hate in your eyes. I should have sent you home to your family. But I didn't. There was honesty in your hatred. Fearlessness in your pain. In your honesty, I saw a reflection of myself. Or rather, of the man I longed to be. So I failed you. I didn't stay away. Then, later, I thought if I had answers, it would be enough. I would no longer care. You would no longer matter. So I continued failing you. Continued wanting more. And now I can't find the words to say what must be said. To convey to you the least of what I owe. When I think of you, I can't find the air to

The letter stopped short there.

Shahrzad puzzled over it for the span of a heartbeat.

Then a conversation from their past echoed around her, like a song from a distant memory:

"And how will you know when you've found this elusive someone?"

"I suspect she will be like air. Like knowing how to breathe."

The letter drifted to the floor, back to its scattered brethren. Everything around Shahrzad fell to shadow and silence. To the bitterness of knowledge and the brilliance of understanding.

In a rush, she was taken back to that awful dawn and the feel of the silk cord around her neck. She forced herself to recall each part of it—the silver light as it crept across the blue blades of grass, the mist in the early morning sun, the penitent soldier with the burly arms, and the old woman with the fluttering shroud. The fear. The anguish. The nothingness. But now, as she closed her eyes, her mind conjured a parallel world of sorrow—of a boy-king at his ebony desk writing a letter to a dying girl, with the sun ascending at his shoulder. Of this boy halting in unexpected awareness, with his hand poised over the parchment. Of him racing down the corridors, with his cousin at his heels. Bursting into a courtyard of silver and grey, punctuated by black ink and burning agony—

Wondering if he was too late.

Swallowing a tortured scream, Shahrzad threw the sleeve and its contents across the shining onyx.

Her own awareness had risen like the dawn at her back. Like a leaden sunrise veiled in a swirl of storm clouds. It was no longer enough to have answers for Shiva's sake. Indeed, it had ceased to be about mere vengeance the moment Khalid's lips touched hers in the alley by the souk. She had wanted there to be a reason for this madness, needed there to be a reason, so that she could be with him. So that she could be by his side, make him smile as she laughed, weave tales by lamplight, and share secrets in the dark. So that she could fall asleep in his arms and awaken to a brilliant tomorrow.

But it was too late.

He was the Mehrdad of her nightmares. She had opened the door. She had seen the bodies hanging from the walls, without explanation. Without justification.

And without one, Shahrzad knew what must be done.

Khalid had to answer for such vile deeds. Such rampant death.

Even if he was her air.

Even if she loved him beyond words.

His guards were on edge and much too close.

Their glaring torches and clattering footfall were not doing service to the torturous ache in his head. Nor were they of benefit to the fire that battled for dominion over his eyes.

When a nervous sentry dropped his sword with a noise to rouse the dead, it took all of Khalid's willpower not to snap the young man's arm from his shoulder.

Instead, Khalid paused in the darkened corridor and pressed his palms to his brows.

"Leave," he grumbled to his guards.

"*Sayyidi*—"

"Leave!" Khalid's temples pounded as the word reverberated down the halls.

The guards glanced at one another before bowing and taking their leave.

Jalal remained against the wall in somber watchfulness.

"That was rather childish," he chastised, once the soldiers had turned the corner.

"You are free to leave, as well." Khalid resumed his trek toward his chamber.

Jalal cut in front of Khalid. "You look terrible." His eyes were bright, and his forehead was lined with worry.

Khalid stared back at him, calm and aloof. "I suppose you expect me to confide in you, following your honest assessment of a rather obvious condition. Forgive me, but I've had a trying evening, Captain al-Khoury."

"I'm truly concerned."

Khalid feigned bemusement. "Don't be."

"If you refuse to talk about what happened tonight, I must continue to press the matter."

"And you will be met with disappointment at every turn."

"No. I won't." Jalal folded his arms across his chest. "You are a disaster. You flinch at the slightest noise, and you nearly ripped that poor boy's head off for dropping his sword."

"The boy was stumbling about, wielding an unsheathed blade. I find it fortunate he didn't trip and impale himself on the cold steel of his own stupidity."

"Your sarcasm gets more brutal with age. And with arrogance. It's not nearly as entertaining now."

Khalid glowered at his cousin. The blood pulsed along his neck and thrummed in his temples. Each beat blurred the lines of his vision.

He shoved past Jalal.

"What were you doing tonight, *sayyidi*?" Jalal called after him. "Do you realize you put our entire kingdom at risk when you discarded your weapon at that hired dog's behest. He could have killed you, and you would have left Khorasan without a ruler. You would have allowed Salim's mercenaries to leave us leaderless, on the brink of potential war with Parthia." He paused pointedly. "All for the sake of a girl—one of so many."

At that, the frayed strands of Khalid's composure tore apart, and he turned the full force of his fury onto Jalal, whirling around and freeing his *shamshir* from its scabbard in a single, fluid motion. He raised the curved edge of the blade until it was positioned a hairsbreadth from Jalal's heart.

Jalal stood still, his serenity at odds with the situation. "You must love her a great deal, Khalid-*jan.*"

After a beat, Khalid lowered his sword, his brow marred by pain and consternation. "Love is—a shade of what I feel."

Jalal grinned, but it did not reach his eyes. "As your cousin, I'm glad to hear it. But, as the captain of your guard, I would be lying if I told you I wasn't alarmed by tonight's events. You are not responsible to only one girl."

"I'm aware of that." Khalid sheathed his sword.

"I'm not so certain you are. If you plan on behaving is such a heedless fashion, I think it's time to tell Shahrzad the truth."

"I disagree; therefore, this discussion is over." Khalid strode down the corridor once more, and Jalal walked at his side.

"She's family now. If you are willing to die for her, then it's time we entrust her with our secret," Jalal pressed in a quiet voice.

"No."

He reached for Khalid's shoulder. "Tell her, Khalid-*jan*. She has a right to know."

"And how would you react to such news?" Khalid shoved his hand aside. "To the knowledge your life hovers on a precipice, bound by a mutable curse?"

"My life is at risk every day. As is yours. Something tells me Shazi does not live in a world that denies this fact."

Khalid's eyebrows flattened. "It doesn't matter. I'm not ready to tell her."

"And you never will be. Because you love her, and we fight to protect those we love." Jalal halted by the corridor leading to Khalid's chamber, and Khalid advanced down the marble and stone without a glance in his direction.

"*Sayyidi*?" Jalal continued from behind him. "Make sure you summon the *faqir* tonight. You are a bowstring ready to snap."

Khalid shoved past the first set of doors into the antechamber and moved toward the entrance of his room. He paused before nodding to one of the guards, who twisted one of the bronze handles and pushed open the polished wood.

Upon crossing the threshold, Khalid found the room completely silent. Utterly still. The only things amiss were the
bloodied strips of linen and the pitcher of water beside the raised
platform—

And the girl asleep in his bed.

Shahrzad lay on her side. Her dark hair was splayed across
dull silk, and her knees were tucked against the lone cushion on
Khalid's bed. A fringe of black lashes curved against the skin beneath her eyes, and her proud, pointed chin was tucked into a
gathering of silk beside her palm.

Khalid sat down with care and refrained from looking at her
for too long. Touching her was not an option.

She was a dangerous, dangerous girl. A plague. A Mountain
of Adamant who tore the iron from ships, sinking them to their
watery graves without a second thought. With a mere smile and
a wrinkle of her nose.

But even knowing this, he surrendered to her pull. Succumbed
to the simple need to be by her side. With a slow exhalation of
breath, Khalid placed his *shamshir* on the floor and eased his body
next to hers. He stared up at the ceiling, at the single flame in the
golden lamp above his head. Even the dim light shining from its
depths pained his eyes. He shuttered his gaze, trying to push past
the weariness and the ever-present torment of the chained beast
roaring inside his head.

Shahrzad shifted in her sleep and turned toward Khalid, as
though drawn by her own inexplicable compulsion. Her hand fell
to his chest, and she settled her brow beside his shoulder with a
muted sigh.

Against his better judgment, Khalid opened his burning eyes to look at her one more time.

This dangerous girl. This captivating beauty.

This destroyer of worlds and creator of wonder.

The urge to touch her now past logic, Khalid's arm moved to encircle her in an embrace. He buried his nose in her hair, in the same scent of lilacs that taunted him from outside his window. The small, graceful hand on his chest drifted higher, beside his heart.

Whatever torment he had to endure. Whatever evil he had to face.

There was nothing that mattered more.

Then he heard a noise in the far corner of the room.

He blinked hard, trying to refocus. His muscles tensed with heightened awareness when a flash of movement blurred across his vision. Khalid squeezed his eyes shut, fighting to clear the lines, fighting to see through the layers of fog and shadow. The pain between his brows grew as his pulse rose to meet the unforeseen challenge.

Another blur of motion flitted across the room, this time in the opposite corner.

Khalid removed his arm from around Shahrzad and reached for the pitcher of water by the platform.

When a new flash of movement caught his attention beside his desk, Khalid heaved the pitcher in its direction and shot to his feet, his *shamshir* in hand.

The sound of the pitcher shattering against the ebony woke Shahrzad, and she sat up with a startled cry.

"Khalid? What's wrong?"

Khalid said nothing as he regarded the stillness around his desk. He blinked again. Hard. His eyes blazed with the fire of a thousand suns. He pressed a palm between his brows and gritted his teeth.

Shahrzad rose from the bed and strode to his side. "Are you— hurt?"

"No. Go back to sleep." It sounded needlessly cruel, even to him.

"You're lying to me." She reached up and wrapped soft fingers around his wrist. "What's wrong?"

"Nothing." Again, his pain lanced through the word, making his response more abrupt than he intended.

She tugged on his arm. "Liar."

"Shahrzad—"

"No. Tell me the truth, or I'm leaving your chamber."

Khalid remained silent, the beast in his head roaring with untold vigor.

Shahrzad choked back a sob. "Again. And again." She spun on her heel and glided toward the ebony doors.

"Stop!" Khalid tried to go after her, but his head throbbed and his sight distorted to such a degree that following her was impossible. With an incoherent slur, Khalid dropped his *shamshir* and sank to his knees, his palms clutching either side of his head.

"Khalid!" Shahrzad gasped. She ran back and crouched beside him. "What is it?"

He could not respond.

Khalid heard her race to the doors and yank one open.

"My lady?" a guard inquired.

"Find Captain—no, General al-Khoury," Shahrzad insisted.

"Right away."

She waited by the door until a soft knock struck a short while later.

"My lady Shahrzad," his uncle began. "Is everything—"

"His head. Please. He's—in a lot of pain." The sound of fear in her voice unnerved Khalid. More than he cared to admit.

"Stay with him. I'll return shortly."

The door closed.

Shahrzad returned to his side. Khalid leaned back against the edge of his bed and braced his elbows on his knees, pressing both palms to his forehead with enough force to paint stars across his vision.

When the door opened once more, Shahrzad stiffened. He felt her draw closer in wary protectiveness.

"*Sayyidi.*" The voice of the *faqir* echoed from above him.

Khalid sighed, his eyes still squeezed shut.

"My lady," his uncle said. "Please come with me."

Her body tensed even further, gearing for battle. "I—"

"Shahrzad-*jan,*" his uncle interjected very gently. "Please."

"No," Khalid rasped. He reached out a hand for her. "She stays."

"Khalid-*jan*—"

Khalid forced opened his screaming eyes and stared up at his uncle.

"My wife stays."

AVA

SHAHRZAD DID NOT KNOW WHAT TO MAKE OF THE scene unfolding before her.

The strange old man garbed in white did not walk with the gait of a normal person. He did not blink, nor did he appear to breathe.

And he was studying her with such piercing intent that it twisted her stomach into a coil of knots.

"*Sayyidi,*" the strange man repeated, shifting closer to Khalid.

Without a word, Khalid bowed his head. The man raised his palms beside Khalid's temples. Then he closed his eyes. Shahrzad felt the air in the room still. A peculiar sensation settled around her heart, sliding chills down her back.

When the strange man opened his eyes once more, they glowed white, like the blinding center of a flame. Between his hands, a warm, red-orange fireburst spread around the entirety of Khalid's brow.

The peculiar feeling in her chest flared, and Shahrzad smothered a gasp. It reminded her of that afternoon last week . . . with the floating carpet.

The circle of light around Khalid's head pulsed yellow, flashing brighter before spiraling up into the darkness. Then it retracted back into the old man's clawed hands.

And the sensation around her heart disappeared.

Khalid exhaled carefully. His shoulders rolled forward, and the tension began easing from his body.

"Thank you," he whispered to the man, his voice parched and raw.

Shahrzad gazed up at this strange wielder of magic. Again, he was staring down at her with an oddly discerning expression.

"Thank you," Shahrzad reiterated, at a loss.

The old man frowned, his unblinking eyes awash with discomfort. "*Sayyidi*—"

"Your counsel is always appreciated. I'm aware of your concerns," Khalid interrupted in a quiet tone.

The old man paused. "It's getting worse. And it will only continue to progress in this fashion."

"Again, I understand."

"Forgive my insolence, *sayyidi,* but you do not. I warned you before, and now my worst fears are coming to fruition. You cannot maintain this farce for much longer. If you do not find a way to sleep—"

"Please." Khalid rose to his feet.

The old man drifted back and bowed with preternatural grace.

"Again, I thank you." Khalid returned the bow and raised his hand to his forehead in respect.

"Do not thank me, *sayyidi,*" the old man replied as he floated to the ebony doors. "My service is to the hope for a great king.

See that you grant him the chance to prove me right." He grasped a bronze handle, stopping to glance at Shahrzad once more before disappearing into the darkness, leaving them alone.

Khalid eased onto the edge of the bed, his eyes bloodshot and his features holding fast to traces of strain.

Shahrzad sat down next to him. She said nothing for a time, and the air grew thick, laden with their unspoken thoughts.

Then he turned his head toward her. "Before—"

"You can't sleep?" she interjected in a small voice.

He inhaled through his nose. "No."

"Why?"

Khalid bent forward, his black hair grazing his forehead.

She reached for his hand. "Tell me."

He peered sideways at her, and his look of misery robbed her of breath.

Shahrzad wrapped both her hands around one of his. "Please, Khalid."

He nodded once. "Before I start, I need you to know how sorry I am."

Her pulse wavered. "For what?"

"For everything. But mostly for what I'm about to tell you."

"I don't—"

"It's a burden, Shazi," he said in a hoarse whisper. "This secret is an encumbrance I never wanted for you. Once you know it, it can't be taken back. Whatever happens, its cold certainty will remain with you. The fear, the worry, the guilt—they become yours."

Shahrzad inhaled carefully. "I won't say I understand, because

I don't. But if it's your burden—if it causes you to suffer—I wish to know."

Khalid studied the stretch of black onyx before him. "Her name was Ava."

"Ava?"

"My first wife. I married her not long after I turned seventeen. It was an arranged marriage. One I arranged to avoid what I considered a far worse fate. How wrong I was."

Khalid laced his fingers through hers.

"I was never meant to rule Khorasan. My brother, Hassan, was raised to take the throne. When he died in battle, it was too late for my father to rectify the years he had spent punishing me for my mother's perceived transgressions. There was no relationship between us—nothing but memories of blood and dreams of retribution. Upon his death, I was as unprepared to rule as any boy filled with hate would be. As you once said—I was predictable. Predictably angry. Predictably jaded."

Shahrzad watched Khalid's weary eyes fade in recollection.

"I was also determined to be everything my father despised in a king. Before he died, he had wanted me to marry Yasmine— to unite the kingdoms of Khorasan and Parthia. Following his death, his advisors continued to push for the match. Even Uncle Aref felt it was a wise, albeit unfortunate, decision. I was adamant in my refusal—to the point where I dismissed my father's remaining advisors and sought my own counsel."

Shahrzad's features tightened. "You despise Yasmine that much?"

Khalid shook his head. "Yasmine is not without her merits,

but I never felt real affection for her. More than that, I could not willingly join my family with that of Salim Ali el-Sharif. When my mother was alive, he treated her like a rich man's whore, and he never failed to exploit any opportunity to speak ill of her after her death. Even as a boy, I remember longing for the day when I would be strong enough to punish him for the things he said." A corner of his lips quirked upward in bitter amusement.

"Revenge isn't what you expected, is it?" Shahrzad asked quietly.

"No. It's not. And it never will be. Revenge won't replace what I've lost."

Shahrzad swallowed, looking away. "Salim must have been very angry about your refusal to marry Yasmine."

"I never refused. It never went that far. When the pressure to marry Yasmine grew—to embolden the ties between our kingdoms and solidify my weak stance as a young caliph—I decided the best way to avoid the insult of an outright refusal was to marry someone else. Ava was from a good family in Rey, and she was kind and smart. Once we were married, I tried to be attentive, but it was difficult. I still had many things to learn about being a king, and I didn't know how to be a husband. Like me, Ava was not the type to readily share her thoughts and feelings, and the moments we spent with each other often drifted to silence. She started to grow distant . . . and sad. Yet I still did not invest the time necessary to learn the reasons. After a few months of marriage, she had withdrawn a great deal, and our interaction was rather limited. In truth, the awkwardness made me even less inclined to seek her out. On the rare occasions I tried to speak with her, she always appeared elsewhere—lost in a world I never sought to understand."

His face had become more worn and haggard as he spoke.

"Everything changed when Ava found out she was pregnant. Her entire demeanor shifted. She began to smile again. Began planning for a future. I thought all would be well and, like a fool, I was glad for it."

Khalid closed his eyes for a moment before he continued.

"We lost the baby a few weeks later. Ava was inconsolable. She stayed in her room for days on end, eating only enough to survive. I would visit her, and she would refuse to speak with me. But she was never angry. Always just sad, with eyes that tore at my soul. One night when I came to see her, she finally sat up in bed and engaged me in conversation. She asked me if I loved her. I nodded because I couldn't bring myself to lie outright. Then she asked me to say it. Just once, because I'd never said it. Her eyes were destroying me—such dark wells of sadness. So I lied. I said the words . . . and she smiled at me."

He shuddered, pressing their joined hands to his forehead.

"It was the last thing I ever said to her. A lie. The worst kind of lie—the kind shrouded in good intentions. The kind cowards use to justify their weakness. I didn't sleep well that night. Something about our exchange unnerved me. The next morning, I went to her room. When no one answered the door, I pushed it open. Her bed was empty. I called out for her, and still I heard nothing."

Khalid paused, his features caught in a storm of remembrance.

"I found her on her balcony with a silk cord about her throat.

She was cold and alone. Gone. I don't remember much else about that morning. All I could think was how she'd died alone, with no one to offer her solace, no one to grant her comfort. No one who cared. Not even her husband."

Shahrzad's eyes burned with unshed tears.

"After we laid her to rest, I received an invitation from her father to meet at his home. Out of guilt and a desire to show her family a measure of respect, I went to see him, against the counsel of those around me. They did not know what her father could possibly want to discuss with me in private. But I dismissed their concerns." Khalid took a deep breath. "Though they were right to have them."

He withdrew his hand from hers and fell to silence.

"Khalid—"

"One hundred lives for the one you took. One life to one dawn. Should you fail but a single morn, I shall take from you your dreams. I shall take from you your city. And I shall take from you these lives, a thousandfold."

Shahrzad listened to him recite these words from memory, his eyes adrift in their meaning.

And realization crashed down on her, like lightning to a crag on a mountaintop.

"A curse?" she whispered. "Ava's father—cursed you?"

"He gave his life to this curse. Before my eyes, he ran a dagger through his heart, paying for the magic with his own blood. To punish me for what I had done to his daughter. For my rampant disregard of his greatest treasure. He wanted to make sure that others would know his pain. That others would despise me as he did. He ordered me to destroy the lives of one hundred families in Rey. To marry their daughters and offer them to the dawn, just like Ava. To take away their promise of a future. And leave them without answers. Without hope. With nothing but hate to keep them alive."

Shahrzad brushed away the hot tears coursing down her cheeks.

Shiva.

"I refused to comply at first. Even after we realized he'd sold his soul to the darkest magic to enact this curse, even after nights without sleep, I couldn't do it. I couldn't begin such a cycle of death and destruction. Then the rains ceased. The wells dried up. And the riverbeds vanished. The people of Rey fell to sickness and starvation. They started to die. And I began to understand."

"I shall take from you your city," Shahrzad murmured, recalling the devastating drought that had destroyed the crops during the last harvesting season.

He nodded. "And I shall take from you these lives, a thousand-fold."

Here it was. At long last. An explanation.

A reason for such senseless death.

Why do I not feel any better?

Shahrzad studied Khalid's profile in the dim light of the lamp above as he continued staring at the floor.

"How many dawns are left?" she asked.

"Not many."

"And what if—what if we fail to comply?"

"I don't know." His posture indicated an invisible weight and its foregone conclusion.

"But—it rained. It's rained several times in the two months I've been at the palace. Perhaps the curse has weakened."

He turned to look at her with a sad half smile. "If that is the case, there is little else I would ask of heaven."

A gnawing sense of awareness began to tug at her core. "Khalid, what if—"

"No. Do not ask what you are about to ask." His voice was harsh and laced with warning.

Her heart tripped about in her chest, matching pace with her newfound fear. "Then you have not even considered—"

"No. I will not consider it." He reached for her with both hands, framing her chin between his palms. "There is no situation in which I will consider it."

She shook her head, though her shoulders trembled and her nails dug into her palms. "You are ridiculous, Khalid Ibn al-Rashid. I am just one girl. You are the Caliph of Khorasan, and you have a responsibility to a kingdom."

"If you are just one girl, I am just one boy."

Shahrzad closed her eyes, unable to hold the fierce light in his gaze.

"Did you hear what I said, Shahrzad al-Khayzuran?"

When she refused to respond, she felt his lips brush across her forehead.

"Look at me," Khalid said, so soft and so close that it washed across her skin in warm assurances and cool desperation.

She opened her eyes.

He rested his brow against hers. "Just one boy and one girl."

Shahrzad forced a pained smile. "If that is the case, there is little else I would ask of heaven."

Khalid pulled her back against the cushion and wrapped his arms around her. She pressed her cheek to his chest.

And they held each other in stillness until a silver dawn broke across the horizon.

OBLIVION

K HALID STUDIED THE PLANS LAID OUT ON THE DESK before him.

The new system of aqueducts directing freshwater from a nearby lake into the city's underground cisterns would be a costly, time-consuming endeavor. His advisors had counseled against such an undertaking for these and a slew of other reasons.

Understandable.

As they were not concerned about an impending drought.

Khalid ran his hand across the parchment, scanning the carefully wrought lines and meticulous lettering of Rey's brightest scholars and engineers.

Such great minds at his disposal. Such vast intelligence at his fingertips.

He was the Caliph of Khorasan. The supposed King of Kings. He commanded a renowned force of soldiers and, for twelve years, he'd trained with some of the best warriors in the kingdom. Twelve years spent honing his craft to become one of the finest swordsmen in Rey. Many considered him a sound strategist as well.

Yet, with all these seeming attributes, he was still powerless to protect what mattered—

His people.

His queen.

He could not reconcile the two. Not without a sacrifice beyond the scope of consideration.

Khalid reflected on the consequences of such selfish behavior. How his unwillingness to consider the life of one girl against so many others would be construed. Would be judged.

Many young girls had already given their lives to this curse. Had died because of Khalid's failure to notice the profound suffering in his first wife. His failure to care.

What right had he to decide whose life was more valuable? Who was he, after all?

A boy-king of eighteen. A cold, unfeeling bastard.

A monster.

He closed his eyes. His hands curled into fists above the parchment.

He would not let the whims of one grief-stricken lunatic dictate his actions any longer.

He would decide. Even if it was abominably selfish. Even if he was judged and punished for it, into eternity.

He would never be a man who failed to care again. He would fight to protect what mattered to him, at all cost.

Save the one thing that mattered most.

Khalid signed the decree to begin construction on the new system of aqueducts. He set it aside and proceeded to the next order of business. As he reviewed the document, the doors to the alcove swung open without a word of warning, and his cousin burst through the entrance.

Khalid's eyebrows rose at this brash display. When his uncle followed a moment later, wearing an expression even more grim than usual, Khalid inhaled and leaned back against the cushions.

The look on Jalal's face was . . . unsettling.

"I assume this is important." Khalid focused his attention on his cousin.

When Jalal said nothing, Khalid sat up.

"*Sayyidi*—" his uncle began.

"There must be an explanation." Jalal's voice faltered as his knuckles clenched white around the battered scroll in his left palm.

"Jalal-*jan*—"

"Please, Father," Jalal rasped over his shoulder. "Let me speak!"

Khalid stood up. "What are you talking about?"

"Promise me you'll give her a chance to explain. I've never known you to break your word. Promise me."

"Give him the report." His uncle edged closer to Jalal with a weary, yet determined set to his jaw.

"Not until he promises." Jalal's insistence bordered on manic.

Khalid strode from behind his desk, his posture rigid. "I am not promising anything until you tell me what this is about."

Jalal hesitated.

"Captain al-Khoury?"

"Shazi . . . and that boy." It was a broken whisper.

An icy fist wrapped around Khalid's throat. Yet he reached out a steady hand. "Give me the report."

"Promise me, Khalid."

"I'm not certain why you think I owe you a promise on her behalf." His voice was unwavering, despite the chilling vise.

"Then promise her."

"What I promise Shahrzad is none of your business. Give me the report."

Jalal exhaled slowly before handing him the scroll. As Khalid unfurled it, a dark weight settled across his chest, like a portent of doom seeking lasting refuge.

He scanned the missive once. The words registered in a far corner of his mind. Khalid's eyes drifted to the top of the parchment again.

And again.

"I'm sorry, Khalid-*jan*." His uncle was kind. "So very sorry. Even I started to believe—wanted to believe—that she was something more."

Jalal shook his head and moved toward Khalid. "She is. Please give her a chance to explain."

"Leave," Khalid commanded quietly.

"Don't let your fear and your distrust ruin this."

His uncle took Jalal by the shoulder.

"She loves you!" Jalal continued, his tone heedless. "This is not what it seems. Maybe it began as something else, but I would bet my life on what it is now. She loves you. Please don't fall to hate. You are not your father. You are so much more. She is so much more."

Khalid turned his back on his cousin, crumpling the scroll in his palm.

And the portent of doom unleashed itself on his body, darkening everything in its path—

Destroying an already condemned soul.

Shahrzad stood at the railing of her balcony, staring up at a sea of winking stars across a soft indigo sky.

She could not bring herself to be alone in her room. Though no traces of carnage remained, it was too soon to lounge within its dimly lit confines, surrounded by the ghosts of skulking shadows.

Shahrzad sighed as she watched a beam of starlight dart across a corner of darkest blue.

She had spent the day wandering the gardens on her own, choosing to forgo Despina's company in order to contemplate the many revelations of the night before without the distractions of the world around her.

Alas, the truth was not as enlightening as she had hoped.

Instead, it was desolate and ugly and cloaked in even more cruelty than she could have imagined.

Her best friend had been murdered for the sake of revenge—a disgusting, twisted revenge inflicted by a crazed man who had lost his child to an unfortunate turn of events. And he, in turn, had chosen to punish others for his pain.

He had punished Khalid for it.

And Khalid had punished the people of Rey.

Shahrzad took a deep breath.

Everything had spiraled down an endless black well because of one man's torment.

She studied her hands against the cool stone railing.

That same desire for revenge had brought her to this palace. Had driven her to hate the boy-king she'd blamed for such suffering.

And now here she was, standing on an abyss.

Khalid was still responsible for Shiva's death. He had given the order. He had sat at his desk and written a letter to Shiva's family while a soldier cinched the air from her body with a silk cord. He had not stopped them from killing her, as he had with Shahrzad. He had allowed it to happen.

Nothing about the facts had changed.

Yet the picture looked different.

Because Shahrzad knew why. Even though it was horrifying and beyond the realm of possibility, a part of her understood that he'd had little choice.

And that one day, he might be forced to make the same decision about her.

The groan of the doors to her chamber drew her attention. Shahrzad tightened the laces of her *shamla* and spun from the balcony. She walked into the center of her room. Tapers of warmly scented ambergris were glowing in the corner.

Khalid stood before the entrance, his profile concealed in part by shadow.

She smiled hesitantly.

He remained as still as a statue.

Her brow furrowed. "Hello?" Her voice sounded strange, even to her—more of a question than a welcome.

"Hello." It was severe and forbidding, hearkening back to a time when stories by lamplight were all they shared. All she could hope to share.

It threw Shahrzad against a wall of ice. "Is something wrong?"

He moved from the darkness toward her.

Something was definitely wrong.

But, though his features were cold and distant, his tiger-eyes rippled with pure emotion.

"Khalid?" Her pulse skipped a beat.

He exhaled with unremitting care. "How long?"

"What?"

He took another step toward her. "How long have you been in love with Tariq Imran al-Ziyad?"

A gasp escaped her before she could stop it. Her heart careened about in her chest, and she felt her knees start to give.

Lie. Lie to him.

The tiger-eyes continued haunting her . . . watching, waiting.

Knowing.

Afraid?

"Since the summer I turned twelve." Her voice broke.

He clenched his fists and twisted back to the darkness.

"I can explain!" Shahrzad reached for him. "I—"

When he turned around, the words died on her lips.

In his right hand was a dagger.

She backed away in horror.

His gaze stayed fixed on the marble at her feet. "Behind the ebony chest in my room is a door with a large brass ring. The handle is unusual. You have to turn it three times to the right, two times to the left, and three more times to the right before it will open. The staircase leads to an underground passage that will take you directly to the stables. Take my horse. His name is Ardeshir."

Shahrzad's confusion overrode her panic. "I don't—"

"Here." He unsheathed the dagger and handed it to her.

She shook her head, continuing to back away.

"Take it." He pressed the hilt into her palm.

"I don't understand."

"Vikram is waiting outside. He'll take you to my chamber. No one will stop you. Take Ardeshir . . . and go." Khalid spoke in a voice barely over a whisper.

Shahrzad clenched the hilt of the dagger, her brow lined, and her heart thundering in her chest—

And then Khalid sank to his knees before her.

"What—what are you doing?" she gasped. "I—"

"Shiva bin-Latief." He said her name with the reverence of a prayer, his head bowed and his eyes closed in shameless deference.

All the air left Shahrzad's body in a single rush of comprehension. She swayed unsteady on her feet before she fell to the floor with the dagger's hilt clutched tight in her hand.

"Get up," he said quietly.

Her chest heaved.

"Get up, Shahrzad al-Khayzuran. You kneel before no one. Least of all me."

"Khalid—"

"Do what you came to do. You owe me no explanation. I deserve none."

Shahrzad released a choked sob, and Khalid grabbed her by the arms.

"Get up." His tone was gentle but firm.

"I can't."

"You can. For Shiva. You are boundless. There is nothing you can't do."

"I can't do this!"

"You can."

"No." She shook her head, staving off the tears.

"Do it. You owe me nothing. I am nothing."

How can you say that? You are . . .

Shahrzad shook her head harder. Her grip on the dagger loosened.

"Shahrzad al-Khayzuran!" The muscles in his jaw constricted. "You are not weak. You are not indecisive. You are strong. Fierce. Capable beyond measure."

She swallowed, steeling herself, searching for a thread of hate, for a dram of rage, for . . . anything.

Shiva.

Khalid stayed resolute in his course. "I took her from you. Nothing I do, nothing I say will ever fix what I've done. If there has to be a choice between us, there isn't one to make, *joonam*. Not for me."

My everything.

Shahrzad rose to her knees and braced her palm against his chest.

"And you expect me to make this choice?" she demanded.

He nodded once, his eyes ablaze.

She curled her fingers into the front of his *qamis*. "You honestly expect me to breathe in a world without air?"

Khalid inhaled sharply as his hands tightened around her arms. "I expect you to be stronger than that."

Shahrzad's features softened. "But . . . there is nothing stronger than this."

Her hold on the dagger was gone. It clattered to the floor. Shahrzad brought her palms to his chest. "Hate. Judgment. Retribution. As you said, revenge will never replace what I have lost. What you have lost. All we have is now. And our promise to make it better."

She wound her fingers into his hair. "There is no one I would rather see the sunrise with than you."

Khalid closed his eyes. She could feel his heart racing. When he was able to meet her gaze again, he slid his hands to her face, brushing his thumb across her cheek with the warm caress of a summer breeze.

They knelt facing each other in silence. Studying each other. Truly seeing each other—without any pretense, without any masks, without any agenda. For the first time, Shahrzad allowed her eyes to linger on every facet of him without the fear of his sharp mind tearing through veils of gossamer and gold—

And seeing the truth.

The small, barely noticeable scar by his left eye. The darkly hostile set to his brows. The pools of liquid amber beneath. The perfect furrow in the center of his lip.

When he caught her staring at his mouth, Khalid exhaled slowly. "Shazi—"

"Be with me tonight," she breathed. "In all ways. Be mine."

His eyes turned to fire. "I've always been yours." He cupped her chin in his palm. "As you've always been mine."

She bristled and started to protest.

"Don't." He returned her biting glare.

"Your possessiveness . . . may present a problem." She knotted her brows together.

The corners of his lips curled upward, ever so slightly.

Shahrzad took Khalid's hand and led him to the bed. Though every part of her body remained acutely aware of the tall, solid presence behind her, she did not feel nervous. She felt calm. A remarkable sense of rightness.

He sat on the edge of the bed, and she stood before him.

Khalid leaned his brow against her stomach. "I won't ask for forgiveness, but I am so very sorry," he said, with the simple brevity she was learning to expect.

She pressed her lips into his soft, dark hair. "I know."

He looked up, and she eased onto his lap, with a knee at either side of his waist. Khalid pulled the hem of his *qamis* over his head, and Shahrzad skimmed her palms across the lean planes of his chest. She paused at a faint line of white along the length of his collarbone.

"Vikram," he explained.

Her eyes narrowed. "The Rajput? He cut you?"

"Why?" It was almost teasing in tone. "Does it bother you?"

She wrinkled her nose.

Khalid drew her closer. "It happens, from time to time. He's better than I am."

"I don't care. Don't let him cut you again."

"I'll do my best." He tilted her chin upward. "What about this?" His thumb ran along an old mark at the underside of her jaw, sending a shiver down her back.

"I fell off a wall when I was thirteen."

"Why were you on a wall?"

"I was trying to prove I could climb it."

"To whom?"

When she did not reply, Khalid tensed. "I see," he muttered. "And the fool just watched you fall?"

"I didn't give him a choice."

A smile ghosted across his lips. "Against all odds, I feel a drop of sympathy . . . amidst a sea of hatred."

"Khalid." She shoved his chest.

"Shahrzad." He caught her hand, his features abrupt in their intensity. "Is this really what you want?"

She stared at him, surprised to see a flicker of vulnerability on his face.

The mighty Caliph of Khorasan. The King of Kings.

Her beautiful monster.

Shahrzad leaned forward and took his lower lip between hers.

She trapped his jaw between her palms and swept her tongue into sun-laved honey.

As he said, there was never a choice in the matter.

One of his hands slid to the small of her back, and she arched herself against him, molding her form to his. The laces of her *shamla* were tugged free, and cool air rushed across her body, followed by the welcome heat of his touch. The feel of his skin against hers.

When his lips moved to her throat—to rest with care beside the wound made by the Fida'i dagger—Shahrzad made a decision.

"I love you," she said.

Khalid lifted his head to hers.

She placed a hand against his cheek. "Beyond words."

His eyes still fixed on her face, he lowered her onto the cushions. Then he covered her hand with his, brushing his lips across her inner wrist.

"My soul sees its equal in you."

All that was before her melted into amber and truth.

And, with a kiss, Shahrzad let herself fall.

For the boy who was an impossible, improbable study in contrasts. The boy who burned her life to cinder, only to remake of it a world unlike any she had ever known.

Tomorrow, she could worry about such a thing as loyalty. Tomorrow, she could worry about the price of such betrayal.

Tonight, all that mattered was this.

Their hands threaded above her head. His low whisper in her ear.

Just one boy and one girl.

This.

Oblivion.

Shahrzad awoke to the scent of roses.

To the scent of home.

A golden sun streamed from between the carved wooden slats of the screens leading to her balcony. She winced at its light and rolled over.

On the silk cushion beside her head was a pale violet rose and a folded piece of parchment. She smiled to herself. Then she lifted the rose and brought it closer.

It was perfect. The circle of winding petals was flawless, and the color was the ideal balance of striking and subdued. Inhaling its heady fragrance, she reached for the piece of parchment and shifted onto her stomach.

Shazi,

I prefer the color blue to any other. The scent of lilacs in your hair is a source of constant torment. I despise figs. Lastly, I will never forget, all the days of my life, the memories of last night—

For nothing, not the sun, not the rain, not even the brightest star in the darkest sky, could begin to compare to the wonder of you.

Khalid

Shahrzad read the letter four times, committing his words to memory. Her smile grew wider with each reading, until it stretched far enough to cause her pain. Then she laughed like an imbecile and quickly chastised herself for it. She placed the rose and the parchment on the stool by her bed and reached to the floor for her discarded *shamla*.

Where is Despina?

Tying her laces, she walked to the door of her handmaiden's chamber and knocked. When no one answered, she twisted the handle and looked inside. It was dark and deserted. She frowned and turned back toward her chamber.

Her frown deepening, she proceeded to bathe and dress in a sleeveless linen *qamis* of vibrant scarlet with matching trowsers. Tiny seed pearls and embellishments of copper and gold were embroidered at the cuffs and along the hem.

As she finished tugging the ivory comb through the last of her strands, one of the double doors opened and slammed shut with a deafening bang.

Shahrzad jumped through the air with a strangled cry.

"Did you miss me?" Despina teased.

"Where were you all morning?" Shahrzad glowered at her handmaiden, snaking her still-damp hair over one shoulder.

Despina cocked her head to the side. "You must be joking, Brat Caliph. I would rather eat my fill of excrement than return to this chamber a moment too soon. Especially at the risk of in-curring a king's wrath."

"What are you talking about?"

"Cease with the displays of false modesty. The entire palace knows about it."

A feeling of warmth crept up Shahrzad's neck. "Knows about what?"

Despina grinned. "The Caliph of Khorasan going into the gardens at dawn alone. And returning with a single rose." She gestured toward the flower on the stool behind Shahrzad. "I think it's safe to assume why."

The heat bloomed onto Shahrzad's face.

Despina groaned. "Are you going to deny it, then? How tedious."

Shahrzad paused. "No. I'm not." She lifted her chin.

"Thank the gods. I thought I would have to suffer through another odious attempt at coyness."

"You're one to speak on such matters."

"Excuse me?"

Shahrzad positioned her hands on her hips and peaked an eyebrow in a perfect imitation of her handmaiden. "Did *you* have a nice evening, Despina-*jan*?"

"Of course I did," Despina said over her shoulder. "I slept quite well."

"I'm happy to hear it. Have you finally mustered the courage to tell the man you love the truth?"

"The man I love? I think you may have hit your head. Perhaps too much unrestrained—"

"Now who's being odiously coy? Honestly, it galls me how both of you continue to play these games and ignore your feelings. He needs to know that you care about him. And he should definitely know about his child. Maybe I can—"

357

"Shahrzad!" Despina spun around, her features contorted in horror. "You can't! You mustn't!"

"Despina—"

"You don't understand! He can't know—anything." Despina's hands shook as she brought them to rest above her stomach.

Shahrzad shot her a gaze of bewilderment. "You're right; I don't understand. He's a good man. He must—love you. Does he not?"

"I . . . don't know." For the first time, the proud, haughty set to Despina's posture faltered. Her shoulders sagged, and she moved to the foot of Shahrzad's bed to lean against the platform. Without a word, Shahrzad sat down on the white marble beside her.

"Anyway, he can't marry me," Despina said in a soft, defeated tone. "I'm—a handmaiden. He's the cousin of the caliph. One day, he will become the next *shahrban.* His father married a princess of Khorasan. He has to marry someone from a good family. Not a handmaiden from Thebes."

"Even if he loves her?"

Despina closed her cerulean eyes. "Even if he loves her."

"I think that's absurd. Have you discussed it with him?"

She shook her head. "He thinks I don't love him. I've said as much."

"Despina!" Shahrzad glared at her handmaiden.

"It's easier that way. If he believes this is just a passing fancy, it will be far simpler for us both to carry on with our lives after the fact."

"Why would you do that to yourself? Why would you lie to him?"

"I believe when you truly love someone, you want what's best for that person."

"I find that not only absurd, but arrogant, as well."

"And I find that amusing, coming from someone as arrogant as you."

"*I'm* arrogant?" Shahrzad sputtered. "I'm not the one assuming to know what's best for a grown man without consulting him first."

Despina smiled sadly.

Shahrzad nudged Despina's shoulder with her own. "I understand how difficult it is, putting your heart in someone else's hands. But, if you don't, how will you ever truly know a person?"

Despina drew her knees to her chest. "His father will despise me. Everyone will think I trapped him into marriage. That I'm a scheming whore."

"I will personally beat senseless the first person to speak ill of you."

Despina arched a dubious brow.

"Don't sneer at me. I may be small, but, when pushed, I can strike out with a surprising amount of force." Shahrzad sniffed. "If you don't believe me, ask Jalal."

"You struck Jalal?" Despina frowned.

Shahrzad shook her head, a smile playing at the edges of her lips.

"Khalid."

"What?" Despina gasped. "You . . . struck the *caliph*?"

"Across the face."

Despina's hand shot to her mouth, and a bubble of laughter burst from her lips.

The two girls remained seated on the floor talking and laughing until a knock at the entrance brought them to their feet. The double doors swung open, and Khalid walked across the threshold with Jalal at his side. A contingent of guards remained in the hall. The *shahrban* waited patiently amongst them.

As always, Khalid moved with an air of imperious grace. His dark *rida'* was fastened over an elaborate silver and gold cuirass. The hilt of his *shamshir* was looped through a black *tikka* sash slung across his narrow hips. He looked menacing and unapproachable—a thousand years, a thousand lives, a thousand tales away.

But Shahrzad knew better.

She met him in the center of the chamber.

His eyes were warm. Her heart soared at the sight.

Despina bowed to Khalid and proceeded without pause toward her small room by the entrance . . . where Jalal stood against the wall, the portrait of casual ease.

It was a vain attempt at indifference, on both their parts.

For Shahrzad bore silent witness to the truth. It was only for an instant, and they never glanced at each other. Yet, she wondered how anyone could miss it—the subtle shift in Jalal's shoulders, and the telltale tilt to Despina's head.

Shahrzad smiled knowingly.

Khalid waited until the door leading to Despina's chamber sealed shut.

"Did you sleep well?" His low voice brought to mind memories of whispered words in the dark.

"I did."

"I'm glad."

"Thank you for the gifts. They were perfect."

"Then they were fitting."

She quirked a slender brow at him, and a corner of his mouth rose.

"I have something else for you," he said.

"What is it?"

"Give me your hand."

"Does it matter which one?"

He shook his head.

She held out her right hand, and he slid a band of muted gold onto its third finger.

It was the mate to his.

Shahrzad ran her left thumb across the embossed standard of two crossed swords. The reigning al-Rashid standard.

Her standard.

As the Calipha of Khorasan.

"Do you mind wearing it? It's—"

"The best gift of all." She looked up to meet his gaze.

And he smiled a smile to shame the sun.

Behind him, the troop of guards stirred.

"*Sayyidi*?" Jalal interrupted with an apologetic glance at Shahrzad. "You should leave soon."

Khalid nodded once in acknowledgment.

"Where are you going?" Shahrzad asked, her forehead creasing.

"A small force is gathering at the border of Khorasan and Parthia under a new banner. The emirs in that region are nervous and wish to discuss strategy, should an altercation arise."

"Oh." She frowned. "How long will you be gone?"

"Two, maybe three weeks."

"I see." Shahrzad chewed on the inside of her cheek, trying to remain silent.

His smile returned. "Two weeks, then."

"Not three?"

"Not three."

"Good."

He regarded her with steady amusement. "Again, I'm glad."

"I'd rather you be careful than glad. And return safe." She dropped her voice. "Or you'll be met with a platter of figs."

His eyes gleamed gold. "My queen." He bowed with a hand to his brow before shifting it over his heart.

Respect. And affection.

As he made his way toward the entrance, disappointment began eking a hole in Shahrzad's spirits.

It was not the kind of good-bye she wanted.

"Khalid?"

He pivoted to face her.

She ran to him and grabbed the front of his *rida'* to pull him down for a kiss.

He froze for a moment, then reached a hand behind her waist to pull her closer.

The guards in the hall shuffled nervously, their swords and

armor jangling together. Jalal's soft laughter echoed from beside the double doors.

Shahrzad did not care.

For this was a kiss of definition. A kiss of understanding.

For a marriage absent pretense. And a love without design.

Khalid's palm pressed against her back. "Ten days."

Her grip on his cloak tightened. "Do you promise?"

"I promise."

ONE ELEMENT OF A STORM

Jahandar rode the dappled mare to the top of a hill overlooking Rey.

The sky above was dark and starless.

Perfect.

He took a deep breath and swung from the saddle. Then he reached into his leather satchel and withdrew the battered, ancient tome from its depths.

It pulsed at his touch.

With careful reverence, he knelt before a small grouping of rocks and set the volume on a flat surface. He lifted the black key from around his neck and inserted it into the rusted lock in the book's center. As soon as he raised the cover, a slow-spreading silver light emanated from the pages.

He was thankful they no longer burned his hands.

Jahandar turned the well-worn vellum until he reached the spell. The words were already committed to memory, but the book's magic assisted him in channeling the power for such a daunting task. He closed his eyes and let the silver light wash across his face and palms, imbuing him with soundless strength. Then he withdrew the dagger from its sheath and ran its tip across the newly formed scar on his left palm. As soon as his blood dripped onto the blade, the metal started to glow a white-hot blue.

He stood and turned back toward the dappled mare. She tossed her mane and snorted, her deep brown eyes wide. Skittish. Jahandar hesitated for a heartbeat.

But people were expecting great things from him.

And he refused to disappoint them again.

Gritting his teeth, he strode forward and sliced the dagger across the mare's throat in a single, quick motion. Hot blood spewed onto his hands in a crimson torrent. The mare staggered to her knees as she struggled against the inevitable. Soon she keeled over; her breaths were shallow at first, then nonexistent.

The blade's edge was fire red, its center burning more brilliant than ever.

Utterly fearsome in its greatness.

He stepped back from the carcass and inhaled through his nose. Then he touched the dagger to the wound on his palm.

The power raged through him, searing into his bones. From atop its throne of mottled stones, the book's silver light pulsed brighter than a star.

Jahandar gasped and dropped the blade as the power collected in his chest, visceral in its magnificence. The ground beneath his feet trembled.

He began to laugh.

Holding his bloodstained arms up to the sky, he muttered the ancient words and watched the clouds churn at his behest. Reveled as they bowed to his whims.

The book's pages fluttered. His wind-whipped beard coiled about his throat.

There would never be cause to disappoint anyone ever again.

Tonight, he would prove his worth, once and for all.

He would rescue his daughter. And save a kingdom.

For he was Jahandar the Great.

Jahandar the All-Powerful.

Jahandar . . . the King of Kings.

The first of the raindrops started to fall.

And Tariq ignored his growing sense of disquiet.

He stood shrouded in darkness, with his back against a wall of discolored mortar and stone. The palace gate was in the distance over his shoulder. It stretched high, constructed of solid wood bound in black iron. Armed sentries were positioned above and below, standing watch from torchlit battlements.

He exhaled, trying to release the tension from his body.

Trying to silence the doubt.

"He really didn't tell you how he plans to breach the gate?" Rahim tugged the hood of his brown *rida'* lower onto his brow.

"For the last time, he said he would create a diversion."

"And you trust him?"

"No," Tariq admitted. "But if he fails, I am no worse off than before."

"Actually, that's false. You have yet to be accused of sedition by association."

"Jahandar-*effendi* would not betray us. In that, I trust him implicitly."

"I wish I possessed your particular brand of optimism," Rahim grumbled.

"And what brand would that be?"

"Idiotic."

"Better idiotic than ineffectual."

"Better alive than dead."

"Run home, Rahim-*jan*," Tariq said. "I can hear your mother calling."

"Insufferable ass."

Tariq grinned, but his chest felt tight.

The hired soldiers standing in the shadows behind Rahim stayed silent, awaiting Tariq's direction.

If only he knew it himself.

He sighed. This would likely prove to be a fool's errand. After all, Jahandar al-Khayzuran did not have a history of reliability. Lost in his grief, he'd failed to be a father to his children following the death of their mother. Then he'd failed his king in his post as an advisor and been demoted for it. And he'd failed Shahrzad when he allowed her to risk her life for revenge.

Nevertheless, Tariq had to try.

The rain fell harder. It was beginning to drip in steady streams from the low-hanging eave above, seeping through his cloak onto his skin.

Rahim edged away from the nearest trickle. "Do you—"

A flash of light flew across the sky, followed by a boom of thunder.

"One thing's for certain; this storm is not helping matters," Rahim said.

Tariq leaned against the wall and closed his eyes.

Rahim cursed at the next crack of thunder. It was loud enough to rattle Tariq's teeth.

People were beginning to stir in the streets. Lamps were being lit in windows across the way.

"Tariq!" Rahim warned sharply.

Tariq spun his head in the direction of the palace and watched in horror as a bolt of lightning struck one of the marbled turrets. It severed the stone into flaming pieces that crashed to the ground with earthshaking thuds.

The guards at the gates shouted in alarm.

"Merciful God," Rahim breathed.

Another flash of white light struck nearby, catching a building on fire. The roar of the resounding thunder jolted Tariq to his very bones.

Now rain pummeled from the heavens in a side-sweeping deluge.

The first of the screams commenced when the next bolt of lightning tore through the roof of a home, sending charred matter and bits of burning rubble into the sky.

The home promptly burst into flame.

And the cries of panic grew louder.

Another blistering flash struck the palace, cleaving more marble from its side. Tariq pushed off the wall.

Rahim seized him by the shoulder. "What are you doing?"

"I'm not watching while that palace is razed. Shahrzad is inside."

Rahim yanked him back. "And your plan is what? To humbly request admittance?"

"No," Tariq shot back in vicious undertone. "My plan is—"

A bolt of lightning struck the center of the gate, blinding him and driving the air from his chest in the same instant. Wood, iron, and ash mingled in the downpour.

Chaos descended around them as the cries of fleeing, terror-stricken people merged with the storm's cacophony. Soldiers spilled through the decimated gates into the city, trying to stanch the fear and maintain order.

"Is this Jahandar-*effendi*'s idea of a diversion?" Rahim shouted in dismay.

Tariq yanked back the hood of his *rida'*. "That's impossible. Jahandar is not capable of this. He struggles to make a flower bloom."

"Then what in God's name is this?" Rahim cringed as another beam of light slashed across the sky and struck the heart of the city.

Fires were erupting everywhere.

Tariq frowned and bit back his mounting premonitions.

"I don't know. But I do know I'm not leaving Shahrzad here." He dragged his hood onto his head and removed the recurve bow from his back.

Shahrzad woke with a start at the first crack of thunder. Her heart lashed about in her chest as she strode to the wooden screens and peered between the carved slats.

It's just a storm.

She walked back to her bed and sat on its edge. Then she began toying with the gold ring on her finger.

Just a storm.

A deafening crash and the sound of rending stone shot her to her feet once more.

Something had struck the palace.

When a clattering of footsteps amassed outside her chamber, Shahrzad grabbed the dagger next to her bed and crouched beside the platform.

The doors swung open without preamble.

"Shahrzad?" Jalal's familiar voice broke through the silence.

She breathed a sigh of relief. "I'm here." She placed the dagger beside the dried rose on the stool and strode forward. Jalal stood in the center of her room with the Rajput and two other guards flanking him.

"Are you hurt?" Jalal asked, his curly hair mussed and his light brown eyes darting every which way.

"No." She hesitated. "Why?"

"The palace was struck by lightning. A turret and a portion of the gardens are on fire."

Her heart thudded in her ears.

Shahrzad balled her hands into fists. "Jalal, do you—"

"It's just a storm, Shazi." He walked closer, full of reassurance. "I wouldn't—"

This time, the very walls of the palace shuddered under the impact. Her bed shifted, and a wooden chest crashed to the floor.

The resulting wave of thunder rippled through Shahrzad's body, making her worry all the more.

She raced down the short hall to her handmaiden's door and yanked it open.

The chamber was empty.

"Where is Despina?" she demanded as soon as she returned to her chamber.

Jalal shrugged. "I don't know."

"Stop it!" she said. "Where is she?"

His eyebrows arched smoothly. Too smoothly. "I'm sure she's fine. Probably just—"

She grabbed his arm and hauled him closer. "Enough of these childish games. Please go find her. I'm worried sick, and I suspect you are as well."

He tensed, his features tight as his eyes flicked across her face. "Again, I'm sure—"

Another boom of thunder cracked through the air, causing the marble at their feet to quake and the wooden screens to unhinge.

"I order you to leave and go find her."

"And I would, my lady. But your order defies that of the king. I'd rather not explain to Khalid why—"

"She's pregnant!"

He stiffened and grasped her by the shoulders. "What did you say?"

I'm sorry, Despina.

"She's pregnant. Please go find her before something happens."

Jalal blinked hard before uttering a colorful string of oaths, many of them directed at Shahrzad.

"Be angry with me later," she insisted. "Just go find her. I'll stay here."

With a wild-eyed glare, he proceeded to hurl commands over his shoulder as he strode toward the entrance.

He stopped just before the threshold. "Shazi?"

"Yes?"

"Thank you." He disappeared down the corridor without waiting for a response.

Shahrzad returned to the foot of her bed, while the Rajput and the two remaining guards stood watch. Again, she fidgeted with the ring on her right hand as the sound and light continued raging outside, making her skin feel hot and cold all at once.

It's raining. The curse has weakened.

This is just a terrible storm. Nothing more.

At the next earsplitting crack of thunder, the unhinged screens to the terrace flew open, exposing the chamber to the elements. Desperate for something to do, Shahrzad moved to latch them shut, but the Rajput held out his arm to stop her. With a brisk nod, he directed one of the guards toward the terrace.

Before the guard had a chance to shutter the screens, he was struck in the chest by an arrow. He staggered to his knees and fell to the floor.

The Rajput seized Shahrzad by the wrist and hauled her behind him. He withdrew his *talwar* from its scabbard with the shrill grate of metal on metal.

Two hooded silhouettes materialized from the terrace.

It took Shahrzad only a moment to recognize the one clutching a recurve bow.

"No!" she cried as Tariq nocked another arrow and fired it at the Rajput. Shahrzad yanked her bodyguard back, and the arrow embedded in his shoulder, just above its intended target. The Rajput did not even flinch.

The other soldier unsheathed his scimitar, and Tariq took him down with a single shot. Then he fitted an arrow to the string and raised it beside his ear, continuing his slow stalk forward.

The Rajput grunted in fury and flourished his weapon.

"Step aside," Tariq demanded in a harsh voice.

Instead, the Rajput eased low into a fighting stance.

"Stop it!" Shahrzad's chest rose and fell in a panic.

Another clap of thunder shook the walls of the palace.

"This is your last chance." Tariq's silver eyes shone in the darkness.

The Rajput laughed with mirthless humor. He raised his sword across his body and stepped toward Tariq.

"Vikram!" Shahrzad pleaded. "Don't do this!"

The Rajput ignored her and leveled the *talwar* at Tariq, preparing to attack.

Tariq loosed the arrow without hesitation. It struck the Rajput in the center of the chest.

"Tariq!" Shahrzad screamed. "Please!"

The Rajput lurched around, his features twisted in disbelief.

Then Tariq brought the wood of his bow down hard across the back of the Rajput's head, and he collapsed to the floor.

Shahrzad stifled a sob.

Tariq regarded her with grim wariness. "Shahrzad—"

"How could you?" It was a choked whisper.

His eyebrows flattened. "He would have killed me."

He was right. But she did not know what to say to her past for destroying all hope of a future.

"Shazi?" Rahim's tone was quiet, his head tilted askew.

"What are you doing here?" Shahrzad's eyes were fixed on her first love.

"I came to take you home," Tariq said.

"You didn't need to come. I—"

His gaze hardened. "I'm not leaving without you."

A flash of lightning struck close by, and a dark fissure erupted on the ceiling, exacerbated by the ensuing thunder.

"This entire palace is about to fall down around our heads," Rahim announced. "We have to get out of here and find Jahandar-*effendi*."

"Baba?" Shahrzad's forehead creased. "Why is my father here?"

Rahim rubbed his palm across the back of his neck. "It's a long story."

A barrage of footsteps echoed in the corridor outside her chamber, and Tariq snatched another arrow from his quiver before taking position between her and the doors. He stood at the ready until the sounds faded away.

"Let's go," Rahim directed.

Shahrzad took a deep breath. "Tariq—"

"I'm not leaving without you!" He spun around and pulled

her against him. "This is not your fight! It never should have been your fight!"

At the next roar of thunder, a piece of the ceiling crashed to the floor. It nearly struck Rahim.

"We're leaving." Tariq held her tight. "Now."

She nodded. Once they were safe beyond the palace walls, she would gather the courage to tell him why she couldn't leave.

Why she didn't want to leave.

He clasped her hand in his and began striding to the doors.

"Wait!" Shahrzad pulled free and ran to her wardrobe to re-move her cloak and Musa-*effendi*'s rug, for she did not want it to succumb to a fire. She threw the cloak around her shoulders and whirled back toward the stool beside her bed to retrieve Khalid's note and her dagger.

At the sight of the now lifeless, pale purple rose, a sudden flicker of remembrance washed across her vision . . . of another rose from her not-so-distant past, coaxed to its tragic demise. Of a well-intentioned gift, falling to pieces, wilting across a marbled floor.

The storm hissed and crackled behind her.

It's not possible. Baba . . . couldn't.

She squeezed her eyelids shut for a moment. Then she placed the note and the dagger in the folds of her cloak and hurried toward the doors.

As Tariq took hold of a handle, Shahrzad placed her hand on his forearm. "How were you planning to make it outside un-detected?"

"Carefully."

She exhaled in a huff. Elbowing him aside, she peered through a crack in the door.

"Stay quiet and follow me." She stepped into the darkened hallway.

With her head down, Shahrzad made her way through the corridors of the palace, hoping no one would notice her new bodyguards.

Hoping they did not cross paths with Jalal.

They traversed another series of hallways before turning abruptly down a smaller corridor with an arched ceiling of distinct white marble.

Her heart sank.

Standing before the doors to Khalid's chamber was a lone guard. He straightened as she approached, but his eyes traveled to her alleged bodyguards and narrowed noticeably.

"My lady," he began with a bow. "How can I help you?"

She smiled warmly at him. "I just wanted to return this parcel to the caliph's chamber." She held up the bundle containing the magic carpet.

"I'd be pleased to assist you. If you would leave the parcel with me—"

Shahrzad shook her head. "I'd rather replace it myself."

"Of course." He nodded, stepping aside.

When Tariq and Rahim moved to accompany her, he held up his hand.

"I'm sorry, my lady, but I cannot allow them entry."

"You can if I say so." Her smile turned sharp.

"Again, I'm sorry, my lady, but only you and Captain al-Khoury are allowed in the caliph's chamber in his absence."

"I believe tonight is a night for exceptions." Shahrzad grasped a bronze handle.

"My lady!" He reached for her arm.

She glared up at him. "Are you going to stop me, then? Because you'll have to use force. I believe you know what happened to the last soldier who touched me against my will. But, by all means, you are welcome to try. I'm certain my husband will be thrilled to learn of this encounter. What was your name again?"

The guard paled. "My lady Shahrzad!"

"That is not your name," she scoffed. "Now, if you value life and limb, you will let us pass."

With a clamoring heart, she took hold of the handle once more and pulled the door open.

Her pulse continued thrashing about as Tariq and Rahim entered Khalid's antechamber. They proceeded without pause through the entrance to his room. It was not until the doors thudded shut behind them that she finally permitted herself to take an unencumbered breath.

Rahim's laugh was as dry as sand. "You are quite the calipha." He leaned a lanky arm against an alabaster wall.

She ignored him and walked toward the black chest.

"I must say, the murdering madman has an impressive chamber." Rahim's dark blue eyes drifted across the onyx and marble. "For a soulless monster."

Shahrzad bit back her retort with effort. She could feel Tariq watching her.

"Help me move this chest aside." She placed her palms against the dark wood.

"Why?" Tariq countered.

"I don't have time to explain!" She pursed her lips. "Do you want the guard to summon Jalal?"

Tariq's eyes flashed, but he directed her back before shoving the chest aside with a grunt.

The hidden door Khalid had mentioned less than two weeks ago was visible now. Shahrzad grasped the brass ring and turned it three times to the right, two times to the left, and three more times to the right before using all her weight to push it open.

"My God," Rahim said. "How did you know about this?"

"Khalid told me." She tried to dismiss the strange look he gave her. "It's dark, so tread with care." Concealing her trepidation, she moved down the stairs leading to the passageway.

The trio hugged the walls of earth and stone as they scurried like vermin under the ground. At the end of the tunnel was a small ladder leading up to a wooden trapdoor. Shahrzad tried to open it, but it refused to budge. Rahim pressed both palms to the rough-hewn surface, and the door eventually swung aside with a whining creak.

They emerged in a shadowed corner of the palace stables.

And a boom of thunder rattled through the earth at their feet. The horses whinnied and thrashed about in their stalls.

"Pick one," Shahrzad stated.

Rahim whistled. "Really? Because I'm told the madman has

a black al-Khamsa from the first of the five. That horse is a prize in and of itself."

Shahrzad whirled on him. "*Not* Ardeshir. You can take any horse from this stable, but not that one."

"Whyever not?"

"Because you are not taking his horse!" Her composure was hanging by a thread.

Rahim put up both hands in a gesture of surrender. "What's wrong with you, Shazi?" Concern marred his features.

"He's not even here." Tariq spoke quietly from the shadows. "The horse is not here. Nor is its master."

"What?" Rahim turned to Tariq.

"Where is he, Shahrzad?" Tariq asked, striding toward her.

"On his way home, Tariq Imran al-Ziyad," a male voice intoned from behind them.

Jalal.

When the captain of the guard emerged from the darkness, he aimed a malicious grin at Tariq.

"I would count yourself lucky," Jalal continued. "Because if Khalid found you with Shahrzad, death would be the least of your worries."

Tariq reached for his bow, intent on his next course of action.

And Shahrzad launched herself in his path, clutching both his wrists.

"No!" Her face was awash in terror.

Tariq's pain compounded further. Now she was even defending the boy-king's family. Defending them against *him.*

Captain al-Khoury's scimitar was unsheathed at his side. He was alone. It would take a single arrow to rid them of his nuisance.

When the boy-king's arrogant cousin strode closer, Shahrzad turned to face him, still holding one of Tariq's wrists in a death grip.

"Jalal," she said, "I can explain."

"There's no need."

"I'm not—"

"I told you; there's no need." He spoke simply. "I trust you."

Her grip on Tariq's wrist tightened impossibly further.

"It's Nasir al-Ziyad's son I don't trust." Captain al-Khoury raised his weapon, its edge gleaming white.

"You can trust him."

"No," Tariq interrupted, "he can't."

Shahrzad glanced over her shoulder, her eyes laced with admonition.

"What are you doing here, Tariq Imran al-Ziyad?" Captain al-Khoury took a step forward, his sword at the ready.

"That should be obvious. I'm here for Shahrzad."

Captain al-Khoury snorted. "Are you? And did you think you could just leave the city with the Caliph of Khorasan? With my cousin's wife?"

"Shahrzad is not staying here. I am not leaving the girl I love in the arms of a monster."

"That's funny. One would think the girl had a choice in the matter."

"You must be joking," Rahim said in a gravelly tone. "Do you honestly think she would choose a madman over Tariq?"

"Enough, Rahim," Tariq cautioned.

"Ask her," Captain al-Khoury said softly. "Ask her if she truly plans to leave Rey with you. Because I know something you are either too stupid or too blind to see."

"And what is that?" Rahim demanded.

"Murderer, monster, madman . . . Khalid may very well be all of those things. But he's also loved. By me and by my father. But, most of all, by Shazi. With her, he is as fiercely loved as he loves."

Shahrzad's body trembled in front of Tariq. Her hold on his wrist was flagging.

"Is he telling the truth?" Rahim asked, bristling at the captain of the guard's familiarity.

She glanced once more over her shoulder, and her eyes shimmered with tears that threatened to course down her cheeks. "Tariq."

No. He could not listen to her say it. Would never listen to her say such a thing.

He dropped the bow and drew her against him. "I know this isn't you. I know something must have happened. But we can fix it. I can fix it. Come home with me. Every day we are apart is a day closer to death. A day wasted on what might have been. I can't stomach it any longer. Come home."

"But," she whispered, "I am home."

"Shazi!" Rahim's face twisted in disbelief. "How can you say that?"

"I'm so sorry. I never, ever wanted to hurt either of you. It's just that—"

"He killed Shiva!" Tariq exploded. "How can you want the boy who killed your best friend? How can you want a cold bastard who killed dozens of young girls and disappears on a lark while his city burns?"

"What did you say?" Shahrzad's voice was deathly quiet. "The city is—burning?"

Tariq's brow furrowed. "The lightning. It caught several buildings on fire."

At this news, Shahrzad shoved Tariq aside and raced to the stable entrance. She hauled back the wooden gate.

And collapsed at the sight.

Half the city was consumed in flames. Smoke billowed into the sky, backlit by flashes of silver lightning. The scent of burning ash mingled with a cloud of rosebushes nearby.

Captain al-Khoury sheathed his sword and crouched beside Shahrzad.

Her look of abject suffering stopped Tariq short.

"Jalal. What have we done?" Her face was unfaltering in its agony.

"No, *delam*. This is not your fault. None of this is your fault." Captain al-Khoury placed each of his hands on either side of her face.

"You have to—" Shahrzad released a shaky breath. "We have to stop this. Before anyone else dies."

"I will do no such thing," Captain al-Khoury replied.

"What have we done?" It was a pathetic, soul-searing entreaty.

Captain al-Khoury hoisted Shahrzad to her feet. "Nothing. You've done nothing."

She shook her head, her features lost and bleak. "Khalid . . . will have to—"

"No. He would never."

"But how can we live like this?" she cried. "I can't. He can't!"

Tariq could stand it no longer. "What are you talking about?"

"Tariq Imran al-Ziyad." Captain al-Khoury continued studying Shahrzad while he spoke. "I have a request."

"The answer is no."

"Don't you want to hear it first?"

Tariq glowered at him in silence.

Captain al-Khoury twisted his head to meet Tariq's gaze. "Take Shahrzad out of Rey."

"That was always my intention."

Shahrzad's eyes glistened. "Jalal—"

"Take her with you." Captain al-Khoury gripped Shahrzad's shoulders.

"No. I can't leave." She fought to set her quaking jaw. "I won't leave. I'm not . . . afraid."

Captain al-Khoury faced her. "Listen to me. For once. I beg you."

Shahrzad began to protest, and a gust of hot air blew back at them, further dispersing the strange perfume of sweet roses and harsh smoke. She closed her eyes tight and pressed a hand to her chest.

"Tariq. Where is my father?" she asked, her voice hoarse.

"Beyond the city," he replied. "Waiting . . . atop a hill."

Her eyes flew open, and she stared at Tariq with an eerie, new-found certainty.

"Take me to him." Without waiting for a response, she brushed past Captain al-Khoury and walked into the stables to saddle a horse.

Tariq turned to watch as she disappeared into the darkness, her posture stiff and her stride perfunctory. He had only begun to process his confusion when Captain al-Khoury seized him by the arm.

Tariq knocked away the arrogant boy's hand. "What—"

"Do you still love her?" He spoke in an urgent whisper.

"That's none of your business."

"Answer me, you fool. Do you?"

Tariq clenched his teeth, returning the captain of the Royal Guard's fierce glare.

"Always."

"Then make sure she never comes back."

BURNING EMBERS

THE TWO RIDERS MET IN THE MIDDLE OF A SKY-darkened desert.

One atop a simple steed of grey, and the other astride a magnificent white stallion.

Behind each stood a cadre of armed soldiers.

The rider with the white stallion spoke first. "I am told we share a common enemy." His voice was rich and patently false.

The other rider returned his measured study.

"So it would seem, my lord."

The first rider smiled with unctuous slowness. "You are as they described, Reza bin-Latief."

"As are you, my lord."

The Sultan of Parthia laughed. "I will take that as a compliment."

"It was meant as such, my lord. Forgive me for failing to convey the sentiment properly, but I did not agree to this meeting for the purpose of exchanging banter with you."

The sultan's laughter echoed into the night. "A man of candor.

I am pleased. Shall we cease with the pleasantries and proceed to business?"

"By all means, my lord."

"What are your intentions regarding my bastard nephew?"

"Suffering. And annihilation."

The sultan's eyes gleamed with a martial light. "I see."

"And what are yours?"

"Humiliation . . . followed by annihilation. Perhaps we could assist one another in our shared objective?"

"My assistance depends on what you have to offer, my lord."

"For now, I can offer money and weapons. Once you secure the border and strengthen your existing forces, I will be open in my support, but until that time, I cannot risk pressing the boy's wrath any further."

"Understandable."

The sultan gestured behind him, and a pair of guards brought forth a small sealed trunk. "A gesture of gold faith. Once these funds are depleted, send word, and I will dispatch more."

Reza nodded. He glanced over his shoulder at his retinue, and two hooded figures stepped forward to collect the gold.

As one figure bent to lift the trunk, the light of a blue desert moon struck against the skin of his forearm.

On it was the mark of the scarab.

Shahrzad,

    I've failed you several times. But there was one moment I failed you beyond measure. It was the day we met. The moment

I took your hand and you looked up at me, with the glory of hate in your eyes. I should have sent you home to your family. But I didn't. There was honesty in your hatred. Fearlessness in your pain. In your honesty, I saw a reflection of myself. Or rather, of the man I longed to be. So I failed you. I didn't stay away. Then, later, I thought if I had answers, it would be enough. I would no longer care. You would no longer matter. So I continued failing you. Continued wanting more. And now I can't find the words to say what must be said. To convey to you the least of what I owe. When I think of you, I can't find the air to breathe. And now, though you are gone, there is no pain or fear. All I am left with is gratitude.

When I was a boy, my mother would tell me that one of the best things in life is the knowledge that your story isn't over yet. Our story may have come to a close, but your story is still yet to be told.

Make it a story worthy of you.

I failed you in one last thing. Here is my chance to rectify it. It was never because I didn't feel it. It was because I swore I would never say it, and a man is nothing if he can't keep his promises.

So I write it to the sky—

I love you, a thousand times over. And I will never apologize for it.

Khalid

Khalid stood at the railing of the rooftop terrace, watching the sun rise across a clear horizon.

His broken palace of marble and stone still smoldered at the edges, cleaved on many sides.

His city was a wasteland of dark plumes and rubble. Of lost promises and heartbreak.

For a breath, he closed his eyes to the ruin.

But only for a breath.

Because it was his city. His choice. His responsibility.

He would never hide from it again.

With renewed purpose, he took the single piece of parchment and held it to the flickering torch nearby.

A corner of the page began to fold into ash, and the flames licked up the sides in shades of azure and orange.

Khalid held the burning letter before him.

Then he released its embers into the wind.

Into a glorious dawn.

GLOSSARY

Akhal-Teke—a breed of horse noted for its metallic sheen; Rahim's horse

al-Khamsa—a desert-bred bloodline of Arabian horse, translated as "the five"; Tariq's horse; Khalid's horse, Ardeshir

Amardha—the biggest city in Parthia; the city in which Salim Ali el-Sharif resides

astragali dice—bone dice of quadruped knucklebones, originally used in astragalomancy, a form of divination

Badawi tribe—nomadic desert tribe, controlled by a sheikh

caliph—the ruler of Khorasan, a term synonymous with "king"; Khalid Ibn al-Rashid

calipha—the wife of the caliph; a term synonymous with "queen"; Shahrzad al-Khayzuran

caliphate—the region ruled by the caliph; Khorasan

Chagatai—a dead language of Central Asian origin

cuirass—upper-body armor consisting of a breastplate and a backplate fastened together

delam—a term of endearment meaning "my heart"

dinar—a form of currency made from gold bullion

effendi—a suffix attached to a name to denote respect

emir—a nobleman of Khorasan, akin to a duke; one of the caliph's bannermen; Nasir al-Ziyad

faqir—a scholar of magic and mysticism

Fida'i—a mercenary marked by the brand of a scarab on the inner forearm

ghalyan—a hookah or water pipe

jahkesh—an insult meaning "whoremonger" or "master pimp"

jan—a term of endearment, a suffix attached to a name to mean "my dear"

joonam—a term of endearment meaning "my everything"

kamancheh—a stringed instrument resembling a violin

Khorasan—a wealthy kingdom, currently ruled by an eighteen-year-old caliph with a murderous past

kohl—an eye cosmetic, traditionally made from ground galena

lavash bread—a type of very thin flatbread

magus—a sorcerer; Musa Zaragoza

malik—the ruler of Assyria, a term synonymous with "king"

mankalah—a leather cuff that spans from wrist to elbow, associated with falconry

mantle—a loose-fitting robe, usually made of an elaborate material such as damask, typically worn by royalty

marg-bahr—a wish of ill will, specifically death or destruction to someone or something

ney—a wind instrument resembling a flute

Parthia—the smaller kingdom adjacent to Khorasan, ruled by Salim Ali el-Sharif

qamis—a loose-fitting, long-sleeved shirt, worn by men and women alike, typically made of linen

Rajput—member of a warrior class; Vikram

Rey—the greatest city of Khorasan; the city of Shahrzad's birth

rida'—a cloak worn over a man's shoulder, covering his shirt; can also include a hood to conceal his face

sahib—a title used in deference, often to denote rank

sama—a practice associated with whirling dervishes

santur—a stringed instrument also known as a hammered dulcimer, struck with a small mallet to produce sound

sayyidi—a term of respect used when addressing the caliph; translated as "my liege" or "my lord" scimitar—a single-edged, curved sword; Tariq's sword; Jalal's sword

Shahrban of Rey—the highest-ranking general in Khorasan, second only to the caliph; General Aref al-Khoury

shamla—an embroidered dressing gown or robe

shamshir—a slender saber with a rather sharp curve to it; Khalid's sword

sheikh—the leader of a Badawi tribe; Omar al-Sadiq

sirwal trowsers—voluminous pants worn by men and women alike, typically gathered at the ankle and secured at the waist by a sash

souk—outdoor market

sultan—the ruler of Parthia, a term synonymous with "king"; Salim Ali el-Sharif

tabarzin—a battle-axe

Taleqan—the fortress of Emir Nasir al-Ziyad; the fourth-richest stronghold in Khorasan; Tariq's home

talwar—a type of curved sword or saber originating from Hindustan; the Rajput's sword

Thebes—a large city in central Greece

tikka sash—a long sash tied about the hips, largely decorative, worn by men and women alike

Tirazis—a city in Khorasan famous for its stone quarries

tombak—a drum resting on the hip

vizier—an advisor to the caliph

ACKNOWLEDGMENTS

I REMEMBER ONCE HEARING THE WORD "JOURNEY" AS being among the most overused to ascribe to a creative endeavor.

Upon reflection, I suppose "odyssey" just doesn't have the right ring to it. Not to mention the whole Homerian thing.

I digress.

This *journey* would not have been possible without a slew of amazing people. I will try my very best to remember each and every one of them, but should I fail in that task, please know it is absolutely my fault, and I shall owe those offended something good in the near future. But not my firstborn child. Because that's been done already.

First, this book would be nothing but a vague notion swimming about in my head were it not for the support and guidance of my agent, Barbara Poelle. B, you were there before I hit the first keystroke on this thing, and it was you who gave me the courage to write it. Mere gratitude seems hollow in face of all that. Nevertheless, thank you, a thousand, thousand times.

As I once said to her when we were under deadline and exchanging e-mails past midnight, there is exactly one other person in the world who has spent almost as much time with these words as I have. To my editor, Stacey Barney, you are my match in all things. Thank you for loving this book and believing in it so strongly from Day One. Then taking it from what it was into what it has become—something infinitely better. I appreciate and respect you more than I can express.

To the phenomenal team at Penguin—to Kate Meltzer, wordsmith and Francophile extraordinaire, to my wonderful publicist Marisa Russell, to Bri Lockhart for all your enthusiasm and support, to Venessa Carson, to Jen Besser, to Theresa Evangelista for the gorgeous cover design, to Marikka Tamura, Cara Petrus, Ana Deboo, Anne Heausler, and Cindy Howle for making sure the words within did proper service to their wonderful inspiration.

To my writing tribe—to Ricki Schultz, Sarah Henning, Joy Callaway, Sarah Lemon, Steph Funk, Alison Bliss, JJ, and Sarah Blair—thank you so much for being there for everything and through everything. I treasure each of you.

To all my fellow 2015 debut-ers—it has been such a privilege to share in this journey with you. A special note of thanks to my 2K15-ers . . . I am in awe of each of you. Also to Sabaa Tahir—thank you for being you.

To the astounding team of folks at We Need Diverse Books—every day I am blown away by our collective passion for this cause. Thank you for all that you do. This is only the beginning.

To Marie Lu for taking me under her wing and being one of the best people I have ever been privileged to know. Your blurb made me cry. And I will always give you the crust. Always.

To Carrie Ryan for being the most epic lunch buddy ever. I'm sure JP and Vic always wonder what it is we talk about for so long. I never know either. But I do know I leave thinking we should do this every week. Thank you, thank you, thank you. For everything and more.

To Heather Baror-Shapiro for taking Shazi out into the world with so much verve and style. I still to this day cannot grasp that my book will be in so many different languages. And it is all because of you.

To my sister, Erica, for being my first reader, for leaving the best notes in the history of ever, and for coming up with the idea for Khalid's letters. Jane Austen has nothing on you (Knightley 4EVA). To Elaine for being my champion and my best friend and my biggest fan. I love you dearly, chica. To my brother Ian for telling me he would read my book when it was "finally" published. I expect a full report next week. To my brother Chris for the laughs and the hugs and the inappropriate GIFs. To my mother for never letting us watch TV during the week, thereby ensuring I would love books and the world of make-believe for all time. To my father for reading to us when we were little. And always doing the voices. To my in-laws for sharing their culture and their love and their food and their jokes with me. I love you both beyond words.

And, lastly, to Vic. You are my reason and my excuse, in all things.

One day, I will write it to the sky.

TURN THE PAGE FOR AN EXCERPT FROM

THE ROSE & THE DAGGER

BOOK TWO IN THE SAGA
OF SHAHRZAD AND KHALID

PROLOGUE

THE GIRL WAS ELEVEN AND THREE-QUARTERS.

Three very important quarters.

They'd been of consequence when her father had left her in charge this morning, with an important task to accomplish. So, with a world-weary sigh, she pushed up her tattered sleeves and heaved another shovelful of dusty rubble into the nearby wheelbarrow.

"It's too heavy," her eight-year-old brother complained as he struggled to move aside another piece of ash-laden debris from within the wreckage of their home. He coughed when a cloud of soot rose from amongst the charred remains.

"Let me help." The girl dropped her shovel with a sharp clang.

"I don't need any help!"

"We should work together, or we won't finish cleaning everything before Baba returns home." She braced her fists on her hips before glaring down at him.

"Look around you!" He threw his hands in the air. "We'll *never* finish cleaning everything."

Her eyes followed his hands.

The clay walls of their home were ripped apart. Broken. Blackened. Their roof opened up to the heavens. To a dull and forlorn sky.

To what once had been a glorious city.

The midday sun lay hidden behind the shattered rooftops of Rey. It cut shadows of light and dark across angry stone and scorched marble. Here and there, still-smoldering piles of rubble served as a harsh reminder of what had taken place only a few short days ago.

The young girl hardened her gaze and stepped closer to her brother.

"If you don't want to help, then wait outside. But I'm going to keep working. Someone has to." Again, she reached for her shovel.

The boy kicked at a nearby stone. It skittered across the packed earth before crashing to a halt at the foot of a hooded stranger standing by the remains of their door.

Tensing her grip on the shovel, the girl eased her brother behind her.

"May I help you . . . ?" She paused. The stranger's black *rida'* was embroidered in silver and gold thread. The scabbard of his sword was finely etched and delicately bejeweled, and his sandals were cut from the highest-quality calfskin.

He was no mere brigand.

The girl stood taller. "May I help you, *sahib*?"

When he did not answer right away, the girl raised her shovel higher, her brow taut and her heart hammering in her chest.

The stranger stepped from beneath the sagging doorjamb. He threw back his hood and raised both his palms in supplication.

Each of his gestures was careful, and he moved with a liquid kind of grace.

As he strode into a weak slice of light, the girl saw his face for the first time.

He was younger than she expected. No more than twenty.

His face approached beautiful. But its angles were too harsh, his expression too severe. The sunlight on his hands revealed something rather at odds with the rest of his finery: the skin of his palms was red and cracked and peeling—evidence of hard labor.

His tired eyes were a tawny gold color. She'd seen eyes like that once. In a painting of a lion.

"I didn't mean to startle you," the stranger said softly. His eyes shifted around the ruin of their one-room abode. "May I speak to your father?"

The girl's suspicion gripped her once more. "He's—not here. He went to stand in line for building supplies."

The stranger nodded. "And your mother?"

"She's dead," her brother said, stirring from behind her. "The roof fell on her during the storm. And she died." There was a daring quality to his words that the girl did not feel. An unmet challenge that came with his youth.

The stranger's severity deepened for an instant. He looked away. His hands fell to his sides.

After a beat, the stranger looked back at them, his eyes unwavering, despite his white-knuckled fists. "Do you have another shovel?"

"Why do *you* need a shovel, rich man?" Her little brother

marched up to the stranger, accusation in each of his barefooted steps.

"Kamyar!" she gasped as she reached for the back of his ragged *qamis*.

The stranger blinked down at her brother before crouching on the packed-earth floor.

"Kamyar, is it?" the stranger asked, a trace of a smile gracing his lips.

Her brother said nothing, though he was barely able to meet the tall stranger's gaze, even from this adjusted vantage point.

"I—I apologize, *sahib*," the girl stammered. "He's a bit insolent."

"Please don't apologize. I rather appreciate insolence, when dispensed by the right person." This time, the stranger did smile, and his features softened demonstrably.

"Yes," her brother interrupted. "My name is Kamyar. What is yours?"

The stranger paused to study her brother for a moment.

"Khalid."

"Why do you want a shovel, Khalid?" her brother demanded again.

"I'd like to help you repair your home."

"Why?"

"Because when we help one another, we are able to accomplish things faster."

Kamyar nodded slowly, then stopped to cant his head to one side. "But this isn't your home. Why should you care?"

"Because Rey is my home. And Rey is your home. If you could help me when I needed help, would you not wish to do so?"

"Yes," Kamyar said without hesitation. "I would."

"Then it's settled." The stranger stood. "Will you share your shovel with me, Kamyar?"

For the rest of the afternoon, the trio worked to clear the floor of charred wood and waterlogged debris. The girl never gave the stranger her name and refused to call him anything but *sahib,* but Kamyar treated him like a long-lost friend with a common enemy. When the stranger gave them water and *lavash* bread to eat, the girl dipped her head and touched her fingertips to her brow in thanks.

A flush rose in her cheeks when the almost-beautiful stranger returned the gesture, without a word.

Soon, the day began bruising into night, and Kamyar wedged himself into a corner, his chin drooping to his chest and his eyes slowly falling shut.

The stranger finished arranging the last of the salvageable pieces of wood by the door and shook the dirt from his *rida'* before pulling the hood of his cloak back over his head.

"Thank you," the girl murmured, knowing that was the least she should do.

He glanced over his shoulder at her. Then the stranger reached into his cloak and removed a small pouch cinched shut by a leather cord.

"Please. Take it."

"No, *sahib*." She shook her head. "I cannot take your money. We've already taken enough of your generosity."

"It isn't much. I'd like for you to take it." His eyes, which had appeared tired at the onset, now looked beyond exhausted.

"Please."

There was something about his face in that moment, hidden as it was in the play of shadows, in the lingering motes of ash and dust . . .

Something about it that signified a deeper suffering than the girl could ever hope to fathom.

She took the small pouch from his hand.

"Thank you," he whispered. As though he were the one in need.

"Shiva," she said. "My name is Shiva."

Disbelief registered on his features for an instant. Then the sharp planes of his face smoothed.

Into an expression of peace.

"Of course it is." He bowed low, with a hand to his brow.

Despite her confusion, she managed to respond in kind, her fingers brushing her forehead. When she looked up again, he had turned the corner.

And disappeared into the wending darkness of night.